Sweet Hope

A Sweet Home Novel

Tillie Cole

Dedication

To my Sweet Home Series readers… what a ride! You've changed my life with your love and support of my beloved Bama gang. I love you all so much it hurts. My sincerest thanks. I am eternally grateful that you gave this author a chance.

To Molly, Cass, Lexi, Ally, Rome, JD, Austin, Axel, Levi and Reece, you will forever hold a place in my heart. I have enjoyed every minute I've spent with you. It's breaking my heart to see you go, but I've sent you off well.

And, finally, to those (like me) who love the villains! I will forever strive to give you bad boys that are saved by love.

xXx

"Sometimes it is the people who no one imagines anything of who do the things that no one can imagine."

Joan Clarke, Mathematician

Prologue

A thick fog swallowed me in darkness.

"Help me," her voice called out. I tried to run forward but my legs wouldn't carry me.

"Please... help me," her weak, broken voice begged once again. Fear pushed me to turn, but everything was too dark. I was blind. I had no light to lead the way.

The dense fog thickened and poured down my throat, clogging my lungs. I couldn't breathe, I couldn't move... I couldn't help her.

"I am afraid... I am so afraid..." she sobbed. Her words whirled in the heavy wind, lashing across my face. My eyes closed, unable to cope with the pain in her voice.

"I can't get to you," I shouted as the heavy fog forced me to the cold ground. My hands raked at the hard dirt as I fought to get free.

"I can't... I can't... Go on... I'm so tired..." she cried. I could hear her fading away.

Panic filled my body. I couldn't lose her. I had to say goodbye.

"No!" I screamed. "Don't leave me!" I clawed harder at the

ground, my fingernails snapping under the pressure. No matter how hard I fought to push forward, nothing happened. My heart pounded in rhythm with the rumbling thunder overhead. Cold blood trickled through my body. I couldn't break way. I couldn't get free... I couldn't get free...

Scalding tears filled my eyes as an agonized pain gripped my heart. "I have to say goodbye," I screamed into the nothingness, "Let me say goodbye!" The skin on my fingers tore and bled as the hard dirt turned into broken glass, the sharp edges slicing deep into my flesh.

"Protect them... always protect them... please… please..." she begged. I could hear the defeat in her voice. She was giving up. She was slipping away.

"No! Wait!" I tried to scream, but no noise came from my mouth. I clawed at my throat, but I couldn't make a sound.

A light appeared in the distance, but it was too far from my reach. Dread filled my mind. She was leaving. She was leaving... and I couldn't say goodbye.

"Wait!" I silently screamed... "I haven't said goodbye!" But I was trapped here, caged under the weight of the black fog on this cold ground, my frantic voice muted, my body paralyzed.

The fog grew thicker and thicker and the light up ahead dimmed from white to gray. "No," I silently cried, "No!"

Relentlessly, the fog closed in, removing the fading light from view and with it all my hope.

She was gone…

2

Suffocating with grief, I fought for breath. But there was no more air, the nothingness of the fog was all consuming.

Rage filled tears trickled down my face as I lay here, defeated. I tried to close my eyes, I tried to push the pain into the back of my mind but guilt remained, splintering me from the inside.

The fog pushed down harder, wrapping me tightly in its hold.

Darkness was consuming me. Darkness was taking my soul.

"Goodbye," I mouthed with my final breath, "I just wanted to say goodbye..."

Jerking upright on my bed, I was panting hard at the dream I'd just had, when I heard, "You got a phone call."

Wiping the sleep from my eyes, I took a deep breath trying to erase the dream that haunted me. My hands were damp with sweat, but I just wiped them on my pants, kicked my feet off the bed and made my way down the hallway to the phone.

"Hello?"

"It's happening."

"What's happening?"

"*You*, Elpi, *you're* happening, *your debut.*"

Every inch of me froze, and I gripped the phone so tightly I thought it might shatter under the pressure.

"Vin—"

3

"You're ready. Your work is ready. Your collection is a masterpiece and must be shared with the world."

"Vin… I appreciate everything you're trying to do for me, but—"

"No buts. It's all arranged. It's been worked out. I've made this happen for you. You need this, Elpi."

I worked hard to cool down; hot blood coursed through my veins. I drew in a long, deep breath.

"You're ready," Vin pushed, his voice this time less business, less coercive, and more supportive.

But I didn't want it. None of it.

"Where's the damn exhibition?" I snapped.

"Elpi. Don't be this way. You're an artist—"

"I'm not a damn artist!" I interrupted through gritted teeth.

"You're an artist!" Vin commanded. "You're the best damn sculptor I've ever worked with. Your work surpasses anything I've ever seen, *including* my own work. You're someone, Elpi. Believe me, you are *someone.*"

"Vin—"

"It'll be in a smaller gallery, in a smaller museum, in an academic setting. It's your first exhibit, and it shouldn't overwhelm you."

"*Where*, Vin?" I asked, exasperated, and ran my hand through my long hair.

"Seattle."

The air sucked out of my lungs as Vin carried on telling me all the good things about Seattle—the art scene, the people, the culture...

"Elpi, I know you'll probably argue about the show being in Seattle, but—"

"I'm in." I interrupted sharply, and was met with Vin's shocked silence from behind the crackling receiver.

"You're in?"

"I'm in."

"No argument? No telling me your art is only for you and no one else? No telling me you want nothing to do with the art world and the people in it?"

"No."

"Right, well... that's... perfect! I've set up a flight for you to come out here in two weeks' time. I'll pick you up from the airport. I'll get you an apartment—"

"Don't bother."

"Don't bother?" Vin questioned slowly.

"I've got somewhere to stay."

"In Seattle?"

"Yeah."

"Where? With who?"

5

"Don't concern you," I said coldly. I felt a hand tap on my back. I turned and nodded at the guy behind me and turned back to speak into the phone. "I gotta go."

"Right. Well, I guess I'll see you in two weeks. But if you need anything, if your 'place' doesn't work out, call me."

I paused, closed my eyes, and tapped my hand twice on the chipped painted wall before me.

"Got it."

Immediately hanging up the phone, dread ripping the shit out of my stomach, I headed down a dark quiet hallway. Raking my long hair out of my face, my nails then scratched down the heavy dark stubble on my face.

Two weeks...

In two weeks, I'd be in Seattle, ready for the next part of my life to begin, but not before having to face a truckload of unresolved shit from my past...

Chapter One
Ally

New York City

Running across the road, I dodged people left and right in my rush to get to my interview on time. The New York weather was humid and sweltering. I was so happy I'd tied my long hair back in a bun.

Gripping tightly onto my purse, I jogged along the sidewalk, frantically checking my watch. My plane had been delayed and getting ready in a Boeing 737's tiny bathroom cubicle wasn't exactly ideal for presenting flawless makeup and hair.

But it was worth it. This was all for the exhibition of my dreams. I intended to nail this interview. There was no choice. I would do anything to curate this show… even fly to the East Coast last minute from California to land it…

7

even leave my beautiful newly-curated Contemporary Art gallery at UCLA in the hands of the Art Director.

Finally reaching the front of the Met, I ran up the stairs in my favorite black Louboutins, straightening out my black sleeveless dress as I reached the top.

Pausing, I inhaled through my nose, and with a slow exhale from my mouth, pulled back my shoulders and walked into the entrance.

In minutes I was whisked away to the private offices by the museum director's assistant and told to wait in a small room dominated by a large wooden table and six chairs. Artwork, from up and coming artists, was hung without rhyme or reason on the white walls. I slumped into a chair, nervously playing with my hands.

Hearing footsteps outside the room, I forced myself to relax and straightened up just as an older man walked into the room.

Vin Galanti. The famous sculptor himself.

Vin was dressed all in tweed, his gray hair a fluffy halo enveloping his head. He looked every inch the eccentric artist.

His light blue eyes met mine and a wide smile spread across his face. "Ms. Lucia!" he greeted. I rose from my seat to take his has outstretched hand.

"Mr. Galanti! It's a pleasure to meet you, sir. I've studied your work in great depth."

Mr. Galanti gestured for me to sit. He sat opposite me. "Please, call me Vin. And I'm very happy to meet you too, Ms. Lucia. I was honored to see the Contemporary Art show you curated in Toronto last year and I was extremely impressed."

"Thank you, Vin," I said in reply, genuinely taken aback by the compliment.

"No, *thank you*. It is truly an honor to meet someone so young who is so passionate about art."

"I am, sir," I said happily, "It's the center of my entire life."

Vin sat forward like an excited child. I had to stop myself from laughing at the grin on his face. "So," he said conspiratorially, "Elpidio..."

"Yes," I croaked, my voice barely audible. The mere thought of curating his work made me feel weak at the knees.

"At last I'm commissioning his first show and I am looking for the right curator to put it all together." His eyes narrowed. "Do you believe this could be you?"

"Yes, sir," I retorted with confidence. "As soon as I heard about the position, I dropped everything to fly out here to meet you. I know I'm the best person for this job.

I've studied his work. I've written academic journals on his methods and on his themes. I've written articles on his rise to fame."

Vin sat back, clasped his hands and nodded his head. He seemed to have lost his enthusiasm. My stomach rolled. I wanted this position so, so much.

"I've read your articles and journals, Ms. Lucia," he said. I waited for him to say more. "You're an exceptional art scholar and you clearly have a passion for my protégé."

"Yes, sir," I replied, "He's one of my favorite contemporary sculptors." I paused at what I'd just said and lowered my eyes to inspect the wooden table. "No, excuse me," I said nervously, "Elpidio is my absolute *favorite* contemporary artist, period."

Vin's head tilted to the side. "Why?" Vin's eyes had lit up with interest.

"Why…" I whispered, contemplating how I could express my love for his work in words. I took in a long breath, thinking through my answer, and opted to speak from the heart. I closed my eyes picturing his sculptures and let my words flow.

"His works… They are both the saddest and most beautiful pieces of art I have ever seen. Every curve of the marble comes from deep within his heart. The themes of his works are both provocative and gutting at the same time. I could get lost in every single one of them, all day, everyday for the rest of my life and never tire of it. They are raw and poetic… so tragic, yet so beautiful. The merest of glances at any one of the pieces evokes a kaleidoscope of emotions from the very depths of the soul. I don't know what else to say except that his work communicates with me like no other," I patted my hand over my heart, "it speaks directly to every fiber of my being. I *feel* his work. I feel it, as though it lives and breathes, just like you and I."

Opening my eyes, I blushed in embarrassment as I realized just how lost to my thoughts I had become. Vin leaned forward again and tapped my hand with his.

"Well, Ms. Lucia, that was quite the answer," Vin said, with a hint of humor in his tone.

Huffing a nervous laugh, I brushed a loose piece of hair from my face. "He's quite the sculptor."

"Yes, he is," Vin said, then sighed a heavy sigh. "He's a genius, a brilliant, brilliant man, though he will never ever think it of himself."

Seeming to forget he was in my company, Vin pulled himself round from his sudden sadness. After several seconds of silence, Vin said, "I'm an old fashioned man, Ms. Lucia. I don't care for formal job interviews and I'm not one for rote scripted replies. I want a curator who

11

understands Elpidio's work, someone who is as passionate about it as I am."

"I've studied each of those pieces more than anyone, *anyone*, Vin. I'm convinced I'm the *only* curator who can design that gallery, the only person who can create a story worthy of his work. I know I can design the perfect space to showcase his talent. I can do this, Vin, believe me I can. I've never failed to deliver before, and I most certainly wouldn't fail with this show."

Vin laughed and once more patted my hand. "Ms. Lucia, after reading your journals and speaking to you today, I am just as convinced of this as you are. But even if I wasn't; listening to you describe how Elpidio's work affects you just now, well, it would have won you the position regardless."

For a moment I let what he'd just said hang in the air. Unable to resist the need for clarification, I asked, "Do I... have I got the position?"

Vin nodded his head once and stood up. "You have indeed. Ms. Lucia. I'm not one to procrastinate. I've already explored your academic credentials and caught up with previous employers. You come highly recommended, you have dedicated your life to curating from what I can gather."

Warmth spread in my chest, and I let myself feel a fleeting moment of pride. I *had* dedicated every moment since college to this career. Even in college, I always knew what my path would be.

Rising to my feet, I offered my hand to Vin, who graciously accepted it. "Thank you, Vin," I said humbly. He gave my hand a firm shake as if to seal the contract.

"When do you need me here in New York? I can be back from California in the next few days if necessary. Is the exhibit here at the Met? The Guggenheim?"

"None of the above," Vin said with a casual wave of his hand as he made his way to the door. I frowned in confusion. "It's going to be small, academic and local to me."

"Okay," I said hesitantly.

Vin glanced back from the door. "It'll be in Seattle, Ms. Lucia, at the University of Washington's art museum. I'm a patron there and I want to garner some exposure for it. Plus, Elpidio would not countenance a big name gallery. He wants intimate."

Intimate… The very sound of Elpidio next to the word *intimate* evoked a warm glow all over my body. I was obsessed with a man I'd never met, no more than a concept. And here I was getting to work physically with his masterpieces—the marble expressions of his soul, the imprints of his heart... in *Seattle*.

"Seattle's perfect," I said, excitement lacing every letter of my words, "I get the sense from his work that Elpidio is not in it for the fame or acclaim of other artists. It's not the prestige of the place. It's the exquisiteness of the art that's the focus." I smiled and dipped my head just picturing those sculptures I'd admired in pictures, only having had the pleasure of seeing one piece in the flesh. "It's going to be amazing; life-changing amazing, for so many people."

"Spoken like a true curator," Vin said fondly. I could hear the smile in his voice.

"No," I said and blushed. "That was spoken by a true fan."

Vin eyed me with curiosity. "You've perfectly described Elpidio, Ms. Lucia. A small museum is ideal for his first show, and you are ideal as its curator. I have a very good feeling about this partnership, Ms. Lucia. A very good feeling indeed."

Smiling, I replied, "As do I, Vin."

"My assistant will be in touch soon with all of the finer details. In the meantime, if you can get to Seattle as soon as possible, we can take it from there."

"Thank you, Vin," I said again, and with the slightest wave of his hand he left the room.

Minutes later, the same assistant saw me out of the museum. As I stood on the top of the Met's impressive steps, I tipped my head back to gaze at the clear summer sky and tried real hard to stop myself from screaming out in happiness.

I'd done it.

I was about to start work with the finest sculptor in the modern era.

I'd landed my dream job.

Returning to the here and now, I pulled out my cell and unlocked the screen. For a minute I stared at the wallpaper, my favorite Elpidio piece, an unnamed white Carrara marble angel.

A bolt of excitement flashed through my body as I pressed two on my speed dial, only to then hear a familiar and loved English accent say, "Hello, stranger!"

"Molls!" I greeted excitedly. "You got a spare room in that mansion of yours? 'Cause your very best friend is coming to stay!"

Chapter Two
Ally

Seattle, Washington

The cab pulled to a stop right on the edge of Lake Washington. I stared up at the stunning white stone mansion set beyond a couple of acres of land, protected by huge iron gates. Molly and Rome's new home.

Rome… I thought and smiled. No way would Molly choose this house.

Grabbing my cases, I rolled them toward the gates, when they suddenly began to open. I beamed a smile and waved at a large camera atop an ornate post on the surrounding white stone wall.

As I walked down the driveway, I marveled at the gardens: lush green grass, ornate water features, trees of every type, and a million flowers brightening up the grounds.

A large set of paved steps came into view, which led to a white door entrance. It flew open just as my hand rose to knock. My lips spread into an ear-splitting smile as my cousin, Rome Prince, appeared in the doorway, his usual sandy long blond hair messy and his brown eyes bright. He was still the epitome of country-boy style as he stood, arms folded, rocking a fitted white T-shirt and faded jeans.

"Hello, cuz," he greeted with a wide smile, his thick accent as Bama as ever as he stepped forward, arms wide, and lifted me off the floor in a bear hug.

I couldn't help but laugh as I hugged him back.

Rome planted me on the floor, and I kissed him on his cheek. "Hello to you too, Mr QB Almighty!"

Rome rolled his eyes and moved past me to grab my luggage. I followed him into the house. My eyes widened as I drank in the foyer, because that's all it could be described as, a foyer. The place was enormous.

"Rome—" I went to say, when I was cut off.

"Ridiculous, isn't it?"

My head turned to the sweeping staircase. Molly Prince was walking down, dressed in a long empire-waist sleeveless purple summer dress. Her long brown hair lay on her shoulders and her pretty face wore a happy smile.

"Molls!" I shouted in excitement and, as Molly descended onto the last step, I wrapped her up in my arms. She immediately hugged me back. "I've missed you!" I confessed, and let her go so we could walk back into the foyer.

"I've missed you too, sweetie," Molly said, squeezing my hand, only to let go when Rome reached out and pulled her to his chest, his arms wrapping around her shoulders from behind. Molly's hands lifted to hold his arms, and *that look* they both had when they were with each other drifted across their faces.

An ache momentarily stabbed at my chest. Looking at how happy they were only emphasized how lonely I felt. Working all the hours God sends could be a good distraction, but as much as I adored my job, it could never replace that heart-stopping, bolt of lightning love I so desperately craved.

"Come on. Let's go and get a drink!" I said cheerily, fighting back my moment of sadness, and let Rome and Molly lead the way to their white country-style kitchen.

Molly must have seen me gaping at the opulence of the room and blushed. "It's too much, isn't it?"

My attention was drawn to my timid friend and her embarrassed expression. "Not at all, darlin'. It's beautiful."

Molly joined me in looking around the room. I adored that she still found it uncomfortable having money. I didn't think she'd ever get used to it. But I couldn't help but think it was an adorable trait to possess.

"She fought me on buying this place, but I wanted somewhere safe for us to live… somewhere for us to start a family," Rome stated.

Molly's eyes, which had been fixed on the table, then shot to her husband's and began to fill with tears.

Rome lifted Molly's hand to his lips. I felt like an intruder on their private and meaningful moment. Molly appeared to shake herself to and cast me a ghost of a smile. "Ally, you must be thirsty. Can I get you a drink?"

"Don't worry, darlin'. I got it covered!" I declared excitedly and ran to my carry-on and pulled out the bottle of champagne I'd bought *en route* to their house.

As I looked up, Molly had turned green and was rushing out of the room. "I… I'm… I'll be back in a moment!" Molly ran out into the hallway. I stood in the middle of the kitchen, eyebrows pulled down.

I turned to face Rome, who was fidgeting on his seat. "She okay, honey?" I asked. "She looked like she was gonna puke."

Rome's eyes tracked the direction Molly had gone. "She's fine." I could see the concern on his face. But

19

Rome had always been all serious and possessive of Molly. His need to keep her safe and cared for stood above anything else in his life.

Feeling awkward at the silence that immediately followed, I asked, "Where are your champagne flutes?"

Rome snapped out of his worry and walked to a cupboard. Reaching up, he pulled out two champagne glasses and set them on the table as I popped the cork. When I went to pour, I stilled.

"Rome, you forgot one. There's only two here."

Rome stiffened beside me, and when I looked up, his eyes were facing the direction Molly had gone. My eyes narrowed, and I nudged him with my elbow. "Hey, cuz! You with me?"

Rome flicked his head to me and ran his hand through his hair. "Yeah, sorry, Al."

"What's up?" I asked. "'Cause y'all are acting real strange."

I stared down at the two champagne glasses and I let out an excited gasp. "Why isn't she drinking?"

Rome opened his mouth, but...

"I'm pregnant." Molly's quiet voice carried from the entranceway to where I stood. Both Rome and I quickly turned our heads to face her. She was pale, and I could tell she'd just vomited.

The air whooshed from my lungs and my hand flew over my mouth. Molly edged forward, and her lip curled in happiness. "I'm sixteen weeks gone…" She looked at Rome and tears of happiness filled her eyes. "Can you believe it? We're pregnant again!"

Tears then spilled down her cheeks. Mine did exactly the same as I ran to my best friend, her hands now shaping the small round bump under her flowing dress. I took her into my arms.

"I'm so happy for you, darlin'," I whispered as I felt Molly grip me tightly.

She was shaking.

I pulled back and wiped her tears with my thumbs. "I'm so damn happy for you."

"Thank you, Ally," she said with an excited laugh. Her whole face shone with excitement. But that expression faltered when her eyes drifted to Rome, who still hadn't moved from his hunched-over position by the countertop. He was watching us closely, but there was pain in his dark stare.

Molly walked away from me, gently squeezing my arm in thanks before she let go and made her way to her husband. Dipping her head, she placed her fingers under his lowered chin and lifted Rome's head before pressing a kiss to his lips.

"I'll be fine," she hushed soothingly.

Rome stared at her for what felt like an age before pulling her onto his lap and wrapping her in his arms. Molly saw me watching in confusion and explained, "I have Preeclampsia, Ally. The pregnancy could be tough, since I shouldn't have developed Preeclampsia this early. Our doctor has given me a list of things I have to do to help myself, but this one here is terrified." She ran her hand through Rome's long hair to emphasize her point. "It's the reason we haven't told anyone sooner. You know, just incase something went wrong again. Lexi and Austin know, but I wanted to wait and tell you to your face. Of course Rome can't stop worrying."

That twist in my gut was back again.

"I'm terrified of losing you," Rome's deep, rough voice said quietly. "No baby is worth that."

Molly's head tilted slowly to the side as she watched him. "You won't lose me. It's all going to be okay. We're going to have a baby and everything will be fine."

They stared into each other's eyes and seemed to speak to each other simply through their connection.

I rocked awkwardly on my feet and moved toward my cases. Molly saw me from the corner of her eye and stood up from Rome's lap.

"Rome, show Ally to her room, baby. I'm going to go and lie down." She rolled her eyes at me. "Doctor's orders. Lots of rest and no stress."

I smiled at her and watched as she headed out of the room. Molly then stopped and turned round. "Oh, I nearly forgot. We've organized a celebration dinner for you tonight, sweetie. Everyone's coming. A big hello to you and your arrival in the Emerald City."

"Molls, I—" I went to argue, worried it was pushing her too far.

"Not you too, Ally! I have enough from my brooding hulking Football stud there, treating me like I'm a fragile doll." Molly pointed at Rome and playfully gave him a scowl. Rome's eyes tightened, being playful back. "I'm fine." Her hand went to her stomach. "We're *both* fine, and I won't have everyone stepping on eggshells around me for the next several months!"

"Yes, ma'am," I said and mock-saluted her.

Molly laughed and shook her head. "And later I want to hear all about this new gallery you're designing at my school, okay?"

"Sure thing," I replied, amused.

Molly nodded in triumph, then carefully walked up the stairs, leaving me alone with Rome. Rome picked up my luggage and quickly headed for the stairs, and I followed.

He led me to a room at the end of a long hallway. When he opened the door, my mouth fell open. It was beautiful; light and airy, an all-white room with a huge en suite featuring the biggest tub I'd ever seen.

"Rome… this is…" I whispered and turned to my cousin, who was leaning against the doorframe, arms folded across his chest.

"Now you stay for as long as you want, you hear? Molly loves having you around. And I don't find it too shabby either."

I stared at my cousin, hearing the catch in his voice as he tried to cover his apprehension over his wife with a joke. I walked over to his tall frame and took hold of his tense arms. "She'll be okay, you know. This baby is a good thing. It's a blessing."

Rome looked down at the floor. "I know it is, Al, and I *am* happy. We've wanted a baby for so long. You know we have. But, Christ, Al, listening to that doctor talk through the risks again and being constantly reminded that her momma died from the same thing Mols has… and…" Rome stopped speaking, and I squeezed my hand on his arm. His nostrils flared and he went on. "And remembering my girl in that damn hospital bed, broken and lost, just kills me. It could happen again. Or it could be worse."

"It won't be, Rome. *Everything* is different this time. You're in a much better place, you're older, you don't have your parents breathing down your neck and all that stress to contend with. And I know *you*. *You* won't let anything happen to that wife of yours ever again."

Rome's lip hooked up into a reluctant grin, and I smiled back.

"I'm gonna be an aunt!" I squealed excitedly, and Rome started laughing. My heart broke at how worried he was but then how excited he was when he finally let his happiness shine through.

"Yeah, yeah, you are. Aunt Ally."

"And you're gonna be a daddy."

He blew out a breath and ran his hands down his face. "Yeah… fuck…"

"And you're gonna be a damn good, one, Rome. The best damn daddy on the planet."

Rome gave me a huge thankful smile, and I could see the pure joy in his expression. I could see just how much he wanted that little baby Molly was carrying.

Rome shook his head in amusement and mussed up my long brown hair with his hand.

"Rome!" I yelled. "Get the hell off!" I tried to slap him away, but he jumped back out of my reach.

"Glad you're here, cuz. It's been too fucking long since we saw y'all," he said, becoming more serious. "We're going out to celebrate in a few hours, so be ready about seven."

Rome walked off before I could say anything, leaving me in this huge guest room. I sat down on the bed.

I was in Seattle, about to take on the exhibition of my life, and to top it all off, I was gonna be an aunt.

This move felt so perfectly right...

Chapter Three
Ally

A few hours later we entered the restaurant, and the waiter took to us to a private room at the back. I was glad, because when we walked through the busy dining room, people began staring at Rome and whispering to one another—star struck on recognizing the Seahawks' starting QB. Molly ducked her head and tried to rush forward, clearly embarrassed, but Rome grabbed her hand, keeping her close to his side. He hated the limelight too.

As we entered the private room, which overlooked the vast beautiful evening view of the Sound, I exhaled, smoothing out my sleeveless black column dress, only to hear my name being called from across the room.

"Ally!"

I beamed a smile at Lexi—one of my best friends—who had risen from her seat and rushed toward me. My heart

27

swelled as she approached, still petite and slight in frame, but looking healthy now that she'd filled out some since College. Her black hair was now long and straight, and grown to the middle of her back. She was wearing a knee-length green dress with long sleeves and ankle boots.

She looked beautiful.

Reaching out, I took Lexi's hands in mine and leaned in to kiss her on her cheek. I squeezed her fingers tightly and stepped back. I had to suppress the urge to pull her in for a hug. Lexi couldn't be touched that way because of her anorexia. Although she was in recovery, it was still a trigger for her to be touched on her back.

"I've missed you," Lexi said softly, cutely smiling up at me.

"I've missed you too, darlin'. I can't believe y'all are living in Seattle now too! It's crazy! Two Bama boys playing for the Seahawks!"

At that moment, Austin Carillo, Rome's best friend, appeared behind his wife and leaned over her to kiss me on my cheek. "Ally," he greeted and, edging back, wrapped his fully tattooed arms around Lexi's shoulders and pulled her against his chest. Austin was the one exception to Lexi's triggers, the only person who could touch her. Austin had saved her life five years ago when she almost lost the battle with her eating disorder, but their love for each other proved to be stronger. He was her reason to live, and she his.

Spotting a messy head of fair hair lingering behind Austin and Lexi, I leaned round, only to see a handsome young guy standing awkwardly. He was well built and athletic. He casted shy eyes my way, and my mouth dropped when I realized who it was...

"Levi? Little Levi Carillo? Is that you, darlin'?" I asked. I met his gray eyes as he raised his head, a deep red blush immediately coating his olive-skinned cheeks.

"Hey, Al," was his quiet reply as I ran to him and threw my arms around his waist, squeezing him hard.

Levi exhaled a quiet laugh from above me, hugging me back. I pushed back and held out his arms, studying how much he'd changed.

"Levi, you got so big and grown up on me!" I joked, and he dipped his eyes to avoid my gaze, a shy smile spreading on his lips. "How old are you now, darlin'?"

"Nineteen, ma'am," he replied. Rome walked behind him and ruffled his hair. Levi nudged him off.

"Well, shit! Nineteen!"

"And one of the best wide receivers you've ever seen," Lexi praised as she reached up to pat his cheek with her slender hand. Levi beamed a wide smile at her, and you

29

could just see the love he had for our little friend radiating out of his every pore.

"Just like your brother, then, huh?" I teased, seeing Austin take a seat at our table next to Rome, Molly and Lexi moving to sit beside each of their husbands.

Linking my arm through Levi's, I said, "Well, looks like you're my date tonight, Lev. You can sit beside me."

Levi fell into step beside me and we sat down. "So you at college, Lev? Are you here in Seattle visiting Austin and Lex?"

"No, ma'am, I still live with them. I attend the University of Washington now; I transferred from UCLA."

I stared at him, feeling somewhat confused. "You didn't wanna stay in LA?"

Austin shifted in his seat as he looked at his younger brother. Levi lowered his head. "I wanted to stay close to my brother and Lexi. That's all. The Huskie's ain't too bad, and we're doing real good this year."

My heart sank as I saw a wash of vulnerability flit across his handsome face.

"Best damn player on that field, hey, little brother?" Austin said, breaking the silence, and Levi lifted his head, blushing at Austin's expression of pride.

"So, Al, Molls and Rome said you're curating some fancy-ass exhibition at the University?" Austin said taking the attention of Levi, just after Rome ordered a round of drinks from the waiter who stood just out of our eyeline.

I laughed at the way he put it. "Yeah, I'm curating some *fancy-ass exhibition*."

"What? It is fancy-ass, right?" Austin said, as Lexi shook her head in exasperation beside him.

"Ignore him. He's all football, football, football, not exactly an art buff," Lexi teased Austin, earning her a threatening scowl.

Lexi batted her hand and looked to me again. "Tell us about it, Al."

"Yeah, tell us about it *Ms. Aliyana Lucia*," Rome said dryly. I used my mama's maiden name for business, and Rome always teased me about it. I just didn't want the Prince Oil stigma following me around. I wanted to be independently successful, not connected with the family name.

My eyes were instantly brimming with excitement. "What can I say? It's my dream come true. This exhibition is the artist's debut show, and I was hand-picked to curate it. I still can't believe it!"

"What does he paint?" Molly asked.

"He doesn't. He's a sculptor." I released a long breath. "He's the most inspiring, courageous, beautifully dark, tortured, talented sculptor I've ever encountered…." I stared out at the darkened view of the Sound, lost in the slideshow of his sculptures running through my head, each more poetic and tragic than the last.

Shaking my head, I met the shocked stares of my friends and anxiously brushed hair from my face. "His work, it's… it's… it's my soul. That's the only way I can explain it. It's life, death, love, tragedy, and everything in between, every human condition… *everything*. His work speaks directly to my heart."

"Ally…" Molly prompted with unshed tears in her eyes. When I felt a wetness on my cheeks, I realized I was crying. Quickly wiping away the tears, I took a deep breath and expelled a nervous laugh. "I *really* love his work."

"I can tell," Rome said affectionately.

"I'm so happy for you," Lexi said excitedly and leaned forward. "What's he like? Is he handsome?" Austin cast a disbelieving look at Lexi, but she either didn't see it or flat out ignored him.

I shrugged. "That's just it, I've never seen him. No one has. He's a complete recluse. I was commissioned by another artist, his mentor, who's fronting the entire thing. He's a patron of the university's art museum and a local to Seattle. It really should have been at a bigger museum, but they wanted to keep it small."

"Vin Galanti?" Molly volunteered.

"Yeah, have you met him?"

"Once or twice." A grin spread on her face. "He's quite the character. He brought some of Plato's original writings to the art museum for a temporary mash-up art/philosophy exhibition they were a part of. I helped with the history and translation of the Latin for the text boards. I adore him."

"So what's his name?" Lexi asked, as the waiter came back with our drinks.

"Name?" I questioned as a glass of champagne was placed before me.

"The sculptor, Mr. Owns Your Soul's name!" she stressed and pouted her lips to stop the smile from lighting up her face.

"Oh, right, sorry. Erm… Elpidio. He goes by Elpidio," I replied.

Austin huffed beside me. "Haven't heard that name in a while."

"You've heard of it?" I questioned.

"It was our nonno's name," Austin replied. "Our mamma's father's name. It's not that common anymore…"

"So it's Italian?" I asked, excited that just a little bit more about the reclusive artist had been revealed.

Austin nodded his head, now too busy eating his breadsticks to elaborate further.

33

"Well, Al," Rome said and sat forward, grabbing his glass of champagne and raising it in the air. "Gotta say, I'm glad you're here with us in Seattle, and good luck with your new job."

Everyone raised their glasses and took a sip.

"I'm so glad to be here too!"

Chapter Four
Elpidio

Seattle, Washington

Vin pulled the car to a stop in front of the address I'd given him. The address I'd clutched onto the entire plane ride here, the ink of that address now smudged on the piece of wilting scrap paper in my hand.

My hands shook as I stared straight ahead, too afraid to look to my right at the house I knew sat there waiting. Everything was silent as I tried to breathe through my nerves. I could feel Vin's eyes watching me.

"Are you okay, Elpi?" he asked, shattering the quiet.

I opened my mouth to answer but no words came out. Nodding my head once, I pulled in a long breath and moved my shaking hand to the door handle. As the door popped open, and without meeting Vin's eyes, I said, "Thanks for picking me up."

"Not a problem, Elpi," he replied. "I'll meet you at he studio tomorrow, yes? Show you the space I've got for you to continue your work."

"Fine," I said in a clipped tone and jumped out the car, slamming the door.

Throwing my bag over my shoulder, I forced myself to lift my head and saw a huge brick mansion in front of me.

My heart hammered too fast, the driveway looking like a damn green mile. I took a step forward, my hands shaking harder as I thought about what waited for me on the other side of that black front door.

Pushing myself to keep moving, the gravel crunched beneath my boots. My stomach clenched and sweat ran down my face under my heavy long hair.

Everything I had left in the world was on the other side of that door. Everything I had left, but nothing I deserved. Questions bombarded my mind: what if they rejected me? What if the only people I loved no longer loved me back? I hadn't seen them in three years, cut them off without any explanation. What if they couldn't forgive me for that? What if I was truly on my own? What the fuck would I do then?

Trying to push the fear from my head, my feet kept forging forward, my breathing increasing the closer I got to the house. Everywhere was quiet, only a few birds singing in the high trees surrounding the property. I hated quiet, it made the shitty thoughts constantly in my head too loud.

Reaching the front door, I tried to listen for any signs of life inside, but I couldn't hear shit. Inside was as silent as it was out here. I wasn't used to it. I was used to shouting, metal doors clanging, and orders being fired… not this nothingness. Not this unsettling peace.

The sound of my rushing blood thundered in my ears and I lifted my hand to knock. But I couldn't stop my hand from shaking. I couldn't fucking stop it shaking. I immediately lowered my head.

I didn't think I could do it. After all this time… what if they didn't want me? My eyes squeezed closed. I was such a fucking pussy!

Clenching my hand into a fist, I took a deep breath, opened my eyes and before I could talk myself out of it, I rapped on the door twice, dropping my hand to wait for an answer.

Too many thoughts were running through my mind as I stood there, feet fixed to ground, trembling like a little fucking girl. Then footsteps sounded on the other side.

Holding my breath, I heard the locks slowly being unlatched and, like time switched to friggin' slow motion, saw the doorknob turn. My hair covered my face as I tried to calm my nerves, but when a pair of feet came into view, I knew who stood there… right in front of me… finally, after all these years.

"Can I help you?"

I closed my eyes on hearing his familiar voice.

Slowly lifting my head, I saw he was even bigger than I remembered. He was dressed in loose gray sweats and a short-sleeved white t-shirt, dark tattoos covering his exposed arms. I forced myself to look up and meet his eyes and I staggered back. It was like I saw him only yesterday, and with that realization, a ton of gutting memories came flooding into my mind; memories I'd try to block out so they didn't fucking drown me in guilt.

His dark hair was longer, not too long, but longer than it had been the last time we'd met. Blowing out a long breath, I dragged my hand through my hair, raking it back, showing more of my bearded face…

And then I saw it, the moment it sank in exactly *who* stood on his doorstep. His brown eyes widened to what seemed unnatural size. He stepped back in shock, his mouth dropping open like he wanted to say something, but no words came out.

"Austin," I rasped out in greeting, glancing away, feeling the most nervous I had in my entire fucking life. Waiting… just waiting for him to push me away.

Austin gripped the edge of the door, staring at me, until I shifted on my feet and nodded my head. I got the meaning of his silence: I wasn't welcome.

"Understood," I said curtly.

I turned to leave just as he stepped forward and whispered, "Axel?"

Austin's voice was strained, laced with emotion. I froze and reluctantly looked over my shoulder.

"Kid," I responded and watched as the shock on his now older face melted into the biggest fucking smile I'd ever seen. Austin launched out of the door and threw his arms around my neck.

I'd never been squeezed so tight.

Austin's trembling hand held the back of my head, crushing me against his body. "Fuck… I can't… I can't believe it's you…" His voice was rough and my throat felt so tight I couldn't speak. Patting Austin on the back, I expected him to pull away, but when I felt his back shaking too, I knew why he wasn't. The kid was crying.

And it fucking broke me.

"*Fratello*, look at me," I said, fighting back my own tears. As always, my kid brother did as I asked—he always had.

Austin kept his eyes down as he faced me, his hands on my shoulders, but I could see the tears dripping from his eyes. Gripping the back of his head, I pulled him back into my chest, whispering, "I fucking missed you, kid."

"Lo giuri?" Austin asked shakily, his voice muffled by my shirt.

I huffed a single laugh. *"Lo giuro."*

Drawing back, Austin looked me over, shaking his head in disbelief. "How... what... Axe, how the hell are you out? How come you're here?"

"Good behavior, Aust."

The pride that flashed over his unshaven cheeks almost undid me. Why he'd always had so much faith in my sorry ass was lost on me.

I didn't deserve it. I didn't deserve him... none of it.

Austin flung his arm around my shoulder and said, "I always knew you could do it. Keep your head down and get straight."

He began leading me into the house and pushed his hand over my long hair. "What the fuck's up with the long hair and beard? Never known you to have anything but a buzz cut."

"Don't know. Just never bothered to cut it."

Austin stopped, and I could feel his hard stare. I eventually looked up and raised my eyebrow. "What?"

"I just hardly recognize you, that's all. It's like you're another person. And…" His brown eyes bored into my left cheek, and I lifted my hand to where my Stidda, my tattooed black star, used to be, the mark that told everyone I was Heighter for life. "You covered it…"

I glanced away. "Yeah…" I replied, no more information needed.

"Why?" He pushed.

"Just did, kid."

"To a crucifix?" he questioned, but I just shrugged. Austin was still staring, but I wasn't going there.

"You got yours took off," I stated proudly.

"It ain't my life no more, Axe. It was 'bout time to let all that shit go." I nodded in understanding, and Austin took that as his cue to move us on into the house.

As we walked through the door, I could feel Austin keep looking at me as if he thought I'd disappear if he didn't keep checking. His arm never left my shoulders.

Austin took my bag and placed it on the black marble floor. I took a look around and had to breathe through the unease I felt at being in such a place. I was used to the thin walls, tin roofs, and plastic windows of trailers, or stone floors and metal gates of cells, not fucking mansions like I was standing in now… a mansion that my kid brother

41

bought all off his own back, from his own talent. It was damn surreal.

Austin slapped me on my back, and I shook my head.

"What?" he asked as I gestured to the large hallway and the TV room that looked like a shittin' movie theatre.

"You did good, kid."

Austin's eyes dipped. "I said I would. Said I'd have a house you could come and live in too, when you got out."

That damn clogged throat was back again, and I knew Austin got that I couldn't speak.

"Austin? Baby? Who was at the door?"

A female voice came drifting out from the right, down a hallway I saw led to the kitchen. Shortly after, a skinny, small black-haired chick appeared.

My stomach flipped. *Shit. Lexi.*

"Baby?" she called again, walking with her head down as she dried a glass with a dishtowel. Austin stiffened beside me. When Lexi looked up, she jumped, startled at what greeted her.

"Ax… Axel…?" she whispered. Her hands began to shake so much that the glass she was holding fell to the floor and shattered.

"Pix," Austin said, and I could hear the worry in his voice. "Shit, Pix, you okay?"

Her huge green eyes went from mine to Austin's as she nodded her head, but it wasn't a damn second before they were back on me.

Austin stood before her and cupped her cheeks, forcing her to look at him. "Baby, look at me."

She did.

"You okay?"

She slowly nodded her head, and Austin wrapped her in his arms as if he were keeping her safe. Safe from me. I knew she'd had problems. Fuck, I knew she'd nearly died. Lev had told me that much when he'd called me from the hospital five years ago and ripped me a new one for letting them all down.

My pulse slammed in my neck as I saw how much she feared me. She was fucking terrified.

"Lexi," I greeted, but my voice was rough.

Her green eyes never left mine as Austin squeezed her tighter.

"Axel," she answered in a shaky voice.

I couldn't stand it.

Taking a step forward, I watched her whole body tense, so I stopped and held up my hands. "Look, Lexi, I wanna say sorry for the way I treated you. It was real bad. I was a fucking dick." I lowered my head, feeling Austin's tension from where I stood. "I ain't that guy no more."

43

Looking back up, Lexi stared at me in silence for the longest time. Then she eventually blew a long breath through her mouth, casting a glance to Austin.

"Pix?" Austin questioned. Lexi reached up and, with her thumb, wiped the wetness still left on Austin's cheeks. I saw tears fill her eyes too.

Sagging her shoulders in defeat, she turned to me and dipped her chin. "It's in the past, Axel. None of us were in a good place back then. We were all doing what we thought we had to do to survive. It needs to stay in the past."

It felt like a huge weight had been lifted off my shoulders.

"Pix," Austin whispered, and I could hear the level of gratitude in his voice. Gratitude for letting his ex-con of a brother walk into their home, fuck, *storm* back into their lives.

Austin wrapped his wife in his arms, and I couldn't take my eyes off them. I'd never really seen how much my brother loved Lexi, or even gave a shit about how much she obviously adored him back. When you're dragged up in hell, I suppose you don't think about what the other side could be like.

But my brother had it. He had it all. He'd taken himself from the cesspool of our trailer park and was living the fucking American Dream.

"Austin? Lexi? You seen my cleats? I need to get to training."

The deep voice sounded from upstairs, and my stomach sank. My heart seemed to skip a beat like I had a damn heart murmur or some shit, because I knew exactly who that voice belonged to.

"Lex? You seen my cleats?"

Footsteps pounded up ahead on the first floor, and Austin and Lexi darted their eyes to each other, then me, the same worried expression on their faces. Just then, a pair of legs began running down the stairs, slowly revealing the tall, built frame of my little brother, Levi.

My lips parted as I realized he was all grown up, his dark-blond hair ruffled like he'd just got outta bed. He was wearing a pair of navy sweats and a sports tank, University of Washington Huskies Football written across the chest. His eyes were downcast as he searched the stairs for his cleats, but he started when he looked up, a shy smile pulling on his mouth.

In an instant, his gray eyes widened, his smile turned into a grimace, hands clenched into fists, and his chest began to heave.

Levi pounded down the stairs and Lexi met him at the bottom step, reaching out to grab his arm. "Levi—"

"What the fuck is he doing here?" Levi said coldly through gritted teeth and wrenched his arm free.

Austin stepped forward and gripped Levi's arm. "Lev—"

"*What* the fuck's he doing here?"

A huge unwanted feeling burrowed out of my chest. Levi was fucking burning with rage.

"Levi, calm the hell down!" Austin demanded, but Levi shook his head in disbelief.

"Calm down? Calm the fuck down? Are you shittin' me?"

"He's our brother, Lev! What the fuck's wrong with you?" Austin shouted, standing in front of Levi. But Levi couldn't calm down.

Levi pushed Austin aside and stepped forward, his eyes lit with fire, and boomed out, "What the fuck're you doing here? Why aren't you still rotting in that cell where you belong?"

Lexi rushed forward and took Levi's arms in her hands. "Levi, please…"

But Levi's eyes were still set on me. The teen who'd come down those stairs looking for his cleats a minute ago, now looked every inch a true Carillo, every inch the ex-

Heighter gang member, every inch the hard little shit I'd forced him to be.

Seeing the hatred he had for me now, when those light-gray eyes used to look at me with nothing but respect and love, destroyed me.

"Levi, look at me," Lexi pushed again, but I took a deep breath and stepped forward, once again clashing gazes with my youngest brother.

"Lexi, it's okay," I said. Her head whipped round in my direction. I could see the panic and upset in her expression, but I flicked a glance to Austin and nodded my head. He returned the gesture.

Reaching forward, Austin took Lexi's hand and pulled her to him, whispering something in her ear.

Sucking in a deep breath, I turned to Levi. "Lev, I know you're pissed—"

"Pissed?" he snapped and moved closer still, his knuckles white from how tight his fists were clenched. "Pissed ain't even close to what I'm feeling about you being here, in *our* home." I watched him take a long breath. "You were meant to be away for another five years. You were never meant to come here."

"He was *always* meant to come here, Lev. Once he got out, this was always gonna be Axel's home... with us," Austin said from behind Levi, and Levi glanced back.

Austin reached out and put his hand on Levi's shoulder. "He's our brother, Levi. We're here for him no matter what. We're Carillos."

I wanted to speak, tried to speak, but I knew if I opened my mouth, I'd break down like a pussy. Austin, that kid always had my back. Even now, after I'd cut off all contact for years, he acted as though we had nothing but good in our past.

Levi's mouth tightened and a look of pure disgust set on his face. "Yeah, we have to be there for him?" He tried to step toward me, but Austin's hand kept him back. It only seemed to piss Levi off more. "Tell me, Austin. Where was our *brother* after Porter OD'd and he ran away? Where was our *brother* when he left you to work next to Gio and sacrifice your degree? Where was our *brother* when our mamma was dying and we nearly lost Pix? And where was our *brother* when we scattered Mamma's ashes in Firenze, the only place she'd ever called home?" Levi said the word "brother" like it meant shit to him, like *I* meant shit to him, and every time he called me out on my sins, it fucking killed me just that little bit more inside.

Why the fuck had I come back? What the hell was I thinking?

"Nah, Aust," Levi said, curling his lip at me like I was a pile of shit he'd just stepped in. "He ain't no brother of

48

ours. He's no Carillo… He's just a fucking loser of an ex-con that's going nowhere in life, and he's come here to use you for money and to drag us back down too."

Red faced, Levi batted off Austin's hand, walked to a closet under the stairs to pick up a training bag, and without another glance, walked right out the front door, leaving Austin, Lexi, and me stunned in silence.

Lexi moved from Austin and ran to the door. "Levi! Wait!" I heard her shout from the driveway, but the sound of a car pulling away on gravel drowned her out, and she ran back in.

"Austin! We need to go after him."

Austin ran a hand down his face and shook his head. "Nah, Pix, leave him. He needs to cool down."

Watching Lexi wipe her eyes and Austin clearly stressed, I shook my head.

I shouldn't be here.

Walking back toward the door, I headed outside, grabbing my bag off the floor.

"Axe, wait!" Austin shouted, and I reluctantly stopped, shoulders sagging. I just wanted to get the fuck away. I wasn't welcome no more.

"Axe, what you doing?" Austin asked, coming to stand before me, blocking my path.

"Look, kid, I should have called first and said I got out. I shouldn't have come here period… I just thought… Fuck, I don't know… I *didn't* think…"

"You thought your brothers would want to see you."

Keeping my eyes to the ground, I nodded. "Yeah, I should've known better. I ruin your lives, don't speak to you for years, then turn up five years earlier than I should've. I get it, kid, I do."

Austin gripped the strap of my bag and picked it off the floor, causing me to look up. I went to argue, when he lifted his hand and cut me off.

"You get *shit*, Axe," he said tightly and glanced back to Lexi, who threw him, then me, a watery smile. Fixing his dark eyes back on mine, he added, "Way I see it, you got out early for doing something good. The Axe I knew always had good in him. He just never made good choices." Austin slung the bag over his shoulder and headed for the stairs, speaking as he went. "But you coming here straight from prison tells me you're finally, for the first time in your life, thinking straight."

Clawing my long hair back from my face, I watched Austin climb the stairs. "Austin, I can get somewhere else to stay. Lev made his feelings 'bout me damn clear. I ain't wanted. I don't wanna be where I ain't wanted."

Austin stopped mid-step but kept his focus straightforward. He said nothing for about twenty seconds and the silence was fucking suffocating.

"I've missed you, Axe," he finally said.

A lump clogged my throat as Austin's voice cracked, and my eyes filled with tears.

"You're my big brother, Axe. It was always me and you. Lev was too young to get it, but everything fell on you and me as kids… I love you. You're my blood. And I don't want you going anywhere without me again."

Glancing away, unable to see Austin breaking, I suddenly felt Lexi next to me. When I glanced up the stairs, Austin had disappeared leaving his wife and me alone.

"He was crushed when you started refusing his visit requests a few years ago, never explaining the reason why…."

I snapped my head to my right only to see Lexi staring off after Austin, before looking back at me.

"He's had so much to deal with: your mamma dying, the draft, moving to San Francisco." Her eyes filled with tears and she wiped at her cheeks. "And me… He had a lot to cope with while I got help… while I got better, which wasn't an easy road." Lexi sniffed, laying her hand on my arm.

"Every day he talks about you. Every day he wonders what you're doing, if you're safe... if your mamma's looking over you."

"Lexi..." I whispered, trailing off as emotion dried my throat. I couldn't handle imagining Austin taking all that on while I rotted in a damn cell, unable to do shit but wish away my life.

"And he's been counting down the days 'til your release so he could be there, at the prison gates, when you got out. He couldn't wait to bring you home."

I briefly closed my eyes and inhaled through my nose. "Fuck, Lexi... but Levi—"

"Is still struggling with your mamma's death. He's too quiet, keeps everything bottled up."

"Yeah? Well, he had no problem making his feelings 'bout me clear enough," I replied.

"And that's why you being here is a blessing."

My eyebrows pulled down in confusion, and Lexi shrugged. "That's the most passionate I've seen Levi since we were all back in Bama. Five years of keeping everything inside. You've just released something within him."

"Hatred," I said, feeling the truth of those words deep in my chest.

Lexi squeezed my hand and began to walk away, only looking back to say, "Love. Only the feeling of love would bring that out in Lev. I know him enough to know that. You only hurt the ones you love. I think you being here will force him to confront things he's tried to bury deep. Having you here will make him have to confront his grief."

Lexi walked toward the kitchen again, and I asked, "Hey, Lexi?"

She turned and smiled sadly.

"Why aren't you kicking me out?" I ducked my head in embarrassment. "I threatened you, scared you... Fuck, I wanted to keep you quiet." Shame, *real* shame ran through me as I met her eyes. "And I wouldn't have hesitated to either, if Aust hadn't stopped me. I... I would have, Lexi. Do you get that? I would've hurt you to protect the Heighters."

Lexi swallowed and I could see a flash of pure fear cross her face. "I know, Axel. I remember your threats just as much as you, and I remember the intent in your eyes as you did so. But I'm working on being stronger, and holding on to hatred will only keep me weak." Her gaze drifted up the stairs again, where I could hear what sounded like closet doors opening and shutting. "And Austin loves you."

I frowned.

Lexi noticed. "Austin puts me first. I'm everything to him. I have been for the longest time now. He's my protector and refuses to let me relapse or be in any kind of danger."

I stared in silence and Lexi blushed. I could see on her face how much she loved my brother. It made me feel uncomfortable. I'd never witnessed that kind of love before and knew one hundred percent that I could never be that important to anybody for as long as I lived.

Lexi sighed. "Axel, if Austin thought you were in any way a danger to me or Levi, you wouldn't be standing here right now. My Austin trusts you, implicitly, and because I know that my husband will never let me fall, I trust you've changed too… I trust the Axel buried deep within you, which has Austin's love, has finally broken his way to the surface."

Lexi circled the wedding ring on her finger. Meeting my gaze, she flicked her chin to the upstairs direction. "You better get upstairs and tell him you're staying. By the sounds of it, he's already unpacked for you. He's been saving you a bedroom since we moved in."

Lexi disappeared into the kitchen and I stayed in the entranceway on my own for a while. Her words ran through my head, and before I even realized it, I was walking up the long spiral staircase and came to a huge hallway with doors leading off in all directions.

Following the hallway to the sound of drawers being pulled open, I couldn't help but look at the photographs lining the walls: Austin at the draft, dressed in a suit, holding his 49ers shirt, then him this summer signing here at the Seahawks. Levi graduating high school, his stidda missing from his cheek. I felt both a mixture of shame and pride at that. Ashamed he'd ever earned one in the first place, but proud it wasn't the guy he was now.

I walked farther toward the room, but a picture at the end, bigger than all the rest, made me freeze in my steps.

Mamma.

Mamma, around the same age as Levi was now, singing on stage in Verona.

I don't know how long I stood there, but when my beard was wet with tears and my feet had grown numb, I knew it'd been a while.

Gutting shame filled my stomach and it almost brought me to my knees.

I'd failed my mamma. She'd asked me—no, *begged*—me to get straight, save my brothers. Instead, I'd condemned them to gang life while she was trapped on her bed with ALS unable to do anything about it. They'd shot people, dealt drugs… and I'd cheered them on all the way.

"It's my favorite," Austin spoke from behind me, but I didn't turn around. I couldn't look away from my mamma's smiling face.

"It was kept in a trunk she had under her bed. I never knew about it. This one, pictures of our grandparents we never met." Austin paused and came to stand at my side. "Pictures of us all as kids... so many damn pictures."

I still didn't speak. I couldn't.

"She knew you loved her," Austin said in a hoarse voice as if he knew what was killing me inside.

I couldn't take any more. I couldn't take any more pain... I couldn't take speaking of my mamma, looking at her so young and healthy, when my last memory of her was caged in her broken body on her tiny, shitty bed. So I wiped my eyes and turned to Austin.

He looked every bit as broken as I felt.

I opened my mouth to speak, when he cut me off. "You're staying, Axe. I ain't letting you leave."

All I could do was nod.

Sighing deep, I slung my arm around Austin's neck, and he led me to the biggest bedroom I'd ever seen. I was used to a claustrophobic six-by-eight foot cell. This was a dream.

"Y'all are unpacked."

"Thanks, kid," I said quietly as I walked to the window, a window that overlooked a still and silent Lake.

I could feel Austin hovering at the door, could feel his stare on my back. "Just ask, Austin," I said, not turning around.

I heard the floorboard creak. "Just... just wondering what your plans are, you know, here in Seattle?"

I huffed a silent laugh to myself. What the hell would he say if I told him the real reason I was in Seattle?

"It's arranged that I'll be working in some fish market by the waterfront." I shrugged. "Conditions of my parole. Start tomorrow."

My kid brother sighed in relief. "I'm proud of you, Axe," he said, and I could hear the sincerity in his voice. "I've still got your old El Camino in my garage. When I moved, I couldn't bear to see it go. Had it tuned up, repainted and reupholstered."

My heart dropped knowing he'd done that to my old car. A car, back in the day, I probably looked after more than my family.

When I turned round to thank him, he was gone. As I stared out the window again, I caught sight of the Husky football stadium in the distance and thought back to Levi...

He ain't no brother of ours. He's no Carillo. He's just a fucking loser of an ex-con that's going nowhere in life, and he's come here to use you for money and to drag us down too.

There was no fucking hope.

Chapter five
Ally

One week later...

Wiping my brow, I sat, staring at the final wooden crate I'd just opened. It stored the last of the Elpidio sculptures shipped up for the show.

I held my breath as I gently removed the protective packages to reveal the single piece of marble that just destroyed me every time I saw it in a magazine or picture. And that one time I flew miles to see it up close.

As the foam packaging slowly gave way to a smooth white marble, tears filled my eyes. I was actually seeing it in the flesh again. In actuality. In all its devastating perfection.

As I cast a glance to my watch, I saw it was fifteen minutes past midnight. I'd been here all day, trying to place

59

the sculptures in their correct positions to test the flow of the exhibit.

The theme of the show was proving difficult to design. I felt like there was a pattern, a natural story to the sculptures, but I'd yet to work them out. I wasn't sure I could do so without some input from the artist himself.

Catching movement from the corner of my eye, I saw Christoph, the night security guard, doing his rounds.

Getting to my feet, Christoph jumped back in shock. "Ms. Lucia, you nearly gave me a heart attack! I didn't see you down there."

"I'm sorry!" I said apologetically. "I'm trying to get the final piece free from its packaging so I can position them correctly tomorrow. It's made from marble and incredibly tall, so…"

Christoph smiled, and came to help me. In just a few minutes we had the wooden crate removed and the packaging dispensed of. As the sculpture was revealed, we both stepped back, and my hand flew to my mouth at the view.

This piece was flawless.

For minutes, all I could do was stare… stare at the six-foot high double-sided white angel, this side's hands reaching out like she was pleading. She held a pile of black ashes in her palms. I knew from my research that what I was looking at now was the broken side of the angel.

Her wings were fraying and clipped and her beautiful face was contorted in pain… *no*, agony. Her body was curled inward, almost like she was struggling to stand straight. What should be a beautiful dress was ripped and torn, sullied with patches of dirt. Her hair was stringy and limp, hanging haphazardly to the middle of her back, and the desolate look in her unnaturally wide eyes… was haunting.

It shattered my heart. It was as though this sculpture had a soul, projecting every emotion the artist felt when he painstakingly carved each curve and expression on the angel's face. I could feel the wracking pain, the inner torture of the broken angel running through my blood.

No picture I had ever seen did this piece justice. To witness it in reality was like being given a gift from heaven itself.

Taking a deep breath, I slowly moved my feet and made my way to the other side, where my emotions completely took hold and tears began pouring down my cheeks.

This angel was stunningly beautiful, a complete contrast to her alter ego. This angel's body was standing straight, full with curves and good health, draped in a pristine Roman-style dress. Her serene smiling face was tipped high to the sky, her thick long hair falling to her waist. I could feel the sensation of the hot sun kissing her cheeks, the warmth enveloping her body like an embrace. Her delicate hands were held up like she was taking flight, her angel wings spread wide. The black ashes that her alter ego held out so desperately, in this formation, were scattered to the ground.

She was breaking free.

My heart beat faster and faster with every passing minute. I was unsure how long I stood there, held in this statue's thrall.

Shaking myself from my trance, I wiped at my eyes and laughed at the extent this sculpture ripped me apart. "Sorry, Christoph, I get a little too emotional with Elpidio's work at times—"

I glanced around the unnamed sculpture, only to see the gallery completely empty, the sounds of my sniffling laughter echoing off the domed glass ceiling.

Laughing again at how I must have scared Christoph away, I ran my hands through my messy ponytail and slapped at my cheeks. I needed to get home. Exhaustion was making me crazy.

Wistfully casting the sculpture one last glance, I made my way to the bathroom to splash water on my face. As I stared in the bathroom mirror's reflection, my heart soared that I was in this position. I was completely and utterly enthralled by this exhibition.

I was convinced that no other show I curate could hold a candle to this one. I was obsessed with these pieces. More than that, I couldn't rid my thoughts of what the artist must have gone through in his life to create them. Nothing good, I was sure. Because of this, my heart bled for him.

Pull yourself together, Ally, I scolded myself and made a move to leave the bathroom to go home.

Just as I was about to exit the museum, I realized I'd forgotten my notepad. I had to work on the floor design when I got home; I still needed to tweak the layout. Nothing I'd done so far had worked. Something was off, which *never* happened to me. Turning on my heel, I briskly walked back to the gallery.

Spotting my notepad lying on top of an empty crate, I made a dash to retrieve it, when from the corner of my eye, I saw a man in the gallery, beside the angel piece.

Fearful at what he was doing here this late at night, I cautiously moved forward to get security but immediately stopped dead. The man was tall, well built and dressed all in black: black jeans, a black long-sleeved shirt, long brown hair tied back in a low bun. But that's not what caused me to stop and stare. The man was as still as the night, as he stood at the main sculpture. His hand stretched and rested upon a spread wing, his head down blocking his face. His shoulders were shaking, as if he were crying. Like he was crying for the angel.

I couldn't move, and my chest grew tight watching this large man seemingly breaking down.

Deciding to tell Christoph, I stepped forward, but the heel of my boot clicked on the polished concrete floor. My eyes snapped to the man, who had now straightened, his face hidden by the large sculpture.

The room was noiseless as we both stood there unmoving, so silent you could hear a pin drop.

"This is a private gallery," I eventually found my voice to say.

The man's shoulders stiffened.

Craning my head, I tried to get a better look at him, but he seemed to anticipate the move and stepped further away from my sight.

"The gallery is closed to visitors. You really shouldn't be here," I added, nervously.

In a second, the man released his hand from the broken wing of the sculpture like it nearly killed him to do so. With his head firmly cast down, he turned and ran out of the gallery.

My heart pounded as I watched him retreat.

What the hell was that? Why did it suddenly feel like I was standing in a vacuum, the air from my lungs dissipated? And more to the point, why was he here this late at night, breaking down in front of the angel?

Shaking myself vigorously, I clutched my notepad and purse, and walked toward the security desk where Christoph was monitoring the screens.

"Christoph?" I called, and he looked up. I sighed and leaned on the desk. "You can't let students sneak into the museum after hours, especially *my* gallery. Many people want to see these pieces up close and will do anything to get a sneak peek."

Christoph frowned. "I assure you, Ms. Lucia, no students are getting in or *have* been getting in."

I closed my eyes in a brief moment of exasperation. "Christoph, they did just now. I just this minute caught a student in the gallery, and he was touching the main sculpture. What if he'd broken it?"

Christoph got to his feet and leaned on the black granite countertop opposite me, confusion still clearly etched on his face. He lifted the sign-in book and read down the names on the page. "No, it was just the two of you who've been here this late."

I was set to argue when his words finally sank into my brain. "The two of us?" I questioned, not understanding to whom he was referring.

Christoph checked the sheet again. "Yeah, you and the artist."

My head jerked to the book he held. "El... Elpidio?" I spluttered in shock.

Something akin to butterflies fluttered in my stomach, and I struggled to talk. "Elpidio the artist whose exhibition I'm curating was *here?*"

Christoph looked at me as if I was insane. I was starting to concern myself with that too.

"Ms. Lucia, Elpidio has been coming in every night around this time to check on the progress. I thought you knew. Vin Galanti cleared it before you both arrived in Seattle."

The notepad in my hand was shaking in time with my trembling, and I placed it down. Elpidio had been coming in every night?

That meant...

"Christoph, was he wearing all black tonight? Does he have dark long hair?"

Christoph nodded. "He always wears black. Never says anything." Christoph leaned forward. "Real dark brooding

66

artist type. And honestly, he scares the shit out of me. He's one intimidating guy."

"Oh my God…" I whispered. I'd just seen him… He was here… He'd been *coming* here and I'd not known…

Abruptly, I covered Christoph's hand with my own. "Christoph, which way did Elpidio go?"

"Out the back door to the staff parking lot. It's where he parks every night."

I immediately began running to the staff exit door. As I swung the door open to the cool night, I watched helplessly as a black muscle car pulled out of the parking lot and raced away from the museum.

As I stood there letting the cool breeze caress my flushed face and soothe my frantic heart, I squeezed my eyes shut. I pictured him standing beside the sculpture, head down, back tense, with his hand gripping the angel's wing as though its touch was the only thing stopping him from dropping to the ground.

My gaze followed the fading lights of his car, and I whispered aloud, "What has happened in your life to make you so broken?"

Chapter Six
Ally

No one could ever know of this moment. This one moment of pure insanity, I had to keep to myself.

It was bordering on ridiculous. Regardless, I found myself in the bathroom of the museum, spreading on a pale-pink shade of lip-gloss on my lips, and brushing out my long dark hair until it fell against my waist. I was dressed simply in an off-the-shoulder gray T-shirt that skimmed my figure and skinny black jeans. I never dressed up to curate a gallery, too much dust and mess. What I was wearing wasn't beyond what I'd ordinarily wear. But there was no doubt, that at thirty minutes past midnight on a weeknight, I normally wouldn't be applying makeup on the off chance a reclusive artist would show his face.

That reclusive artist I couldn't get out of my head. That reclusive artist I dreamt about last night. That reclusive artist who had been weeping while holding on to a marble angel's broken wing. That tall, broad, sullen artist who had fled at the very sound of my voice.

I was a bag of nerves simply thinking about what it would be like to meet Elpidio in person. I prayed to all that was holy that he wouldn't be a pompous ass. I didn't want my dream of this man shattered.

Checking one last time that I looked good, I walked back toward the gallery, glancing to the security desk to see if Christoph was there. He wasn't. Which probably meant Elpidio was a no-show.

Dammit. Seeing me must have scared him off last night. If only I'd known he'd been coming at night, I could have introduced myself… I could have finally met the man whose work had stolen my heart.

Head down in disappointment, I walked slowly to the gallery and moved the dark curtains aside, entering the private workspace. Bridgette, the Museum Director, had arranged to put the curtains up this afternoon after my many complaints about art students and visitors trying to take in an early showing.

As the curtains closed behind me, I jumped in surprise when I caught movement ahead.

My eyes slowly traveled upward to a pair of legs clad in black jeans, to a sculpted waist and torso covered in a

69

short-sleeved black shirt splashed in what looked like
marble dust.

My heart was in my throat as I drank in large arm
muscles, sculpted and pronounced under heavily tattooed
olive skin. My gaze drifted to a muscular tattooed neck,
partially covered by a dark short scruffy beard and
shoulder-length dark brown hair.

Elpidio…

I had to blink to believe the man I'd wanted to meet for
years was really standing right in front of me. I forgot how
to breathe. I forgot how to speak, move, or anything else
that should come naturally to a human being.

Elpidio's head was down, avoiding my gaze, but I knew
he knew I was here. Every inch of his body was taut, as if
ready to spring.

My voice failed to work as I watched his broad chest rise
and fall. Then, with deliberate slowness, he exhaled harshly
through his nostrils and lifted his head.

I nearly staggered back.

He was… dark. There was no other adjective I could
think of to do him justice. Dark, aggressively tattooed, and
absolutely yet unconventionally… *beautiful*.

Elpidio was as inspiring to look at as his sculptures, and
when his almost-black eyes pierced mine, I released a pent
up shuddering breath.

I thought my legs would give way as I watched those curious onyx irises rove all over my body. I trembled under his scrutiny, knees weak, heart fluttering.

Italian, I thought. Austin had been right. Elpidio definitely looked Italian.

It felt as though minutes passed in silence as we stood motionless, not knowing what to say.

Trying to salvage a modicum of professionalism, I snapped out of my stupor and stepped forward, timidly holding out my hand.

"Hello…" I said in a cracking voice.

Elpidio's stern gaze never once drifted from mine, his dark eyes stabbing. "I'm Aliyana. You… you must be Elpidio?"

In a second, I witnessed paleness spread on his cheeks and his eyes dropped to the ground, his shoulder-length brown hair falling to cover his face. He was protecting his anonymity. Vin had told me how uncomfortable he was with any acclaim or recognition. His mentor clearly wasn't lying.

"It's okay," I rushed out. "I'm the curator of your exhibition. Your being here stays with me. I'm ethically bound to protect your anonymity if you so wish."

Elpidio's shoulders seemed to relax some at that, and sighing reluctantly, he raked back his long hair from his face and raised his head.

This time I could see him more clearly. He was ruggedly edgy, and on his left cheek, he wore a tattoo of a black crucifix just below his eye. He simply screamed danger. His eyes were unnervingly assessing as though he had no trust in me, or toward anyone else for that matter.

Suddenly, Elpidio reached forward and encased his hand in mine. When our hands touched, I lightly gasped, the heat of his palm searing. I'd forgotten I'd been holding my hand out to greet him, too entranced by his unrefined looks and silent temperament.

"Aliyana," he said gruffly. My heart skipped a beat on hearing his husky drawl.

"Elpidio," I flustered. "I can't tell you how happy I am to finally meet you," I said breathlessly. His mouth tightened as though my enthusiasm were lost on him or irritated him. I couldn't decide.

Clearing my throat, I released his grip and gestured to the developing exhibit. "What do you think?" I asked nervously, a subtle tremble in my voice. I moved beside him to face the gallery. "I'm an avid admirer of your work, so this is truly a dream come true for me to design this exhibit."

Elpidio remained silent, so I turned back to him, and his dark eyes were narrowed as though in displeasure as our gazes collided. A flush of heat spread through my body under his heavy attention. I could feel my cheeks blazing.

"Is something wrong?" I asked, nervously threading my fingers through my long hair.

Elpidio's expression stayed blank, the further narrowing of his eyes the only change in his look. Elpidio turned his gaze back to the expanse of gallery and slowly tilted his head, studiously scrutinizing something in front of us. Reflecting his stance, I tried to follow his gaze and see what he was seeing.

Elpidio glanced at me again, and for a moment, I felt like I'd seen him before. That split second glimpse of his dark eyes revealing a familiarity to his face. But then the moment was gone as quickly as it came and he walked forward.

Elpidio stopped at his sculpture of a man folded over, head cradled in hands, legs tucked into his chest… and tragically, every inch of his body was pierced with black painted marbled knives, the knives cracking the white Cararra marble as though he were being torn apart by the blades.

"Elpidio?" I questioned, and he looked up at me.

"Elpi," he said coolly, and a shiver rippled down my spine at his dominating tone.

"Elpi… okay," I whispered in reply. The way he stared at my lips a little too long, flustered me.

Reaching out his hand, he ran his calloused tattooed fingers along the curve of the sculpture's back and looked at an empty space in the corner of the room.

I watched him closely examine his pieces with precise care.

Elpidio suddenly stood and pointed to the far corner. "This one should go there."

My heart raced with excitement as I moved to join him, leaning over his shoulder to see the exact spot to which he was pointing. As I stood there breathing lightly, I sensed his body growing tense at our close proximity. This close, he smelled faintly of cigarette smoke and the oaky cedar musk of his cologne.

He smelled good… *too* good. So good it was pushing the boundaries of my professional conduct.

The heavy muscles and cords in Elpidio's arms tightened. He ran his hand through his hair once more. I surmised that he did this when he was feeling nervous.

"Is there a particular reason for you wanting the piece to be in that corner?" I asked.

Elpidio tipped back his head and stared out the glass domed ceiling. I followed suit, my eyebrows pulled down in confusion.

"The sun will pour in through the roof for most of the day. If we angle it just right, the rays will cut across sculpture and reflect the knives on the floor, like I'd planned."

The more he spoke, the more I picked up on the devastation in Elpidio's deep timbre. By the end of his explanation, I found I was no longer looking at the domed ceiling, but at him and the expression of deep sorrow etched upon his face.

For a brief moment, Elpidio closed his eyes, and I could feel the sadness pulsing from him.

In an instant, my heart broke for him. I had no idea why, but he definitely seemed to be suffering.

Seconds went by in silence, yet I couldn't stop watching his face. This mysterious sculptor was more intriguing in person than I could ever have imagined. Intriguing but troubled... intimidating... a man about whom my every instinct told me to steer clear.

Not wanting to intrude on what seemed like a personal moment, I forced myself to focus on the sculpture.

"Do you agree?" Elpidio eventually asked.

"I love it," I said quietly and moved so the full moon and all its light was in sight. As I looked at the shadows cast on the floor, my eyes widened.

My attention returned to Elpidio, who stood with his bulky arms crossed over his chest. His harsh gaze was focused on me.

"I'll agree with whatever you want, but…" I trailed off, leaning down further to check I was correct.

Elpidio tensed. "What?" he snapped.

I reared back slightly at his sharpness. Elpidio then sighed, his tanned cheeks flushing red as he rocked unsurely on his feet. It was as if he were insecure, like he wasn't used to having someone discuss his art on a personal level with him… like he was completely out of his depth.

But that couldn't be right. Although this was his first show, he must surely be used to people discussing his art, both academically and publically. He'd been sculpting for a couple of years.

Sighing, I straightened up. "Well, with the sun's rays shining down, it will look like he's bleeding."

Elpidio craned his neck to the sculpture but didn't move.

"Come here and see," I urged, and reluctantly, Elpidio moved to my side and crouched down, careful our bodies didn't touch. I knew the instant he saw what I was referring to, as a quiet exhalation escaped his lips.

Elpidio ran his hand down his face. "It does," he agreed in a graveled voice.

"Does the effect of bleeding fit with what inspired the piece? We don't want to change what it's meant to represent," I asked. Elpidio hadn't named any of his masterpieces, nor provided any background on what inspired them, what the art was meant to portray. As a sculptor, its conception could only ever be explained by one person, *him*. But as the curator, not knowing anything about the sculptures' backgrounds made them a nightmare to stage.

"Completely," he replied breathlessly. Seeming completely taken aback, Elpidio sat on the floor, content to watch the moon-shadows project what looked like black rivulets trailing along the concrete below.

Slumping to my knees beside him, I waited for him to speak. I was used to artists having unconventional methods when exhibiting their work, but Elpidio appeared to be completely at a loss with this process.

Leaning forward, I traced a long a black shadow on the polished concrete floor with my finger to gain some form of composure. When I looked back up, Elpidio was watching me. His gaze was a touch softer than before and his expression was warm.

"Sorry," I said quickly. "I know I can get carried away at times. Your work…" I sighed and flushed red in embarrassment. "It makes me all kinds of crazy." I sputtered a nervous laugh and went back to tracing the shadows near my knees.

Elpidio didn't speak for several seconds, but then asked, "What do you think he's bleeding?" Surprised, I glanced at him. Elpidio jerked his chin to the marble statue of the man before us.

"*What* do I think he's bleeding?" I asked, confused.

He gave me a stern nod.

As I studied the sculpture, his form bent over as though in agony, I said, "Pain? Blood? Rejection?"

Elpidio's eyes were unfocused, lost in concentration.

"Is that right? Is it pain? Blood? Something else?"

Elpidio's eyes abruptly met mine. "Guilt."

Guilt…

I looked at the sculpture again, this time with fresh eyes. Now I felt the guilt. Each dagger, a sin the man should not have committed… The marble man was breaking apart because of his guilt.

"You… you ever felt guilt like that, Aliyana?"

My heart fluttered at the way Elpidio spoke my name, his tongue wrapping around the Spanish pronunciation perfectly. As I met his eyes, his gaze implored me to answer his question.

Sadly I shook my head. I didn't carry anything close to the level of guilt portrayed in this piece. In fact, I doubted many did.

Teeth clenched, Elpidio abruptly got to his feet and darted for the exit.

"Are you leaving?" I asked, my voice laced with disappointment. Elpidio stopped dead in his tracks.

"Yes," he growled low. His voice was broken, but I didn't think it was in anger, more in distress.

I sensed how badly he wanted to leave. His hands clenched into fists at his sides and his broad muscled back bunched impossibly tight under the thin material of his shirt.

I didn't want him to go. I wanted him to explain every piece to me like he did with the man split by daggers. I wanted to see this world he'd created through *his* eyes. I wanted to talk to the man whose work I cherished *more* than any collection I'd ever studied or seen. I wanted him to explain his life-journey so I could create the exhibition his genius deserved. And if I were being true to myself, I wanted to get to know him too.

"Please," I whispered desperately and Elpidio cautiously turned to face me.

The expression he wore wasn't welcoming. In fact, it could only be described as downright threatening. But I had an insatiable need to know *more*. I didn't know Elpidio, not at all. But something inside of me wanted to help him heal.

One thing was true. I knew his work. I'd had a glimpse of the real man inside through every curve of his marble creations. He could hide behind the tattoos and long hair, but he couldn't hide what he displayed in plain sight. His sculptures were him screaming to the world that he was flawed.

"You never name your work," I stated as Elpidio's eyes tensed in overt agitation. I stepped forward, looking up nervously through my long lashes. "Your work… you never give them titles."

Elpidio shrugged, but that flash of insecurity—or was it reluctance?—I'd seen earlier, again washed across his face. I stepped forward again. He didn't back away as we stood toe to toe.

My hands were shaking. He was so beautifully fascinating… that Latin skin, those forbidding facial tattoos, the heavy coating of ink that covered the real man who lay beneath.

"Why?" I asked. "Why leave your beautiful pieces nameless? Naming them gives them life. A baptism of your creation, so to speak."

He glared at me. I swallowed hard, feeling rattled. But Elpidio, this time, leaned forward to me, and a chill ran down my spine in anticipation of what he would do.

"Naming them makes it all too fucking real," he whispered, his hot breath skirting past my face.

"I don't underst—" I went to argue, but Elpidio cut me off with his severe expression.

"I don't fucking deserve all this. I deserve none of this shit… Believe me… I never fucking wanted it… but I got it all the damn same."

I inhaled a ragged breath as his large body towered over me. I fluttered my eyes to meet his. His almost-ebony eyes flared with heat.

"That's not true," I whispered. His work, more than anyone's, deserved to be on display. People should see his works of art.

"You don't know me, girl," he disagreed through gritted teeth.

"I know your work," I countered, my heart breaking into a sprint at his surge of aggression and his condescending use of the word 'girl.' "More than anyone else, I *know* your work…"

Elpidio watched me so intently that I thought I might collapse under the weight of his stare. Then, to my utter surprise, he dropped his scowl and his eyes dulled with defeat. His hand reached up and took a strand of my long hair between his finger and thumb, rubbing them together, before his gaze locked on to mine.

The air seemed as thick as the densest fog around us, until Elpidio dropped my hair as though it were a naked flame. A startled, disbelieving expression set clearly on his face, like he was shocked he'd just touched me.

He quickly turned on his heel.

This time I knew he was leaving, regardless of my protest. As he threw open the heavy curtains, I asked, "The titles…?"

Elpidio's fist wrapped around the black material and his head dropped. "Do you really need them that much?" he asked shortly.

A flicker of hope sparked in my chest. "They would help me… immensely. People like to put a name to a sculpture, and they love it if there's some explanation behind its creation. The press like it too, so they can reference their favorite piece in their reviews. I've already had requests for that from some major industry heavy hitters."

"Fuck sake," he hissed under his breath, but I heard it. I waited on tenterhooks for his answer, every part of me

trembling from our strange encounter, when he finally dropped his shoulders. "Fine, whatever."

"Thank you," I replied, my stomach swirling with butterflies.

Elpidio drew the curtains. "I'll come by 'round the same time tomorrow night."

"Okay," I replied, heat infusing my blood at the thought of working with him again.

Just as he turned to leave, I quickly asked, "Elpidio?"

He stopped but didn't turn.

"Any chance you're from Bama?" His shoulders stiffened. "I only ask because I'm from Birmingham, and I picked up on your accent too."

He hesitated. "Mobile," he reluctantly replied, quietly. A small smile spread on my lips at the thought we were from the same state, when he added, "It's Elpi. *Elpi*," he emphasized.

"Okay," I whispered, wanting to say more. But then Elpi pounded through the parted curtains, leaving me next to the sculpture we'd just discussed. As it sat in the glare of the silver moonlight, I gave a long drawn-out exhale, as a cold shiver of realization engulfed me.

Elpidio, *Elpi*, is this pained, wounded man laying on the floor, the man bleeding guilt…

Chapter Seven
Axel

"You don't know me, girl,"

"I know your work." Aliyana's Spanish eyes flared with conviction. "More than anyone else, I know your work..."

As I circled the untouched slab of marble before me, my chest bare and sweaty from my recent workout, the curator's words kept circling around my head. *"I know your work... More than anyone else, I know your work..."*

Aliyana. Damn Aliyana Lucia for getting in my fucking head.

From the minute I'd seen her two nights ago in the gallery, catching me by the marble angel, I'd been shocked fucking speechless.

I'd never seen any chick look like her. I'd never seen anyone with eyes that bright, hair that dark, or a smile that fucking blinding. In the past, I'd gotten pussy whenever I'd wanted. Plenty of Italiano trash whores around the trailer park to sink into for a quick wet fuck. But never had a chick of her standing paid me one bit of attention. Fuck, I'd barely even seen a woman in five years, let alone got laid… Then she's the first one to pay me any attention, tripping over her words as though I was the greatest thing on Earth.

Then last night, Aliyana waited for me to show up. *Me.* I could barely fucking wrap my head round that fact. I should've stayed away. I never wanted anyone involved with this shitty exhibition to ever know what I looked like. But morbid curiosity of what my show could look like drew me back to that damn gallery night after night… curious to see the sculptures I'd spent months creating, sculptures I hadn't seen in so long… and there she was, looking at me with her stunning fucking face, all excited to meet fucking *Elpidio.*

Elpidio, a fictional artist. Elpidio, the sculptor that the prissy fucking art world had fallen in love with. But no one, *no one*—but Vin—knew Elpidio was actually Axel Carillo. Some fucked-up ex-con from a trailer park. And no fucker had time for him.

Axel Carillo, the thirty-year-old ex con who got a reduced sentence for selling out a drug supplier to the feds. Axel Carillo, the once famed second-in-command to the

Heighters, the hardest and most brutal gang member to own that piece of turf. And Axel Carillo, the fuck-up of a man that broke his dying mamma's heart and led the two best brothers a guy could ask for to ruin.

Axel Carillo deserved to live in fucking misery for what he'd done.

Axel Carillo deserved to be treated like scum.

Axel Carillo didn't deserve another chance at life.

Nah, Aliyana Lucia may think the sun shined out of Elpidio's ass, but my brothers knew the real me. They knew who I really was deep down. Shit, the way Levi treated me every time he saw me told me that much.

Only two hours ago had he shown me just how much he couldn't stand me, and he didn't hold back his words while he did so…

*****

Sitting at the breakfast table, I sipped my black coffee, like I did every day, watching as Lexi cooked at the stove, Austin's arms wrapped around her waist. They didn't give a shit I was in here, or at least Austin didn't. There he stood with his lips kissing along Lexi's neck.

As much as I didn't want to see my little brother slobbering all over his skinny wife, I loved seeing him this happy.

At that moment, Lexi turned her head to face me and immediately blushed. Austin followed her gaze and started laughing when he saw what had his little woman so embarrassed.

"You're too fuckin' cute, Pix," Austin said and, pressing a kiss on Lexi's cheek, came to sit opposite me. Lexi plated up their eggs and sat down beside her husband, slowly lifting her fork to cut up her food. She kept her eyes downcast as she methodically chewed on each forkful of eggs. I caught Austin checking on her from time to time, his hand dropping down to lay on her leg.

For a minute, my gut clenched as I thought of how much my mamma would've loved to have seen her pride and joy this happy. And she would've fucking doted on Lexi. She'd have been the daughter Mamma'd never had.

That one thought of my mamma had my eyes closing and my throat fighting a huge lump.

"You good, Axe?" Austin asked.

My eyes snapped open, and I could see his eyebrows pulled down as he watched me.

"Yeah," I replied huskily, coughing and shifting on my seat.

Austin eyed me skeptically but didn't push it. "So," Austin said, getting up from the table to get us more coffee. As he filled my cup and sat back down, I waited for what he wanted to say. "You've been working real long hours at that market. Seems like all the fucking time."

As always my heart beat hard when Austin brought up my cover. I fucking hated lying to them all, but I just couldn't tell them what I was really doing in Seattle.

"Picking up more shifts. Working as much as I can," I mumbled vaguely.

"Overnight?" Austin questioned.

"A guy I work with has a place nearby. I sometimes crash there. But I work night shifts too."

"A guy you work with?" Austin probed, and Lexi looked up, worry in her eyes. Austin shifted on his seat. "An ex-con?"

My eyes narrowed at my little brother. "What if he is?" I asked. "So am I, Aust."

Austin opened his mouth to reply, when another voice cut in instead. "Of course he is, Aust. Axe only hangs with fucking losers. Remember Gio? He was Axe's puppet master back in Bama, hey?"

I closed my eyes briefly and tried to breathe through Lev's oncoming rant. He launched into them daily, his words trying to crop me the fuck down.

"They're probably not working late. He's probably back selling coke. The only thing he was ever good at. A snow entrepreneur."

Every part of me froze at the mention of my dealing, and I turned to glare at Levi, who was leaning back against the granite countertop, making a protein shake. My baby brother was shooting daggers at me with his gray eyes.

It'd been like this since I'd arrived. Most days he ignored me, the rest of the time he tried to shoot me down, tried to make me feel like the fucking loser they all believed I was.

The first few days, I put up with his shit, tried to coast the tide of anger. But recently, I'd been crashing at my studio more. Had Vin put in a bed for me there. Didn't wanna be here, where I wasn't wanted. Didn't wanna fuck up Lev's life more than I already had.

"Levi, stop!" Lexi said tiredly, but I put up my hand to stop her.

I locked gazes with my fratellino. *"Believe it or not, kid, I ain't into that shit no more."*

A knowing smirk spread on Levi's mouth. "Yeah, Axe? You reformed now?"

"Si, Lev, I am. Just trying to get on with my life."

Levi gripped the shaker in his hand and stepped forward, his face beaming red. "You know, I used to believe that God looked after good people, but looking at you sitting here in this house after everything you did to me, Aust, and Lex just doesn't sit right." Lev leaned forward, and for a minute, I thought the kid was gonna try and hit me, but he pulled back last minute. "You killed people, Axe, for nothing more than turf. You made Austin and me shoot guys from the Kings, and what makes me more pissed than anything is Mamma fucking died. Mamma, the best woman that ever existed, fucking died while you got to live. You!*"*

My chest tightened as I watched tears fill Lev's eyes. I wanted to do nothing more than stand up and fucking pull him to my chest and tell him I was sorry. But no way would he let me do that.

"Lev, you'd better wind your fucking neck in, now," Austin warned. Lev darted his eyes to Austin, then focused back on me.

"It's okay, Aust. Let him say what he wants. He obviously wants to get it off his chest," I said coolly, which only served to piss Lev off more.

"Axel, no one should be spoken to like that," Lexi said quietly, and it was the only time in his whole performance that I saw Lev lose his tough thug act.

Never breaking Levi's gaze, I shook my head at Lexi. "Let him say whatever he wants to say, Lexi. It's been a long time coming."

Levi's gray eyes lit with fire, and I was sure if he had a gun, I'd be taking a shot of lead to the head. He leaned down farther. "Work at your fucking fish market, Axe. But know nothing you do will ever make me forgive you. You're nothing but trash."

Levi walked out of the house, and I sat at the table, still gripping my coffee, the mug almost cracking under my tight grip.

"Axe, fuck, he shouldn't have said all that about Mamma—" Austin tried to say, but I stood, cutting him off, washed my cup out in the sink, and placed it on the drainer.

Closing my eyes and inhaling to fight back the fucking devastation washing through me, I said, "He's right, Aust. Everything he said was right." I looked up to see Austin and Lexi watching me with sympathetic eyes.

I didn't want no fucking pity. It only pissed me off more. I wasn't a damn charity case.

Pushing off the counter, I walked past my brother and wife, but not before saying, "If I could trade places with Mamma, I'd do it in a heartbeat. I deserve to be dead. I ain't never done nothing good in my whole life. Lev's right. I'm trash."

*****

Feeling the cold metal of the hammer in my hands, I began slamming it down on the large chunks of gray-veined Pavonazzo marble that I wouldn't need on this sculpture. With each blow I felt each one of Levi's words strike my chest like I was being torn apart.

What the hell have I done to that kid?

I'd fucking destroyed him, that's what. Me, the guy who was meant to have protected him, had fucking destroyed him.

Marble dust clouded the room. Looking at the clay cast I'd created as a template for the real thing, I took my hammer and smashed it straight through the center, two clay pieces crashing to the floor.

The hammer hung at my side. I panted with exertion, the muscles in my arms throbbing with the heavy weight of the tool.

I remained still, staring at the marble. Before I knew it, I'd picked up my pointed chisel and began chipping out a new outline. A certain image pushed its way into my mind, my hands giving it life.

I worked like a crazed man. Hours and hours passed as I chipped at the marble, the definition eventually taking form.

I worked so long that the gray skies gave way to the black of night and a strong wind pelted the long windows of the studio overlooking the Sound.

Muscles aching, body exhausted, I took a step back, assessing the sculpture. I had to turn away. I couldn't bear to look at it.

As I turned, my eyes filled with water. My normal uncontrollable anger took hold, sparked by a truckload of self-hatred. Then, I noticed Vin standing in the doorway, staring at the unfinished sculpture, a blank expression on his old face.

"How long have you been there?" I asked, gritting my teeth as I went to pick up a towel I'd thrown on my tools. I wiped my face.

"A while," Vin said, as he shuffled his ageing body into the room, his wooden cane by his side. I tensed as he came closer. I hated anyone seeing my work at any point, but especially when it was in progress. I couldn't take the judgment.

Vin walked to the sculpture with drawn eyebrows and slowly circled it. I ignored him and walked to pick up my pack of smokes. I lit one and took a long drag.

Vin shuffled over to me, I could see him looking about the sparse studio. His eyes targeted the large double bed in the far corner.

"You've been staying here a lot?" he asked.

"I work late."

Vin nodded, but I could see the concern in his eyes. I blew out a long cloud of smoke.

I didn't get why anyone fucking cared.

"I know you work late, Elpi. It's nearing one in the morning."

I ran my hand down my face. Shit, I'd been here all damn day.

I slowly turned my head to look at Vin. "Nearly one *a.m.*?"

"Yes, it's twelve forty-five," he replied in confusion. "I've been out at dinner with friends and thought I'd drop by. I just knew you'd be awake. I have to go back to New York in the morning, so wanted to say a quick goodbye. My work will keep me away until nearer the opening of your show."

93

Stubbing out my smoke, I reached for my black shirt which was pitted in marble dust and clay and slid on my black boots. "Okay. Bye."

"Where are you going in such a rush?" Vin asked as I reached for my wallet and keys for the El Camino.

"The gallery."

"Ah. You're still going every night," Vin mused, and I stopped dead.

"You know I've been going?"

He nodded. "I signed you up as a night visitor before you even arrived. I knew you couldn't resist. It's a good thing. It tells me you're not as indifferent to this exhibition as you try to make out."

I kept my silence, feeling like a fucking douche. Yeah, I gave a shit.

"And you're going now to check on its progress?"

I stared at Vin and knew the old bastard wouldn't stop pushing me until I spoke. "I'm gonna go give titles to my pieces."

Vin's mouth spread in the biggest fucking smile ever. "Elpi! I'm so glad. The titles will give them life!" Then he frowned. "But why now? You've refused for so long."

My stomach rolled as Aliyana's face came to my mind. Looking down, I scratched at my beard. "The curator caught me there last night and asked me to name them. I

94

agreed. She was… persistent," I trailed off; for some reason I felt lighter when I pictured her eager face.

Glancing at the unfinished sculpture set in plaster in the middle of the studio, I already knew what I'd name that one…

"You've met Aliyana?" Vin's question pulled me back to the here and now.

"Last night."

Something close to humor flashed in Vin's eyes and he fought a smile. That knowing look just pissed me the fuck off.

"What?" I asked sharply.

Vin held up his hands. "Nothing."

I glared at him, then took another smoke and slipped it between my lips. I pushed past Vin. "I'm out."

As I left the studio, I swore I heard Vin laughing.

Opening door to the dark, wet night, I ducked my head as I ran out into the rain and jumped into my black 1969 El Camino. I breathed deep as the rain thundered off my muscle car's roof. The smoke from my cigarette filled up the newly upholstered cabin.

Looking in the rearview mirror, I pulled out the band that kept my long hair tied back and let my damp hair down. Marble dust covered every inch of me. I shook my head asking myself why I even gave a shit how I looked.

Of course I knew why I gave a shit. The reason was about five feet six, had a fucking body to die for, long dark-brown hair that fell to the middle of her back, and the biggest Spanish eyes I'd ever seen. Yeah, that's why I gave a shit. A hot woman that *got* my work.

Leaving my smoke dangling from my bottom lip, I stared at my reflection. *Go get this done, Axe. Leave the chick alone. Name the sculptures. Tell her enough background info to shut her up about the text boards. Then leave and never go back.*

*****

Entering the back staff entrance, I flicked my chin to the night security guard who was always at his desk. The guy ducked his head behind the desk to break any eye contact. He was terrified of me. Didn't surprise me; most people were. All except Vin, and maybe Aliyana. Vin because he wasn't exactly sane, and Aliyana? Fuck knows why.

Noticing the black curtains were shut, I then heard some Spanish-sounding pop music playing from inside.

Taking a deep breath and wishing to God I'd had another smoke to calm me down, I opened the curtain and stepped into the gallery. It looked so different from last night. All the wooden crates and packaging from the sculptures were gone. Only my sculptures and the rigs to position them remained. Handwritten notes were scattered on the floor around each piece.

Hearing off-key singing from the back of the room, I followed the fucking brutal sound. As I rounded the corner, Aliyana Lucia was there dressed in an oversized white shirt, tight black leggings, pink Doc Martens, with her dark hair tied in a messy knot on top of her head.

I couldn't take my eyes off her.

But the outfit and her looks weren't what had me entranced. She was holding a paintbrush in her hand, painting what looked like tester pots of tones of white onto the back wall, while shaking her hips, badly singing, *"Amor Prohibido murmuran por las calles. Porque somos de distintas sociedades…"* in perfect Spanish. She was having fun, letting loose…

My eyebrows pulled down. In all my life, I don't think I'd ever been around anyone who ever just had fun. *I'd* never had fun…

An unfamiliar feeling of warmth spread in my chest as I stared at Aliyana. I watched her belting out the lyrics, her brush strokes keeping time to the beat.

For the first time in my life, I wanted to feel that happy, if only for a minute, I wanted to know what that level of freedom felt like. It looked… *nice…* Aliyana, standing there swaying her hips, not a damn care in the world, was

97

like feeling a ray of light shining on your face when you'd been stuck in a dark pit your whole life.

After a few minutes just watching, mesmerized, I straightened up, dropped my smirk, folded my arms across my chest, and cleared my throat.

Aliyana froze mid-brushstroke and slowly turned her head. Her beautiful face was spattered with white paint, and her brown eyes were almost Disney-level huge as they landed on me. Her olive skin shaded to a bright red. She carefully lowered the brush to the tray on a cart beside her, whispering something to herself under her breath.

My cheeks twitched, and I had to stop myself from laughing at her reaction to finding me here.

Fuck. She looked mortified.

"Elpidio, I didn't think you were coming," she said, all flustered, her hand over her chest.

Fuck me, she was gorgeous. I'd thought so last night, but now, like this...?

I held her stare, watching as her chest began to rise and fall under my attention, it went faster and faster the longer we held gazes. Long dark lashes fluttered in nerves and my fists involuntary clenched together against my chest at the action.

"*Elpi,*" I reminded her icily.

Aliyana's eyes flared with embarrassment and her face flushed even more than before. She reached up to play with her hair. At the sudden movement, her partly unbuttoned shirt gaped at the neck, allowing me to glimpse her tan skin and the top of her firm tits under her white lace bra. I almost groaned at the sight, but I was rooted to the spot, just fucking dumbstruck by this chick.

"I'm sorry, Elpi," she rushed out. "You did remind me about your name last night. I wasn't thinking."

I immediately felt like a dick on hearing the apology in her soft voice, but I stayed silent as Aliyana hurried to switch the music off.

I remained frozen to the spot as she took a long deep breath, her back to me, shoulders tensed as a deafening silence hit us both. But she pulled herself together and turned to me with that beautiful smiling face of hers.

"I'm so happy you made it," she said, moving toward me. Her dark eyes ran down my body, from my messy long hair to my clay-covered black shirt and black ripped jeans. Aliyana's full pink lips twitched, two deep-set dimples on either cheek popping out. Hesitantly, she reached up her hand toward the ends of my hair. Every part of me froze and my breath clogged my throat as I watched her swallow nervously.

It'd been years since a woman had touched me. And never one that looked like her.

As her slim finger drifted past my cheek, I caught her scent… jasmine. Mamma used to burn jasmine incense in the trailer. I didn't know if that was the reason, but for the first time in a long time, I felt myself relax around someone. Strangely, it felt like home.

Aliyana took a piece of my hair between her index finger and thumb. Her pink lips parted slightly and her warm breath spread all over my face.

I… liked her this close… touching me.

A second later, Aliyana pulled away her hand and she held it up in front of my eyes for me to see.

"Marble," she whispered, her dimples deepening as her lips gently pouted, eyes narrowed in suspicion. "You must have been real busy today. You're covered."

Something in my face must have caused her back off, because she dropped my hair and stepped back.

I gritted my teeth. I had no idea how to do all this shit. Women, this exhibition… be fucking normal.

"So have you?"

"What?"

"Been working all day."

I could see the excitement in her eyes. I nodded my head before glancing away, putting my hands in my pockets.

I moved toward the dagger piece we'd discussed last night. It was now in the corner I'd suggested, high up on a plinth. There was a huge spotlight shining down on it. I frowned.

"If you don't want it elevated, we can change it," Aliyana suddenly said from beside me. Her scent of jasmine drifted past me again, my lips tightening at having her so close. She ran her hand over the white plinth, really studying the piece. "I asked it to be put higher to really maximize the effect of the rivulets. And I put the spotlight here tonight so you could see how it would look in the daylight. See?"

I bent down and immediately saw she was right. As I stood up again, Aliyana was biting her finger between her teeth.

"Well?" she asked.

"It's perfect," I rasped. It genuinely was. In the glare of the spotlight, rivulets ran down the sculpted man, off the plinth, and shadowed about two feet along the floor. The skin on my back pricked as I felt Aliyana watching me.

"So you approve?"

"Fuck… yeah… it's…" I trailed off, not knowing how to express what it made me feel. I was never good with words. Not unless I was threatening you to pay up for your crack or I'd crowbar your fucking knees.

Aliyana's hands clasped together and a proud expression settled on her face. That look made me step back. Get some distance.

I'd made her happy. I wasn't sure how to deal with that. Happiness and me didn't really sit right.

"So…" Aliyana said as she circled, gesturing to the statue. "Have you thought about its title?"

As I stared at that man, the rivulets nearly drowning his frame, the shadows looking like gushes of running blood, only one title came to mind. "Exsanguination," I whispered before I'd time to think about it.

Aliyana tensed. Fuck. It was probably a stupid title. I was so shit at this whole art thing.

"The draining of blood?" Aliyana mused quietly. My eyes snapped to hers, but she was staring at the sculpture, an empathetic look on her face. "Exsanguination…" she murmured under her breath. Her shining eyes met mine.

"Of guilt," I explained, my voice breaking. "Of every sin this man committed… of his actions that caused people pain… actions he can never take back. Those daggers are there for life."

Aliyana sucked in a breath, and I dipped my head, feeling the truth of every word I'd just spilled cut into my black heart.

"And what was the inspiration?" she pushed tentatively.

I sighed and pushed my hair back from my face. I glanced to Aliyana, but I couldn't take seeing the sorrow on her fucking beautiful face. "Shit, girl," I snapped without caution. My eyes closed briefly as I tried to rein in these feelings, these fucking choking feelings I'd never dared let loose.

"You really need to know how I thought of this fucked-up piece? You need every damn sordid detail?" It came out harsher than I'd intended, but I wasn't real comfortable with revealing this shit to anyone.

"Just something would be good." Aliyana nervously inched closer to me, her voice barely above a whisper. "Like, how did you think of it? That should suffice for the text boards."

Slowly inhaling through my nose, I dropped my head so my hair covered my face. "The guy's a sinner. A guy that's done some real fucked-up shit, but by the time he realized all the pain he'd caused others, it was too late. He'd already done the worst. He'd already ruined people… ruined lives… destroyed people's innocence, changed people, forever changed people's souls …"

In my mind, I saw Levi as a fourteen-year-old kid, me standing behind him, pointing out a member of a rival gang, a King. Levi held in his hands a Beretta. His little fingers were fucking shaking, face white with fear, scared shitless, but I ignored it all. Gio had nodded his head at me, ordering my little brother to earn the Heighter stidda, the star tattoo on a Heighter's left cheek that showed you'd passed the initiation… by shooting a King.

I watched my twenty-five-year-old self stand behind Levi like a damn demon at his back, whispering in his ear for him to hurry. Lifting his slim arm to aim at our rival and ordered *now* as Levi did what I'd said and fired a bullet straight into the fucker.

But more than anything, I could see Levi turn to face me. I could still feel how fucking proud I was of him, that he'd proved himself to my "brothers"—the gang that was my everything and always had been since I was twelve. But I could also see the change in Levi's face. The young kid Austin and Mamma cherished, forever changed, as his victim lay bleeding out on the ground.

"Elpi?" Aliyana questioned at my silence.

Feeling a tear drop run down my cheek, over the crucifix tattoo that now covered *my* stidda, I added, "Every dagger is a crime he committed, the guilt flooding everyone and everything around him. Fucking never-ending guilt."

A hallow feeling set in my gut, and I glanced up to the sculpture. "But the daggers will never leave. The guilt will keep on pouring out. The wounds will never close… the cracks, the fractures on his body, will never heal."

The sudden silence in the large gallery suffocated me, making me want to do nothing but cut and run, leave this fucking exhibition and my pain for someone else to deal with. But as I heard Aliyana's quiet controlled breathing beside me, I couldn't move.

For the first time ever, someone was sharing in this pain with me. A virtual stranger. And I didn't know what the hell to do with how damn good that felt. I'd vowed to never let anyone in. I didn't understand why I'd broken that vow with *her*.

Lifting my dirty hands, I unsubtly wiped away the few tears I'd failed to stop from spilling down my face and turned my back on the sculpture, on the sculpture that was all *me*. Tipping back my head, I stared out of the domed ceiling at the millions of stars. I suddenly didn't feel so tortured as I pictured Austin and me as kids, Levi just a baby in my arms. Just a couple of young brothers, *best friends*, sitting on the roof of our trailer, lying back and watching the stars…

*****

Austin's little hand pointed up to the dark sky. "Those three right there are Orion's belt. Can you see them, Axe? The three stars in a row? And those right there are the Pleiades, or the Seven Sisters. But

105

to see all seven stars at once, you have to close your eyes, then open them real quick, 'cause some of them instantly fade away, leaving only a few left over," he told me.

I looked to my eight-year-old kid brother as I held Levi in my arms. Austin was nothing but gangly limbs and big brown eyes, a mini me, and I laughed. "How d'you know all this, Aust?"

He shrugged and turned bright red. "I read it in a book at school. I've read lots of them."

"You like the stars?" I asked.

He blushed bright red. "Yeah. They make me feel happy."

It went silent, and I knew he was embarrassed telling me that. Austin was a thinker; he was smart.

Looking at the sky again, I pointed at a star. "What's that one, kid?"

Austin moved closer to me and followed my finger. "That's Sirius, Axe," he told me excitedly.

His face looked over at me. "You like the stars, Axe?"

"I like you telling me about them, kid," I replied, smiling.

Austin settled back down, just as we heard our papa come home drunk from the trailer park bar and start screaming at Mamma. Mamma immediately started crying, begging him not to hurt her. I felt Austin stiffen beside me and his breathing changed. He was terrified. He always got scared of our papa when he came home trashed. It was the reason I brought him up here, to distract him.

Reaching down, I wrapped my arm round his shoulder and pulled him to my side. I fucking hated our loser of a papa. All he wanted to do was hurt us. So I made a promise to myself to always do anything to protect my brothers.

"Come on, kid. Tell me more." I pushed, feeling Austin grab onto my shirt and squeeze it real tight as a glass smashed inside the trailer and my mamma screamed out in pain.

With a shaky voice, Austin pointed at a bright star. "Th… that's M-Mars…"

"Nah, really?" I asked. "Is it made from chocolate too?"

I felt Austin weakly start to laugh beside me. "No, Axe, but it's red and big, and some people think aliens live on it…"

"Really? Aliens?" I asked excitedly, pulling Austin and Levi in closer.

Austin released my shirt, and I knew he'd managed to block out the beating of Mamma inside and I exhaled in relief. "You see, Mars, it's made of red rock, Axe…"

*****

And that's how we got through the bad times. The three of us lost in the stars, the night sky taking us away from the shitty trailer we called home.

Watching the night sky became our thing, until *my* thing became the gang, my crew brothers in the Heighters taking over my life… and I dragged little innocent Austin along for the ride. He'd trusted me, and I'd turned him into a coke-dealing thug at the age of twelve… just like me.

Austin, Levi and me never looked at the stars like that again.

I missed it.

I fucking missed Austin and the relationship we used to have… one I never got to start with Levi when he was old enough to understand.

As I stared at the sky through the glass, my eyes fell on Orion's Belt. I couldn't go there right now. Couldn't keep thinking of our lives before everything went wrong.

A hand running softly down my back had me whipping around. Aliyana's concerned eyes were wide as she stared up at me, her hand stilling on my back. I could feel the heat of her imprint on my skin like it was a hot branding iron searing my flesh.

"Are you…?" Her fingers moved, stroking at my muscled back, making my skin feel like it was on fire. "Are you okay?"

My instinct was to pull away and tell her to go to hell. Push her away like I did everyone, but as looked into her eyes, I couldn't fucking move… I wanted those hands to move lower, to touch every part of me.

Aliyana's hand moved up, her fingers brushing past my hair until her index finger ran over my short beard. "Elpi?"

Reaching up, I gripped her hand to throw it off my face. Her breath hitched as our hands touched, but I held on… Fuck knows why, but I held her hand against my cheek, my heart slamming crazy fast in my chest.

A flush of red raced up from Aliyana's chest to her neck and cheeks. Her tongue ran over her full pink lips and her eyelids lowered as she stared at me, just breathing… the two of us just fucking breathing.

"Elpi…" Aliyana hushed and began moving toward me. I stared at those full lips and wanted nothing more than to kiss her, to slam her up against the wall and fuck her until neither of us could stand.

But I couldn't… *We* couldn't.

Squeezing her hand, I pulled it from my face and laid it at her side. Disappointment showed in her hurt expression, and I reluctantly moved to the middle of the gallery, giving us some space.

"Elpi?" Aliyana called from behind me. As I faced her, she was playing with a loose strand of hair that had fallen from her band. She looked so goddamn cute and innocent, looking at me with those huge exotic eyes, her long lashes fluttering against her high cheeks. "Are you okay to talk about the others?" she asked shyly.

No, I wanted to say. *I'm done with all this exhibition shit, dredging up things from my past that I don't ever wanna face.*

Instead, I took a deep breath and nodded.

A relieved smile spread on her face, and she moved to stand beside me. I immediately felt her warmth, and the air became thick around us. Aliyana dipped her head and blushed, and I knew she felt the weird pull between us too.

Why did everything in my life have to be so fucking complicated?

"So which one should we do next?" she asked.

"I don't care," I said, my hands in pockets, feeling my smokes… I really wanted a damn smoke.

Aliyana started walking straight for my biggest piece, *the* piece, and I stopped dead in my tracks. It took Aliyana a second to realize I wasn't behind her. In fact, I'd turned my back, feeling like a damn crack had splintered through my chest.

I couldn't deal with facing what that sculpture meant to me right now.

"Elpi, what—"

"I'm not going there," I snapped.

"Okay," Aliyana said cautiously. "Do you want to choose another one?"

I closed my eyes and felt myself relax. Making myself scan the room, almost all the pieces tore me apart. All of them had meaning… meanings that were too hard to face. But I could get through a few.

Walking to a smaller piece, an hourglass with a hand reaching up through the sand, I motioned with a nudge of my head for Aliyana to join me.

"This one's okay?" she asked, and I threw her a single nod. "Do we have a title?"

As I looked at the hand of the man drowning in the sand, I felt the suffocation, the impossible situation he was in… the heavy sand pulling him further and further down…

"Downfall," I blurted out.

Just like before, I felt Aliyana's eyes scrutinizing my face, probably trying to read me more, but this time I stayed stoic.

"Downfall," she repeated, scribbling in her notepad. "And the inspiration?"

*****

After the sixth piece, I felt emotionally and physically drained.

"Do you want to call it quits for tonight?" Aliyana asked followed by a yawn.

Exhaling a relieved sigh, I ran my hands down my exhausted face. "Yeah," I replied, and for the first time since I'd come into the gallery, my muscles seemed to lose tension… then began aching like fuck.

As I worked out the cricks in my neck, I heard Aliyana move beside me. I stared down at her. She was blushing.

She was affected by me… And I liked that more than I should have.

"So…" she said quietly, edging even closer. My palms began sweating as she approached. My heart thundering in my chest. "Thank you for doing this tonight. I can't believe how powerful your words are against your already breathtaking works of art."

I fought a smirk. Coming from any other curator, I was sure it would've been just a line to crawl up the sculptor's ass, but not her. I saw in her eyes that she loved all this crap. And even crazier, she loved my work… the twisted, fucked-up sculptures from my mind.

How that was possible I had no idea. I was convinced if she actually knew who I was, what I'd done, she'd see the sculptures in a completely different light; repulsion, and a fucking lame attempt to gain forgiveness.

"It's late, or early, depending on how you want to look at it," she laughed and shyly stared at the floor.

I frowned, wondering why she was still talking. When she looked up at me through her long lashes, the view of her in face in the moonlight stole my breath. If I were a painter, I would've created a damn masterpiece off that one stunning memory alone.

"Are you hungry?" My frown deepened, and I watched her swallow. Her hand lifted to twirl that same loose strand of hair around her finger. "I… I mean, would you like to get breakfast with me? That is if you're hungry?" she asked nervously.

I opened my mouth to say no, when my stomach growled. Truth was, I was fucking starving.

Aliyana, on hearing my stomach, paused, then smiled a dimpled megawatt smile, the beauty of it nearly knocking me the fuck out. This time, there was no smirk, just a reluctant smile spreading on my lips.

It felt strange to smile. I hadn't in so long.

"Elpi," Aliyana said through a uncontained laugh. "You actually smiled!" Her face was all lit up like lights at Christmas, and I shook my head.

"Yeah, don't get used to it. It's a rare occurrence."

Aliyana stepped back and put her hand on her chest. "And you have a sense of humor too?"

I watched her laughing, and my chest tightened to the point I thought the muscles would tear underneath my skin.

As Aliyana gradually lost her laughter, she stepped even closer to me, her tits brushing against my shirt. I wasn't smiling anymore. No, now I was breathing hard, fighting the urge to take her in my arms and smash my lips to hers.

Aliyana blinked, then blinked again without saying a word, only to then offer, "Breakfast?"

Lifting my hand, I couldn't help but take that long strand of hair that fell over her cheek and tuck it back into her messy knot.

Hearing Aliyana's breath hitch at my touch, I couldn't resist leaning down, inhaling the scent of her hair… lavender.

Aliyana's firm tits brushed against my thin T-shirt, her slim thigh pressing firm against my hard cock. Her warm, minty breath blew over my cheek, bristling my beard, when I reached into my back pocket, pulling out my car keys.

"I'll drive," I said roughly, moving back, snapping the unbearable tension that had cocooned us.

Breathless, Aliyana pressed her hand against her stomach, getting her bearings. "Okay," she managed to say and fell into step behind me as I burst through the curtains, hightailed it out of the exit and gasped in the cool Seattle air, light rain splashing against my heated face.

Hearing the door close behind me, I pulled out a smoke and placed it between my lips. I inhaled a long, sweet drag, the smoke filling my lungs, calming me the fuck down.

Without glancing behind me, I pounded pavement to my car and opened the passenger door, leaving it open for Aliyana. As I slumped into the driver's seat, Aliyana dropped down beside me, her brown eyes still glazed from our moment under the dome.

Lifting my smoke, I inhaled a long drag, then flicked the ash into the ashtray on the dash. "Where we going?" I asked, looking straight ahead through the blurred-with-rain windshield. "I don't know Seattle yet."

Aliyana sucked in a breath. "Neither do I. I can only think of one place."

"Is it private, you know, not busy with a shitload of folk?"

"It's small."

Switching on the ignition, I stubbed out my Marlboro cherry, lit another smoke, and let it sit on my bottom lip.

"Direct me."

Chapter Eight
Axel

The longer we drove, the more I knew I shouldn't be here with this woman. But I was, and honestly, I wasn't gonna be going anywhere. I was going to breakfast with Aliyana for no other reason than I *couldn't* go anywhere else. She'd asked, and I'd agreed. There was no other choice.

"It's just over there," Aliyana said, pointing to a small café tucked away on the waterfront. I laughed to myself. It was just three blocks from my studio.

In minutes, I'd parked the El Camino and we got out, the sunrise starting to break. No one was around except the market workers setting up for the day and early buyers waiting for the fresh fish to come in from the boats.

Aliyana and I entered the café overlooking the Sound, where we were told to pick wherever we wanted to sit. The guys who ran the place were still setting up, so I walked ahead of Aliyana to the farthest corner and sat down. The place was full of Italian flags, the servers Latino in their features and clearly Italian too.

I wondered if she'd picked this place because she'd worked out my heritage or whether it was because she just liked the coffee.

As I dropped to the seat, Aliyana sat down opposite me and took another glance around the empty café. We were alone. Good.

"This okay for you? This *empty* café?" she asked with a teasing smile.

"Yeah," I replied, and she smiled wider at my curt response.

And there she went again, amused at my attitude. Most people would have given up on trying to talk to me by now, but it was like she didn't get that I liked to be left alone. That I didn't want people round me… I wanted to just fucking *be*.

"You're not one for small talk, are you?"

Aliyana's eyes looked tired. Fuck, I knew mine did too, but hers didn't lose their playful glint as she stared at me, awaiting my answer.

"Not really."

She laughed again.

A server came to us then, calling back to a server in the kitchen to set up the patio. He'd spoken in perfect Italian. The waiter arrived at our table, his eyes flaring as they fell on Aliyana.

The guy flushed bright red and fumbled his notepad and pen in his hand. Something tightened in my stomach as Aliyana smiled up at him and the fucker flashed her a toothy smile.

Feeling fucked off that this asshole was hovering, I sat back in my chair and glared. He soon met my eyes, and when he did, his eyes immediately dropped to the notepad and he nervously asked us what we wanted.

"*Caffè doppio e una brioche alla crema,*" I ordered.

The server looked up and, although his expression was still guarded, he asked, "*Tu parli Italiano?*"

"*Sì,*" I replied.

"*Da dove vieni?*" he asked, wanting to know where I was from.

"*No, sono Americano. I miei genitori loro sono Italiani,*" I said, telling him my mamma and papa were Italian, not me.

Fuck, I'd barely spoken Italian in years. Couldn't bring myself to. I only ever spoke Italian to Mamma and my brothers. But since getting out of prison, it hadn't felt right. Mamma was gone. I couldn't bring myself to speak her mother tongue for more than a few sentences without it gutting me inside.

The server must have seen my body stiffen and my eyes drop to the table as he moved on to talk to Aliyana. I didn't even hear what she ordered, too busy trying to breathe through the pain ripping me apart.

The feel of Aliyana's warm hand placed over mine had my eyes darting up to clash with hers.

"Are you okay? You went real quiet on me just now. I was calling your name, but you were lost in your thoughts."

"I'm good."

We sat in silence while the server brought our coffees. Once he'd left us alone, Aliyana took a packet of sugar, poured it into her coffee, then fiddled with the packet.

"So." She broke the silence. "You speak fluent Italian?"

"Yes."

"I've been told Elpidio is an old Italian name." She lifted her latte to her lips, but her eyes never left mine, imploring me to answer her question.

"My folks were Italian, so I speak it. Bilingual," I replied evasively, throwing my double espresso down my throat and signaling to the server to bring me another.

"*Yo también*," Ally said, and I swear my dick hardened in response to her purring that fucking Spanish my way.

Her face lit up, and she added, "*Hablo español, no italiano, aunque puedo entender algo de lo que dijiste.*"

Fuck porn. A chick as hot as Aliyana Lucia sitting in front of me, hair ruffled in a messy knot and shirt gaping, talking to me in Spanish was the hottest thing I'd ever fucking seen.

I figured out from certain words in that sentence that she spoke Spanish and not Italian, though she could understand a lot of what I'd said. I couldn't help but flick my chin in appreciation. I could kind of get what she was saying to me too. At least a little.

She laughed at me, and it hit me that she'd pulled me away from drowning in dark thoughts about my mamma. She'd pulled me through… again.

The server stood beside our table with a tray full of pastries and coffee. "You can put that down, *ragazzo*," I said, and the server dropped the tray in front of us.

"*Gracias*," Aliyana said in a friendly tone as he handed her a croissant smothered in Nutella.

I couldn't take my eyes off her as she picked lumps of the flaky croissant and put them in her mouth, licking the chocolate spread off her fingers.

She had no fucking clue how beautiful she was… and the effect she had on men.

"You got a man?" I suddenly blurted.

Aliyana froze, her tongue just about to lick a blob of Nutella from her thumb. A blush coating her cheeks, she lowered her hand and grabbed for a napkin.

Clearing her throat, she shook her head and whispered, "No."

As she whispered the word, I felt myself relax. I hadn't even realized I'd been bracing myself for her to tell me she had some rich, good-looking fuck as a boyfriend… someone who treated her like a queen.

"Why?" I asked abruptly, and Aliyana jerked back in her chair. I shifted on mine too, hearing a second too late how aggressive that sounded. Aliyana's eyes had dropped to the table.

I was such a fuck-up.

Leaning forward, elbows on the table, I added, "Just thought a woman like you would have a line of men a mile long following you 'round." I ran my hand down my beard, fucking embarrassed. I was shoving my foot further into my mouth at every turn.

And this was why I preferred to be left the hell alone.

A smile tugged on Aliyana's mouth and she shrugged. "Just never met a man that I really connected with, you know? Never felt that bolt of lightning that leaves me breathless, I suppose."

"No boyfriends?" I asked, now curious.

Her nose crinkled up, those dimples of hers popping out all over the place. "Not really. I've kinda thrown myself into my work these last few years. Never met a man who's my type." The way she blushed bright red and fiddled with the empty sugar packet again had me itching to ask what was her type.

After seconds of wondering, I finally just fucking asked. "And what's that?"

Aliyana took a deep breath, her full tits pushing against her shirt, and met my eyes. "A man who's protective, strong, dark… artistic, passionate… cultured…" She trailed off, rubbing her pink lips together, and I froze.

Her brown eyes pierced mine like she could see through to my fucking dark soul. I shifted under her scrutiny and felt my heart begin to race.

Forcing myself to look away, I picked up my brioche and ate it in silence. That fog of tension was back around us again, but I pushed it out of my mind. I just needed to get through this breakfast.

"Can I ask a question?" Aliyana said, and I sat back in my chair, my brioche now demolished. I flicked my chin in response, giving her the okay. "Why don't you want anyone to know who you are?"

And there it was. The one question everyone wanted to know. Why was *Elpidio* a recluse?

I shrugged. "Not into the whole fame thing."

"Then why the exhibition? And why now?" She pushed.

Glancing out over the Puget Sound, I raked my hair back with my fingers. What was I meant to say? *I was locked up for distributing 'class A' drugs on the University of Alabama's property, and in the process, nearly ruined my brother's shot at the NFL. Oh, that's right, you don't know. My brother is Austin Carillo, number eighty-three for the Seahawks and regarded one of the best wide receivers in the country. But that's now. A few years back, I was running a street crew dealing drugs. Oh, and I sold some fucked-up snow to a Tide player and he OD'd. So I've been serving ten years inside but got out a couple weeks ago after only five years because I ratted out a big-time cocaine supplier.*

I couldn't tell her none of that shit, so I answered, "Vin wanted it, and I told him as long as I didn't have to deal with people, he could do what the fuck he wanted."

Aliyana's head tilted to the side as she regarded me. "And how and where did you meet Vin? I can't imagine you ran in the same circles."

If only she knew.

She edged forward, waiting for my answer.

"Around."

"Around?" she questioned.

"Around," I said a bit firmer to let her know I wasn't saying shit.

Slumping back in her chair, she began eating again, only pausing to quietly say, "You've gotten me more than intrigued, Elpi."

My forehead pulled down to a frown.

She must have seen my expression and added, "Your artwork floors me, so tragically beautiful." My gut clenched as she spoke those words. *Tragically beautiful...*

She dropped her croissant, letting out a single laugh. "I remember the first time I saw a picture of one of your sculptures. It was a piece in a magazine on Vin Galanti, and he did nothing but talk about his protégé, the reclusive and mysterious Elpidio. He'd just loaned one of your pieces to the Met as part of a marble statue contemporary exhibit, an exhibit of sculptors who still adhered to the old-fashioned hammer and chisel techniques." Aliyana's eyes lost their focus as she pushed her fingers through a small pile of sugar granules that had fallen from the packet she'd used earlier.

"Vin showed your first piece, the only work I'd seen in pictures from you." A tiny smile pulled on her lips. "And the piece that is still my favorite today."

I knew which one she meant. The only piece I could barely look at now without breaking.

"The angel..." she said, and I could hear the love for it in her voice. I expected to feel the usual slam of grief I never failed to experience whenever I thought of that piece and what it represented.

But Aliyana sitting here now, telling me she loved the piece, that it was her favorite out of all my sculptures, made me feel... proud... humbled... fucking floored. Floored that out of everything I'd created, Aliyana loved my mamma's dedication most.

"I was in Austin, Texas, at The Blanton Museum of Art, but when I learned that your piece would be at the Met, I jumped on a plane and flew out for a whistle-stop stay of forty-eight hours just to see it up close." She laughed. "The same thing I did to get this job actually."

That blush was back on her cheeks, only this time I enjoyed every dip of her eyes, the flush of her cheeks, the quiet sighs she exhaled. I was just enjoying Aliyana, period.

"It sounds stupid, Elpi, but seeing your angel changed me. I don't know what it was, but... but... ah, it doesn't matter," she said in embarrassment.

"Tell me," I ordered gruffly. I really needed her to finish that fucking sentence. I needed to understand what she saw in my sculptures that had her so moved.

Aliyana took a long, drawn-out swallow but met my gaze with her brown eyes and said, "I felt *you*. I felt you in its every curve. I felt like I was looking straight into your soul. I felt the love you poured into that sculpture... It made me reassess everything in my life… It made me want *more*… it's difficult for me to explain."

I sucked in a sharp breath, my hands moving upward to rub over my eyes. "Aliyana…" I growled out, but not from anger, but from the fact that she was telling me things I didn't deserve… that she didn't want to get wrapped up in.

"Did I say too much?"

I drew my hands down my face. "Aliyana… if you saw the real me… if you saw straight into my soul, you wouldn't be sitting here with me now."

Aliyana's eyes widened. "What do you mean by that?" Her voice was now shaking. I'd scared her. Good. She *should* be scared of me. I wasn't the right kinda guy for her. I'd only just met her, but I knew she should be setting her standards a fucking mile higher than me.

"Exactly what I said. If you knew the real me, what I've done in my life, you'd be running away right the fuck now."

"Wh-what have you done?" Her eyebrows pulled down to form a frown. "Why are you so hard on yourself?"

"Penance. A whole lotta fucking penance I need to pay."

"But I can't believe that of you."

"You're wrong."

She shook her head adamantly. "But—" She went to argue.

Slamming my fist down on the table, I gritted my teeth, cutting off whatever she was gonna say. "You know fuck all 'bout me, girl," I hissed, my voice too low to be anything other than a rumbling threat. "You might think you know my art, but you know shit about me."

Straightening in my chair, I waved to get the server's attention, motioning for the check.

Aliyana didn't say anything else. In fact, she picked up her purse and walked straight out of the café.

The servers watched her go, nudging each other as they stared at her ass. I jumped from my seat, pulled out a fifty, and pounded over to where the Italian punks stood gaping and slammed the note on the countertop.

As soon as they laid eyes on me, they backed off, hands held high. Their faces drained to white, seeing how much they were fucking me off and I marched out of the café to see Aliyana beside my Camino. I pulled out a smoke and, as always, placed it between my lips, taking a soothing drag. For once, I embraced the shower of rain that was pouring from the always-gray sky.

As I reached the car, Aliyana kept her head down and slid silently into the passenger seat.

My stomach rolled.

I'd really fucking hurt her.

By the time we got back to the gallery, I'd burned through three smokes and a shit ton of guilt. But it was for the best. I was no one a girl should get with, especially one as good as her.

As I pulled the car to the shadowed side entrance, I waited for her to get out. But she didn't move. The air in the cabin of the Camino seemed to crackle with electricity, and the heat of the stagnant tobacco-filled air built until it was unbearable. I could hear every single breath that came out of Aliyana's mouth, and with every soft inhale and exhale, my cock seemed to harden more and more, the feel of it trapped under my jeans almost painful. I risked a glance to the right. Aliyana faced forward, gripping her purse tightly on her lap with both hands.

It was only meant to be a glance, one last look at her before she left my car. I was only intending to drop her off here at the gallery, leave, and never come back.

"I need the title and information about the angel sculpture. Could you come by one night to get it done?" Aliyana said. I couldn't fucking stand how sad she sounded.

I nodded mutely, unable to speak, and turned to stare out the windshield again. But as Aliyana started to reach for the handle on the door, something inside of me snapped. I couldn't take how upset she was at me. I couldn't take her leaving and not knowing how she fucking tasted.

Before I knew it, my hand reached out to my right, and wrapping my fingers around Aliyana's arm, I pulled her against my chest, only briefly catching her eyes widen and her mouth suck in a shocked gasp, before I crushed my lips to hers.

Moving my hands from her arms, I wrapped one at the back of her slim neck and the other to fist her hair. As I forced my tongue into her mouth, both of us groaned at our tongues clashing together.

She tasted amazing, and any part of me that wanted to take this slow was overridden the second her hands dropped her purse to the floor and lifted the bottom of my shirt to my stomach. Grunting as her palm scalded my skin, I pulled her closer still with my hand on her neck until her tits were pressed against my chest. Aliyana released a breathy moan, her fingers tensing until her nails scraped down my stomach, my skin burning at the marks she was making… the marks trailing down my stomach to the top of my jeans.

My cock was pressing against the zipper, fucking begging for her hand, my tongue fighting against hers for dominance. But as soon as Aliyana's fingers began tearing open my button, I froze.

Fuck.

We had to stop.

What the hell was I thinking?

Aliyana broke away from my mouth, her full lips and wet tongue moving down to lick and nip down my neck. Under her hands, the button on the top of my jeans popped open, and she began pulling down my zipper… the jeans the only barrier between her and my dick.

Squeezing my eyes shut, knowing what I was gonna do was gonna be painful, I trapped her hands between mine. Aliyana's head snapped up, and unable to resist, I pressed my palms on her cheeks and smashed our mouths together one last time, before pushing her back and ordering, "Go."

Aliyana fought for breath as I sat with my shirt pulled up and my zipper half down. "But—"

"GO!" I said louder, shifting back to fasten my jeans, my hands lifting to grip the steering wheel. Aliyana inhaled a sharp breath, but I didn't look her way. If I did, she'd be laid on this seat and her pussy would be strangling my cock in about ten seconds flat.

A moment later, I heard the door quietly open and close.

Shutting my eyes, I fought back the sick feeling pulsing through my body. But all I saw was a pair of big brown eyes telling me they could see straight into my soul, that they *felt* me.

In thirty minutes, I was back in my studio, strong coffee brewing in the pot, pulling my shirt and jeans off as I jumped into the shower.

As the scalding hot water drummed on my head, steam billowing around the small room, all I could picture was Aliyana's face smiling at me like she didn't see all my sins. Speaking Spanish to me, her tongue rolling the words, the taste of her Nutella-flavored mouth on my tongue, and the feel of her hands trailing down to fist my cock.

Fuck! What was with this chick? Why was she getting to me like this?

Grabbing for the body wash, I squeezed the green gel out into my hand and ran the fresh-scented soap over my body. But the more I scrubbed the marble scum from my skin, the more images of Aliyana flashed through my head: her eyes, her mouth, her cute-as-fuck dimples popping out on her cheeks as she smiled at me... her breathless voice as she told me she'd flown across the country just to see one of my sculptures up close... and those tits pressing against her shirt, her chest flushed red from looking at me, and the moans she spilled into my mouth from my kiss.

Without conscious thought, my hand wrapped around my stiff cock and I began stroking it up and down. Groaning out loud, picturing Aliyana's long slim fingers gripping my dick instead of mine, my forehead dropped to lean on the damp tiles. Working my hand faster, my breath coming out in harsh pants, I pictured her naked beneath me, me pinning her down so she couldn't move, and fucking her hard... and I was gone. One thought of sinking into her wet pussy had cum spurting in waves over my hand, a long grunt echoing off the tiled shower cubicle.

Jerking my cock slower, I worked myself down, my legs still shaking from how damn good that felt... how much I came just imagining having her on her back, her slim legs wrapped around my waist.

But then reality hit and the demons of my past came thundering back into my chest, knocking the breath from my lungs, bringing the usual feelings of hate, sadness, and guilt to every cell...

Drying off, I slipped on a pair of sweats and returned, exhausted but unable to sleep, to my current work in progress and began chipping away at the little boy's face... the young, torn face crying bullets... bullets that I'd made him fire when he didn't want to... ruining his damn life.

As I pounded the hammer against the head of the pointed chisel, I pushed Aliyana's smiling face and haunting eyes from my mind.

I had to forget what had happened between us. There was no way I would fucking ruin her too.

Chapter Nine
Ally

Two weeks later…

So this is it? This is where he stays? I thought to myself, looking at the sculpting studio from my car. The address Vin had given me led me to the waterfront, not too far from Pike Market.

The night was dark and beside me on the seat of my rental was a box filled with the draft text boards and titles. I'd called Vin to ask him to sign off on them, but he'd insisted he was too busy on the East Coast and that I should take them to Elpi himself… at his studio… the studio overlooking the Puget Sound… after two weeks of hearing nothing from him.

As always, the skies were overcast, a slight breeze in the air, but the day was dry. Checking the address in my email from Vin again, I sighed. This was the right place...

I was procrastinating.

A large white square building stood before me. It looked like a small factory, the windows were large but blacked out on this side. It was tucked away down a small pathway, offering beautiful sea views. Vin had said this was his studio, the one he'd used for years, but he gifted it to Elpidio for this exhibition.

My heart beat faster as I watched the wooden double door for any signs of life. There was nothing, meaning I had to get out of the damn car and knock, show Elpi the text boards and get him to give me permission to use them.

Taking a fortifying breath, I opened the car door, shivering at the cold chill seeping through the thin material of my lilac maxi dress and short, fitted black leather biker jacket. My hair was straight and loose, the light breeze causing it to drift across my face.

Reaching across to the passenger seat, I pulled out the box housing the boards and, locking the car, slowly walked across the street to stand at the large wooden door.

Loud music was pumping from inside, and my stomach tightened with nerves. I wanted to see Elpi more than anything in the world, but I doubted he really wanted to see me. My knees shook as I lifted my hand and knocked on the door.

As I waited, I glanced round the small street, noting it was deathly quiet. It suited Elpi completely. A lonely studio on a lonely street for a loner sculptor.

The music continued to blare inside, and there was no sign of Elpi. Trying again, but knocking harder this time, I waited about five minutes before it sank in that he couldn't hear me.

Feeling colder and colder by the minute, I glanced up the empty street again before shifting the box under one arm and tried the doorknob.

It turned.

The door creaked open, betraying the age of the studio, and revealed a long empty hallway leading in only one direction.

Taking the heavy box in both hands, I edged into the hallway, kicking the door shut with my foot, and called, "Hello?"

My voice was no contender against the blaring heavy rock coming from a room at the end of the corridor. Straightening my shoulders, I forced my feet forward and suppressed my nerves. The closer I got to the end of the hallway, the more I doubted my decision to come here. It was his private space. He most definitely would not want me intruding.

But as I thought to leave, I heard the poetic sound of a chisel chipping away at marble and I stilled.

I wanted to see him work. To observe an artist at work was a rare privilege. And more than that, I wanted, no, *needed* to see Elpidio again.

I couldn't help it. I felt a pull within me that refused to let me turn round and leave.

Rubbing my lips together, I bent to place the box of text board drafts on the ground and crept forward to stand in the door-less doorway... And the sight that greeted me took my breath away.

Elpidio stood in the center of the room, dressed only in a pair of black ripped jeans, his top half bare, every inch of his olive skin covered in what looked like thousands of tattoos. There wasn't one bit of naked skin showing. I'd never seen anyone so covered in ink in all my life. But aside from the tattoos, which had me gripping the doorframe with rigid fingers, were the thick defined muscles protruding over his shoulder blades, the cut pieces of flesh damp with the sheen of sweat, flexing with every blow from the hammer in his hands.

His bulging thighs were rigid as he stood his ground, carefully sculpting the back of a marble slab which looked to be the image of a young boy with a larger boy at his back whispering in his ear.

The heavy rock music filled the room, and before I knew it, my feet were carrying my forward like a moth to naked flame. The closer I got, the more I noticed.

Elpidio's back was marred with scars. In fact, all of his skin had scars, both long and short, raised and flat, red and white. But one long, jagged scar ran along the back of his thick neck... a neck that was visible now it was free from the curtain of dark hair which was tied on the middle of his skull in a loose bun.

That made me smile. I'd always thought his long hair was like his protection, his mask. It pleased me to see when he was sculpting it was pulled off his face... like he was free of all constraints, pouring his soul into his carefully-crafted masterpieces.

It was overwhelming to see such a ripped and tortured man so raw and unkempt, but passionate all at the same time...

Feeling safe to step closer still, curious to catch a glimpse of what he was creating, I stepped forward, just as there was a change in music. The three-second pause between songs betrayed my presence as my foot pressed down on a creaky old floorboard, the sound of the groan echoing off the walls in the expansive space.

Like he was expecting a blow to the back, Elpidio whipped round, his chisel angled like a weapon. I froze, a slice of fear spearing down my spine.

Elpidio's eyes widened as he saw me rooted to the spot, eyes shining with shock. His harsh and violent expression changed in an instant. He dropped his chisel to the ground as his dark stare bored into me.

We didn't move. We didn't speak. We just stared, our breathing increasing in speed. As my teeth ran over my bottom lip, I allowed my gaze to drift down his heavily tattooed and bulky muscled chest, his ripped and prominent abs glistening with the effects of his labor. His tapered waist boasted a sexy, defined 'V' showcased by his low-riding black jeans.

As my eyes journeyed back north, heat spread between my legs, and I groaned out loud feeling the unbearable pressure pulsing in my core.

Strands of loose hair fell over Elpi's face, making him look like a forbidden dream. As our eyes met once more, the temperature in the room seemed to soar with the intense attraction that crackled between us.

I swayed on my feet, unsure of what to say or do, when on a pained groan, Elpi rushed forward, thrusting his large frame against my body and smashed his lips against mine, one hand clasping my hair and the other gripping my ass in an unyielding hold. I couldn't move, couldn't do anything but be trampled by this man, this strong and commanding man making me lose all rational thought.

The taste of tobacco and beer filled my mouth as he moved his hand from my ass to begin tearing off my jacket. I gasped as my lips broke from his mouth, my jacket landing in a heap on the floor as another rock song pounded through the large speakers from the sound system across the room.

Elpi didn't miss a beat, moving his lips to trace down my neck, his hands freeing from my hair to rip down the straps of my dress and bra. My breasts instantly hardened as they were exposed to the chilly room.

My eyes rolled back as Elpi released a satisfied groan and, pushing my breasts together with his rough, large hands, he sucked my puckered nipple into his mouth, the feel of his teeth scraping my breast causing my pussy to grow even wetter.

"Elpi, yes!" I hissed as he sucked hard, causing me to cry out, my legs shaking in need.

Fully gorged on my flesh, he released my nipple with a pop and with flat hands, pushed me backward until my back hit the wall. He paused in his onslaught only to sear me with a desperate look, his hungry expression almost melting me into a puddle on the ground.

As a crescendo sounded on the heavy metal song, he used both hands to pull my dress down to the floor, taking my silk panties with it.

I was completely bared to him.

Elpi took a silent step back, his tattooed chest rising high with the severity of his labored breathing. I hadn't dared push off the wall, his hard dark-brown eyes keeping me locked in place.

I released a shuddered breath as I drank in his large body, feeling nothing but beautiful as his nostrils flared while his eyes traced my every curve.

Seeing a swollen bulge beneath his jeans, my thighs tensed together, searching for release as he snapped open the button on his waistband and pulled down the zipper.

A thin cropping of dark hair came into view as his jeans dropped down his muscled thighs, his long cock springing free, hard and ready to fuck me.

"Elpi…" I whispered and braced myself as he kicked his jeans to the side, his bun holding back his long hair affording me the opportunity to see every angle of his beautifully severe face. He stormed forward, his damp chest pinning me against the cold wall as the hard thumping rhythm of Marilyn Manson's "Tainted Love" assaulted the room.

Reaching down, he lifted my feet off the floor by gripping my thighs, my back scraping against the wall. He never once broke my gaze and said nothing as his dick began running along my pussy, the friction on my clit causing me to cry out.

I was ready. I was wet and ready and more than eager for him to take me, to fuck me against this wall with the ferociousness I knew he harbored deep inside. A ferociousness I knew he needed to release. A ferociousness I wanted him to unleash inside me.

"You on something?" he growled as he pressed forward, his hard nipples scratching against mine.

My eyes fluttered as I tried to form an answer. But when he ground his hips harder, his cock rubbing my clit, causing me to dig my nails into his neck, I couldn't even speak.

Elpi froze, and I tried to work my hips to heighten that addictive feeling of almost reaching my peak.

"You on something? I don't have a rubber," Elpi barked, repeating his question. His voice this time had dropped an octave, sounding more guttural, like he swallowed broken glass, causing excited shivers to cover every inch of my exposed body.

"The shot…" I whispered quietly. "I'm on the shot."

"Good," was all the warning I got before he used his strength to lift me higher, then in one swift motion impaled me on his cock. I groaned at the feel of his thickness filling me so impossibly full. His masculine musky scent filled my nose and I sank my teeth into his shoulder as a tsunami of pleasure engulfed me.

The rhythm of the song increased, Elpi using the beat of the crashing drums to control his thrusts. His grunts were guttural as he pounded hard, the tip of his cock pushing unrelentingly inside me. His solid muscles twitched under his skin and he tucked his head into the crook of my neck, his hard grunts increasing in volume.

My thighs ached from the force of his grip. My back burned from the hard wall on my naked flesh. Inside of me was lit with fire, my core building higher and higher, so much that I felt I couldn't bear it. As Marilyn Manson's voice heightened in pitch, Elpi's hips became frantic as we thrashed against the wall, my pussy feeling every inch of his naked flesh pushing deep within me.

My fingers raked his shoulders as my moans changed from short and breathy to loud and drawn out. "Elpi!" I cried as an impossible pressure built between my legs.

He didn't say anything in reply to my pleas, his hips now slamming furiously into me. He groaned so harshly it sounded as though he were snarling into my neck.

As he pulled back one last time, then plunged back within me twice as strongly as before, it was my undoing.

Back and legs stiffening, I screamed out my release, my channel contracting, milking Elpi as he never once faltered in his thrusts.

My eyes shut of their own accord as I tucked my nose into his neck, lapping at his flushed skin. His movements became more erratic, his growls increasing. Opening his mouth, his lips latched on my lower neck. Sucking hard, he roared against my skin, pulling the covered flesh into his hot mouth as his cock swelled. I felt the dizzy at the sensation of his release.

My clit pulsed as his hips slowly rocked within me, his cock jerking in tandem with his hitched breaths against my neck.

As the fog of pleasure began to clear, my hands still grasping onto his slick tattooed skin, I blinked back the shock of what'd just happened.

I'd fucked Elpidio… I'd *fucked* Elpidio… Frantic, unbarred, hard sex… the best sex of my life.

Unsure of how he would react, I braced myself for his rejection, but to my complete surprise, he reared back his head, his gaze colliding with mine.

As always, nothing was voiced aloud, but by the floored expression set on his hard face, I knew he was feeling as raw and exposed as me. And as he inched his head forward, running his nose gently down my flushed cheek, his eyes closing as he did so, it brought me to tears. I'd never seen this side of him before… the almost tender side I always believed was buried deep beneath the hard exterior.

As Elpi's warm breath drifted down my neck, he stepped back, taking me from against the wall. Turning me round, his cock still deep inside me, my thighs still wrapped around his waist, he walked slowly across the room. As we moved, I couldn't resist smiling and pushed a stray strand of hair behind his ear. Flashing me a quick glance, his dark eyes shined with warmth at my gesture, and his mouth twitched.

He'd liked me touching him this way.

Suddenly finding us across the room, Elpi lowered me down to a soft bed underneath ceiling-to-floor length windows, which showcased a picturesque view of the Sound.

This view of the Sound could not hold a candle to the man hovering over me as I lay on perfectly straightened white sheets. He stared down at me for several seconds before leaning down and pressing his mouth against mine, his hips finally moving as he slid from inside me.

Taking hold of my wrists, without breaking from my lips, he wrapped each one of my arms behind his neck, his lips languorously caressing mine.

Feeling a heady wave of emotion swelling in my chest at that unexpected act, I ran my fingertips along his neck, finding the path of the long jagged scar.

Dismissing the questions forming in my mind about how he came by such a horrific injury, I melted into his hold, basking in the afterglow of our love making… enjoying the simple pleasure of lying here, my lips fused to the man who had affected me like no other.

Chapter Ten
Axel

She tasted of mint.

She smelled of Jasmine.

She'd drilled through to my fucking soul... the tainted soul I never ever wanted anyone to see.

Aliyana's hot tongue fought against mine, her hands dragging lazily up and down my back. But I didn't want lazy. I wanted her squirming under me. I wanted her screaming my name, clawing at my back, bringing me back to fucking life after five years of nothing but my own fucked-up heart for company... after years of nothing but numbness.

Grinding my hips against her wet pussy, I ate her moans filling my mouth. Suddenly, I rolled us over until Aliyana was straddling my waist, her hooded glazed eyes and her swollen mouth parting as she stared down at me. Taking a fresh towel from beside my bed, I ran it between her legs, removing any evidence of me from within her, loving how her face flushed at the action.

I'd never seen anything so fucking sexy in all my life as her straddling my waist. Her tits were the perfect size for my hands, and I lifted my hands to feel them against my rough palms. Aliyana rolled her head back and moaned, my cock hardening again as it pushed against her round firm ass.

I needed to taste her. Needed to feel her wet cunt against my tongue.

In less than a second, I gripped Aliyana's thighs, and with one pull, I used my strength to drag her up over my chest and cover my face. Gripping her thighs tightly, I smashed her pussy to my mouth. My tongue immediately plunged into her hole, only withdrawing to find her swollen clit and I sucked it into my mouth.

"*Fuck!* Elpi!" Aliyana screamed. I looked up in time to see her palms slap against the white wall behind the bed as her hips began to rock against my tongue, her thighs tightening with my every lick and suck.

Feeling my cock harder than before, I groaned, really fucking needing it to be touched. Glancing back at my hips grinding up against thin air, Aliyana's flushed face stared back at mine. She pushed her hands off the wall and whispered, "Let me turn round."

Too busy eating at her pussy, her taste addicting, I didn't move. But as my eyes closed, I felt a finger run softly across my forehead, causing them to snap back open.

Aliyana's beautiful face met my eyes, her tongue running along her pink lips. Her breathing hitched as I pulled on a long suck of her clit. Aliyana gave out a long moan and I felt her clit pulsing against the flatness of my tongue.

"Elpi… please… I want to taste you too… I want your cock in my mouth as you lick me. I want you to come in my throat as I come down yours."

Fuck. Hearing those words slip from her perfect fucking mouth had my dick jerking, reaching and straining, for the feel of lips surrounding its tip.

Not wanting to miss a beat, I released my iron grasp on her thighs and, lifting her hips, using all the strength in my arms, swung her round by her waist to sit back on my face. Gripping the smooth cheeks of her ass and finding her slit scalding hot, I crushed my mouth against it and pushed my thumb inside.

Aliyana's tits pressed against my abs, and I grunted loudly as her soft hands wrapped around the base of my cock. On a moan, Aliyana took the tip of my dick in her hot mouth, taking me in as far as she could.

The feel of her mouth sucking at my cock almost undid me, pressure already building in my balls as Aliyana cupped them in her palm.

My tongue worked faster at her clit, keeping time with her tongue moving up and down my dick. Wanting to hear her screaming out my name, I plunged another finger into her pussy.

Aliyana moaned, her thighs spreading farther apart at my shoulders, mashing her cunt to my face as far as it could go.

All I could taste was her.

All I could think of was her naked body, her gaze not seeing a loser ex-con below her, but the *real* me...

Aliyana's head suddenly lowered and the tip of my dick hit the back of her throat. At the feel of her hands tightening on my sac, pre-cum leaked into her mouth, Aliyana groaning as she swallowed it down.

I was gonna come. Her making noises like that guaranteed I was gonna come... hard.

I could feel heat building, the dull ache creeping up my thighs. Needing her to come too, I worked my tongue harder against her clit and crooked my fingers in her pussy.

Aliyana jerked against my face and released a scream. Her thighs tightened and her hips rocked furiously against my face as my fingers plunged back and forth.

Her hand, that was wrapped around the base of my cock, pumped me faster. Her palm was slick against my hot skin as her tongue lapped at my tip.

As her lips engulfed my dick, she gave one last suck, and I roared against her clit, feeling my cum shoot into her mouth. Aliyana moaned around my cock, her pussy tightening as it contracted around my fingers.

I drank at her pussy, swallowing down her taste, as Aliyana lapped her gentle tongue up and down my dick.

I collapsed back against the pillow and I pulled my fingers out from her pussy. Our heavy breathing seemed to fill up every inch of the studio, my large speakers crackling from the lack of music being played from my still connected phone.

With a satisfied sigh, Aliyana slumped to press her cheek on the inside of my right thigh.

For a few minutes, as I stared at the ceiling, I allowed myself to enjoy this moment. I didn't let the pain of my past slam into my chest. I didn't let my mamma's gaunt face haunt my mind or Levi's hatred of me twist my stomach… I lay here, still tasting Aliyana on my tongue, smelling her Jasmine scent on my damp skin, enjoying the feel of her warm slow breath flowing over my leg.

She was fucking perfection.

She was light. A blazing golden light. When you're locked in perpetual darkness, you'll do anything to fucking chase that light.

La mia luce…

Minutes passed and neither of us spoke. But a strange urge pumped through my blood… I wanted to look into her eyes. I wanted to see those dimples pop on her cheeks as she looked up at me through her stupidly long lashes, a huge blinding smile on her mouth. And for the first time ever, I wanted somebody to be in my arms… No, I wanted *her* in my arms.

I wanted this chick to move up the bed and just fucking *be* in my arms.

Acting on impulse, I sat up, leaned forward and tucked my arm under Aliyana's flat stomach. I pulled her backward, positioning her to lie beside me.

I smiled at Aliyana gasping in shock as I moved her sleepy body to lie beside me. Then my heart exploded in my chest as a shy blush dusted her cheeks as I hooked my arm around her neck and pulled her to lie half across my chest.

I stared upward, feeling disturbed by how much I liked her hand pressed flat over my chest. My body froze at being this close to a woman. But my fingers clutched a thin strand of Aliyana's long hair, rolling the softness between my thumb and index finger.

More minutes passed in silence and I thought she'd fallen asleep. With my free hand, I reached out to my side table and picked up my smokes. Placing a Marlboro Red in my mouth, I lit up the stick and inhaled, blowing out the smoke through my nose. As I was about to take another drag, a finger tiptoed over my beard and guided me to look to my right… straight into Aliyana's doting doe eyes.

Fuck. How was it possible that a pair of eyes could tell you so much? How was it possible that a pair of dark eyes could bring me to my fucking knees with one glance?

"Hey," she said, her cheeks blushing.

Taking another drag, letting the smoke fill my lungs, I ran my fingers along the soft naked skin of her shoulder. "Mm…" I grunted gruffly.

Her eyes flitted down, then blinked back up at me. "I didn't expect this would happen when I came by tonight." Her blush intensified and I realized she was nervous. Nervous of my rejection.

Aliyana's hand ran down my sternum, down over my abs, and paused, before stroking back and forth on my lower stomach just above my dick. My muscles tensed at the feeling and Aliyana smiled up at me, then pressed a single kiss to my pec.

Balancing my smoke on my lower lip, I put my palm on her cheek and said, "Never did either." Aliyana pursed her lips, her eyes widening with hurt, when I added, "But I'm sure fucking glad it did."

Aliyana smiled wide, her white teeth sparkling. Then she did the impossible… She made me laugh, that one happy damn grin of hers made me fucking laugh. It wasn't a lot, one grunt that could barely even pass as a laugh, but she brought it out of me. Somehow, she could bring a shit ton of emotion outta me.

Aliyana leaned up on her elbow, her tits pushing against my bicep. Taking the smoke from my mouth, she took a drag herself. And yeah, her smoking? Nothing fucking hotter than seeing those full lips wrapped round the cherry.

As she placed the smoke back between my lips and lay back on my chest, I took another drag and, exhaling, asked, "You smoke?"

She shook her head. "Not really. Only occasionally when I have a drink." She tipped up her chin. "Or when I've had sex."

I knew she was joking, but a fucking insane wave of jealousy swept through me, and I bit out, "You fuck a lot of guys?"

Aliyana's head drew back as if I'd struck her, but I couldn't help it. The thought of her with another guy had me spinning.

"No, I don't!" she hissed. "Do you fuck a lot of girls?"

Feeling the tight coil begin to unwind in my gut, I tossed my still lit smoke on the floor and replied, "Not in years."

Aliyana's mouth dropped open and her lashes fluttered in shock. "You haven't been with anyone in *years*?"

I didn't answer her question, but my mouth tightened and my eyes narrowed.

Aliyana wasn't deterred. Inching closer, putting her palm on my cheek, she asked, "Why? Why haven't you been with anyone for so long? I don't doubt you could get some serious interest."

I shook my head, telling her without words that we weren't going there, and releasing my arm from round her shoulder, I sat up, dragging my hand down my face.

This conversation was getting way too close to things I didn't ever want to talk about with her.

I heard Aliyana sigh in defeat from behind me, then I felt her cheek press against my back. I closed my eyes and breathed. I more than liked the feel of her touch.

"Why won't you talk to me?" she whispered. I felt the pain in her voice slice through my heart. "I wouldn't tell another soul anything you revealed."

Dropping my head and finally losing the wall I kept around me at all times, I whispered back, "'Cause I really can't fucking stand the thought of you hating me."

Aliyana rolled her cheek until her forehead pressed against my shoulder blade. "I could never hate you."

"You *could* and you *would* if you knew the fucked-up shit I've done."

She didn't respond for several seconds, but then her arms slid around my waist and pulled me down to the bed. Flattening me to the mattress, hands on my shoulders, she straddled my waist, leaned down, and pressed her lips to mine. But the kiss was softer this time; she wasn't letting me take her mouth aggressively like I had every time we'd kissed before... No, this chick was determined to make me *feel*, dredging up shit I'd buried down deep.

Breaking from the kiss, Aliyana put her hands on my cheeks and said, "You are worth your weight in gold, Elpi. You *are* someone, someone real special."

My nostrils flared as I fought back a lump clogging up my throat. She had no fucking idea how much that meant to me. She was dead wrong. But still, those words fucking pierced me.

Shifting her legs off my waist, Aliyana jumped off the bed and wrapped a bed sheet around her chest. I didn't move from my place on the bed, choosing to watch her as

155

she walked about the room. Her inquisitive eyes drank in every part of my studio: my tool station, the area where I molded the clay templates of my sculptures, the desk that normally held my sketches... and finally, her eyes fixed on my current work in progress.

My stomach clenched as I watched her cautiously approach the nearly finished piece, her experienced curator eyes assessing every inch of it. And I saw every single emotion slide across her gaze: excitement, curiosity... then sadness, real gutting sadness.

As Aliyana circled the sculpture, she stopped when she reached the front, and I noted her mouth dropping open as the full effect of the sculpture came into view. Her eyes filled with water and she stepped closer to the finished young boy unsteadily holding a gun in his tiny hands, his unnaturally wide eyes crying blood and bullets. Then I watched as her gaze traveled to the twenty-something man behind him, holding the little boy's gun arm steady, pushing him to fire.

The marble man wasn't finished yet. His face wasn't yet carved. I hadn't quite brought myself to add his features. *My* features on that fucking guy I didn't recognize as me no more, forcing his baby brother to kill...

I tensed, waiting for the damn storm of questions Aliyana would no doubt ask about its inspiration, but to my surprise, she simply wiped her eyes, not once glancing my way. Instead she moved to the far side of the room, to the big-ass piano Vin had sitting in here.

As Aliyana's hand ran over the shiny black grand her head whipped round to me. "Is this yours?" she asked breathlessly.

"Vin's," I replied, my eyebrows furrowed with curiosity as I watched her stroke it like it was a precious stone.

Aliyana turned back to the piano and made her way to its front. She lifted the lid to reveal the keys. "It's beautiful," she admired in awe and looked to me again. "It's a Steinway concert grand."

Shuffling further forward on the bed, I rolled onto my side, my hand propping up my head. "You play?"

Aliyana nodded, still star struck by the damn piano, and laughed once. "I've played my whole life. My mama does too, and she taught me. But we only had a regular piano... nothing like this." Aliyana sat on the piano stool and caressed the white and black ivories.

"The piano was my life when I was a kid. And I still love to play. Still love to get lost in the melody of my favorite piece." Aliyana bent forward and inhaled, her face lighting up. "It's gorgeous."

I didn't know what it was, maybe the passion and joy I saw dancing in her eyes, but I couldn't tear my gaze away from her as she sat on that dusty leather stool covered only in a sheet, a sheet that we'd just fucked on. Her long hair was messy and fell loosely over her shoulder.

She looked like a painting.

Aliyana released both hands from the sheet, causing it to fall to her waist. I bit back a groan as her round tits were bared. But Aliyana didn't notice me watching her. Instead, she flexed her hands, and with an excited smile pulling on her lips, she positioned her fingers above the keys.

I held my breath as the first note rang out, her eyes focused as she tested the sound, her feet shifting forward to press on the pedals.

Then, closing her eyes, a serene expression spread across her beautiful face. Aliyana began to play... perfectly play a piece of music like she was trained by Mozart or some shit. A piece of music that couldn't have suited her, and her infectious attitude any better. The notes were laced with hope, love and joy... like a lullaby, but more powerful. The melodic notes made me feel like my life could get better. Because that's what Aliyana did, she made me feel like my life could get better.

I had no idea why, but this piece of music she was playing, started to bring tears to my eyes, like a motherfucking pussy. It was like she was telling me with

158

song how she felt about me... about us... about what
we'd just done.

I focused on Aliyana playing that music, her facial
expressions changing with every new section: from happy
to sad, from tearful to complete adoration. I'd never seen
anyone look like they belonged somewhere as much she
did on the stool in front of that piano, playing the most
fucking beautiful piece of music I'd ever heard.

I was completely wrapped up in everything that was her.
Her long, slim fingers slowed to play a quieter, less
complicated section of the song, her head swaying from
side to side, lost in the notes. At that sight, something
seized my body, ran like lava through my blood. A thing I
hadn't dared let myself feel for... I didn't honestly know if
I ever *had* felt it before...

Hope.

Being with Aliyana like this... her accepting soul only
seeing me for me and not my past, a fucking unwarranted
blind faith... she filled me with *hope*.

Lei era speranza... She *was* hope. *La mia luce*... my light.

It reminded me of what my mamma would hope for me
when the gang had me deep in its clutches. I'd kiss her
good-bye, heading out to meet Gio and my crew as
Mamma lay unmoving in her small bed, her ALS keeping
her body hostage. She'd watch me with those huge sad

eyes, eyes that prayed for our lives to be better, and she'd brokenly whisper, *Io prego perché tu possa trovare la tua luce, mio figlio smarrito…* I pray you find your light, my lost son…

My heart beat faster as the memory invaded my mind, constricting my chest. Aliyana's fingers slowed as if she could sense I was fucking falling apart inside, the sweet sounding melody gradually coming to it's close.

Something inside me took over, and unable to stop myself, I slid off the bed and silently crossed the room. I moved to stand behind Aliyana just as her fingers on one hand danced over the higher keys of the piano, the final high-pitched note hanging in the air.

Before she'd even had a chance to move her hands from the keys and her bare feet from the pedals, I took her chin in my hand from behind, turning her face to press her lips against mine. The pressure in my chest disappeared as soon as her sweet taste entered my mouth.

Shocked at my action, Aliyana moaned into my mouth, her arm rising up to wrap round my neck. Without breaking the kiss, I hooked my arm around her waist and lifted her off the stool, her back flush against my front. I walked us forward just a few steps to the side of the piano, our tongues still clashing. Unable to wait any longer, I leaned her forward to press her stomach against the cold wood of the grand, still keeping her lips on mine. Hooking her right leg over the inside of my elbow, I raised it enough to open up her pussy, and in one steady push, slid my cock deep inside her. I wasn't rushing this. I wasn't fucking her now... It was something *more*... because she was *more*...

Aliyana slipped her mouth from mine as she quietly cried out my name. "Elpi..."

Slowly gliding up my arm, her free hand lay on top of mine over her stomach. As I rocked within her, my thighs burning from the feel, Aliyana lifted my hand and entwined her fingers within mine.

Dragging in a breath at the feel of her small hand squeezing mine so gently had me fighting to not drop to my knees and fucking beg her to never leave this room. We didn't need the world outside. We had this room. We had just her and me in this room.

When Aliyana glanced back to meet my eyes, I paused inside her and stared right back. There was no music playing to drown everything out, no words said to break the silence... It was the most intense and meaningful moment of my life. Here, deep inside this woman who only knew the man I was now, not the unfeeling bastard I was before, was my *more*.

I'd never once thought that I deserved a second chance, never wanted one. As far as I was concerned, I deserved to

161

spend the rest of my life miserable for what I'd done. But here, deep inside the most beautiful woman I'd ever seen, the woman who just *got me*, I was bartering with God to let me keep her... just for a while... to keep feeling... *this*... whatever *this* was...

"*Tu sei bella...*" You are beautiful, I whispered and noticed Aliyana's eyes glisten. She careened forward and pressed a brief kiss on my lips, then tilted her head to the side, urging me to kiss down her neck. My hips started rocking again, Aliyana lightly panting with every drawn-out thrust.

Aliyana tightened her grip around my neck, and with our entwined fingers holding tight, I built up speed, taking us further and further to the edge.

Minutes later, our damp skin scalding hot, Aliyana quietly moaned as she came. Her eyes fluttered closed and, after two more thrusts, I tucked my nose into her hair and came too.

"Elpi..." Aliyana murmured quietly, and I tightened my arm around her waist. I held her as close as I physically could. And Aliyana let me. Let me hold on to our connection without saying a word.

"What was that music you played?" I suddenly asked. "Just now, what was that?"

"Yiruma's "Kiss the Rain,"" she answered breathlessly, her tired body sagging in my arms.

I committed the title of that song to memory. "Kiss the Rain."

Pulling out of her, I scooped her up in my arms, only stopping to lift the sheet off the floor, and carried her back to my bed. As we lay down, Aliyana softly peppered kisses all over my face before resting her cheek affectionately on my chest.

"I've missed you, Elpi…" she whispered sleepily.

I squeezed her closer to my side, wishing I could tell her I'd missed her too. Instead, I curtly ordered, "You're staying here tonight."

Aliyana nuzzled into my chest and I felt the muscles in her cheeks pull into a smile. "From the first time I ever saw your angel sculpture, it seared my heart… I always knew if I could meet you in the flesh, your soul would do the same."

The words she spoke might as well have been a fucking Hail Mary from God himself, a free pass for the fucked-up sins of my past. But that could never be true. I had to pay the piper. I'd ruined lives. Karma didn't work this way, giving you everything you could dream of without paying some kind of price.

I pressed my cheek on the top of her head and closed my eyes.

It was the first time I'd slept right through the night without waking up to cold sweats and an unbearable anger killing me inside.

Chapter Eleven

Ally

As I woke to the bright sun filtering through the large windows of the studio, the rays lighting up his muscled naked body, it felt like I was caught in a dream.

Elpidio's strong arms were still holding me close; he'd never let go all night. I treasured the touch of this closed off, tortured man, but felt a deep pit swell in my stomach.

What was he hiding about himself that was so terrible?

What was haunting his genius mind, pushing anyone away from getting too close? Warning me to stay away?

Lifting my fingers, I traced them gently over his rugged face, focusing my attention on the black crucifix which dominated his left cheek. The lines looked like he'd done it himself, the center of the cross seeming to cover something underneath.

165

Eyes following fingers, I ran them down his short, soft beard to his neck, tattoos covering every inch of skin. Unfamiliar symbols, images of Italy and cryptic words featured in most of the designs. These designs led to similar works on his chest, the centerpiece an intricate rosary falling to his sternum.

It was beautiful.

But on closer inspection, my eyebrows furrowed as I studied a number of slash scars and what looked like stab wounds on his abs and stomach.

They all looked bad, but none as painful-looking as the one on the back of his neck.

How the hell did he get them all?

I thought back to the numerous questions about his past which had gone unanswered: the tragic background to his sculptures, the tightly pristine made bed when I walked into the studio last night, the scars, and the fact he hadn't been with a woman in years.

As I cast my eyes over his current sculpture, the boy with a gun, crying blood and bullet tears, one thought came to mind: Was he military? Was that why he was so closed off? So jaded by people... by life?

A loud beep sounded from across the room, the shrill noise waking Elpi, his dark sleepy eyes blinking open. I held my breath as he looked down. His eyebrows knitted together as if he was confused by seeing me sprawled across his chest. But when a hint of a smile hooked on the corner of his top lip, I felt a swarm of butterflies invade my stomach.

"Hi," I whispered.

"Alright," he whispered back in his sexy deep drawl. Leaning his mouth down to meet mine, our lips touched just as my cell sounded again.

Groaning at the interruption, I reared back. "I have to go," I announced, reluctantly.

Elpi looked over to the large clock hanging on the far wall and nodded. His face darkened like a bad thought had run through his mind, but then it disappeared just as quickly as it came.

Pressing a final playful kiss on his hard abs, I rolled off the side of the bed, hissing as my bare feet hit the freezing cold tiled floor. As I moved to stand, Elpi's hand caught my arm, causing me to glance back at him.

The conflict that played across his face confused me, but then on a reluctant sigh, he said, "Come back tonight." It appeared to pain him to utter those words. My heart melted, knowing what displaying so much vulnerability must have cost him emotionally.

The butterflies in my stomach swooped and dipped again and, smiling, I nodded my head. "It'll be late, though. I'm out with friends all day and most of the night."

He threw me a curt nod, his face remaining unmoved and serious. Reaching out my hand, I threaded his fingers through mine. "I wish I didn't have to go."

As he squeezed my hands, I blushed. I knew that was him telling me he wished I didn't have to go either.

Resenting having to attend the Seahawks' season opening game today, I forced myself to leave the bed and dress.

Elpi sat up on the bed, the sheet riding low on his hips as he lit up a cigarette and held it between his lips, looking like a darker, more disturbed version of James Dean.

He was living, breathing poetry. Not love poetry, but the poetry which tears out your heart, rips it to shreds, pushes it back into your chest, and makes you question what the hell just obliterated your soul?

I couldn't tear my gaze away from him as I pulled up my dress over my breasts, his man bun seductively awry, his ripped tattoo-covered abs tensing as his arm moved up and down to hold his cigarette as he inhaled. When he blew out the smoke, small lines etched round his eyes; the severe effect screamed *danger*. I was completely infatuated with this man.

Elpidio caught me staring as he scratched his nails over the skin on his broad chest. His eyes lit with blatant desire, and he flicked his chin. "Get the fuck outta here or you won't be going nowhere."

Exhaling a shuddering breath at his curt demand, I strode to the bed, where Elpi balanced the cigarette on his full bottom lip—an action that was beginning to destroy me at how damn sexy it was.

When I stopped a foot away, Elpi reached out his hand to grip my hips, then jerked me closer until I lay sprawled over his body. Releasing one of his hands, he moved his cigarette from his mouth and blew out the smoke, the thick cloud billowing past my face, the rich tobacco scent mixed with his natural musk eliciting a groan from the back of my throat.

"You're fucking coming back tonight," he growled, making sure I knew to obey his command. At the uncensored heat in his eyes, all I could do was nod in agreement as his hand on my hip trailed down to run a finger along the outline of my pussy.

Forcing myself to bite back a moan and walk away, I picked up my purse from the floor and headed out without looking back.

As I opened the door of the studio, I sharply sucked in breath, letting the cool air calm me down. As I exhaled, I tipped my head to the sky and laughed in happiness.

My heart felt alive. My soul felt… my soul felt… *fused*… melded to Elpidio's. There was no explanation other than I understood there was a good man beneath all the tattoos and the barrier he deployed to keep people at arm's length. A good man whose soul smiled when I played my favorite piece of music on the piano, a piece that meant so much to my heart. He'd *had* to make love to me…

Fused.

Nothing else described this new sensation of completion within me.

Hearing my cell beep again, I growled at the interruption. Jogging to my car, I opened up my messages. There were two.

MOLLY: IT'S GAME DAY!!!

And again…

MOLLY: I've tried to call you three times, but there's no response. And I noticed you didn't come home last night… after you went to Elpidio's… So I'm assuming things went well? YAY! But we need to leave in an hour if we're to make the game. Rome would love you there.

I smiled as I read Molly's last text and sent her quick response that I was on my way home. She was going to grill me for details. I just knew it.

*****

"Holy shit, Molls! How the other half live, hey?" I said, shaking my head at the opulence of the décor as Molly led the way into Rome's private suite in the CenturyLink stadium. I walked to the floor-to-ceiling wall of glass offering a perfect view of the field and whistled low. It was amazing. From this position, we would have the best view of the game.

Typical Rome. Buying an expensive suite just so his pregnant wife would be safe and warm while he played.

For a minute, I looked down at my pale-pink knee-length chiffon shirtdress, my black fitted blazer, and my favorite pair of brown cowboy boots that I'd had for years. My hair was tied with chopsticks and I wore large silver loops in my ears.

I'd asked Molly a million times if what I was wearing was okay. She assured me it was. But Molly really couldn't give two shits about what she or I looked like, never had. What she didn't see, however, was that she always looked beautiful no matter what she wore. And today was no exception, as she sported a long black dress, the clingy jersey material showcasing her growing bump and stunning figure. Her long brown hair was curly and flowing down her back, her square-framed Chanel glasses complimenting her pretty face.

Hearing someone enter the suite, I turned to see Lexi and Levi walk in. Lexi beamed a huge smile at us all, waving excitedly as she wore her "Carillo" Seahawks home jersey with a pair of jeans. Levi was wearing the navy-and-green jersey too. I expected him to come and say hello. Instead, he jerked his chin in a brief greeting and walked to the far side of the suite to sag down in a chair.

Frowning at his strange behavior, I held out my hands to Lexi and kissed her cheek. "How're you doing, darlin?" I asked.

"Good, you?" she answered, but I could see she was distracted about something.

Blushing, I dipped my head. "I'm real good."

Lexi cocked her head to the side as she regarded me. "What—"

"She's been out all night, Lex," Molly interrupted from beside us, and Lexi's eyes widened in interest.

"Who with? Do tell?" Lexi asked, leading me to a couch in the corner of the room. Molly followed and we all sat down.

"Taking a deep breath, I couldn't fight the smile pulling on my face. "Elpidio," I confessed, and Lexi's thrilled smile reflected my own.

"The reclusive artist?" she asked, curiously.

"Yes," I replied, giggling.

"And?" Molly asked. "What happened last night? You've said nothing about it yet. You've kept me on tenterhooks!"

I shrugged. I wasn't sure how to explain what Elpi and I had shared. It wasn't normal by any stretch of the imagination, and honestly, by both his looks and closed-off attitude to seemingly everyone but me, I knew my friends would warn me to stay away.

Lexi and Molly were waiting anxiously for my answer, so I simply said, "It was the best night of my life. He's beyond anything I could ever have imagined."

Molly reached over me and pulled me in for a happy hug, and Lexi could do nothing but smile. I laughed at Molly's reaction when a server came by to hand us glasses of champagne.

As I reached out for my flute, I noticed Levi slumped further into his chair, looking out over the field, with headphones on, music blaring, blocking out the world, lost in thought. He looked miserable. My eyebrows pulled down.

"Lex?" I called and, stopping her conversation about Austin's debut today with Molly, she turned to face me.

I nudged my head in the direction of Levi. "What's wrong with Lev? He looks as miserable as sin and barely said hello when y'all walked in."

Lexi ran her tiny hand, sporting black nail varnish, down her face, glancing sympathetically at Levi, then back to us. "Axel," she said on an exasperated sigh.

I grimaced. "Shit. Yeah. Molly and Rome told me he'd got out of prison. How's all that going? I haven't had time to ask you much about it."

"Axel's quiet, don't say much at all. Keeps to himself. I actually kinda feel sorry for him. He's always on his own." I leaned forward to pat Lexi's hand. She squeezed my fingers. "But Levi... Levi's just angry all the time. And it breaks me seeing him this way... *both* of them this way. Axel tries to speak to Levi, he's really trying to make amends, but Lev just explodes if he does. It's hopeless."

"And what's wrong with him today? It's Austin's debut for the Seahawks. I thought he'd be excited. And they're playing Reece's team too, so he'll get to see him again."

"He is," Lexi answered, "but Axel's due here any minute. Austin wanted Axe here so bad he begged him to show up. It tore me apart seeing how excited Austin was that Axe was gonna finally see him play in the NFL. That husband of mine hero-worships his big brother. Even after everything they've gone through, he loves him to death."

"Axel's coming here today?" I asked in a wary voice, my eyes widening. I instantly felt uneasy. I'd never met the guy or even laid eyes on him, but I knew he was nothing but trouble with a capital T. Shit, he'd just gotten out of prison for Christ's sake.

Lexi nodded. "Like I said, Austin wanted Axel here. And credit where credit's due, Axel's really trying. He's keeping out of trouble and his head down. He's working at this fish market the prison organized as part of his parole, all the hours God sends. But even still, Levi just can't forgive him yet. I think he's afraid to trust him and love him like he needs, just to have Axel fall back to his old ways. Levi's lost too much too young. I think he's trying to protect his heart from more pain. But I want them to be a family again so bad. I'll do anything to make that happen, for all their sakes."

As I listened to my little friend, I felt a swell of pride fill my chest. She'd conquered so much from being so young, brought herself back from the brink of death, *twice*, managed to become a successful business woman by helping others suffering from eating disorders, and now, she was desperately trying to pull together a group of brothers torn apart by years of nothing but acts of selfishness and grief.

The three of us were sitting in silence when Lexi's cell phone beeped. She looked down and moved to get to her feet. "Axel's outside. I'm going down to meet him. I'll bring him up here to watch the game."

Lexi walked across the suite to Levi and tapped him on the shoulder. Levi moved the headphones from his ears. "Axel's outside, sweetie. You wanna come and get him with me?"

Levi's eyes frosted with venom and, putting the headphones on his head, he said, "Just fucking leave him out there, Lex."

Lexi's shoulders sagged, and without looking Molly's way or mine, she left the suite to meet Axel.

I blew a long breath out of my mouth, and Molly shook her head. "It's a mess," she said, and taking a sip of my champagne, I nodded in agreement.

"So tell me all about the ins and outs of this gallery you're designing. It feels like it's been forever since we've had a real chance to catch up."

"Well…" I started and launched into the goings on of the last few weeks and the ups and downs of constructing the Elpidio show.

Too busy talking to Molly, my back to the entrance of the private suite, I didn't see Lexi walking in behind us until Molly's golden-brown eyes looked up over her glasses and she adopted a nervous expression. Twisting in my seat, I saw Lexi in front of me.

"Ally, Molly," Lexi said, and I stood from the couch, seeing someone enter the suite in my peripheral vision. Suddenly, my cell rang from inside my purse, and I saw it was the museum.

"Sorry, Lex, let me take this," I said and rushed to the far side of the room out of sight. The call ended up taking ten minutes, a carpenter stressing about the measurements of a plinth he was building.

Walking back into the room, my gaze got lost at the screaming Seahawks crowd on their feet and the cheerleaders running on the field. I headed to where Lexi sat, seeing her pixie face turn to me. Lexi immediately got to her feet, and I saw Molly raise her eyebrows toward a guy sitting behind Lexi. I could hardly see him as he sat in a dark corner, just his bulky arm propping his head up on the arm of the chair visible from where I stood.

"Sorry about that, darlin'," I said. "I'm on the clock twenty-four-seven at the minute!"

"No problem," Lexi said and motioned behind her. "Ally, I'd like you to meet Axel, Austin's older brother."

Feeling nervous at meeting the guy responsible for so much of my friends' pain, my hands actually shook. The guy behind Lexi reluctantly got to his feet. His broad back was covered in a long-sleeved black shirt, the arms rolled up to his elbows, and his hair was covered in a oversized black beanie hanging low in the back, covering his neck.

Shit, I thought. He was huge. Probably bigger than Austin in terms of his muscle size.

Lexi moved to the side, and I took a deep breath as the notorious bad boy of Bama turned to face me, and as my eyes slammed to meet a pair of dark Italian eyes… a pair of *familiar* dark Italian eyes that were etched into my heart…

All the blood drained from my face.

No… It's… it's not possible…

Elpi's tanned bearded face turned ashen as I stared at him, mouth gaping and his always-stern eyes widened in alarm.

We both stood there, frozen to the spot.

Unmoving.

Silent.

Just staring…

Elpidio is… Axel Carillo?

I flitted a glance to the left and caught sight of Lexi's worried face.

Forcing myself to react, I held out my shaky hand. Elpi, I mean *Axel's* mouth tightened at the action.

"Hi," I whispered shakily, flinching as his warm palm met mine and sent the usual bolt of electricity shooting up my spine.

Axel dipped his head in greeting, just as Lexi added, "This is Ally Prince, Axel, Rome Prince's cousin."

Axel's hand tightened in mine at Lexi's announcement, and I could see the disdain for my cousin written all over his face.

I pulled back my hand and my gaze involuntary ran down Axel's large body. A body I now knew intimately.

The announcer took to the mic across the field, working the strong crowd into a crazed frenzy. The Seahawks team was coming out.

But I couldn't move.

"Ally! Quickly, or you'll miss Rome and Austin coming out of the tunnel," Molly said, and Lexi rushed to sit beside her, leaving Axel and me locked in a tense gaze.

"Ally!" Molly called again. Finally able to move my feet, I staggered toward where my best friend sat, glancing back to see Axel moving to the farthest seat on the other side of the long paneled glass… the seat that offered him the perfect view of me. And he kept staring. I felt his eyes on me as clearly as I could feel the subtle heat from the vent beside my feet blowing in hot air.

I couldn't believe it.

My heart cried as I looked out of the window... I was completely infatuated with Axel Carillo.

Feeling his gaze burning through my eyelids, I reluctantly looked up, just as Molly and Lexi jumped to their feet. Levi had moved beside Lexi, leaving Axel sitting on the opposite side of the suite on his own.

That alone made my heart squeeze. He appeared every inch the outcast, his own brother blatantly rejecting him... the black sheep of the Carillos, lost and scorned, forced to be on his own.

A hand suddenly lay on my shoulder. Molly was looking at me. "Ally, they're just about to announce Austin and Rome. Reece is already on the field for the Redskins."

I focused on the field and pride raced through my veins seeing the banners and jerseys reading "Prince 7." My cousin had come through so much and deserved all of this. I also saw Reece, strutting on the side of the field, ever the egomaniac. I hadn't seen him once since college.

I smiled in forced excitement as fireworks and pyrotechnics burst through CenturyLink, music blaring through the speakers. Reaching down, I took Molly's hand, gripping it tightly. I needed her support. Not through excitement for Rome's first game of the season, but for keeping me composed at the revelation I'd just experienced.

Elpidio was Axel.

My heart was shattered.

Molly and Lexi both had tears in their eyes, waiting for their husbands to take the field, and when I looked to Lexi's side, Levi was gripping her hand too. There was nothing but adoration on his handsome face for his brother, Austin, as he awaited the announcement of the newest Seahawk. But a pit swallowed my stomach when I saw his clear disregard for Axel.

I thought of the little boy sculpture, and I fought not to break down and sob at all the realizations rushing through my mind.

It's Axel and Levi…

The announcer revved up the crowd, as he began his introduction of Austin. I heard Lexi hold her breath as they ran through her husband's football accolades. Levi lifted Lexi's hand and pressed it to his chest, a huge smile pulled on his normally shy face as the crowd roared their approval and welcome for their new wide receiver.

Seconds later, to a line of flaming pyrotechnics, Austin Carillo ran onto the field. Lexi silently cried in happiness beside me, but that's not what nearly brought me to tears

181

too… No, that honor belonged to a tall, lonely figure standing on his own at the farthest side of the room. A lonely figure with his muscled arms folded across his broad chest, the most heartbreaking expression of pride on his face, as he watched his brother hold his helmet up to the crowd. An awed flicker of a smirk pulled on his lips as I watched whispers of tears tumble down his cheeks.

Axel Carillo *cared*… Axel Carillo cared more than anyone thought about his brother… his family… more than I could ever have thought possible from the hellish reputation that travelled with him.

Pain racked my body. I was crushed that Elpidio was really Axel Carillo. How the hell could this be? It felt like the universe was playing a mean trick on me.

As if feeling my hard stare, Axel's eyes darted to mine, his proud flicker of a smile dropping in embarrassment at being caught, and he quickly wiped at his eyes, looking away from me.

Molly's hand squeezed mine, and as I met her eyes, she was looking between Axel and me with a strange expression on her face.

Leaning close to my ear, I stiffened as Molly went to say something, when the stadium positively lifted in volume, the announcer barely audible over the fans' screams. Molly pulled away, her eyes immediately fixed on the players' tunnel as Rome was announced. To the line of scantily clad cheerleaders waving pompoms and fireworks lighting up the stadium, Rome Prince took the field.

Molly exhaled, and I watched her eyes fix on her husband as he stopped dead in the middle of the frenzy, pure love in her stare as her hand ran over her round stomach. Rome faced our suite, and holding his helmet in his hand, pressed his fingers to his lips in Molly's direction. Molly sniffed back her sobs and returned the gesture. Rome smiled and tapped his chest over his heart. He ran toward Austin, throwing his hand around Austin's shoulders.

Molly laughed, choking on emotion. "Sorry, guys, it's my hormones," she said, wiping her cheeks.

Releasing her hand and wiping at her cheeks with my thumb, I said, "Nah, it's just you two."

Molly laughed, and we sat down.

Truth was I wanted a love like theirs… a soul-shattering, leave you breathless kind of love…

That thought had my eyes instinctively searching for Elpi under my lashes and we immediately locked gazes. He was still watching me, that intense, see-into-my-soul Italian stare of his was burning into mine.

The whistle sounded on the field, making me jump, forcing me to look away from the man I feared I'd already lost my heart to. I made myself watch the game and tried not to think of all the wrongs he'd done in his past… the mountain of wrongs… the wrongs I wasn't sure I could ever get past…

Chapter Twelve
Ally

The Seahawks won. Austin even scored a debut touchdown, but I couldn't bring myself to look at Elpi's reaction. In fact, the longer I sat in this chair, the more I couldn't take the tension pulsing between us.

"Ally?"

Blinking fast, realizing Lexi was calling my name, I glanced to my side. Lexi leaned forward, waving for me to lean forward too.

"You okay?" she whispered, and cautiously watched Axel as he stared out the window at the emptying field.

I nodded, but Lexi said, "He won't hurt you, you know."

My forehead pulled down in confusion. "What are you—"

"You've been staring at Axel all game, and I know it's because you're scared. He *looks* scary, all those scars and tattoos, and those dark eyes that look like they can incinerate people where they stand. But he won't hurt you. You can be assured of that."

Shocked that I'd obviously been paying Axel so much attention, I simply nodded and sat back in my seat, praying Rome and Austin would hurry and get up here so we could leave.

I needed time to think. I just needed time to friggin' deal...

Then Axel got up from his chair and I froze.

My hands grew damp as I watched Axel scan the room, and Molly and Lexi watched him too. Axel's head was downcast and his fists were clenching and unclenching. He acted nervous about something, and the reason for that nervousness was soon revealed when he walked to Levi.

"You wanna go get a drink or something to eat with me, kid?" he asked, and my pulse raced, seeing the flare of hope spark in his eyes.

But Levi ignored him and kept his head down. Levi's face was stone as his jaw clenched.

"Lev?" Axel prompted and reached out to touch Levi's shoulder.

Levi ripped his shoulder away. "I ain't going nowhere with you."

The expression of raw hurt that ghosted across Axel's face was my undoing. It cut to the core and carved a pit of sympathy in my stomach the size of the Grand Canyon. I fought the urge to jump to my feet and hold him in my arms.

"I'll have a water please, Axe, if you're going to the bar?" Lexi said, and Axel nodded, seemingly thankful for something to do after being so harshly shunned. He moved to leave the suite, but not before he flickered his eyes to me, desperate hurt glinting in his gaze.

When Axel had left the room, Lexi faced Levi. "Lev, did you have to be like that?" she said, clear disappointment in her tone.

Levi shrugged. "I didn't want a damn drink."

Lexi sighed and dropped her head.

Molly shuffled forward to comfort Lexi, when Rome walked into the suite.

Rome, as always, bee-lined for Molly and, wrapping his arms around her, pulled her in for a kiss.

Austin walked in the room shortly after Rome, and immediately his eyes began to search the suite. We all knew he was looking for Axel.

Austin, seeing his wife clapping her hands at him in congratulations, laughed and, taking her face in his hands, brought her in for a kiss. As he broke away, he whispered,

"*Ti amo tantissimo*," in her ear, making her blush, then next took Levi in his arms.

"You were fucking unreal, Aust," Levi said proudly.

"Thanks, Lev," Austin replied, and just at that moment, the suite door opened and Axel stepped through carrying a bottle of water for Lexi.

Rome, who had just hugged me, stiffened. But Austin, Austin's whole face lit up as he crossed the room and threw his arms around Axel's neck. Axel's assessing eyes looked up to all of us watching, and he awkwardly pushed Austin back after tapping his back.

"You came, Axe," Austin said in relief.

Axe tapped his hand on Austin's face. "You know it, kid," Axel replied. "*Sei stato grande, fratello.*"

"*Grazie,* Axe, *grazie,*" Austin replied.

Slinging an arm around Axel's shoulder, Austin led him back toward us. "We having drinks here first, then catching dinner?" he asked, looking to Rome.

Rome's eyes narrowed and focused on Axel. Axel's eyes were glaring at my cousin just as fiercely.

"Axe," Rome greeted coldly.

"Rome," Axel greeted back.

Austin tensed as he looked between his brother and best friend, but Rome broke the tension when he turned to Austin and said, "Dinner sounds good," and sat down, pulling Molly to sit on his lap. Lexi moved next to Austin where he immediately sloped his arm around her neck.

Axel stayed next to Austin, drinking a beer, and listened to his brother's rundown of the game. Levi watched on, unwilling to join them, but by the look on his face, clearly wanting to.

"I hate that fuck," Rome said from beside me, too low for Axel to hear and my heart fell at his words.

"Rome," Molly censured.

"What? After everything he's done, Austin just welcomes him back? No questions asked?"

A sudden anger built within me as I listened to my cousin being so unforgiving toward Axel, and just as I was about to jump to Axel's defense, someone walked into the suite.

"Well, look at this, it's like a friggin' UA reunion!"

My attention followed the voice and, there at the door, was Reece. I couldn't help but smile as he stood there, beer in hand looking as preppy as always with his clean cut blond hair and thousand-dollar smile. He'd filled out some since college, but was still just as handsome.

Reece entered and slapped hands with Austin, Levi and Rome, hugged Molly, then turned his huge smile to me.

"Ally," he said playfully. "You haven't changed bit," he added as he wrapped me in his arms. As I looked over

189

Reece's shoulder, loosely hugging him back, Axel was glaring at us, and in that glare I saw the real Axel Carillo. I saw the infamous ex-leader of the Heighters, the guy who took no shit. And this version of him, I actually feared.

Pulling me back by my arms, Reece leaned forward, and taking me by surprise, jokingly planted a kiss on my lips.

Pushing on his chest, I broke from the kiss. "Reece! Get the hell off!"

Reece winked at me. "Shit. You're still my dream girl, Al. Still just as hot as ever." I shook my head at him in reprimand, but couldn't help but laugh. At twenty-three, he was still a hopeless flirt. I kind of missed having him around.

"Reece, get the fuck off my cousin, you horny little shit," Rome said, amused.

Reece laughed, holding out his hands. "I'm off. I just couldn't help myself." He turned to me and his eyebrows danced. I laughed again. He'd always made me laugh. The guy was as laidback as they came.

Reece slung his arms around my neck and turned us to face all the old gang. "So, are we going out tonight? I fly back out to D.C., tomorrow and want to see what the Seattle nightlife's like."

"We can grab dinner, but I'm taking Molls home after," Rome said.

"Same for us," I heard Austin say.

Reece sighed dramatically. "Y'all are getting real boring as you get old. I never get to see y'all and you're already bailing on me." He squeezed me tighter. "Just you and me then Al," he joked and kissed my cheek again. "I'm sure we can figure out something entertaining to do."

I went to open my mouth to cry off the entire night, dinner included, when I heard Austin call, "Axe? Where you going?"

When I looked round I saw Axel heading out of the door, his pack of smokes clutched tightly in his hand.

"What happened?" Lexi asked Austin.

He shook his head in confusion. "No damn idea."

My heart pounded as the group all moved to sit around a table and the server brought us drinks. But I couldn't take my mind of Elpi... Axel... whatever the fuck he wanted to call himself. I knew he'd left because of Reece.

The air in the suite became suffocating. Needing to take a break and deal with the revelations of tonight, I excused myself and fled in the direction of the bathroom. As I walked out of the suite and down the long empty hallway, I rounded the corner to the bathroom, where Axel was heading my way.

The two of us stopped dead.

Our gazes clashed.

He looked livid.

Our chests were panting hard, and as I forced myself to shift to the left, Axel gripped my arm and dragged me into the bathroom, locking the door behind us.

I backed away toward the farthest wall as his dark gaze turned on me; he looked liked the devil himself, his chest puffed up and lips pulled tight.

"Who's that fucker that was all over you?" he demanded, inching forward. I backed up against the cold tiled wall. "Who was that little blond prick? You fucking him? Why the fuck were his lips on yours?"

"Who is *he*?" I whispered incredulously, anger lacing my voice at his attitude. "Who is *he*?" I shrilled louder. "He's an old friend! Someone I haven't seen in years!"

Axel's lips ran over his teeth, visibly shaking. I stepped forward as he stared me down, his eyes blazing with anger. "Who the fuck are *you*, *Elpidio*?"

"Don't," he warned, icily.

"Don't?" I snapped, "*Don't?* You're Axel Carillo! Axel *fucking* Carillo! Jesus!" I ran my hand over my forehead when Axel didn't say a word. "You're the reason my friend almost lost his scholarship with the Tide. You ran away and left him to deal with everything on his own. You left him to deal drugs just to make money for your family! You threatened to 'shut up' my best friend who was battling

Anorexia! And you hate my cousin, like you'd kill each other if you got the chance, hate each other! And…"

I choked on the sob which was working its way up my throat.

"And what?" he asked through gritted teeth. "Don't fucking stop now when you're laying all this shit at my feet."

I met his expressionless eyes and said, "And you've been in prison! Shit, Elpi! What we've shared these past weeks… what we shared last night… and you're fucking Axel Carillo! You were meant to be *Elpidio*! You were the only guy that I've ever felt that fucking bolt of lightening in my heart with, and you turn out to be… *him! You!*"

Axel reared back as if I'd slapped him and my breathing stuttered at the amount of pain etched on his face. "And you're Ally Prince," he said tightly, but I could hear the hurt radiating in his voice. I'd hurt him. Really hurt him.

"I've heard of you, *Ally*. I know your fucking cousin, remember. I know what family you come from. Your rich-assed oil family." I opened my mouth to speak, to tell him he knew shit about me, when he said, "*You* were meant to be *Aliyana Lucia*… the woman that I tried to push away, but you kept coming back anyway, fucking *melting* me. You were meant to be Aliyana, the only woman, no, the only *person* who knows what I've been doing with my life for the last few years while inside, trying to keep my head down and not fucking suffocate under my guilt. You were meant to be the woman who claimed to *feel* my work. And you were meant to be the woman that told me that I was worth my weight in gold even though I told you I had a fucked up past. I'd warned you! I'd told you I was less than scum."

My heart sank as he spoke those words, because I did say that. I *was* that person. But all this time, we were both pretending to be someone else. I wasn't sure at this point if any of what we shared was real. I was so damn hurt... so shocked... so confused that I'd lost my heart to a criminal. A man I'd been led to believe was a ruthless, soulless prick.

Our heavy breathing filled up the bathroom. And, after a stabbing expression flitted across Axel's face, he turned on his heel and stormed toward the door, turning the lock.

Suddenly panicking that he was leaving, my heart overrode my head and I called out, "Elpi!"

He stopped dead in his tracks, glanced back, and with pure pain in his eyes, said, "Turns out I was right, Aliyana. No fucker can forgive my past, no matter how hard I try to move on. Ain't no redemption for me. You lied when you said I could be forgiven, Aliyana. You lied to my fucking face. Worst part is, I believed you. I believed you might be my light in this whole fucking mess." Eyebrows pulled down, his facial expression became severe. "That's what fucking hurts most."

He opened the door and left, before I could even summon the words to beg him to wait, to talk this out.

Sliding slowly down the wall I slumped into a messy heap. I couldn't holdback the heavy flow of tears.

Chapter Thirteen
Axel

"Who the fuck are **you, Elpidio?***"*

Aliyana's, no, Ally fucking *Prince's* words haunted my mind. No, they had taken *possession* of my goddamn mind as I drove my Camino like a damn bat of hell toward my studio. I'd bailed on Austin and Levi. I hadn't told anyone I was leaving. I couldn't. I couldn't face everyone in that damn rich-assed suite, everyone who wished I wasn't there. The people who thought I was trash, looked at me like they wanted nothing more for me than to disappear… Aliyana and Molly looking at me like I was gonna walk up to them, pull out a gun and fucking murder them.

Aliyana! Christ, how could she fear me now? Now that I'd shown her the real me?

Did none of them fucking get that I did what I did in my past for my famiglia? I took the only path available to me and kept my famiglia going, I kept my mamma's medication flowing in. And yeah, I fucking paid in blood, *King* blood… but what the hell else was I meant to do? I was a kid on my fucking own trying to fix problems I couldn't fucking fix…

Seeing a red neon sign for a liquor store, I abruptly turned right and screeched my car to a stop. Storming out of my car into the store, I headed straight for the rows of whiskey. And grabbed a bottle of Patron and Jägermeister while I was at it.

I needed to drown in liquor for a while.

I wanted to forget who I was for a while… at least for tonight. Forget it all. The last few weeks, the last few years… everything… just for a fucking while.

But as I walked to the cash register, the damn Spanish record blaring through tinny speakers changed, the familiar Latino tune making me stop dead in my tracks.

It seemed as much as I wanted to forget, God had other plans.

Closing my eyes, I could still see Aliyana dancing to this song, "Amor Prohibito", standing in her white shirt and pink Doc Martin pink boots, swinging her hips as she painted the wall of the gallery.

Hearing the little Mexican guy unlatch something from behind the counter, I opened my eyes to find him

197

watching me, a terrified expression in his eyes. His hand was tucked under the caged counter. I really had to work hard not to lose my shit.

I'd tried real fucking hard inside to learn how to rein in my anger. But at times, I struggled, *really* struggled with it.

Marching forward, the man's face paled as I slammed the three bottles on the counter and pulled out some cash. He swallowed, then shakily reached out his hand to take the cash.

Narrowing my eyes, I snapped, "Keep the change," before grabbing the bottles and skulked out of the door.

As the cool evening air hit my face, I paused, muscles tensing as I tried to calm down. Gasping for breath, I headed to my car.

As I slid into the driver's seat, I glanced to my right seeing a group of guys hanging out the back of the strip mall. My stomach churned. Everyone of them was dressed in dark loose clothes, crew tattoos covering every inch of their skin… and inked teardrops running down their cheeks, proving who they belonged to.

Staring at the brothers laughing as they stood together, dealing coke or whatever the fuck it was they were pushing, I felt a moment of nostalgia. The only time I'd ever felt like I belonged in this life was with the Heighters.

With Gio.

A sharp pain sliced through my gut at the thought of Gio. He'd pulled me from my shit life and had given me something to live for. I spent every day with him, he was my best friend... and I'd had him killed. The fact of which fucking haunted me every minute of every day.

I'd had to get my best friend killed to protect my brothers. No one knew what the guilt of that did to me.

I huffed a laugh to myself. My brothers that I'd done everything for didn't even want me. Gio's death buried any ties to my crew. And now I had a price on my head... and a damn ugly scar on the back of my neck to show how close my old crew brothers came to cashing in on it.

Moving my bottles of liquor to the passenger seat, I reached into the glove compartment and took out a roll of fifties I kept in there.

I stared at the crew again, and before I talked myself out of it, I headed in their direction.

A member of the crew clearly saw me coming, and pushed to the front of his brothers, his face stern and ready to take me on. I smirked as he did. The asshole had no idea who I was, who he was fucking with if things went south.

"What the fuck do you want?" the pint-sized punk asked as I joined them in the shadows.

Smiling coldly at the little Hispanic leader's ballsy attitude, I reached into my pocket. All the brothers staggered back, reaching to the front of their jeans to pull out their guns. Without flinching, I pulled out my roll of fifties and held it up.

"Snow," I said coldly. The leader relaxed and gestured, calling off his boys.

Handing me a couple of bags filled with white powder, the leader pressed them into my palm, the feel of those plastic packets so familiar that, weirdly, it soothed me. Turning on my heel, the leader shouted, "You with a crew? You got enough markings that say you are."

Stopping, I glanced back, seeing the camaraderie amongst the guys standing protectively around their leader. I missed that. That shit was family to me. That was life.

"Not no more," I replied sharply, feeling that long scar at the back of my neck burning like the day it was made.

Walking quickly, I got to my car, shoved the bags of coke into my jeans, cracked open the Jim Beam and drove back to the studio.

Kicking open the old wooden door to the studio, I pounded through holding the stash of liquor to my chest, whiskey already open, half empty from my ride home. The amber liquid was warming my chest, giving me a perfect fucking buzz. The studio was dark and cold and completely silent.

Silence… I couldn't stand fucking silence.

Stumbling through the hallway, tripping over old boxes and lumps of discarded marble, I eventually reached the entrance of my studio, but not before stumping my foot on a large box just beside the doorway.

Frowning in confusion at what it was, I staggered to the workstation beside my work-in-progress, dumped my liquor on the wooden top, pulled out half of my coke, leaving the other bag for later. I threw it down beside the glass bottles of mind numbing perfection.

Flicking on a lamp on the workstation, I walked back to the hallway, picked up the strange box and brought it into the studio. Dropping the box next to my current sculpture, I grabbed the bottle of whiskey and slumped down to the floor. Taking four long gulps of Beam, I placed the bottle beside me and ripped the box open.

The contents immediately came into view and chased the breath from my lungs. The titles and text boards for my show.

Closing my eyes, I inhaled through my nose and used my hands to push myself to my feet.

Silent… it was all too fucking silent.

Reaching into my back pocket, I pulled out my phone, attempting to open my music, when all I could see were a shit ton of missed calls and text messages from Austin…

AUSTIN: Where are you, Axe? You still here at the stadium?

AUSTIN: Been looking for you all over. Where are you? Want to take you out for dinner.

AUSTIN: Back home now. I'm worried. Why did you take off without telling me? Did something happen?

Feeling a rush of guilt pass through my chest, I pushed it from my mind the minute I pictured that blond Redskins punk kissing Aliyana on the lips, her fucking bright smile and huge brown eyes looking up at him afterward, and her hand pressing on his chest. Then…

*You were the only guy that I've ever felt that fucking bolt of lightning in my heart with, and you turn out to be… **him! You!***

Feeling like I'd taken a hit to my stomach at the replay of her words, her words that were right on the fucking money, I plugged in my speakers and let the heavy bass beats of Linkin Park pound through the studio.

Looking at the box sitting on the floor, I made my way forward, grabbing the Patron as I did so. Dropping my ass to the tiled floor, the room beginning to spin, I ripped off the top and took a long drink like it was water and not real good fucking Tequila.

Lining up the Patron next to the whiskey, I reached into the box, pulling out the title reading 'Exsanguination'. My stomach muscles involuntary tightened seeing the title of one of my pieces there in black and white.

It somehow made all this shit real.

Placing the title plaque by my feet, I then picked up a larger board. The lettering was the same non-descript font, the color scheme black against white. But there was a lot more writing, and I began to read…

"The sculptor's inspiration for his dark and highly emotional 'Exsanguination' piece is one born of man's intense inner conflict with guilt. The subject's fetal position is due to his inability to face his grief, his inner turmoil bringing him physically to his knees. Each carefully black painted dagger plunged into the cracked Carrara marble portrays the heavy burden of sin on a soul, the reparation of man's deliberate violation of morality. The punishing daggers are irremovable and a permanent reminder to the subject that his crimes can never be forgotten or redeemed. Nor can he ever be saved. He bleeds his guilt in an eternal ever-flowing state of desolation."

As I finished reading the last word, I dropped the board to the floor and slumped back against my newest sculpture, feeling like my chest had been ripped open, exposed for everyone to look inside.

203

How the fuck did she know to write the board that way? How to write what I was feeling this way? How the fuck did she know how to read my work and *me* perfectly? Like a goddamn fucking book.

Feeling like my lungs were being squeezed in a fist that I couldn't friggin' fight off, I pulled out my smokes and lit one up. Taking alternate long hits of my Marlboro and huge swigs of my whiskey, I looked up and stared at the young marble boy holding a gun, crying red painted bullets and a fucking uncontrollable rage swept through me.

With every drag of my smoke and every swallow of whiskey, I was pushed farther and farther to the edge. Images of Levi's rejection tortured my mind. Aliyana's damn disgusted face when she realized it was me, Axel Carillo, not her precious *Elpidio*, Molly's hand shaking in pure fucking fear as she took mine in hers. And that cunt, Rome Prince's stupid fucking scowl as he glared at me with nothing but hatred, acting like he was Austin's blood, not me.

Fuck them.

FUCK THEM ALL!

Standing, I began to pace back and forth on the studio floor, gripping the glass neck of the whiskey bottle tighter in my hand, the ash from my nearly-done Marlboro falling on my chest.

My heart beat faster and faster keeping rhythm with the heavy metal of Pantera's "Walk" now vibrating off the walls.

I was done. I was done with trying to prove to everyone that I'd changed. I was done with this art bullshit, with motherfucking Elpidio!

I didn't know how to do 'normal'. Because I wasn't fucking normal! Never had been. Having a drunk abusive cunt of a papa, a cripple as a mother, and forced to be the man of the house at ten years of age kinda fucks up a kid's idea of 'normal'.

Draining the rest of the whiskey, I threw my head back and screamed out my fury, launching the bottle against the wall, hearing it smash.

Spitting my finished smoke to the ground, I marched to the workstation and poured a packet of coke onto the top, reaching into my back pocket for my driving license. Taking the rectangular piece of plastic, I chopped the powder into lines, that sense of excitement swirling in my stomach just imagining the hit that would follow.

I'd never got addicted to this shit, too busy pushing it on the streets, but I'd sure as fuck take a line every now and then, when things got bad. I liked the buzz, the damn mind-numbing buzz the magic dust takes away.

And I needed that now more than ever.

205

"...You've been in prison! Shit, Elpi! What we've shared these past weeks... what we shared last night... and you're fucking Axel Carillo!"

Aliyana's words throbbed in my skull, her disappointment feeling like the worst kind of migraine. I lifted my head to try and shake off the damn pain, only for my gaze to settle on the image of that fucking sculpture.

Levi...

Levi who couldn't look at me with anything other than fucking contempt... The memory of him shooting me down today cut me in half.

With the whiskey running thick in my blood and that motherfucking sculpture torturing my mind, something inside of me snapped.

Seeing my hammer lying on the workstation, I picked it up, feeling the cold metal in the palm of my hands and turned to the almost completed sculpture. Wanting nothing more than to have it gone from my sight... gone from my fucking life, I positioned myself behind it, raised my hammer and—

"ELPI!!!! *NO!*"

Freezing on hearing *her* voice cut through the loud music and my drunk ass mind, I snapped my head to the doorway, only to see Aliyana friggin' Lucia staring at me, mouth open and her hands held out trying to stop my destruction of this pathetic sculpture.

At first sight of her stood there in that short pink dress, cowboy boots and her dark hair pulled back, my cock hardened to a painful level in my jeans. But then the more I stared, the more the fire built in my chest.

My hands began to violently shake. Dropping the hammer onto the ground, I whipped to face her, my arms rigid at my side.

"What the fuck do *you* want?" I snarled.

Everybody from my past expected me to be Axel Carillo? The dark fucked-up prick who only brought pain?

THIS was fucking Axel Carillo! I could BE Axel fucking Carillo!

Aliyana's mouth dropped open at my question and her face drained of blood. I stepped one step closer, and she stepped one step back. My top lip curled in sick humor. I almost could smell her fear from all the way over here.

"What's wrong, little girl? You scared?" I said in a low, graveled voice, my eyes narrowing. "You scared of *me*?"

Aliyana inhaled a terrified breath, her hand lifted to stroke the hair back from her face, and for one moment, at that simple action, I could tell she *was* really scared… and, for that *one* damn moment, my anger seemed to fucking fade to vapor.

Part of me really didn't want this chick to fear me. But remembering that blond prick kissing her lips, and the fucking repulsion in her eyes on finding out her precious *Elpidio* was really the black sheep Carillo, had me right back to incensed.

I didn't need none of them. I'd survived this long on my own. I could do it again. I could do it all on my fucking own.

Seeming to pluck up courage from somewhere, Aliyana walked forward, her face nervous. "Elpi, please…"

And that did it. Her breathy plea using that fucking false name ruined me. She knew who I really was, but she still couldn't bring herself to say it.

Axel Carillo.

Axel. Carillo.

I'M AXEL FUCKING CARILLO!

Storming forward, I fought hard to loosen my constricting chest at how fucking good she looked. I wanted her gone. Fucking gone from my life and not torturing me by standing here in my studio… in my fucking personal space, after she'd done everything but spit in my face back at the game.

Pounding forward, Aliyana backed up, the heels of her cowboy boots clicking on the floor until her back hit the wall. Slamming my hands over her head, I caged her in, those huge doe eyes nearly destroying me.

"Why're you here?" I demanded. Even to me my voice sounded lethal.

"Elpi… you've been drinking," she said, clearly smelling my breath. But I froze, not because she'd figured I'd just inhaled a fifth of Jim Beam, but because she'd just called me that fucking name again!

"I'm not fucking ELPI!" I roared, Aliyana flinching below me. "My name's *AXEL*. A-X-E-L! FUCKING AXEL CARILLO!"

Aliyana's breath quickened as I roared. I expected her run. I wanted her to run in fear. Fear the fucked up Axel Carillo from the Heighters… just like every fucker else did.

But instead, as my livid eyes bored into hers, she lifted her trembling hand and nervously placed it on my chest, right over where my heart was fucking racing.

I was dumbstruck… I could deal with her fear, with her running scared… even with her screams, I was used to causing fear in people. But what I couldn't handle, what I couldn't fucking take was her affection at a moment like this… couldn't take the damn understanding in her tearful dark eyes.

Swallowing hard, I hissed as her hot palm cut through the material of my shirt and a pink flush colored her perfect cheeks.

"Axel…" she whispered, her accent clear and strong, "Axel Carillo…"

No… NO! NO! She couldn't do this to me.

She couldn't give me hope… I really couldn't deal with motherfucking hope… anything but *hope*…

Staggering back as though I'd been burned, I drunkenly stumbled over the text boards on the floor. Aliyana followed me, her eyes never moving from mine. Unable to keep looking at her sad face, I turned, then froze… I had no-fucking-where else to go.

A hand pressed against my back, then I heard a short sharp inhale. Tensing at Aliyana's gasp, I closed my eyes and braced for her to tell me that she was done. That she was leaving and never coming back. That she was gonna tell my brothers what I'd been doing. But that's what I wanted, right? Her gone and outta my life? I asked myself, knowing that the truth to that answer was a huge fucking *NO*.

"Axel…" Aliyana said on a pained sigh, her hand leaving my skin. It felt like I'd lost all warmth as that hand was removed.

Turning slowly, I saw Aliyana at my workstation. Her attention was on the bottles of liquor lined up… but then my stomach dropped when I saw it wasn't what'd caught her attention.

The lines of coke…

Standing stock still, I waited for her to look at me, and when she did, there was nothing but pained disappointment in her expression.

I'd never felt so much like Italian trash as I did at that moment. I looked exactly like the man she thought I was. A fucking junkie loser.

"Axel…" she whispered sadly, "what have you done?"

As I watched her eyes brimming with tears, I shook my head, and stumbled toward the other end of the studio near my bed. But as I tried to get some damn distance, the tight grip of her hand on my arm spun me around.

I was done.

Done with it all.

"What?" I shouted, ripping my arm free.

Aliyana swallowed back her apprehension and stepped toward me, her jasmine scent immediately filling my lungs.

"Have you taken it?" she asked me quietly, pointing at the lines of snow.

Flames ran in my veins and I bent down, to growl, "Why the fuck do you care? Why the fuck are you even here, *Ally*

Prince? Just fuck off back to your preppy douche friends and your blond shit of a cheap lay. 'Cause that seems to be your thing right? Fucking guy after guy? Wasn't but last night I was all up in your wet cunt, then you let the Redskin's QB get all up in that pussy not yet twelve hours later!"

It was quick, 'bout as quick as a flash of light, but Aliyana's face filled with uncontrollable anger and, before she'd even realized it, she slapped me hard across my face.

On instinct, my face fucking burning hot from the force of her hit, I reached out and grabbed her slim wrist, wrenching her chest to my chest.

"You gotta motherfucking death wish?" I hissed between gritted teeth.

Dark brown eyes flared, and Aliyana spat out, "Fuck you, *Axel!*"

My lips tensed. "*Now* I'm Axel? Now you're fucking pissed, I'm Axel?" My breathing came hard, as did hers, her hard full tits scraping against my body. I lowered my mouth close to her face and snapped, "Get the fuck out."

Throwing her arm away, I turned to walk toward my bed, my damn head spinning with too much whiskey, when Aliyana shouted, "I didn't fuck Reece, you unfeeling bastard!"

My feet ground to halt but I didn't face her.

Unfeeling bastard…? That was a fucking joke. I'd give anything not to feel for just a damn minute.

"You complete fucking asshole! I came here to see *you*! I *had* to see *you*! Even knowing you're *Axel fucking Carillo*, a man I know I should stay the hell away from…" she breathed fast, but my heart was sprinting faster waiting for whatever else she had to say, "I just…" I heard her step closer, then felt her warm breath on my back filter through my shirt, shivers running down my spine, "I just couldn't… *Christ*, Axel, I just couldn't stay away…"

It was then that I realized I hadn't really breathed since I'd left that game, since we'd argued in that bathroom. But hearing her whisper those words had my shoulders sagging. I turned slowly to face her.

As our eyes met, I could see she was just as revved up as me, some damn insane poison running through our bodies keeping us close. Aliyana's gaze pierced mine and she added, in a defeated voice, "How the hell could I ever want anyone else now I've had you?"

The air seemed to go completely still around us, the pulse pounding in my neck making me feel so fucking alive. Feeling a bolt of lightning burning through my body, we both lurched forward at the same time, our mouths instantly fusing together as her hands started attacking me, ripping off my clothes.

213

Briefly breaking our kiss, Aliyana dragged my shirt over my head, my beanie going with it. Unable to taste her on my tongue, I wrapped my hand in her hair and pulled her mouth to mine, my tongue pushing inside. I groaned at her hot wet tongue furiously brushing past mine as her nails raked at my bare skin.

Lifting my hands, I ripped apart Aliyana's shirt, the buttons flying to the floor, her bra following a second later. As I moved to pull off the rest of her dress gathered at her waist, Aliyana pushed on my shoulders, my mouth breaking from hers as I fell to the bed, my ass hitting the mattress with a dull thud.

I almost came seeing her standing above me, brown eyes bright, her hair messy and falling over her shoulder. And those fucking perfect tits bare, with what remained of her dress hanging limply around her waist, just undid me.

Her cowboy boots were rooted to the ground, her legs slightly apart. Her lips rubbed together as she drank me in, her dimples looking so damn big on her pink cheeks.

On a groan, Aliyana leapt forward, climbing on my lap, her hands instantly ripping down my zipper and freeing my hard cock.

Christ... I grunted as her hot palm began stroking my dick up and down. Aliyana's mouth slammed to mine. It wasn't soft or gentle; no, she was fucking my mouth with her tongue. Just as her hips lifted, she pulled her panties aside, and putting my cock at her wet slit, she slammed down hard, taking me into her tight pussy in one quick move.

"Fuck!" I shouted, lifting her dress to slap my hands against her firm ass. Moaning loudly at my touch, Aliyana hammered down on my cock, rolling her hips so that I almost came in seconds.

This chick was fucking *me*. She was fucking me hard… she was owning me… she was fucking me as *Axel Carillo*…

With that realization seeping into my drunken mind, I used my hands on her ass to sink her down further onto my cock. Her teeth bit my bottom lip as her breathing became erratic, and her hands pulled at my messy hair, almost to the point of pain. But I liked this. Shit… I fucking loved this, *her*, this damn wild writhing on my lap.

Throwing her head back, her eyes closed as she moaned and cried out from the feel of us together. Leaning forward, I took a red hard nipple in my mouth and sucked. When my teeth scraped against her flesh, Aliyana pushed my head further into her tits as her pussy began to squeeze my dick.

Pulling my head back, I watched her face flush so damn sexy as she came, nails digging into my shoulders. I knew she'd drawn blood, but I didn't care. Feeling my balls tighten, I gripped her ass tighter as her mouth sagged, her eyes crashed to mine and she screamed, "Axel!", as she came.

Her pussy felt like a vise as she milked me dry, my cum filling her so fast that my neck corded tight with the strain.

"Shit!" I hissed on a gasp, my hips jerking with the force of how damn good that felt. Aliyana's hands tightened around my head, and my cheek rested against her damp tits as I worked on slowing my pulse, my heart, hell, the million thoughts running through my head.

Just as José Gonzalez began singing "Heartbeats" through the speaker, Aliyana put her palms on my bearded cheeks and pushed me back, tilting up my face to look straight at hers. "I should, but I don't care that you're Axel. I just want to be here with you... like this... feeling this lightning between us."

Exhaling a long breath, I glanced away and closed my eyes. "Fuck, girl..." I trailed off. "I ain't used to all this."

"What?" Aliyana asked nervously, trying to use her fingers below my chin to turn my head. "Used to what?"

But I couldn't face her. I weren't sure I wanted to see how much feeling this... this *much good*... just outright terrified me.

"Axel... please..." Aliynana begged.

Lifting my head, I met her wide gaze. Taking her hand from my palm, I brushed it across my lips, pressing a kiss to the warm skin, then slid it down my neck and over my heart.

Aliyana sucked in a breath and a pink flush flooded her cheeks. "It's beating so fast," she whispered.

I didn't give a reaction, but as her searching eyes probed, I sighed and rasped, "I ain't used to feeling good things… I can't ever face feeling much of anything… I've done too much bad shit, enough to drown me…" Aliyana's eyes glistened and, leaning in, she pressed three barely-there kisses along my cheek. Closing my eyes at that foreign act of tenderness, something in me caved, and I whispered, "but with you… I feel… I feel … *everything, every-fucking-thing*… right here…" I pressed her hand harder against my heart.

I wasn't sentimental. Truth was, I was a cold-hearted bastard. I wasn't real good with words, confessing my feelings or all that other sappy shit chicks loved. But that didn't mean my sinner's heart didn't *feel*, didn't race when she was near… when she smiled at me… when she plain understood what I was feeling deep inside, without me saying a damn word. She gave this cold heart of mine life. She gave it light. She was its fucking rhythmic beat.

"Axel…" Aliyana murmured, before gently pressing her lips to mine. This kiss was different than anything before. Because this kiss was given even though all our cards lay on the table.

Breaking the kiss, Aliyana pressed her forehead to mine, then carefully she stood up. I pulled in a long breath as my cock left her pussy, but I couldn't take my eyes from her as she pulled her dress down until it pooled at her feet. My fists clenched the bed linen as she stood before me in just her pale pink panties and cowboy boots.

I knew that for the rest of my life, the image of the most perfect chick on the planet, undressing just for me, would be forever branded on my brain.

Shucking the brown boots, Aliyana then hooked her fingers on the sides of her panties and slowly pushed them down her legs. Once completely naked, she stepped toward me, holding out her hand. Putting my palm in hers, and trusting someone completely for the first time ever, I stood.

Aliyana looked up at me through heavy eyelids, releasing my hand, only to drop them to my already-undone jeans. Putting her palms on my chest, she ran her fingers down my abs, over my stomach and hooked her fingers into my waistband. Slowly, Aliyana pulled down my jeans until they joined her clothes on the floor.

Retaking my hand, she pulled back the sheet of the bed and crawled in, guiding me to follow. I did it without question. Shit. I'd follow this chick anywhere.

As I lay down facing Aliyana, she squeezed my hand and cast me a nervous smile.

"Shit, Aliyana," I said, bringing our joined hands to my lips.

"You're Axel Carillo," she whispered in disbelief, making my lips freeze on the soft skin on the back of her hand. "I'm not supposed to want you…" she said shakily, and I felt my heart sink.

Aliyana must have read something on my face, because she shuffled closer until our bodies were flush and we shared the same air. "…But I can't help it. You're not the man everyone says you are… are you?"

Feeling my heartbeat pick up speed, I combed back the hair from her face and said, "I'm exactly who they think I am."

Aliyana swallowed, a droplet of sweat from our fuck rolling down her olive-skinned slim neck. "No… you're punishing yourself for the actions you desperately took to save your family, not embracing the good man you are now." My stomach clenched at the sincere belief she had in me and I closed my eyes.

Aliyana's hand pressed on my cheek. "Look at me," she urged. When I didn't do as she wanted, she rolled me onto my back, her tits pressing against my chest. "Axel, look at me," she pushed harder.

Reluctantly opening my eyes, Aliyana's searching gaze was assessing my face. "Answer this," she said. I waited for her question. "Did you take that coke you bought tonight?"

My eyebrows furrowed and I tried to turn away, but her hands on my face refused to budge. "Answer me," she insisted. "Did you take it?"

My jaw clenched, but seeing she wasn't gonna drop it, I rasped. "No, I didn't. You fucking happy?"

The smile that then followed my reluctant confession floored me. Gently holding her wrists, I added, "But if you hadn't shown up, I would've."

That smiled disappeared and her eyes glanced away. "I don't believe you would have," she disagreed.

"You don't know me as well as you think then, do you?"

Aliyana's face melted into a sad expression and she nodded, moving her finger to run over my scowl. "I do. Tell me," she watched as her finger traced the edges of my beard, "where did you get it? The coke?"

Narrowing my eyes, I shrugged and said, "Some street crew I saw near a liquor store."

Aliyana's eyes flared for a second, before she looked all sad again.

"What?" I snapped. I fucking hated pity. Hatred I could deal with, pity, I couldn't fucking stand.

"A street crew?" she questioned, "Like the Heighters?"

My muscles tensed. "So if it was? Fuck! Why you asking anyway?"

"Axel," she said softly, running her finger over my crucifix… the crucifix that used to be my stidda. I used to be so damn proud of that black star tattoo on my left cheek, proud that my crew had my loyalty, my trust.

"You were hurt after the game… after Levi's public rejection… after mine…" her expression fell at that, a guilty expression on her face, "and you ran back to the only thing you know. To the only life you've ever lived here on the outside."

My breathing paused at how right she read me. She always had, ever since the moment she first saw my art.

"Axel?" she pushed, waiting for my reply.

Dropping my gaze to her pink painted fingernails, I confessed, "I don't know how to do it…"

"Do what, *querido*?" Ally blushed as she called me that. I had no idea what she'd said, but I'd sure as fuck liked the way it sounded. It sounded like a term of endearment… it sounded as though she cared. Ain't no woman ever give a shit about me before.

Lifting my hand, I pulled the chopsticks from her hair, long dark locks falling over my chest. I combed my fingers through the silky strands.

"Axel, You don't know how to do what?"

Smelling the lavender shampoo on her hair, I said, "Be normal... get people to trust me... believe in me... give me a second chance. How do you exist in this world without having to fight? Without pain?"

Aliyana's eyes misted over and she shifted so she was fully lying on top of me, her legs in between mine. "You've never known how to be pain free, have you? Have you ever been happy?"

Hating the sympathy in her gaze, I turned my head, fire burning in my gut. "Don't," I hissed.

But she kept going. "You were brought up fighting your whole life, joined a gang because that's what kids did where you came from, then you spent your time caring for your sick mamma, Aust and Lev. And then..."

Swallowing my pride, I finished, "Then I got locked up."

"Axel... You've never known true happiness..." A tear fell from Aliyana's eyes. I dried it with the pad of my thumb. I couldn't believe that she was crying for me. I couldn't believe those tears were for me. Ain't no one but my mamma ever cried for me before. But mamma cried for the state of my soul, for the parents of the men I'd killed… but not Aliyana, she cried for the fucked up man that never knew happiness.

Unable to see Aliyana breaking, and for once, speaking without guard, I hushed out, *"Sono felice insieme a te."*

Aliyana stilled and her brown eyes met mine, her mouth slightly open in shock. " Axel… did you…?"

I shrugged and Aliyana pressed her hand over my racing heart. A smile twitched on her full lips clearly feeling it race and she asked, "You're… you're happy with me?"

Exhaling a pent up breath, I confessed, *"Sì."*

"Axel," she cried and her eye lashes fluttered fast as she fought back tears. Lifting her body higher, her finger ran over my lips, and she said, *"Bésame."* Before I even knew what she'd said, she crushed her mouth to mine.

Holding Aliyana to my mouth, we kissed lazily as I ran my fingers up her spine, loving the feeling of her shivering at my touch. There should be a sculpture created for her. She was perfect.

As Aliyana slid her lips from mine, I rolled us until we were facing each other and her hands ran over the nape of my neck.

Her expression changed and I could feel her fingers tracing my scar. "Axel?" I grunted in reply, my chest

223

tightening at what I knew she was gonna ask. "How did you get this scar?"

She must have felt me tense. She pulled me closer and whispered, "Please, tell me… stop keeping everything hidden. You can trust me."

Laying my head back against the pillow, Aliyana shuffled closer. "I got it in prison," I said vaguely.

Aliyana's eyes widened. "How? What happened?"

Closing my eyes, I thought of that day and without opening my lids, stayed in the darkness and said, "My old crew brothers that were inside got me alone and came at me. I knew the day would come when they'd get their revenge on me. No one turns on a crew brother, but I did, and they wanted blood for blood."

I could hear Aliyana's breathing quicken. But like a damn fountain, this shit just began pouring outta me. "We were in the yard, them over one side and I was keeping my head down. I'd managed to steer clear of them, for 'bout two years, but when Alessio, the old Heighter leader's brother got put away for life, I knew it was only a matter of time before they came to take me out. That fucker was evil, and he wanted me dead for what happened to his little brother, Gio—"

"What happened to his brother?"

My eyes snapped open and my hands started shaking. Fuck, why were my hands shaking?

Aliyana noticed my hands and clasped them in hers. Losing the color from her face, she pushed, "Axel? What happened to Gio?"

I didn't want to tell her, but she needed to know what I'd done in my past. She needed to know what fucked up guy she was laying beside.

"I had him killed," I whispered. Aliyana's hands gripped mine so tight it started to stop the blood flow.

"You… you…"

"Had him killed," I confessed.

"Axel, why?" she whispered in disbelief. I could hear the shock in her voice. The truth was, she'd never fully understand how I could take lives. Only folks brought up in crew life ever would. How could people brought up in a sweet ass home with healthy legit parents ever understand how a kid has to fight—sometimes 'til the death—for survival?

I stared out of the windows at the dark night, the stars bright in the sky and my stomach dropped as I thought of my best friend, everything we went through together.

"To save my brothers," I rasped. "I had to have him killed to give my brothers the chance of a better life. Gio was my best friend, my brother in arms. He was the closest

225

person to me, but I knew that when I went inside, he'd go after Austin and Levi. He was obsessed with having the Carillo's by his side. And once you'd got the stidda, you were crew. You were Heighter for life. Only way out was death. If you tried to leave, you were—"

"Killed…" she interrupted and, meeting her eyes, I nodded my head.

"Yeah. Levi and Austin were fully initiated, full members, stidda's inked on their left cheeks, bound to the crew for life. I knew the only way they could be free was to take Gio out. So I called our rival's leader. The King crew I'd dedicated my whole life to fighting and told him when and where to find Gio. My best friend and crew brother was killed exactly when and where I'd said the Kings could find him. Gio was shot dead at my hands, but Austin and Levi were free." I sighed. "It was the best thing I've ever done for them. The blood on my hands ain't ever gonna wash away, but at least my brothers are out and living good lives… lives I could never have given them. I'd dragged them into that gang, it was only right I got them the fuck out. It just took me too damn long to see the fucking light."

Aliyana was silent, Hinder's "Lips of An Angel" playing through the speakers, the only sound in the studio.

"You had your best friend killed…" she murmured somberly. I had to look away, suddenly consumed with grief.

"I can't imagine having to make that choice. It would be like me choosing to kill Molly to save Rome. It would be… *impossible*. I couldn't live with myself."

The constant weight that pressed on my chest lightened some as she understood what my everyday was like. I heard the sadness in her voice. She fucking understood what having Gio killed did to me, *still* did to me. She understood the gravity of the hardest choice I'd ever made.

Aliyana's lips pressed on my skin giving me strength and she asked, "How did you meet Gio? How did you even get involved with that gang?"

Whether I wanted to or not, that question took me straight back to the past…

Chapter Fourteen
Axel

Westside Heights Trailer Park
Tuscaloosa, Alabama

Eighteen years ago…

Walking into the trailer, a two-year-old Levi wriggling in my arms, I saw Austin sitting on the couch, his head down and crying.

As I approached him I could see blood on his face and a bruise forming on his eye. "Aust? What's happened?" I asked and rushed to bend down in front of him. I put Levi on the floor, passing him a broken toy truck, then turned to Austin and forced his hands from his face. Austin tried to fight me seeing him, but I was stronger and he couldn't fight me off. As I pulled down his hands, Austin didn't meet my eyes, but I could see the state of his face.

Anger made me shake. "Who did this to you?" I snapped. Austin winced as I pressed my fingers against his swelling eye.

"Austin!" I shouted, Levi jumping in shock at my angry voice as he played on the floor.

"I don't wanna talk about it," Austin said, his voice catching because he was crying.

"Well I do," I said and wiped his tears away with my thumbs. "Tell me who hit you. I'm gonna kill them!"

Austin lifted his head and sighed. "Just some older kids from school, Axe. You don't know them."

"Why did they hit you?" I asked. Reaching for a dishtowel, I began wiping away the blood off his face. Levi pulled himself up to stand on the sofa, crawling into Austin's lap.

"Hey, fratellino,*" Austin greeted Levi and he hugged Levi to his chest, Levi's chubby arms hugging him back.*

"Austin?" I pushed again. "Why did they beat you up?"

Austin's eyes narrowed. "Have you seen me, Axe?" Austin used his hand to point to his clothes. "I'm poor. My clothes are all too small, my sneakers are old and they hurt my feet, but Papa won't let Mamma buy us new clothes. The kids at school… they make fun of me."

Dropping the towel to the floor, I pressed my hand over my stomach. It felt like someone had kicked me... They make fun of me...

229

"I get it everyday, Axe. I ain't you. No one's scared of me."

Austin's head dropped, his tears splashing on his dirty jeans. "I hate our lives! I hate Papa. I hate that he beats Mamma, makes her work all the time and then spends all the money on drink."

As I stared at my little brothers, both of them dressed in faded clothes, all of us going hungry, something in me snapped. Jumping to my feet, my insides felt like they were on fire.

"Axe?" Austin's beaten face was looking up at me from the couch. He was scared.

"Stay with Lev," I ordered and rushed out of the trailer. I was so angry. So damn angry! Before I knew it, I was sprinting through the trailer park. I kept my eyes staring forward as I ran to the park's bar, ignoring the Heighters all watching me rush pass them as I pushed through the entrance to the bar.

I stood still and looked for my papa. Hearing a woman laugh, my eyes went to the sound. The laughing woman was sitting on Papa's lap.

Storming over to where he was, I stood beside him and pushed on his big arm. His eyes snapped to mine and disgust built on his face.

"What the fuck are you doing here, boy?" he slurred drunkenly.

Sucking in a deep breath, I said, "I need money. Austin and Levi need clothes and we need food."

My papa's gaze darkened as I said that and he pushed me hard on my chest. I stumbled back as he and the woman laughed.

Gritting my teeth, I ran at my papa and pushed him back. "They need clothes! It's not fair!" I shouted. "Austin's getting beat up at school because of it!"

The bar went silent as my papa stared down at me. His skin began turning red and I started backing away. My stomach dropped as I realized what I'd just done. I'd made him mad. Real mad.

In a second Papa had thrown the half naked woman off his lap and reached out to grab me by my neck. He dragged me out of the bar and burst through the doors out into the cool night.

Papa's free hand gripped onto my hair and he pulled me to face him. "You little cunt! You're gonna pay for fucking with me!"

His hand let go of my hair and he punched me on the jaw, the pain making my legs weaken then drop to the ground. My scalp burned as my papa kept tight hold of my hair and punched me again in my stomach. He let go of my hair and I fell down. Closing my eyes, I curled my body trying to protect myself from the kick I knew would come next, when suddenly, I heard someone dragging my papa backwards.

Opening my eyes, I saw Remo Marino, the leader of the Heighters, holding my papa by his arms. "What the fuck you doing to that kid, old man?" he asked and I could see my papa fighting to get free.

"Get the fuck off me, you piece of shit!" he shouted back. But then more of the Heighters surrounded him and began throwing punches.

I tried to sit up, not knowing what to do, when a hand pressed on my shoulder. My head whipped to my right, when I saw Gio Marino

231

beside me. I tried to get away from him. My mamma had told me to stay away from the Heighter crew, said they were nothing but trouble.

"Relax, ragazzo," Gio said. "I ain't gonna hurt you."

"You're not?" I asked. My voice was croaky and my eyes went back to the rest of the gang that were kicking my papa on the ground.

"Papa," I whispered and staggered to my feet. Gio joined me and wrapped his arm around my shoulder, forcing me to stay where I was.

The Heighters began moving from my papa, and my eyes widened when I saw him rolling in pain on the ground, covered in blood. I'd never seen my papa look so weak before.

My gaze never left my papa, but when someone moved in front of me I looked up. Remo Marino.

"Axel Carillo, yeah?" he asked and I nodded my head, looking behind Remo to all the other Heighters watching me. I knew they were all Heighters because of the black star on their left cheeks.

"He hit you like that a lot?" Remo asked. My attention came back to the older Heighter leader and I nodded my head. I didn't dare lie to him.

"I... I needed money for my little brothers. They need clothes. Papa wouldn't give me it." I dropped my head in shame. "I lost it and came after him... I was stupid. It's my fault he hit me."

Remo looked back over his shoulder at my papa trying to get to his feet and shook his head. "Fucking hate assholes like that. And you ain't stupid, kid. You did good." Gio's arm tightened around my shoulder and I saw Gio nod his head to Remo's raised eyebrow.

I didn't understand what that look meant.

"Filippo, get the kid some cash," Remo said to a guy stood beside him. Filippo reached into his pocket, pulled out a roll of cash and placed it in my hands.

My mouth dropped at the amount of money he'd given me. It must have been hundreds of dollars. I met Remo's eyes again. "You wanna keep earning soldi like that?"

Staring down at the cash again, I nodded my head.

"Good," Remo said. He flicked his chin toward Gio. "You know my little cousin, Gio, Axel?"

I looked to Gio. "A little."

"I'll watch out for him, Rem. I'll show him how business is done."

Remo nodded his head. "Bene." Gio took his arm from around my shoulder and Remo stepped away. "Be back here tomorrow after school, Axel, and we can get you earning a shit ton more cash than that."

Excitement washed through me at the thought of getting more cash. I could help my mamma. I could help my brothers.

The Heighters all began to walk away except for Gio.

"Why? Why are you helping me? I don't understand?" I asked and Gio smiled.

"You're Italiano, fratello. *We look after our own." He shrugged. "And the way you took on your old man today shows you got balls. Ain't afraid to fight for a cause. You'll do well with us. We'll take care of you, have your back."*

233

At his words, I breathed out a long breath. "Grazie," I said sincerely. "Grazie mille."

Gio came beside me and threw his arm around my neck again. We began walking toward my trailer, back to my brothers, when I looked behind me to my papa on the floor. "What about my papa? He'll beat on us again after this. I'll pay for what you did."

Gio laughed. "He ain't gonna touch you again, Axel. He knows better than to fuck with the Heighers. You run with us now, ragazzo. If he even breathes wrong your way, Remo will make sure he never does it again."

"Papa ain't gonna touch my mamma and brothers again?" I asked in relief.

Gio shook his head and I felt a smile pull on my lips.

Gio laughed at my reaction and nodded his head. "I'll be with you all the way, ragazzo. Now, let's go get those brothers of yours some new clothes..."

*****

Aliyana was silent as I finished speaking, my damn heart feeling bruised as I thought about that day. The day the Heighters changed my life.

"They protected you from your drunk abusive papa...?" Aliyana said. "They helped you clothe Austin and Levi?"

"Yeah," I replied roughly.

234

"Axel…" Aliyana's watery voice said, "Your life was so sad. No wonder you gravitated toward them. They gave you hope that it would all be okay."

I shook my head. "It was more than that. They *saved* me. They kept my family going, they had my back… I fucking owed them everything."

"And your papa?"

"Left two weeks later. Moved in with that slut that was on his lap. It was the best fucking day of my life. I knew it was Remo and the Heighters that had made him leave." I huffed a laugh. "They saved us all."

"God, Axel. I don't know what to say. You were so young. So young to be dealing with all of that on your own."

"I didn't feel young back then. I was twelve but felt twenty-seven."

"And Gio? You became close?"

I couldn't help but still feel that bond I'd had with my best friend at her question. "He was always with me after that day. He never left my side. Taught me everything I needed to know to survive, to make money. He was the only person who never let me down. From the day we met until the day he died, he had my back without question." My body tensed as I remembered the moment I'd heard he'd died… died at my hands. I'd felt like I'd been cut open remembering our friendship. I'd felt like the biggest prick on the face of the planet.

"And I gave him up to our rivals to save Aust and Lev… I still ain't made peace with that. Don't think I ever will. I've never had anyone that close to me since, doubt I ever will again."

I heard Ally sniffing, and when I looked into her teary eyes, I felt every bit of sadness leak out of me that I'd kept locked away for so long over losing my friend.

I was guilty of killing the guy that saved my life to save the blood of my blood.

"And the scar?" Ally suddenly prompted. "On your neck."

I shrugged. "A fight broke out in the yard. Alessio and the rest of the Heighters used it as cover to come at me." I winced, still seeing them all approaching, fucking eight of them against *me*. "I fought them off as best I could, but two of the fuckers pinned me against the fence. Alessio pulled the knife out and, just as the guards started filling the yard, he sliced the knife down my neck." I gripped tighter onto Aliyana's hand, for some reason, needing the damn support. "They ran while I dropped to the floor and started bleeding out."

"My God…" Aliyana said. "How did you not die?"

My chest tightened. "It was close. Had surgery and spent weeks and weeks in the infirmary."

"*Christ*, Axel… And Austin and Levi? Why were they not told? I can't believe they wouldn't care."

My vision lost focus as I stared at nothing.

"Axel, please," Aliyana pushed. Seeing her face needing the answers, I cussed under my breath.

"When I found out Alessio was being sent down, I cut off all ties to my brothers. Claimed I had no next of kin to the prison, everything."

"I don't understand?" Aliyana said. Her cute ass face was all scrunched up. Lifting my hand I ran my tattooed finger down her cheek, circling a deep dimple and said, "Alessio is a sadistic asshole, one seriously crazy motherfucker. Killed for more than just turf, that bastard killed for fun. And I'd got his boy, his little brother, shot. That guy was gonna be coming for me, in any way he could."

"Austin and Levi…" she trailed off, getting why I did what I did.

"Lev had stopped coming to see me by then, he was just a kid and hated me, but Austin was still coming whenever he could. I knew him and Levi and Lexi were living a good fucking life in Cisco. Lev was at a good school, Austin was starting for the 49ers, Lexi was eating better and started

237

her own treatment center…" Water filled my eyes and I coughed to straighten my voice. "I was so damn proud."

"Oh Axel," Aliyana said and kissed my shoulder.

Gripping onto Aliyana's hair, I finished. "There was no way I was gonna compromise all that they had now, the life my mamma wanted for them, so I cut all ties. Alessio and his fucking boys wouldn't get any chance to get at my brothers unless they crossed the country and I knew the fuckers didn't have the funds to go that far. If they got my brothers, it'd be when they were coming to see me. That shit wasn't gonna fly."

"So Austin never knew you stopped seeing him to save them?"

I shook my head to indicate 'no'.

"They also never knew you were harmed… that you could have died?"

"No, and they never will," I said sternly.

Edging closer, Aliyana pressed her lips to mine, kissing me three times. Lifting just above my face, she asked, "They should know what you went through to save them, Axel. If they only knew, if Lev knew—"

"I didn't save them, Aliyana, I condemned them. When they were kids, I made deals with the Heighters to get them fighting beside me in the street war, thinking it was fucking important. Like a damn piece of shit trailer park was ever fucking important. But my brothers, nah, they weren't like me. They were smart, they were talented... they were going somewhere in life. That is, once they got the hell away from me."

Aliyana's face darkened. "Axel, you're the most talented person I know, look at what you create," she said. I had to fight a smile at the conviction in her voice as she pointed to my work in progress.

But that smile quickly dropped when I cupped her cheeks and said, "I'm not a good person, Aliyana. I'm fucked up. I've got a real dark soul and more sins piled at my door than the Devil himself. You should be running away from me, not willingly running into the darkness holding my fucking hand."

"It's too late," she said quietly, "You've already consumed me. There is no turning back from you, not now. My hand's never letting go of yours, eternal darkness or not."

"Then I pity you."

Aliyana's mouth parted and she sucked in a sharp breath. I pulled the pad of my thumb over her bottom lip and said, "I've killed people. Do you get that? I've put men in hospital. I've ruined lives... ain't no redemption out there for me. There's no beauty, no fairytale to be found by being *fused* to me."

239

Aliyana shook her head and a determined look spread on her face. But then, something passed over her face as she looked to my marble boy crying bullets, and facing me again, she said softly, "The most beautiful art is often born from the most desperate of circumstances." And in that one sentence, she obliterated my stone heart to pieces.

"Fuck, girl," I growled, fighting over-emotion, but Aliyana pressed her finger on my lips before I could say anything else.

"Your art is your redemption, Axel. *Elpidio* is your rebirth, your second chance at life. You are a victim of circumstance, not a sinner by choice."

Feeling my throat clog so tight I felt I would choke, I fought to gasp for air, only to whisper, "*La mia luce*," as I stared at this woman beside me, completely fucking astounded by her defense of a loser like me.

Aliyana's face blushed and she dipped her head to my chest, her arms wrapped around my waist. Reaching out to my side table, I picked up a smoke and lit it. I took a long a drag.

"I can't smell smoke now without thinking of you," Aliyana murmured. I ran my hand through her hair and she asked, "Why is there a crucifix now covering your Heighter star?"

Stiffening, I took another drag and said, "A couple of years after I went into prison, my Heighter inmates came into my cell and scrubbed it out with a needle and ink. They'd heard Alessio was coming in and didn't want him to think they'd let me off for two years without some form of payback. I didn't even bother fighting back, just let them erase a gang I no longer wanted to belong to anyway. After the shanking a few months later, I got a needle and ink off my cellmate and changed it completely."

"But why a crucifix?" Aliyana asked carefully.

Sighing, I said, "Mamma used to cross my forehead with holy water every night when I was a kid. I don't know why, but when I picked up that needle that had erased my past, the image was in my head and before I knew it, a cross was on my face."

"Axel," Aliyana said, and lifted her head. "About your mamma—"

Covering her mouth, I shook my head. "No more. Fuck, girl, I can't take no more talking about all this shit tonight. I've told you more than I'd ever planned to ever tell anyone. I need you to leave it alone now."

I just couldn't go there about my mamma. It was one part of my locked heart I never wanted to open. I wouldn't be able to take the guilt.

241

Aliyana nodded, getting I couldn't talk no more. My head was spinning with whiskey, but more than that, it was spinning that Aliyana came back to me knowing who I was.

Smoothing back the lines on my forehead Aliyana confessed, "I can't believe that I am completely and utterly infatuated with Axel Carillo."

I froze at her confession, my heart slamming against my ribs and, smiling, she peppered kisses all over my neck. "No one will be happy about us. They won't understand. But I can't bring myself to care."

She might not. But I did.

I could hear the sadness in her voice when she thought of her friends, of her fucking cousin finding out she was my woman. They wouldn't go for it.

Needing to protect her, I said, "They can't ever know, Aliyana. It's better all 'round if they never know 'bout us. I don't want them thinking bad of you for wanting me."

Aliyana nodded, then her head tilted to the side and she smiled. "I do want you, Axel. Flaws and all. And call me *Ally*, okay? Outside of work only my mama calls me Aliyana."

I took one last drag of my smoke, flicked the cherry to the floor then rolled Ally onto her back, working my hips between her legs. "No more talking. I want in that wet pussy again."

Chapter Fifteen
Ally

One month later….

"You good, darlin', you don't look too well?"

I'd been standing in the hallway waiting for Molly to come down the stairs to go to Austin and Lexi's, and I frowned when she appeared at the top of the stairs looking weak and frail.

Molly batted her hand in front of her face. "Ally, I'm fine, just tired," she said, but my eyes narrowed in concern. Over the past few days she'd been real quiet and tired. I was worried, and by the way Rome wouldn't leave her alone, fussing twenty-four-seven, I knew he was too.

"You ready to go?" she asked. I nodded my head, not wanting to push my concerns. Molly didn't like to be fussed or pitied.

Cassie and Jimmy-Don had arrived from Texas for a visit and they were staying with the Carillo's.

The Carillo's… including *my* Carillo. My dark and tortured Axel Carillo. The man I had fallen head over heels for.

Tonight, Lexi was throwing her best friend and husband, Cassie and Jimmy-Don, a small party to welcome them to Seattle. Of course I was going, they were some of my best friends after all, but after not seeing Axel in nearly two days because of work commitments, I also couldn't wait to go to see him… to hopefully steal a moment to hold him… to just be in close proximity.

After weeks of being almost nightly in his bed, I was addicted. More than that, I was captivated, obsessed and completely enamored.

He was my fast becoming my everything—my sun, my stars, my moon, *everything.* Although I believed he felt the same way about me, I was never completely convinced. Axel Carillo was a fortress, an enigma. His cold demeanor spoke of him being one way but with me, in bed, when he stroked my hair or pulled me close after making love into the shelter of his thick arms, I felt it in him *more.* He still didn't open up much, had never again talked of his past, kept his feelings buried deep, but I knew I made him happy, and on occasion, I was able to make him smile…

There was nothing more beautiful than a smiling Axel Carillo.

I yearned for him to open up to me. I could see he was haunted. He barely slept. He worked every hour God sent on his heartbreaking sculptures, as if purging his past. I knew that if he just shared his demons with me, he could perhaps begin to heal, but for now, I was content to just have him in my life. I knew, that to many, the idea of being in this man's company would be a living nightmare. But, to me, being in his strong arms was the sweetest of dreams… my heartfelt wish come true… my bolt of lightning.

"I'm ready, darlin'," I said to Molly. I tried not to show my growing excitement at seeing my man in a matter of minutes, as we walked outside toward my rental underneath a drizzly Seattle sky.

Striding slowly next to Molly, we got in the car and my heart began to race as I pictured his hard stare penetrating mine. Only the two of us aware of our forbidden relationship. It made everything we shared so much more intense, like we knew every moment spent kissing, discussing art and joined to one another was *more* because it was solely for us.

"You look beautiful tonight," Molly said, her head leaning back against the leather headrest, her hand running gently over her growing stomach.

I blushed as I ran my hands down my knee length black high-waisted pencil skirt; my white three-quarter sleeved crop top showed about an inch of flesh between it and my skirt. My hair was down and curled, pinned to one side, and on my feet I had my four-inch black painted leather Louboutins.

I had dressed for Axel. And literally couldn't wait for him to see me. I wanted to see that flare of desperation in his eyes, the one he shows when I'm naked before him, his sculptor's hands stroking every inch of my body as though I was a muse.

"Just thought I'd make an effort," I said with a nonchalant shrug when I caught Molly curiously watching my face.

Molly smiled in reply, but I could tell by her assessing gaze that her genius mind was working overtime. I changed the conversation to the latest developments at the gallery, trying to throw her off the scent. In ten short minutes, we arrived at the Carillo residence.

It made me laugh when I realized weeks ago how close they lived to Molly and Rome. Not that Axel stayed here much now, he'd practically moved into his studio, running from his unresolved problems with Levi… but mainly so we could be together. I knew Austin and Lexi questioned where he was most nights, I'd heard them talking in hushed whispers, worried Axel was up to no good again, but they didn't push it. I think Austin was afraid if he did ask, Axel would close himself off completely. He was probably right; Axel's shield was about as easy to break into as Fort Knox.

I wished he'd tell them about his art, about the fact that he'd changed his life and was an exceptional man, with an unrivaled talent, but he wouldn't. Instead, he'd rather they think he worked at a fish market, paying back society for his illegal wrongs.

He kept himself in such a state of self-loathing that it broke my heart. He deserved the world, but until the day came that he welcomed that world in, I bestowed on him all the grace I could muster.

As Molly and I got out the car, the front door opened and Rome came hurrying out, his eyes immediately seeking out his wife. He'd been at Seahawks training with Austin, then came straight here. Jimmy-Don had gone with them, and I'd agreed to bring Molly.

"Baby, you okay?" I heard Rome ask Molly as he helped her out of the car. "You don't look so good."

"Rome, don't start. I'm fine," Molly remarked in exasperation, but Rome flickered a concerned look toward me. I shrugged. Honestly, I didn't think she looked well either, but she was one stubborn woman who insisted she came.

Hanging behind Molly and Rome, I scanned the windows for signs of life. We slowly entered the house, and as soon as I did, my eyes sought out Axel. My stomach dropped in disappointment when he was nowhere to be seen. I was like an addict, craving just a glimpse of his brooding form.

Rome took the lead, holding Molly, and led us to the left into a huge TV room. On the couch right in front of me was a pregnant Cassie, her blonde hair and red cheeks as bright as ever.

As soon as her eyes clocked mine, she hurriedly rose from the couch and plastered on the biggest smile. "Ally friggin' Prince!" she bellowed out in her loud Texan accent, her usual rhinestone jeans and plaid shirt covering her large baby bump.

"Cassie!" I squealed in excitement and crossed the room to take her in my arms. "I've missed you so much, girl!" I said in her ear and she held me in her tight strong grip.

Cassie pushed me back and, looking down my body, whistled low. "Shit, girl! Just when I thought you couldn't get any hotter, you go and fucking hit it outta the park. You make me wanna buy a strap on and DP your ass."

Frowning, I shook my head and tried to accept her words for what they were: a compliment!

Bending down, I rubbed my hand over her stomach and glanced up at her smiling face. "You look amazing, darlin'. I can't believe you're pregnant again! What's this now, number three?"

She shrugged on a 'eh', and pointed at JD, "Yep, number three. Blame it on this one, he can't keep his damn hands off me. Which I get by the way, I'm one fucking hot bitch."

Laughing at her usual boisterous antics, I looked round Cass to see JD stood beside Austin and Levi, all drinking beers, watching a basketball game on Austin's wide screen.

Shifting around Cass, I moved to the ever-smiling JD and crushed him in a bear hug. "How're you, darlin'?" I asked and stepped back.

"Not too bad, Al, how're you? Heard you're curating some fancy ass exhibition here in Seattle."

I rolled my eyes and looked at Austin who was smiling. "Let me guess, Austin told you that?"

Next to me Levi started laughing as Austin shrugged. "Well it is, right? Fancy ass, I mean."

Shaking my head, but smiling at how they viewed the art world, I threw my arm around Levi's shoulder, ruffling his sandy hair. "Don't you laugh, Lev, you're meant to be more cultured than this sorry lot!"

Levi laughed, then his face beamed bright red as he glanced down to my outfit. "You look real pretty, Ally," he said quietly, and my heart swelled. He was such a good kid. But then my heart quickly deflated as I wished I could make him see that Axel was a good man too. A man who had done more for his brothers than they knew. A man who loved them so much, but didn't know how to express it, because he'd never been shown how.

Faking a smile, I hugged him hard and replied, "And you're not too shabby yourself, Lev. Tell me, you got a girl yet? The chicks at college must be clamoring after you. If I was younger, you'd have been on my radar." I winked.

He gave me his usual shy smile and shook his head. "No, ma'am, no girls as yet." Austin was watching Lev as his younger brother closed in on himself. I could see the racking worry in his gaze.

"Hey Ally!" Hearing Lexi enter the room, I turned and walked to kiss her on the cheek. Within minutes I had a glass of Moscato in hand and was crushed beside Cassie on the couch, Molly and Lexi sitting in chairs in front of us.

Glimpsing something flicker in the darkened hallway, my heart began to race when I caught sight of Axel, hiding in the shadows, watching me. Knowing he could see me, I smiled in his direction and I caught his lip hook into a smirk as he stepped further into the light. God, he was beautiful. As always, he was dressed all in black, his long hair falling like a curtain over his face, but those dark eyes I loved so much stayed on me, drinking me in, making me feel like the most beautiful woman in the world.

God, I wanted to go to him. I wanted my friends to welcome him into the room, talk to him because they liked him and he belonged to me. I wanted them to watch me openly walk up to him and kiss him without shame. I wanted them to accept him because we belonged to one another, no matter how difficult it was for them to understand.

But I knew it couldn't be. My friends, *his brothers*, wouldn't understand. So instead, I had to make do with furtive glimpses into the shadows, where the man who held my heart hid from the world... the world that had shunned him... the world that, at age thirty, he didn't understand.

"Axel?"

My every muscle froze on hearing Axel's name being called from behind me. I turned to see Austin rushing forward, a huge smile on his face.

Glancing back to the shadows, I saw Axel trying to duck his head and get away, but it was too late, Austin had already seen him.

"Axe!" Austin called, "Come have a beer with us... with *me*." He belatedly corrected himself, clearly embarrassed at his slip.

Rome's eyes narrowed as he stood beside Lev and JD. Levi cast his eyes down on seeing his big brother and Rome muttered something to himself.

Anger burned in my veins at my cousin's change of mood. Thankfully, Austin stood before Axel, a hopeful look on his face. "I didn't think you'd come down when I invited you to join us earlier. I'm so damn glad you did, *fratello*."

My heart sank when I heard how happy Austin was that Axel had shown face. Because I knew Axel would never have come down here to sit with us. He shunned any contact with people or crowds. Yet here he was, skulking in the safety of the dark just so he could watch me.

Suddenly I felt like crying. Axel should feel welcome in his own family's house. He shouldn't have to keep what he felt for me a secret, for fear of my friends turning their backs on me... because of the man I'd chosen to lo—

My hand flew to my chest as I realized what I'd been just about to admit. I couldn't... I didn't, not yet, right? It was impossible... it was...

Shit... it was true...

I glanced up to check no one had noticed my strange reaction, and nobody had... until I locked gazes with a familiar pair of golden eyes, Molly Prince's golden eyed gaze was firmly glued on me.

Forcing my attention back to the darkened hallway, I was convinced Axel would refuse to come in. He'd make some lame excuse and bail. I knew this was his idea of hell, so I had to prevent my mouth from dropping open when, rather awkwardly, he walked fully into the light. He looked so damn sexy and brooding that, for a moment, I couldn't catch my breath.

I did love him. I loved this tortured man before me with a breathless intensity.

Austin, clearly also in shock at his brother's appearance, threw an arm around Axel's shoulder and led him toward a bucket of beer, handing over a bottle of Bud.

"That's Axel?" Cassie whispered from beside me. Swerving in my place on the couch to face her, I silently nodded my head. I wanted to tell her it was *my* Axel, *my* Elpidio, the man who'd brought me to life with his deep soul and magnetic dark force, but I couldn't.

Watching Cass assess my man, I braced for her to talk shit about him, feeling like she'd be stabbing me with a dagger in the process, but in typical Cassie fashion, she did the opposite.

"Fuck me, that guy is sin on a stick!" Cassie exclaimed with an impassioned sigh.

Molly and Lexi shook their heads at Cassie whose eyes bugged out at Axel. Her blue eyes tracked every inch of his built body, a body I now knew better than my own, his every tattoo etched in my memory.

"I mean, that long almost-black hair, the beard, the tattoos on his neck and face… the whole *I'm an ex-gangster, I could kill you on the spot and I've served hard time thing?* Whew!" Cass fanned herself with her hand, "If I wasn't pregnant and married I'd be all up in that bad boy shit! I'd sure as hell rehabilitate him!"

Jimmy-Don was staring at Cass in exasperation. After all, she was being her typically loud self. I forced down a swig of my wine for fear I'd burst out laughing… especially when I looked at Austin and Axel who were staring at Cass with mutual expressions of disbelief. At least Austin was; Axel just glared at her, his jaw clenching.

Austin, deciding to ignore Cass, nodded to Axel in the direction of JD, Rome and Lev. When Axel reluctantly looked over at the three men, they were all watching him

with wary expressions, none of which exactly looked
welcoming.

Axel pointed his beer at the seat nearest to me, under the
TV. "I'll just watch the game," he said gruffly. He sounded
his usual hard tough self, but I could detect the pain and
hurt in his gaze and his voice. Levi's actions made it clear
he wanted Axel nowhere near him.

Hearing Cass sigh again, I looked in her direction and
she was still fanning herself, staring hungrily at my man.
She turned to me and mouthed, *"That voice!"*

Part of me was glad that Cass felt the way she did. It
gave me hope that Axel and I weren't a lost cause.

"So, Ally," Cass said, leaning back against the couch as
Axel slumped into the chair… the chair that offered a
perfect view of me. Hell, he was sat exactly opposite.

I turned to Cass. "Yeah, darlin'?"

"Rumor has it, you got yourself a new beau?" Cass's
eyebrows danced, but my cheeks flamed when I saw Axel
freeze in my peripheral vision.

"Yes," I whispered and took a sip of my wine, trying to
avoid follow-up questions.

"*So*, what's he like? Some reclusive artist, right?"

Feeling my breathing hollow out, I nodded my head.
"Yes."

Cassie slapped her thigh loudly and groaned in frustration at my short answers. "Ally, I'm pregnant and have been with JD for what seems like forever. Molly's knocked up too and Lexi and Austin, well, she's his little Pix and he's her bad boy. They don't see anyone else, so we need to live the single life vicariously through you. So spill it, I need details! Mama needs some gossip!"

Flashing a glance to Axel, I debated what to say. I was worried I would be too transparent and our secret would be found out. Axel raised his bottle of beer to his mouth and cast a glance back at me. That one hungry look alone melted me on the spot. I thought I caught a flicker of amusement in his dark eyes, but from here I couldn't be sure.

Shit. I had no idea how to get out of this.

Feeling Cass's laser stare burning through me, I sighed in defeat and asked, "What do you want to know, Cass? I don't really wanna talk about it… it's private."

When she smiled excitedly, I knew I shouldn't have spoken.

She screwed up her face, deep in thought, then pursing her lips, she asked, "What's he like in bed? Hung? Fuck of the century?"

Choking on my sip of wine, I spluttered a cough and looked to Lexi and Molly who were trying real not to laugh at Cass.

"Cass!" Lexi admonished, her lips pursed in humor, "Stop it!"

Cassie's face scrunched up in confusion. "What?"

"You can't ask things like that, Cass," Molly said tiredly, causing me to momentarily forget my exasperation at Cass and grow concerned for her instead.

"Yeah, I can. We're all friends here! And I friggin' heard you and Bullet fucking and screaming more than I wanted to back in College, so there's no need for shyness now, Mol! Ain't no secret you're at it like bunnies!" Cass's hand landed on my arm as Molly's eyes bugged out. Rome coughed behind us, and Cass plowed on regardless. "*Well?* The sex? How is it?"

Blowing out a breath, I could feel my face flame, but I replied quietly, "The best of my life, Cass. It's... *he's*, amazing. There, you happy now?"

Cassie grinned and I dipped my head to look at Axel, who was staring at me, his gaze lit with the heat I'd come to adore. He wanted me. And, *Christ*, I wanted him too.

"And looks? What does he look like? I need a visual," Cass asked.

"He's dark, beautiful, muscled… pretty damn near perfect," I whispered, realizing that I was betraying more of how I felt about Axel than intended. "Putting it simply, he's the most incredible and staggering man I've met, in *all* ways, not just physically, though he's beyond words in that department too."

"Well, shit, Al!" Cass said, for once, her voice at low volume, "I didn't know you were *gone* for the guy, like fallen head over heels, gone. I thought it was just sex?"

My heartbeat accelerated to match the speed of a Hummingbird's wings, and I blinked too fast. Cass's arm threaded over my shoulders. "You really like this mysterious guy, huh?"

Inhaling a shuddering breath, I cast a side-glance to Axel who was gripping the neck of his bottle with a fierce intensity, waiting with bated breath for my reply.

"He's stolen my heart," I whispered, "It's hopelessly and irreparably fused to his."

"Ally…" Lexi hushed out and I saw water fill her eyes. "I had no idea…"

Feeling the room aquire a deafening silence, I looked up to see all my friends staring at me in surprise. Clearing my throat, I nervously asked, "What y'all staring at me for? She asked me, I was just being honest."

Molly sat forward capturing my attention. "Just never seen you this smitten with a guy before, sweetie. It's a blessing to witness."

As I stared into the golden brown eyes of my best friend, I said, "That's because he's not just any guy, he's my *more*, my bolt of lightning, the one I've been waiting for all my life." A smile pulled on my lips as I stared at the floor and I whispered, "*Él es mi corazón.*"

I knew they couldn't understand that I'd just called Axel my heart, and I was glad, it was my admission to myself.

When I looked across the room, Axel was sitting forward in his chair, his elbows on his knees. Then, as if feeling my stare, and unable to cope with such a declaration, wordlessly, he got to his feet and walked out of the room.

Feeling like the air had been stolen from my lungs, I drained the rest of my wine and got to my feet too. "If you'll excuse me a moment," I requested, "I'm going to the bathroom."

Leaving my friends to mull over my confession, I walked into the hallway and, on my left, I saw Axel enter the kitchen.

As I looked down at the empty glass in my hand, I knew, if caught, I could use that as my excuse for being in the kitchen with Axel. I simply needed more wine. That was plausible, right?

Not giving it anymore thought, I entered the large kitchen, immediately spotting Axel. He was bent over, hands placed firmly on the countertop. His back was rising and falling with deep controlled breaths.

Checking no one was behind me, I walked forward and stood beside him. Axel jumped on sensing my presence. His guarded expression melted into one of deep want when he saw it was me.

Without taking his hands off the counter, his eyes slowly undressed me. I could feel my nipples harden under his harsh scrutiny. "Fuck, Ally," he rasped, his deep voice guttural, and I could see a bulge forming beneath his jeans. "You're fucking killing me looking like that. Fucking nearly took you on the TV room floor."

Clenching my thighs together at the effect his words were having on me, I turned and pretended to search a cupboard up high. I could feel Axel's hard stare on me as I reached up, faking a search for more wine, knowing my stomach was showing and my breasts were pushing out as my back arched.

Hearing a low groan, my breathing paused when Axel brushed past my back with his front as though he was innocently passing by me to reach for a glass.

Shivers ran down my spine at his hard touch and I bit back a moan as his warm breath drifted by my neck. As if that alone didn't have me yearning for him to press me up against the counter and fuck me from behind, the scrape of his lips and teeth on the skin of my nape sure did.

Slamming my palm on the granite surface to steady my feet, he ordered almost inaudibly, "You better leave those shoes on tonight when I get you alone. I want you in nothing but them, your hair as it is now and those heels stabbing into my back."

Shakily opening another cupboard door, I kept up the pretense of searching for *anything*, when his arm pushed past mine, his skin scalding.

"You're getting me alone?" I asked, knowing he, and only he, would be able to hear me.

Axel's head leaned closer to mine. Licking along the shell of my ear with his hot tongue, my eyes fluttering closed, he growled. "You fucking bet I am. Didn't have you last night and didn't like it. I..." he cleared his throat and I heard him pause in breath, "I... missed you, *carina*..."

Completely shocked that an admission so heartfelt came out of his usually non-confessional mouth, such tender, honest words, when he rarely gave *anything* away, made me tearful. "Axel..."

I forced myself to hold it together, but my heart was so full of emotion and my blood so charged with need that I didn't think it would be possible. Axel didn't move from my side. In fact his large hand drifted across my stomach, wandering fingers first running along my exposed skin, then drifting down to trace the outline of my pussy as his lips drifted from my ear to nip at my neck.

"Did you mean it?" he whispered and my eyes fluttered open.

"Mean what?" I asked breathlessly.

"That I've stolen your heart," he hushed. I could hear the reluctance in his voice at how much he wanted to know, "that it's hopelessly fused to mine."

Warmth filled my chest as he repeated my completely honest words back to me. Sliding behind me, his unyielding arm around my waist grinding my ass against his hard crotch, he pushed, "Well, did you? I need to fucking know…"

I could feel his heart beating rapidly against my back. I smiled. He was nervous. Axel Carillo, with me wrapped in his strong tattooed arms, desperately wanted my words to be true. He needed someone to care about him so strongly… he needed to be… *wanted.*

"Yes," I murmured in a quiet voice, knowing that I could tell him so much more if I wasn't so afraid. "I meant every single word. You have completely consumed, possessed and made me yours, *querido. Todo tuyo…*"

Axel's grip on my waist bordered on painful and his hips rocket against my ass with more force, making us both moan. Hard his cock was teasing my already-wet pussy.

Gasping and scraping my fingernails against his hands, Axel was suddenly dragging me across the room toward the pantry. Once there, he slammed my back up against the wall, his hands keeping my wrists pinned up above my head. My chest heaved and he groaned on seeing my breasts swell with his attention.

"I feel like fucking you hard, right here, right now, against this wall, *la mia luce.* I want to feel you strangling my cock so fucking bad."

I licked my lips, so turned on I couldn't stand the torture, *the sweetest of tortures*, but torture nonetheless. I wanted what he offered too. I needed him inside me. I needed that feeling of a lightning bolt piercing through my body, the one I only ever felt when I came with him.

"Axel…" I sighed, my eyelids hooded as his full, moist mouth descended on mine. The short hairs from his beard teased my lips as they lightly feathered against mine, the taste of beer still prominent round his mouth. Then on an unrestrained groan, Axel surged forward and took my lips with his, his movements furious. They offered a promise… a promise of what lay ahead for us tonight when we were alone… when we could be together with no restraints.

Needing more, always needing more from this man, I pushed my insistent tongue through his lips until my tongue caressed his.

Axel, showing a strength I failed to possess, broke away on a pained growl. Dropping his hand to frame my face with his palm, an intricate spider web tattoo covering the skin, he said, "Text me when you want to leave, I'll be outside waiting for you. I want you to myself tonight."

Nodding numbly, my legs shaking like a newborn foal, I pulled my arms from Axel's hold and straightened my skirt and hair. Axel's hard gaze watched me the entire time. I lifted my hand to rest on his chest and confirmed, "Tonight, *querido*."

Just as I turned to leave, Axel nudged his chin in the direction of my shoes. "Remember, they stay the fuck on."

Nodding silently in agreement, fighting the instinctive urge I had to not fall into his arms and beg him to take me at this second, I forced myself to walk back into the TV room where everyone was still talking. They didn't know I'd just experienced one of the most erotic moments of my life with the man I'd just betrothed my heart to.

Throwing on a smile, I slumped beside Cass, she linked her arm through mine, and I asked, "So, what did I miss?"

*****

The night seemed to drag by as I listened to all the conversations my friends made, but I felt disconnected. In my head, I was back in that kitchen with Axel. I was being stripped of my clothes. I was being devoured by his hungry mouth and wet tongue… And I was clutching onto his back as I cried out my release.

Molly and Rome left after a few hours, Molly finally admitting that she wasn't feeling too well. She'd looked uncomfortable all night. I was genuinely worried for her.

Finally, when midnight hit, I rose from my chair, calling off early under the pretense of having to get up early for the gallery. It wasn't completely a lie, I would be at the gallery tomorrow, but first I had to spend quality time with the sculptor.

As I got outside, a shadow moved to my side and I smiled knowing that Axel had received my text. As I pressed the fob to open my car, I climbed inside, my pulse thundering as the passenger side door opened too. Axel quickly slipped into the seat, switching off the interior lights, plunging us into darkness.

The air in the car seemed to thicken with electricity. Placing his hand on my knee, Axel squeezed my leg and growled a single command.

"Drive."

Licking along my lips at the heat of his touch, I said, "I just need to go grab my overnight bag from Rome's. I'm at the gallery early tomorrow for the final positioning of your newest sculpture. Then we'll be almost done."

Axel's hand froze on mine. "I can't come with you to Rome's, the fucker hates me, and if he sees you with me...." he trailed off. I could hear the concern for me in his voice.

Drifting my fingers down his cheek, I said, "Just stay in the car, I'll be in and out in less than five minutes. He and Molly will be in bed anyway. They'll never know." I looked across at Axel. His facial expression was glacial. Leaning across the seat, I pressed a kiss to his bearded cheek and assured him, "It'll be fine. No one will know you're with me..." I smiled and added, "then you can take me back to the studio where I'll be all yours, to do with whatever you please..."

Axel grasped my head in his hands and pulled me in for a brief hard kiss. Breathless, he ordered, "Fucking drive fast."

I pulled out of the Carillos' driveway as fast as I could, and in record time, arrived at Rome's electric gates where I furiously pressed the fob for them to open.

Every time we halted at a stop sign, I'd had to fight to not pull back the seat and beg Axel to just fuck me in this car. I'd never had, nor had I ever felt, this before; an irrational need to give myself to a man wholeheartedly for no other reason than wanting him as close as we could physically get.

The gates opened slowly. Seeing Axel grip the thighs of his jeans, I tore down the graveled driveway and slammed the car in park.

Looking to Axel, I said, "I'll be back in five minutes." Just as I gripped the handle and cracked open the driver's door, the house door flew open. I heard a pained groan from Rome and my blood ran cold.

My eyes narrowed on the darkened entrance, trying to see what was happening. Suddenly Rome ran out the door... Molly lying lifeless in his arms.

"ALLY!" he shouted as he headed for my car, fear lacing his voice. I sprinted from the car...

"Rome?" I asked nervously. I caught the gutting expression on his face as Molly, dressed in a long silken nightgown, hung pale and unresponsive in his arms.

"Help me!" he begged, "She won't wake up! I can't fucking wake her up!"

Tears began pouring down my face. I froze not knowing what to do. Rome was shaking as he pressed his wife to his chest, sobs ripping from his throat. "Baby," he whispered, his fingers running over her face, "Baby... please... wake up..."

Choking on my cries, Rome looked up at me. The utter helplessness etched on his face brought me to my knees. "Ally," he cried, "I can't lose her, not my Mol, I can't..." He broke off and rocked her to his chest.

I tried to think, I tried to unscramble my frantic mind as I stared at my unconscious friend. I couldn't think rationally, couldn't think clearly.

Suddenly, the sound of the car door opening had my head turning to where Axel was walking round the car. Rome's head lifted up as he spotted the movement. His eyes frosted over.

Before my cousin could speak, Axel threw open the car's back door, and looked at Rome. "Get in," he ordered, "I'll get y'all to the hospital."

Rome, clearly needing someone to take charge, ran forward and slid very carefully onto the backseat, all the time murmuring to Molly for her to wake up.

I met Axel's eyes as he opened the passenger side door. My mouth opened but no words came. Quickly rubbing the tears from my face with the pads of his thumbs, his expression softened and he said, "Get in, *carina*. We've gotta go."

Nodding numbly, I dropped into the passenger seat and turned to see Rome pressing kisses along Molly's forehead, cheeks and lips. His face contorted in agonized pain. A loud cry escaped his mouth as he rocked back and forth with Molly on his lap, looking every bit as helpless as I felt.

In seconds, Axel was gunning down the driveway, heading to the hospital. "It's… It's… gonna b-be o-okay," I stuttered to Rome in between sobs.

He looked into my eyes. "What… what if she dies? *Christ*, Ally, what if I lose her and the baby… I can't… I can't… I wouldn't survive… I… "

Reaching out my hand, I laid it on his and squeezed tightly. "She's gonna be just fine." My eyes lowered to take in Molly's prominent baby bump. I added, "They both are. I promise."

Feeling a hand stroke soothingly along my thigh, my gaze darted to Axel who was concentrating intently on the road. My heart felt like it would burst. He wasn't one for showing affection, but that one gesture, that one touch of support made my eyes fill with tears of gratitude for having him in my life.

"Text Austin and Lexi, *carina*," Axel whispered. I nodded my head, doing what he asked. My hands were shaking like leaves in a storm as I fumbled with the touch screen. I managed to string a sentence together, telling our friends what had happened. Seconds later, a reply came from Lexi saying they would meet us at the hospital.

As I turned my attention back to Rome, he looked... broken. Memories of the night in College when Molly had lost their first child ran through my mind. He couldn't do that again. Molly was his universe... she was his *more*.

As I sat, I intently watched Rome beg his wife to be okay. I knew he hadn't registered exactly who was driving us to the hospital or why Axel was in my car to begin with. But I knew one thing for sure; when Molly pulled through, because she *would* pull through, Rome would now know who had captured my heart... and before the night was over, so would all my friends...

Chapter Sixteen
Ally

Rome and Molly were rushed straight through into the OB unit as soon as we arrived. Molly had begun to move slightly—the fidgeting of her fingers and low breathy moans, but it was enough to give me hope that she would be okay. Axel and I had parked up the car and made our way inside, a nurse telling us to go to the waiting room.

As I walked, lost in a daze, Axel guiding me through a maze of sterile hallways, I began to notice nurses and doctors warily eying Axel. He kept his head down, seeming to block it all out, but *I* noticed. They were judging him. They were seeing the tattoos on his face, his intricately inked arms and hands. Add this to the fact he was heavily muscled and formidable in size, they were obviously viewing him as dangerous.

Each security guard we met turned their head as Axel walked by, eyes assessing. And with each encounter I grew more and more annoyed. My best friend could barely wake up, my cousin was falling to pieces, and the man who had kept his cool and brought us to help, was being judged a threat to people in this hospital.

Feeling my hands clench in frustration, my heart began to race. As we passed two security guards in an empty hallway, they turned on their heels and began to trail us as we made our way to the unit where Molly had been taken. My emotions wrought, I decided I'd had enough.

Spinning round, I met the shocked eyes of the two men, and confidently asked, "Why are you following us?"

They stood stoic trying to stare me down. As Axel placed his hand on my arm to pull me back, their gazes focused on him. It broke me. The way they were staring at this man who was fast becoming my world, who'd had nothing but chaos and tragedy in his young life, well, it shattered my heart.

Wrenching my arm from Axel's firm grip, I stepped forward only imagining how I must have looked with my hair in disarray and black mascara tracks dried on my cheeks. "Is it because of *him*?" I asked coolly pointing at Axel whose face expressed no emotion.

"Just doing our jobs, miss," the larger of the two replied.

273

I laughed without humor and stepped forward again. "Well before you judge my *boyfriend*, know that this man has just saved the life of a pregnant woman who couldn't wake up. He's a good man. Has more talent in his little finger than you two could ever dream of. And just because he looks the way he does, you think it appropriate to stalk us while we are heading to hear if our friend is going to be okay?" I hissed and seethed as their faces remained impassive.

"*La mia luce*," Axel said from behind me, his voice stern and low, "*Vieni qua.*" My heart raced faster and faster still as I stayed on the spot, glaring. Then Axel threaded his hand through mine, shocking me to all hell.

My gaze automatically went to our joined hands. I sucked in a breath at his public display of affection.

Axel had never held my hand. He never came near me when people were around... not like we were ever really around people anyhow, but this surprising action left me completely speechless.

Axel used his hold on my hand to pull me close to his chest and he pushed his free hand through my hair. Our dark gazes collided and he whispered, "We need to go upstairs to check on Molly. We need to meet Lexi and Austin. Don't do this, just leave it alone."

Water filled my eyes at how calm and accepting he was at the way people regarded him without even knowing him. I couldn't bear it. He was worth so much more than people thought. Yes, he had the gang tattoos. He looked, to most people, sinister and dark, but he was so much more than the armor he wore. I wanted to scream from the rooftops that he was so so much more! He was creative, artistic... and even though he tried to portray himself otherwise, he was a good man who cared for his own.

He cared... somehow I had to make him realize it too. I had to crack open the high wall he had built around him.

Wanting to wrap my arms around his neck and hold him close, I resisted. "But they shouldn't be allowed to take one look at you and judge you as a danger. They can't do that! It's not fair!"

Axel's eyes closed momentarily and he inhaled. "Ally," he said as he breathed out slowly, "Fuck them. Let them follow us. They're nothing to me... I'm used to it."

As a tear fell over my cheek at this injustice, I let Axel lead me away, staring up at his expressionless face as his fingers tightly held mine.

He was so used to being looked down upon by anyone outside his gang, that he didn't bat an eyelid when it happened, even when it was so uncalled for. At that moment I understood this closed off man just a little more.

He didn't know how to be in this everyday world.

He was brought up in a no good trailer park on the wrong side of town. He was the eldest son to a drunken and abusive papa who hit him and his mother regularly. He joined the Heighters as a child because that's all that was available to him at the time... but he was a child for fuck's sake! Conditioned to live their way... he'd made mistakes, *big* mistakes. I got that; still couldn't wrap my head around most of it. But he'd served his time. He'd survived being a target, attacked in prison for abandoning his gang to save his brothers. His brothers who had no idea what he'd endured to make sure they could escape their shit lives and be free. And despite all that, this lost man life had been so unfair to, had found his calling and completely changed his life with the simple tools of a hammer and chisel.

He'd influenced so many lives already with his art... including mine. He couldn't see it yet, but he'd completely changed my life in every conceivable way.

This man, clutching my hand like a vise to save me from getting in trouble in his defense, deserved people to give him a chance. I was enraged that he accepted so casually people's blatant dismissive and hostile behavior toward him.

Grinding my feet to a stop, my emotions forfeiting my logic, I glanced behind and realized that the security guards were no longer trailing us. Axel had stopped too, his attention still forward focused but I could see his jaw working underneath his beard. I could see his neck muscles straining in anger.

"Why do you let people treat you that way?" I asked, hearing the cutting edge fueling my voice.

Axel's lower neck muscles bunched, his traps and thick arms seeming to increase in size as his eyes squeezed shut. He blew a slow calming breath through his nostrils, his olive skin flushing with red.

When he didn't say anything in reply, I added, "It's not fair how they look at you. Because you look this way, they assume you're a gangbanger who's going to cause nothing but trouble. It makes me sick!" He still didn't respond, so I stepped closer to him and made him look into my eyes. "Why are you staying silent? Say something, Goddammit! Why are you not saying a damn word?"

Axel's hand became bruising in mine. With a frustrated grunt, he spun, dragging me along the empty hallway, until he stopped in front of a door with the sign 'Store Room.'

277

Turning the doorknob, he pulled me through and released my hand. He began to pace the floor. I watched him carefully, but adrenaline was still pumping wildly in my blood.

Running a hand over my face, I asked, "Why are we in here?"

Axel stopped dead and, spinning to face me, his face contorting in rage, he reached over my shoulder to the door and snapped the lock shut.

Using his chest, he pushed me back against a set of metal shelves. "You don't think I care?" he hissed low.

I swallowed… I'd pushed him to his breaking point.

"You don't think every time one of those cunts, like those asshole guards, looks at me like I'm nothing more than trash, I don't wanna turn around and fuck them up? Because I do! I fucking hate *everyone*. I hate people and their fucking *'I'm above you'* attitudes, the *'this guy is gonna hurt me'* opinion of me when they see me walking down the street. I have an anger inside of me that I'm pretty fucking sure will never leave, an anger if unleashed it on fuckers like that, I'd end up killing. And I would kill them, I know it. I wouldn't be able to stop. 'Cause that's what I've been fighting my whole life, assholes like that! Judging me and fucking wanting me to fail, to disappear so I wouldn't be society's problem anymore."

"Axel, that's not right—"

Raising his hands to the metal shelves, he hit his hand against the top one and snapped, "And I don't need you to fucking defend me!"

My eyes widened and any anger I was holding dissipated, only sorrow creeping in as his words took over. "I couldn't take it. You're not the man they see! They're so wrong about you!"

Axel laughed in my face, but it was a dark mocking laugh. He shook his head, looking at me like I was stupid. "They're *not* wrong!" he bellowed. "They're fucking right! I *am* the man they think I am! I've been that man for so long I don't know how to *be* anyone else. You just don't let yourself see the real me! You're blinded by all this art, *Elpidio* shit!" he rushed forward and cupped my face in his hands. "Wake the fuck up, Ally! I'm Axel Carillo. I'm bad, I'm no good for you… Jesus Christ! I'm a motherfucking coke dealer! You keep trying to make out I'm this great guy, looking up at me with those big ol' doe eyes like I'm your sun, but I'm the damn opposite! I'm midnight! I'm a fucking eclipse that steals the light! I've done it to everyone in my sorry piece of shit life! Look at Austin! Levi! My mamm—"

Axel's voice cut off, breaking with emotion as he tried to utter his mother's name. He paled; even saying her name irreparably crushed him.

He *cared*…

"You're more than that," I argued, gripping his arm and pulling him round to face me. "Don't you dare pull this shit on me, Axel. Not *me*." I took in a shuddering breath as he watched me with an unmoving tough expression chiseled on his rugged face. "Don't you dare do this. The man I'm with *is* a good man."

His hands gripped his long hair. "You have no fucking idea. You like the idea that I'm this reformed bad boy turned sculptor you've given your heart to. The truth is, there's no reformation for me, Ally. I just cover the evil inside me real well. When I went to jail, I had to learn to deal with prison life real damn quick. I had to learn to rein in the anger or risk being killed. I had to pretend to be a good guy so I could get the fuck out alive… you have no idea what it was like…"

"Shut up," I snapped. Axel's muscles began twitching at how tightly he was tensing in response to my attitude.

"What the fuck did you just say?" he questioned through gritted teeth.

Unafraid, I met his feet, looked him right in the eyes and said, "I said *shut up*."

Axel Carillo stood there, his pumped up body radiating waves of pure menace, but he didn't scare me. This was what he did. He *intimidated*. He evoked *fear*. He chased people away. But deep down, he was a frightened little boy who didn't know anything else to do in life but fight; fight to protect his family and those he loved, fight against a society which had forgotten about him, which had brushed him aside since birth.

"You need to back the fuck off, Aliyana. Right now. I'm warning you," he said, threateningly. Slowly, I shook my head, pushing my nerves down deep so they wouldn't show. Axel's nostrils flared. I knew I had him where I needed him to be. He had no idea what to do with me right now, no idea what do now I was standing up to his typically successful bulling ways. Because I *knew* him. There was no way in hell he would hurt me… I could see it in his eyes… I could feel it with every beat of my heart.

"I won't back off. I won't let you do this," I pushed harder.

His eyes narrowed, small lines appearing on the edges of his lash lines.

"Let me ask you something. And this time, actually *give* me an answer," I demanded. Axel watched me like a hunter watches his prey, but I didn't let myself falter. "Why did you start dealing drugs for the Heighters? Not

281

why you joined the gang, I know that, but why you started dealing coke when you were older?"

In this quiet room, I heard his teeth grinding together. I could see his pulse throbbing on his neck. I knew this is what he needed. He needed to see for himself that he wasn't inherently evil. Being innately evil and having evil thrust upon you were competently different things.

"Answer me," I snapped.

Clenching his fists, he hissed, "Because I was crew, and that's what we did to protect our turf. The best of us sold the coke, the rest of us looked out for cops, for threats from our rivals."

"Bullshit," I challenged. Fire lit up his eyes. I prodded his chest. "Tell me the *real* reason. Why did *you* deal drugs? Not the gang, *you*. Why did *you* recruit Austin *and* Levi into the crew so young?"

"For money," he answered icily and a ray of hope burst in my chest. He wasn't outright lying to me anymore, simply evading the truth.

"Money for what?" I continued.

A flash of pain stabbed across his stony expression. His eyes began to blaze. "Don't," he pushed. This time I almost stopped driving this. I could see the pain he didn't want to face clawing to the surface.

"*Why* Axel?" I insisted, gripping the material of his shirt in my hands.

He remained silent. I was pretty sure he *couldn't* speak.

"Was it to get money for your mamma's treatment after she was diagnosed with ALS? Was it to get as much money as you could to save her from being in so much pain? Was it so she didn't have to die in agony? Is that why you needed the money?"

Axel's mouth parted. He dragged in a ragged breath as a single tear ran down his face, his lips ever so slightly quivering. In sympathy, tears flooded down my cheeks too. Axel didn't know it, but I saw his mother… I was there, in the room, when she died. I wanted to tell him, but I knew he wasn't ready for that confession yet.

But I couldn't stop now. I'd made a small crack in his impenetrable armor; it was about damn time that armor was obliterated.

It was time to let in the light.

"You did," I said firmly. "You drafted your brothers in to the Heighters because you couldn't do it on your own. You needed help but you were afraid to ask for it. Had no one to ask, anyhow. You were alone, you were '*Axel Carillo*', the man the Heighters used for intimidation. The guy all the rival gangs feared above anyone else. So how could you beg someone for help when you were always the guy to show no emotion or remorse? Yes, a part of you wanted Austin and Levi involved because you loved that crew. They were your family. They had your back when no one else did. They would kill for you, no questions asked. They were always there when no one else was. And you wanted that sense of family for Austin and Levi too. Because you *love* them. You *love* them more than anyone or anything in this world. They're all you have left and it was the only way you knew how to keep them close and try and save your mamma at the same time. You thought it would keep y'all together as a family."

Axel's heart was slamming against his chest as he stared over my head, unable to meet my gaze. But I knew he was listening, as his hand reached up for mine and gripped my wrists tightly. It was in nothing else but support.

"But you couldn't save your mamma," I said in a quieter supportive tone, using my thumb to gently stroke the skin on his hand, "the Heighters were ruining Austin and Levi's lives. You ran away from the cops back when Porter OD'ed, and unbeknownst to you, left Austin and Lev to deal with your mamma's final days. But you came back and saved Austin from doing hard time. You came back to save your brothers over the crew who'd been your only real family for so long. Because you did it all for family. Everything you do is for family. You've repeatedly sacrificed your chance at happiness so they can keep theirs."

I slid my hands around his neck and traced the long scar, the scar from the shanking that nearly killed him. "You endured five years of hell for your brothers. And even though you found your life's passion within that nightmare, your sculptures cry desperate pleas for forgiveness. Your sculptures are guilt ridden cries of pain... deep sorrow... deep anguish and sadness for things you believe you cannot move on from... or face up to..."

I was referring specifically to the marble angel. It was still the only finished piece he'd never explained to me. But I knew what it was about, that angel. The dual-faced broken and liberated angel was his mamma.

"Ally..." he whispered, his hands shaking as they held me.

Skirting my palm to lay on his cheek, I said, "I know you, Axel Carillo, *querido*. You're not the villain in this story, you're the beautifully flawed hero. You're the dark hero who has been sacrificing himself all along so others would be safe... and you did it all fully understanding that no one could ever know. But *I* know, and *I* don't care what anyone thinks of me for giving my heart to you."

"They're all gonna know now," he rasped, his voice sounding as though he'd swallowed yards of razor wire.

285

"Your friends, my brothers, will all know we're together after this, after tonight… and they ain't gonna understand why. When all this shit clears with Molly, they're gonna try and make you leave me. They're gonna want to tear us apart."

Tilting my head to the side, I could see the hurt and the apprehension… and was there… *fear*, in his voice? The realization warmed my soul…he didn't want to lose me. My heart became so full of love I could barely breathe… *he didn't want to lose me…*

Edging to his mouth slowly, I brushed my lips along his, hearing him sigh at that same feeling which always jolted through our bodies whenever we touched.

"*Rayo*…" I whispered against his warm mouth, unable to stop my smile.

"What?" he asked as his hand caressed my spine.

I smiled wider, the action causing him to inhale a quick breath. "Lightning," I explained. "Together, we make… *lightning*… it's the only way I can explain what feeling goes through me when I see you, talk to you… touch you… make love to you…"

Axel was silent at my words, until his hand wrapped tightly around my waist. "*Fulmine*," he translated into Italian. My legs quaked at his perfect pronunciation, such a beautiful language slipping from his lips. "*Si…*" he said on a deep sigh, "*La mia fulmine… la mia luce…*"

"Kiss me," I replied. Axel pressed us closer together, our bodies once again *fused*.

Our lips wandered along cheeks and necks until at last they met in a sensuous kiss… the most perfect of soft kisses. More was said in this single kiss than our endless nights of lovemaking.

As our lips parted, our breaths coming strong, I assured Axel, "No one can make me leave you. I don't care what they say. You're mine, *all* mine. Your troubles are my troubles. Your sins are now my sins."

Axel shook his head as if he couldn't believe what I'd just promised. He lifted my hand, turning my arm to kiss the inside of my wrists. "You're my sacrament. The holy water my mamma used to bless me with, a pleading benediction slipping from her lips, now runs in your veins." He dropped my arm only to use his thumbs to smudge the tears from my eyes and suck the collected tears into his mouth. As his lips released the pad of his thumb, he finished, "it falls with every tear you shed for me."

"Axel," I quietly sobbed. He pressed a kiss to both of my cheeks before wrapping me in his arms. It was a simple embrace. An embrace that most couples innocently share almost absentmindedly, but Axel had never let me in before this moment to share such a loving act.

It meant something... no, it meant *everything*... it meant he had let me in... *finally*.

As I wrapped my arms around his waist and melted against his chest, he told me, "You're my reawakening." Almost choking on his final sentence, he crushed me even tighter. I frowned at what had him so upset, when he opened up to me... about the topic he couldn't ever bring himself to mention before now. "You're the wish my... mamma... had for my darkening soul... the thing she would say to me every night before I left to push snow... *io prego perché tu possa trovare la tua luce, mio figlio smarrito*... I pray you find your light, my lost son..."

Pain crashed into my chest at the cutting, forlorn timbre to his voice. I cried. With words so touching how could I not?

Axel kissed my head and added, "And I *have* found it, *carina. La mia fulmine... la mia luce... la mia vita*... the only person who sees my clear reflection in the fogged mirror that is my life."

Chapter Seventeen
Axel

Not wanting to leave this storeroom to face the world outside, I reluctantly dropped my arms from around Ally, and instantly felt cold.

"We'd better go see how Molly's doing," I suggested, my finger stroking across her chin.

Ally moved back and silently nodded. Lowering her hand she retook mine. Her eyelashes fluttered up and she asked, "Is… is this still okay?"

Bringing our joined hands to my lips, I kissed the back of her hand as I studied her hopeful face… her *hopeful* face. I studied each line and curve, an image stirring in mind. An impression, a spark… like it *always* started.

I thought about how Ally had always looked at me like this. I thought back to the time I saw my mamma's sculpture sitting alone in that empty gallery looking so lonely that it made me crumble. And then, from behind the marble, there she was like a damn bright light, her beautiful face, the most beautiful face I'd ever seen, staring at me in silence… making me no longer alone. I should have known then, maybe I did in some way, that this would be the woman to change my life.

Months ago I was lost, drowning in a sea of guilt and fucking crippling sadness. Though I was fighting to break the surface, I couldn't ever get free. Every fucker I knew was watching me from the sideline, letting me drown, but not her. Not *la mia luce*. I thought she might throw me a lifeline, or at least try to pull me through. What I didn't expect her to do was jump in and tread water beside me… waiting, just *waiting* until I was ready to follow her to the shore.

I squeezed Ally's hand. "It's more than fucking okay," I replied. And there it was, that blinding smile. That smile giving me hope that maybe this life would work out after all.

"Ready?" Ally asked, with a nervous smile.

Part of me said that I should let her go, that I shouldn't put her through the shit that no doubt everyone was gonna put her through for being with me. But the other part of me, the selfish part, which for once in my life *wanted* to have something just for me, refused to fucking let go.

I was going with the selfish part. I wasn't giving her up for nothing or nobody.

"Ready," I replied. Together we walked out of the storeroom and down the hallway to the OB unit. As we entered the unit, the nurse at the nurse's station directed us to the waiting room. As we approached the closed door, I glanced down and could see the apprehension on Ally's face. She was nervous and I felt nothing but guilt.

Sighing, I dropped my head and tried to let go of her hand. Ally looked up at me in alarm, and squeezed our hands tighter. "No," she said firmly, "we're facing this together. I'm choosing to take whatever they throw at us."

Yanking her to my chest, I kissed the top of her head. Ally turned the doorknob, straightened her shoulders and walked through, pulling me in behind her. Low voices had been talking. When I looked up, Austin, Lexi, Levi, JD and Cassie were sitting on plastic chairs… talking… but they were all now real fucking quiet as they looked our way.

The silence dragged on and Ally stepped closer to my side. When I lifted my eyes, every fucker in the room was staring at us… at our joined hands… At Ally Prince with Axel Carillo.

The first person I clashed eyes with was Austin, who was frowning in confusion, Lexi sat on his lap, her mouth dropped open.

Clearing her throat, Ally asked, "How's Molly?"

Moving on from Austin, I next met eyes with Levi who was looking between Ally and me, back and forth, back and forth. No one looked happy. No one was answering Ally's question.

My stomach dropped and Ally's face paled as we heard, "Molly's stable. Her condition's now progressed to Eclampsia, that's why she collapsed. Her blood pressure was way too high."

I recognized Rome Prince's voice from behind us. Ally tensed. Using my hold on her hand to pull her into my side, we turned so everyone could see us. I wrapped my arm around her shoulders and lifted my chin just daring any of these fuckers to say something.

Ally melted into my side and gripped onto my shirt. She looked up at Rome in relief. "Molly's gonna be okay?"

He had his arms folded over his chest and I could tell that he was about to lose his shit. "She's sleeping, but she'll be fine," he replied tightly.

I heard Ally sigh deeply and I moved my mouth to her ear to whisper, "She's gonna be okay, *carina.*"

"Firstly," Rome looked right at me and said, "I wanna thank you for bringing Molly and me here. I fucking fell apart, but you brought us here and she's safe now. I can't repay that."

Ally relaxed hearing her cousin's sincere thank you, but then Rome dropped his hand and looked to her. "But secondly," he shook his head in disbelief, "You're with Axel, Al? Are you fucking kidding me?"

Ally's eyes tightened and she looked at me. "Yes, I'm with Axel," she replied, nothing but pride in her voice.

"You told us you were with that artist. You fucking lied?" he half-asked, half-challenged, looking like he couldn't wrap his head around everything that was happening.

Ally's hand froze on mine. My heart pounded wondering what the hell she was going to say to that.

"Yes," Ally whispered, "I lied… I lied to y'all because I knew you wouldn't approve."

I exhaled sharply as Ally lied to her cousin to protect my secret, when Rome's mouth dropped open. "Ally, what the fuck are you thinking?" he asked loudly. Ally sucked in a hurt breath. "Have you lost your fucking mind?"

"No," Ally whispered, "I'm thinking real clear. For the first time ever, I'm thinking perfectly clear… and I want him. I'm *with* him."

Rome's eyes narrowed, when Lexi spoke up. "There's no artist? Axel's the guy you've really fallen for?" There was nothing but concern on Lexi's face. That kinda fucking gutted me. I knew we weren't close. I knew she still expected me to fail in life, but I didn't expect to see fear in her eyes over my being with her friend.

"Yes," Ally told Lexi who darted a glance to Cassie who, surprisingly, for once, seemed to have shit all to say.

"You don't ever have a boyfriend, and when you finally get one, you chose a fucking drug dealing ex-con?" Rome snapped. Anger started build in my blood as I heard Ally start to cry. My breath was growing faster and faster, and as Rome's eyes met mine, I stepped forward. I was gonna kill this fucker for upsetting my woman.

Ally stepped forward putting her hands on my chest. "No, *querido*, stop."

"Shit, Ally!" Rome exclaimed. I stepped forward just then Austin moved in front of me and faced his best friend.

"Quit it, Rome, *now*," Austin ordered. Rome stopped dead and by the expression on his face, I could tell he couldn't believe what my kid brother was doing... having my back... I almost couldn't believe it either.

"Are you serious, eighty-three? After everything he did to you, to Lexi, to Lev, you're gonna defend him being with my cousin? *My cousin!*"

Austin's jaw worked and I felt like shit. I could see him hating the fact that he was hurting Rome, but I could also see how much he wanted to defend me. "Rome, I'm just as shocked as you at them being together, and honestly, I ain't sure what to think of it right now. But Axel's been doing real good. So just back the fuck off with all the hating for a damn second, yeah?"

"Back the fuck off?" Rome repeated through gritted teeth. "*Back the fuck off?* He's trash. He's always been trash. He always will be trash... and Ally?" Rome looked right at Ally and said, "He'll make you trash too. You've already been lying for his ass to your family and best friends."

And that right there broke me. Ally was anything but trash. And I knew the guy was in pain, his wife was sick, and he looked like shit. But nobody was calling Ally trash, cousin or not.

Leaping forward, I nearly got a good crack on Rome's face but Austin managed to hold me back. JD was on Rome as he tried to rush at me. Just as he did the door to the waiting room flew open and the two guards, from before, walked in.

As soon as they saw me being restrained their eyes darkened. Ally rushed to me and put her palms on my face. "Axel, please, calm down," she whispered. As I looked at her face, I could see she was more than upset, then I looked down at my hand still in a fist. I ripped my arms from Austin and wrapped them around Ally's shoulders.

"Sir, we need you to leave," the bigger of the two guards said to me. I could feel Ally crying into my chest. I nodded to the guy that I would go. Glancing back, I saw Austin with his hands behind his head, watching me… but I could also tell that even he didn't approve of me with Ally. The one person who I thought had my back really fucking didn't. When it came down to it, he still thought me unworthy.

"*Carina*," I said, "You stay with your friends. I'll leave. You need to be here for Molly."

Ally's head snapped up and her eyes looked huge. "No," she replied. I caught Cassie cussing from behind.

Ally threaded her hands through mine and turned to her friends, Rome watching us like a hawk. Straightening up, she announced, "I lied about who I was with because I knew y'all would act this way. Yes, I'm with Axel, and I don't care what any of you have to say." She looked across to Rome and he shook his head at her in disbelief. "I know he's done wrong in his past. I know that y'all will find it hard to forget it, but he's a good man." Her face flushed and she added, "And I'm twenty-seven for Christ's sake! I'm old enough to choose who I want. And I *choose* him. I don't need, nor do I seek your approval."

All her friends gaped. I'd never seen a bunch of people look so friggin' shocked. Then, to make things worse,

Rome stepped forward and said, "I'd rather you were with anyone but him. Anyone's better than a crack dealing junkie that will lead you straight to hell."

Ally's head snapped to Rome, her eyes darkened and she said, "Yeah? Well I don't *want* anyone else, Axel," she looked up at me and hit me with a watery smile, "he completely owns my heart."

"Ally…" Lexi whispered from our side, her hands to her mouth, tears in her eyes. And I couldn't speak, my chest was too tight at her proudly standing by my side. She was *proud* to be at my side. What kind of fucked up world had I landed in where Ally Prince was standing proudly at my side?

Ally turned to Lexi. "Please can you keep me informed of Molly's recovery, Lex? Tell her that I'll see her real soon, and I'm sorry I couldn't stay." Lexi nodded, looking worryingly at Austin. Ally then looked to her cousin. "I know you don't approve, Rome. And I want to stay for Molls, but I get that you're pissed at me right now and need us to leave. Because if Axel goes, so do I. But know that I ain't the kid you feel you gotta protect no more. And I don't need you to approve my choices." She took a breath and continued, "If you want me to leave your house, I will. I understand."

Rome's jaw clenched as he glared at me, but when his eyes fell on his cousin, they softened some. "You don't have to leave, Al. You know that, but I can't get on board with you and him being together. I got no idea how it happened or how long you've been together. But I know he's fucking poison, Al. He might be doing okay now, but he'll fuck up again. I've seen him do it from when we were kids. He's Heighter for life."

"He's not, Rome," she said coolly. "You have no idea how amazing he really is."

With that, we turned and walked down the hallway, leaving all her friends behind. We never spoke as we got in the car, we never talked as we drove to my studio.

Wasn't much to say anyhow.

*****

As we walked into the studio, Ally had her arms wrapped around her waist like she was cold. I stepped back, watching her as she stood still just staring out of the window. She was so damn beautiful I almost couldn't stand it.

Putting her rental car keys on the table, I moved to stand behind her and turned her in my arms. Her normally bright face was so pale and most of her makeup was gone from how much she'd cried.

As I drank in her unusually sad face, my stomach rolled.

I did this to her.

I did this to everyone. Fucking destroyed their lives, made them sad… made them leave the people they loved.

Rome was right, I *was* poison. And I probably would fuck up again. It's what I did best.

"Don't," Ally suddenly said in a hoarse voice, pulling my attention back to the moment. I didn't say anything in response. She wouldn't like what I had to say anyway.

Ally's hand pressed in my cheek, drawing me in. "Whatever you're thinking, stop."

"We shouldn't be together," I replied, even though it was fucking tearing me apart inside to say so.

Dropping her hand from my face, Ally walked toward my bed and began undressing. My dick immediately started hardening as she pulled off her top, a white lace bra underneath. And when her hands began pulling down the zipper of her skirt, her tanned firm ass appearing as she only wore a tiny white thong, I had to close my eyes just to keep my shit together.

Managing to gain some sort of composure, I strode across the room to Ally, fighting for breath as she unclasped her bra and it fell to the floor… only her thong remained and those sexy as fuck heels still on her feet.

I froze, completely unable to move. Then Ally turned and faced me. She threw the pins from her hair on the floor to let her long hair fall down her back.

She looked like a damn siren and I was so fucking screwed.

I could see in her eyes that she knew what I was trying to do. She'd clearly anticipated that I was standing here about to push her away. To save her from losing her best friends because she'd fallen for me. But I could also tell by the determined look in those eyes, that she wasn't gonna let me do shit.

Moving her hands to the hem of my shirt, she lifted it over my head and leaned forward to press her lips against my hot skin. Her soft, swollen lips ran across my pecs and down to my nipple where she sucked it into her mouth. She then continued down until she reached the zipper on my jeans.

Carefully unzipping me, she pushed my jeans down and took tight hold of my solid cock. I breathed through my nostrils as she straightened to whisper in my ear, "Stop trying to run me off. I choose you. I want to be with you, Axel Carillo. And if you keep trying to push me away, I'm gonna unleash the fiery Latina living within me and *make* you friggin' listen."

As she drew back her head, her eyebrow was raised in challenge and her natural color was coming back to her cheeks. I couldn't help but hook my lip up in a smirk, and Ally had to purse her lips to stop from laughing too.

"Unleash the fiery Latina?" I asked in a gruff voice, as that skilled Latina hand of hers began working my dick back and forth.

"*Sí*," she whispered in her cum-worthy Spanish accent and, taking my hand, I pushed it down into the tiny triangle of her thong, slipping my fingers through her wet pussy, eventually finding her clit. Using the pad of my finger, I began moving it in circles, loving hearing her gasp.

As our hands worked each other faster, I pushed her hair aside to hush out, "Don't forget I'm Latino too. I can give as much as I get."

Ally's eyes were hooded with hunger when I moved my head back and met her gaze. "It's… It's… why it's like… this… between us…" she said between shallow breaths.

"Mmm?" was all I could say in question. I held her hair bunched in my hands, my hips beginning to rock as a flush chased up her skin.

"This… explosiveness we have… it's why we fight… scream… then fuck like we ain't gonna see tomorrow…

301

fuck with all that fiery passion… it's the Latin blood… within us… it's the… Latin fire…" she managed to say, before a cry had her words cutting off as I sunk a finger into her hole.

She was right. We fought with each other, butted heads, screamed… but that only fueled the attraction we had for each other.

We were lighting…

Unable to see anymore through the damn sex fog she'd put me in, I knocked her hand from my cock and, withdrawing my hand from her cunt, ripped her thong in two until all she was wearing was her natural tan and those fucking spiked heels.

Ally's eyes were wide as I stepped into her, flesh against flesh. "I told you I was gonna fuck you in those heels," I said in a low voice, and I watched as millions of goose bumps covered her skin.

Ally's tits heaved with her breathing, and on a sigh, she said, "So fuck me then."

Smiling at that Latina inside being unleashed, I picked her up by her thighs. Striding across the room, Ally dragged her teeth along my traps making me groan. Hitting my workstation, I used one hand to clear the desk and lowered Ally to the surface, her back immediately spraying up marble dust.

Ally's brown eyes were glazed with lust as she looked up at me. Unable to not touch her anymore, I sucked her tit, rolling her hard nipple into my mouth.

"Axel... *Mi Dios*..." she moaned, her pussy grinding against my hard dick. The faster her hips moved, the more I needed in. Breaking from her tit, I took Ally's thighs in my hands and pulled her to the edge of the countertop. Never taking my eyes off hers, I wrapped her legs around my back, hissing when the spiked heels of her shoes dug in to my flesh. My eyes flared and Ally smiled in victory.

"You said you wanted them digging into your back... well, they're in your back, now what?"

Grunting as she tensed her legs, the sharp sting of pain from her heels shooting straight to my dick, I braced at her entrance and pushed straight inside.

"Christ!" Ally screamed as her hands raked at my biceps, but I was too gone, too fucking wrapped up in this chick beneath me, the only chick to ever have been standing proudly at my side.

I pounded into her, my stomach clenching and thighs tensing as her head thrashed around in the dust. Her dark hair was lapping up white dust, smudges paling out her flushed face. But the more she thrashed, the more I stared. She looked like a living sculpture. She looked like the best sculpture I'd ever seen.

Back arching, Ally's moans came longer and her arms fell from my bicep and lay across her head. Dust settled on her flat, toned stomach, and unable to resist, I spread my palm over her covered skin, pumping harder and harder with every stroke. Ally's eyes were closed as I felt her pussy tighten and start to contract. Then, her whole body tensing, her mouth dropped open as she screamed out her release. Unable to take the sight of her beneath me, and my dick unable to take the pressure of her tight pussy, I came harder than I ever had done in my life, Ally's eyes shooting open to watch me.

Gasping for breath in the aftermath, I lifted my hand and, using my thumb, lightly traced the dust covering most of Ally's face with my fingertips, and I knew, without a shadow of doubt that I'd be adding one final piece to the exhibit.

Ally let me touch her face, she let me shift her head from side to side as I studied her angles and features. And I knew right then, that this piece would change it all. This piece would be the first one to break the mold.

It would be the one to set me free.

When my hand dropped from her face, my heart began to race in excitement for what I was going to create, Ally moved her heels from my back. I immediately felt blood drip down the back of my thighs.

I hissed and Ally's eyes widened. "Shit… Axel, I'm so sorry."

Lowering my head to take her full bottom lip between my teeth, I pushed into her one last time and dropped her lip from my teeth to say, "Don't be. That was fucking incredible."

Ally's returning smile almost knocked me on my ass. Picking her up again, I walked us to the bed, but not before Ally grabbed the new bottle of whiskey I'd just brought from my table and took it with us.

She held it tightly in her arms. Ally shrugged. "I think we need it after tonight."

As I lowered us to the bed and we crawled under the covers, dawn began to break. Ally waited until I sat against the headboard, then reached over me to the bedside table. She took a smoke from my nearly empty packet, placed it between her lips and lit it. As the end burned orange, Ally took in a drag, only to blow it out of her lips and place the smoke between my lips. As she hovered above me on all fours and I took a long drag, her eyebrow raised. "They're real bad for you, you know."

Taking the smoke from between my lips with my finger and thumb, I exhaled. "Yeah, I heard that once."

Ally started laughing harder this time, but stopped to press kisses down my stomach. I ran my hand through her hair and Ally lifted her head to say, "I can never get enough of you. It's impossible."

My heart beat faster and I reached for the bottle of whiskey. As Ally's head tilted to the side to gaze at me, I said, "I'm real bad for you, you know."

Ally held her breath for a moment, losing her smile. She lowered her mouth to my chest and moved up to my lips, only to whisper back, "Yeah, I heard that once."

I huffed a laugh as Ally sat back, eyeing me playfully. "Just once?" I asked.

She pretended to think, her finger to her lips. "Or twice, or three times…" she laughed, but quickly lost her humor, "or a million."

My stomach tensed at the sad tone in her voice. I balanced the smoke between my lips and took the bottle of Tennessee heaven from her hands. I unscrewed the cap and, moving the smoke from my lips, took a swig of the whiskey and handed it to Ally. She took three long swallows before tearing it from her mouth to gasp at the burn in her throat and chest.

As she lay back on her ankles after drinking down the whiskey, her eyes scanned around the room. When she saw the state of the workstation, she looked down at her hair and lifted it in her hands. She laughed.

"I'm a mess," she said, trying to swat the dust off her hair and skin.

She wasn't a mess. In fact, if she wasn't here right now, I'd be taking a new slab of marble, beginning to sculpt the image already haunting my damn head.

Ally's shoulders slumped. Running her finger round and round the top of the bottle, she said, "The exhibit is almost done, Axel."

That sadness was back in her voice and she couldn't lift her eyes to me.

"Yeah?"

Ally nodded her head, her eyes downcast. She lifted her head and, looking at me, said, "I'll get another commission after this one is done."

Realization hit… she'd be leaving Seattle.

"Where will you go?" I asked.

"Wherever I get a job." I nodded, unable speak, feeling like a thousand daggers were cracking open my chest. I really didn't want her to leave.

"And you, Axel? Where will you go?"

My back stiffened and I stilled. I hadn't even given it any thought. I only ever thought of the here and now. That I needed to be in Seattle…

"Don't know," I replied.

Ally regarded me. "You won't go back to Bama?"

307

I firmly shook my head.

Ally frowned. "Why?"

I glanced away, not wanting to talk about it, but Ally crawled forward and straddled my waist, pushing the hair back from my face with her hands. "Axel, tell me why. For God's sake, you have to start sharing things with me. Tell me about your life. What's going on in that complex head of yours?"

Sighing, I lay my hand on Ally's soft thigh and said, "I'll be killed."

Ally's hand topped stroking my hair and the color drained from her face. "You'll be…"

"Killed," I finished for her and sucked in another smoke. Ally watched me. I could see her hand begin to tremble. "Hey," I said, taking her hand in mine. "Don't—"

"Who will kill you?" she interrupted. I could see the fear in her face.

I hesitated, not wanting her to be dragged into anything, but she leaned forward and pressed her forehead to mine. "Tell me… share this with me. Don't deal with it on your own. I'm here… I'm right here... with you… *for* you."

My fingers tightened on her thigh and I realized that I finally wanted to tell her what I'd always kept to myself.

"Axel, please," she begged and, not wanting to be alone no more, I looked her in the eye.

"You know how many years I got, Ally?"

"Ten," she said.

"But I only served five," I added.

Ally's eyebrows pulled down. "I assumed you got out for good behavior."

"Part of it was," I said. "I kept my head down, tried to stay out of everyone's way."

"Then what else? What else got you out early?"

"I gave up names."

Ally's forehead pulled down in confusion. "What names?"

Running my hand down my face, I said, "Drug dealers that supplied to the Heighters. Feds knew I could give them the names and addresses of the big coke hitters and where they kept their stash. I had nothing to lose in giving them up. The feds promised me a half sentence if I did, so I agreed. The suppliers were the ones that gave us the messed up coke that made Porter OD. Those fuckers deserved to go down."

"And that's who wants you dead?"

I laughed without humor. "Probably, but that's not who I know is fucking *intent* on it. If the feds did their jobs right, the dealers won't know it was me that gave them up. They'll be serving life now anyway."

"Then who…?" Ally trailed off.

309

"Remo. Gio's older cousin, the old Heighter leader. He was as close to Gio as Austin and Lev are to me, so he's pissed. He had to move up state years ago when a beef with the Kings got outta hand. He needed to lay low for a while. That's where he was when all the shit went down with the Heighter deal and Porter's overdose. Gio told me I had to get out of town for a while, lay low too. So I went and stayed with Remo. He was real good to me. Helped me hide out undetected. But when Lev called me and said that Mamma had died, Lexi was suffering from anorexia and in hospital, and Austin had been arrested, I knew I had to come home. I should never have fucking run away like a pussy anyhow.

"When I said I was going back home, Remo tried to stop me, he knew Gio needed me to keep the crew strong. I was the main reason most of our rivals left us alone. He knew they'd be vulnerable without me around. So I knocked him the fuck out to get away, came back to Tuscaloosa and handed myself in. I knew Remo would be after me. No one fucked with Remo. Then after I organized for Gio... to be taken down, Remo made sure I got a message inside that if I got out, I was as good as dead. I fucking ruined them all. They'd saved me from my papa, from that shit life, and now Remo was gonna make me pay for fucking everything up."

Ally winced as I mentioned Gio's death, and maybe mine, but she ignored it and asked, "And Remo, he knows you're out of prison now? He knows you're in Seattle?" Her voice had gotten higher and higher the more she spoke.

I shrugged. "He'll know by now, no doubt. Some of the guards were easy to buy off. Someone will have sent word."

"Then you have to tell someone!" she half-shouted, her cheeks pale and her face panicked. "The police, someone."

I cupped her face to calm her down. "He ain't got the money to get out here and he's wanted by the feds. He won't dare risk it. He doesn't know where in Seattle I am, and he definitely doesn't know about the exhibition and… *Elpidio* and all that shit."

"*Christ*, Axel…" Ally said, her voice cracking. "I… I'm so afraid for you…"

My gut twisted at the pain in her voice. "Don't be. I've gotten through tougher shit. People have wanted me dead for years. I've gotten real good at dodging bullets." I tried to make it sound like a joke, but Ally wasn't biting.

Taking the whiskey, I shoved it in her hands. "You better take a drink."

Doing as I said, Ally knocked a shit load of the amber liquid down her throat. But when she lowered the bottle, I could still see the concern in her expression.

"Fuck, Ally," I said and, taking her arms, pushed her down beside me and crushed my mouth to hers. Within seconds she'd melted under me and I pulled back. "Don't over-think all this."

Her eyes filled with tears and her fingers wrapped around the long hair falling in front of my face. "You never get a break, do you? There's always something that haunts you."

The sadness in her voice cut me deep. Swallowing back the lump that was clogging my throat, I said, "I did this all to myself, *carina*. I caused the war, this is the fallout. It's karma."

"You deserve better," she whispered. I could see how she much she believed that in her expression. I had no idea what I did to deserve her.

I closed my eyes as her words sank in.

"I got more than I deserve. One brother is married to a chick he loves more than life and he's playing in the NFL. The other is *heading* to the NFL. I got a woman, and I'll never understand it, who fucking wants to be with me. And I get to create what I love for a living. What more could I want?"

"For people to trust you. For your brothers to know you're a sculptor, for your brothers to accept you again… for you to be at peace, to be happy."

Shuddering a breath, I said, "I ain't sure any of that will ever happen, and if it doesn't, it's fine. I got more than most folks got."

I could see Ally wanting to say more, but I really didn't wanna talk about this shit no more. She could see it my expression.

"Lay beside me," she said, with an exasperated sigh.

Slumping down to her left, I cracked a hint of a grin when she lifted my arm around her shoulders and cuddled in.

"Crazy night, huh?" she said, her finger tracing down the rosary tattoo on my chest.

"You could say that."

"They'll come round," she said, keeping that positivity she just seemed to exude.

I stayed silent. I wasn't so convinced.

"Axel?" Ally said quietly.

"Mmm?"

"Will you now tell me how you begin sculpting? You know, in prison? I'd love to hear more about the creative side of you."

Warmth filled my chest as I thought back to the first day I walked into the prison classroom. Some guy was there to teach us art. The warden, fuck, and the state, hoping it would help us cons deal with our anger.

Ally shifted in my arms to rest her chin on her fist as it lay on my chest. Her eyes were filled with anticipation and excitement. I was about to open up to her about my art. And I would *finally* talk about it. It was a while since I'd seen that look in her eyes. When I was just *Elpidio* to her it was there all the time. Now she knew I was Axel, most of the time she looked worried or, worse, sad.

"You really wanna know all this boring stuff?" I asked.

Ally nodded against her fist. "Nothing is boring when it comes to your sculptures. Finding out how an artist began his journey is always the most interesting thing to me. How he found the spark that unleashed his passion."

"Okay," I said jokingly, like she was weird.

Ally nudged me, laughing. "I know I'm a geek, but I wanna know all the same."

Her free hand reached for my hand which was casually lying on my stomach. She threaded her fingers through mine. As I looked down, Ally beamed a huge smile.

"How I got started…" I said, and taking a deep breath, I began. "I'd just been shanked and was in the infirmary recovering." I shook my head at the memory. "Shit, I was

314

in there for what felt like forever; a ton of guards and psychologists coming in day and night trying to get me to talk, to rat on my old crew, but I wouldn't. First rule of surviving in that place was to keep your damn mouth shut. So I did. I didn't talk to no one, was constantly alone with my thoughts. It was laid up unable to move where really started questioning shit. You know, what I'd done in my life, all the wrongs, not many rights… and my family, what I'd done to the only three people who'd ever really gave a shit about me—unconditionally. But the more I thought about my past, the more the guilt flooded in and started tearing me apart."

Ally squeezed my hand, as though in encouragement. I kept going. "I couldn't cope with seeing the fucking light, I suppose. It was the first time in my life I'd been forced to lay there and think. It's real easy not to feel a damn bit guilty about choices you've made when you're always on the move; hustling, dealing snow, you know, the usual."

Ally cast me a wry grin at that. She looked so damn perfect staring at me right now, her perfect face placed on her fist, her face open and accepting of everything I was saying. She was a fucking dream come true.

"Keep going," she urged, and I lifted our joined hands to kiss at her soft skin.

Staring down at her fingers, I continued. "The more I thought about everything I'd done, the more angry I became. Real angry, Ally. I couldn't deal with all the memories. They started giving me damn nightmares, still do. The guilt, it was unbearable.

"When I was physically getting better, one of the nurses who was real good to me, asked me about my tattoos. She asked me who designed them, and I told her it was me." Ally's eyes ran over my tattoos and her gaze darted to meet mine.

"You designed all these yourself?"

I nodded and Ally's mouth dropped open. "They're so beautiful, so intricate."

I could actually feel my cheeks burning at her praise. "I designed most of Austin's too."

Ally shook her head and smiled. "So you can draw?"

I shrugged again and Ally leaned up to kiss my lips, whispering against my mouth, "You amaze me, every single day there is something new."

Pulling back, she re-took her place with her hand on her fist, her dark hair now brushed over to one side, falling over her shoulder. And that was the shot. That, right there, was the image. This was her at her most beautiful.

"Axel, you were saying the nurse talked to you about your tattoos?"

Snapping back to the here-and-now, I said, "Yeah…
erm… right, so, yeah, the nurse knew I could draw. She
told the docs, the shrink, and the next thing I know
they've enrolled me in an art program. At first I was
pissed. I'd taken a business class and was doing okay. Aust
was proud of that, so I wanted to keep going. But from
that first day in that class, something within me just
clicked." I stared off to my tools hanging on my wall. "My
whole life I'd been so busy dealing, working for the gang,
that I hadn't tried to find out what I could be good at. Ten
seconds in that room and I knew I'd found my 'thing'."

"Amazing…" Ally sighed. "A blessing in disguise."

"Yeah… I started drawing anything I could. I was okay
at sketching, shit at painting, but when the teacher, a guy
called Daryl, brought in clay, me and it, just fit.

"Before long, I was making clay sculptures. Pouring all
my anger out into those pieces." I laughed, remembering
the look on Daryl's face when I'd finished the first proper
piece. "Daryl kept driving me more and more, until a few
months later, he asked the warden if he could teach me
how to sculpt marble. I had no real interest in it. But then
one day, he brought me in a book of marble statues. I
opened it at a random page. The very first thing I saw was
Antonio Canova's—"

"*Psyche Revived by Cupid's Kiss*," Ally interrupted, her face all animated and glowing.

"Yeah," I agreed, then frowned. "You like it too?"

Passion flared in her dark eyes. "It's my second favorite marble sculpture of all time."

My eyes narrowed when her face flushed with embarrassment. I wondered what her favorite was, but something in me stopped me from asking.

"Anyway, when I saw that sculpture, I looked up the artist, an Italian. An Italian who worked with Carrara marble." I dropped my gaze. The Italian flag and the Firenzian Fleur de Lys tattoos on my arm both caught my eye.

As I stared at the green, white and red, a sense of pride flowed through my veins; the same sense I had on seeing the man who carved that sculpture was also Italian.

"I felt a link to my heritage as I looked at that sculpture. But more than that, I understood everything the sculptor wanted to portray in his work. I didn't know shit about the story of Cupid and Psyche, but from that one sculpture I knew they loved each other… desperately. I got so much from that one statue.

"I told Daryl I wanted to try it and went from there. I had a ton of disasters over the next year. Daryl wanted me to use modern tools, but I refused. I'd become obsessed with Antonio Canova, so I insisted on only using the tools he used."

I huffed. "Turns out that was a good thing. It gave me an edge, a uniqueness against other modern sculptors today."

"But how did your work get noticed?" Ally asked, her face all impressed. I could feel the love for the art-form radiating from her smile.

"Daryl had a friend who knew Vin Galanti. He took photos of my sculptures and sent them to his friend, who sent them on to Vin. Next thing I know I had a visitation request from Vin and that was it. He became my mentor, took my sculptures from Prison, stored them at his studio in New York... then I got word he was showing one at the Met. I fucking went apeshit. I never wanted my work shown. They were mine, they were my guilt, my past, everything."

"But Vin did it anyway," Ally confirmed.

I shook my head. "Yeah, the fucker did. And after that, everything changed. People knew who I was. At least they knew 'Elpidio's' work, 'Elpidio's' name was suddenly known in the art world."

"And 'Elpidio'?" Ally asked. "He was your—"

"*Nonno*... Mamma's papa. I never met him, but..." That usual stab dragged through my stomach when I thought of my mamma. It was getting harder and harder to keep all the shit back that surrounded the woman who wanted nothing more than for me to succeed. Instead all I'd done was fail, over and over and over... I'd been an epic fuck-up as her son.

"*Querido?* Are you okay?" Ally asked me softly. When I met her warm eyes, I knew that she understood who I was thinking about. But I still couldn't go there yet... not even with Ally.

Not yet.

"My... Mamma used to talk about *Nonno* all the time. She loved him. She said he was a good hardworking man. I was using the Italian technique, I was using Carrara marble, so his name felt right to use. Fuck, my own papa's name would only be a curse."

"Elpidio... It's perfect, it really it is," Ally murmured. I could suddenly see the way she was looking at me had changed.

I drew my head back, and asked, "What?"

Ally crawled over me and tucked her head into my neck. She looked like she wanted to say something to me, but for some reason she was holding it back.

"You are so much more than anyone knows. You should give yourself way more credit than you do."

I didn't say anything as we lay there. For a long time I thought Ally had fallen asleep until she said, "I'm going to do everything in my power to persuade your brothers to see the man you are today."

I stilled. "I don't want them knowing about my sculptures."

Ally sighed. "I know. I won't pretend to understand why, but I accept it… reluctantly. But I'm still gonna try everything else."

I felt my heart would burst through my chest as she said that. Ally's cell beeped. In a flash she was across the room opening it up.

Relief spread over her face.

"Good news?" I asked.

"It's Rome. Molly's gonna be okay. She's gonna have a tough couple of months, but for now, she's good."

Ally walked back to the bed and sat on the edge of the mattress. Looking back at me, she said, "I'm tired, but at the same time, I don't think I can sleep."

"I got an idea then," I said, and I watched as fire lit in Ally's dark eyes.

"Yeah?" she said and turned her body to crawl over me. After she'd kissed me, I held her head in my hands and whispered, "Play for me."

Ally reared back in surprise. "What?"

Feeling like a damn pussy, I said, "Play the piano… for me."

Ally's expression changed from surprised to embarrassed to wonder. "You want me to play the piano for you?"

I threw her a single nod. Ally cast a glance to the piano, then back to me. "What do you want me to play?"

"What you played me before… *Kiss the Rain.*"

Her smile washed away any embarrassment I felt and she said, "You remembered the title?"

Pulling her face in to press kisses all over her cheeks and neck, I whispered, "I remember everything, every single fucking thing from that night. Every single fucking thing…"

Ally, surprising me to all hell, wrapped her hands around my neck and squeezed me in the biggest damn hug I'd ever felt… I never ever wanted to let her go.

When she released me, Ally said, "You're in every part of my heart, Mr. Carillo, in every single part…" before getting up from the bed, leaving me lying here like a dumbstruck fool.

What does she mean by that… That I'm in all of her heart?

Before I had a chance to think it over, I heard Ally sit at the piano and test out the keys like she did the last time. There she sat, naked, her tanned skin flushed, her dark hair falling to her waist.

Eyes closed, her hands stretched over the keys. Then the opening chords to that song fucking sent an arrow through my heart. The image of my woman sweetly smiling at me with her chin on her fist, big brown eyes watching me, like no one had ever looked at me before, filled my mind.

My hands itched to create.

My heart raced for me to sketch.

As Ally's eyes closed and a happy smile spread on her lips, I picked up a pad of sketch paper and a pencil from my bedside table...

And I started to draw... to draw the outline of the only sculpture I knew I would never tire of staring at.

Chapter Eighteen
Ally

"That's it, guys. The only two things left for me to do is get the final text boards drawn up and to arrange for the cleaners to polish the gallery until it damn near sparkles!"

I stood in the center of the art gallery with my team. I stared at the finished exhibition with a lump in my throat... it was simply *stunning*.

Axel's pieces exquisitely occupied the white open space; each one at a different height, each one lit perfectly with colored lighting or with subtle painted backdrops. It was a journey, a journey through the complex tortured emotions of a sculptor... a sculptor who had yet to see its beauty... yet to see his heart-aching creations on display for the all the world to see.

As my team gathered around, a soft applause rang out as we all congratulated one another on a job well done. But a louder clap came from the rear. As we turned round Vin Galanti emerged through the black curtains with tears streaming down his face.

He was back from New York in time for the opening night, now only in a few days' time.

"Vin!" I called, as he pushed through the dispersing group.

Fixing his attention on me, he hurried toward me, hand over heart. "Ms. Lucia… I'm speechless…" he said, clearly in awe, then a huge smile spread on his face.

"I'm real happy with it too. It's my best work yet."

Vin looked to me, his pale eyes kind. "And Elpidio?"

I blushed, thinking of Axel, and replied, "I'm hoping to show him the display tonight."

Vin smiled sweetly. It was then I knew *he* knew we were an item. I wondered if Axel had told him.

"Maybe he'll finally see the light, hmm? Finally realize that he's worth all this effort," he said hopefully. I took a deep breath, silently sharing Vin's hope.

I *hoped* that seeing all his work displayed in such a beautiful setting would help him come clean to his brothers about what he'd been doing… about everything…

Glancing at the clock on the wall, I turned to Vin. "I gotta go, Vin. I'll see you in a couple of days for the opening, yes?"

Vin patted my hand, but he was too lost in the exhibition to reply. As he walked forward, he suddenly glanced back to say fondly, "From the first time I was sent a picture of his angel sculpture, I knew he was special. I knew that he wasn't just a gang member serving time." Emotion welled up in me as I saw Vin's eyes glisten. "He was so closed off when I met him, so broken and angry with the world. His sculptures were so sad, so heartbreaking... but the man I saw earlier today, carving marble outside my studio overlooking the Sound, well, he was changed. I might even stretch it to say he was peaceful... perhaps even happy."

Vin smiled at me to signal that he knew I was the reason for Axel's emotional change... the sentiment brought a lump to my throat.

"Did you see what he was carving? He refuses to tell me. He keeps it hidden outside the studio under a padlocked tarp so I can't even take a peek," I asked.

Vin's watery smile spread into a wide grin. "I saw it... but my lips are sealed."

I groaned in frustration and threw Vin a wave as I grabbed my purse and ran out the door.

I made it to Axel's studio in record time.

From the moment I entered the studio, I felt a chill in the room. The open doors led to the patch of grass overlooking the water. I could hear Axel chipping at the marble. I was desperate to go outside, but he'd asked me not to. As a curator I respected his creative process and his need for privacy. But as his girlfriend, I couldn't stand it!

Axel walked through a second later dressed in a long black sleeved shirt with a padded vest over the top. His black oversized beanie smothered his head. And, as always, a Marlboro cigarette balanced between his lips.

He was so damn sexy.

Walking over to me, he moved the cigarette from his mouth so I could kiss his lips. "Mmm… that's better," I murmured when we broke away. Playfully, I returned his cigarette between his lips.

Waving my keys, Axel took a long breath and nodded his head. That was him telling me he was ready to go, but the at the same time he really wasn't.

Levi had a game today for the Huskies. Axel had been desperate to see his brother play. We knew he was the star player. Unsurprisingly, Levi hadn't ever asked Axel to go watch. I'd decided that was bullshit.

I was making Axel go today. He wanted to see Levi play, so I'd made damn sure it would happen… with just a little help.

I could see the apprehension flaring on Axel's face. Tracing my fingers down his cool cheek, I said, "In the end, he'll appreciate that you went."

Axel turned his cheek into my hand, but his eyes stayed on mine. "He won't, he'll hate that I was there, but we'll go anyway. Nothing else has worked."

*****

The stadium was packed when we arrived at the gates. Axel was tense and kept his head down as we pushed through a throng of excited fans. He hated crowds, practically panicked whenever we had to be around this many people. I led the way. Unknown to Axel, I'd arranged for us to sit in the family section.

Seeing a small crowd gathered around two people, I waved my hand at Lexi. She was standing beside Austin as he signed autographs for the Husky fans.

Axel, seeing me wave, lifted his head. His fingers squeezed mine in a death grip when he saw that Austin and Lexi were waiting for us.

Without glancing back at him, I pushed through to where they stood. Lexi cast me a nervous smile. Austin nudged his chin at me, then at his anxious older brother.

"Hey, guys!" I greeted, Axel's hand refusing to let go of mine as he hovered by my side. Lexi stepped forward and pressed a kiss on my cheek.

Axel dipped his head at Lex, then his gaze wandered to Austin who was still signing autographs. He suddenly inhaled and his dark eyes softened. My heart thumped faster at his reaction to Austin who was now speaking to the fans, with a kind smile on in face. Axel was so proud of him. I knew how to read Axel's slight changes of expression by now. They were subtle, but they were extremely revealing.

Austin met eyes with Axel and smiled wider, asking his fans to wait a second. Austin approached Axel and threw his arms around him. Awkwardly, Axel hugged him back with one hand. Austin drew back. "Happy to see you, *fratello*. You ain't been answering my calls since the hospital the other night." Austin then looked to me and his eyes tensed. It was as though he was working out how I'd gotten to be with his brother.

Stepping forward, I hugged Austin. A fan appeared beside him and asked, "Austin, is that your brother?"

Axel stiffened as the fan looked upon him. The fan backed away as soon as Axel automatically switched to his 'normal' intimidating expression.

"Yeah, he's my big brother," Austin replied proudly. Axel's cheek twitched. He was getting emotional.

The fan's eyes narrowed on Axel. "Does he play football?"

Austin stopped in signing her shirt. "Nah."

"Then what does he do?" she asked excitedly and Austin's eyes widened. Axel cussed under his breath and looked away.

Just when I thought Axel would turn and walk away, Lexi stepped forward and laid her hand on Austin's arm. "Baby, we need to go."

Axel and Austin both relaxed as the fans moved away after a few last minute pictures. We walked through the gates into the huge stadium.

Axel stopped dead as we reached the side of the field and drank in the atmosphere, the crowd, the music, the chants… the students and fans wearing the name 'Carillo' on their backs.

"Shit…" Axel said quietly and when I looked to my right, Austin and Lexi were watching Axel. I could see the happiness in their eyes that he was finally witnessing this. His baby brother playing at this level.

"Crazy, huh?" Austin said, but Axel didn't look at his brother. Instead, his face took on a regretful expression and he whispered, "I should have watched you at the Tide."

I sucked in my bottom lip just to try and keep it from quivering. Axel's hand was iron tight in mine and I knew that it had cost him his pride to admit that to Austin.

I was so proud of him. Austin was dumbstruck. He too was wearing a look of disbelief… but there was real emotion in that stare. For Austin, I knew that Axel saying anything about the past was a surprise.

Lexi's green eyes appeared huge on her pixie face and her mouth was slightly apart. Obviously feeling my stare, she met my eyes and her lips widened into a shaky but thankful smile.

Austin released his arm from around his wife and stepped up to Axel. I tried to shake off Axel's hand, but he kept his grip. Knowing he needed this time with Austin, I squeezed my fingers in support and lifted to press a kiss on his cheek. "Talk to Austin," I whispered so only he could hear. Closing his eyes in defeat, Axel opened them again and reluctantly let go.

Austin laid his hand on Axel's shoulder. "I would've loved you there, Axe," he rasped.

Axel's head dropped. Austin stepped forward and put his hand on Axel's face. "But you can see me play now, Axe. You'll get to see Lev play too. That's all that matters."

Unable to stop a tear slipping from the corner of my eye, I turned and pretended to check our ticket to see where we were seated.

A slim arm threaded through mine. When I glanced to the side, Lexi was looking up at me. She leaned in and pressed her cheek against my bicep. I held my breath. Lexi never let anyone get this close to her except for Austin and, occasionally, Levi.

It only served to make the situation that much more special.

"Darlin'?" I managed to push out as Lexi and I began walking to our seats, Axel and Austin following behind.

Lexi tightened her hold on my arm and said, "I'm not gonna pretend to understand you and Axel, but then, I ain't one to talk. God knows Austin and I had our secrets when we fell in love." Looking up at me, she sniffed and said, "but… just… thank you…"

My eyebrows furrowed in confusion but Lexi said no more.

Arriving at our seats, I motioned to sit beside Lexi when Axel reached out and took my hand. "No, you sit beside me," he said in a gruff curt voice.

Lexi looked at him in alarm. I knew it was because of his sharp demand. But only I knew Axel was uncomfortable in crowds… only I knew that he needed me to sit beside him to help him relax.

Austin pushed himself back against his chair as I passed him to sit by Axel's side. I could see in his expression that he was furiously trying to work out my close relationship with Axel, but I ignored it.

As I stood in front of Axel, I saw his shoulders sag in relief. Just as I went to sit beside him, he leaned forward and pressed his lips against mine.

I could feel Lexi and Austin's attention fixed on us, but I didn't care. Nobody knew what we shared. No one knew what we meant to each other.

Sitting down next to Axel, he put his heavily muscled arm around my shoulder and pulled me into his side. I loved it. I loved how he needed me... I just loved him— more than even I could comprehend.

As the cheerleaders and band finished their pre-game show, Austin asked, "So, Axe, how's the work on the market?"

Axel's muscled tensed. I kept my gaze forward. I hated that he was about to lie to his brother.

"Good. Busy. Keeping my head down," Axel replied keeping things vague.

I risked a glance to Austin whose head was tipped to the side and his eyes narrowed. I panicked that he knew something was up with Axel's cover story. Axel barely went home; Austin had to figure that more than strange.

"Good to hear it, *fratello*," Austin replied and sat back in his seat. I almost laughed as Austin and Lexi kept watching us like we were a couple of caged animals in a damn zoo.

"How's Molly today, Ally?" Lexi asked, leaning over Austin to do so.

"Better. She's already marking term papers from her bed. Rome's not happy with that, but we both know he'll give her anything she wants. She's on stronger medication. I'd say that she's already feeling like her old self."

Molly had been discharged from hospital earlier today. I made sure I was there to greet her. Rome had obviously told her about Axel, and in typical Molly fashion, she'd told me she was happy I was happy. Rome scoffed at that, but then Molly had never been one to judge people. I loved her for that.

Just then, the crowd jumped to their feet as the team was announced. Axel stood, pulling me with him. I lifted my hand to hold his that draped over my shoulder. His heart was racing as he waited for his brother run out. When Levi appeared on the field, I heard him exhale loudly.

As Levi ran to the sideline, tears filled Axel's brown eyes. As they tracked down his cheeks, I reached up and wiped them away with my thumb. Axel squeezed me tighter, just as Austin's arm wrapped around Axel on his other side. When I glanced up at Austin, tears were running down his cheeks too. Putting his hand on the side of Axel's head he pulled Axel to lean against him.

I watched the two older Carillo brothers, broken inside
by tragedy and circumstance. Both were alike in their
Italian looks and personality and my heart filled with hope.
Bridges were being built, shattered hearts were being glued
back together… blood ties were being strengthened.

The crowd roared as the players took their positions.
Levi was in sight. Just before he put on his helmet, his gray
eyes sought out Austin and Lexi, a smile pulling on his
lips… until they wandered to Axel in Austin's arms. Those
gray eyes that were normally so sweet and guarded,
suddenly blazed with contempt.

I wasn't sure Axel and Austin had seen it, but I had.
When I glanced to Lexi, the sadness and stress on her face
told me she had too.

My stomach sank.

I wasn't sure this was going to go as well as I'd hoped.

*****

The game came to close with the Huskies up by ten.
Levi had played amazingly well. He scored two
touchdowns and was named MVP. I couldn't have
imagined a better day for Axel to watch his little brother
play. But although Levi had played so well, he'd also been
aggressive. Overly aggressive. He fought with other

players, stormed up and down the touchline. The entire time, Austin cussed at his brother to calm down.

Only once did Axel look to me during the game, and I could see regret in his expression. He was regretting our coming here.

As the crowd began to disperse, the four of us sat and watched Levi stand central in the field, crouched down on one knee with his head cast down. His teammates and coach all passed by him, but they all left him alone. Levi and the four of us seemed to be the only people left in the large stadium.

We all knew Levi was livid that Axel and I were here without his permission. I couldn't help but think that whatever was between them had to be confronted finally...

"We better go down and see him," Lexi eventually said. Austin agreed, though with hesitation in his voice.

"We'd better get going," Axel said, and I sighed. He and Levi had barely interacted the whole time he'd been out of prison. Hell, Levi stopped seeing Axel in prison after only a few visits, so they'd pretty much not spoken a word in over five years, unless it was Levi tearing Axel apart.

The tension between them was palpable. It was horrible to be around.

Silence followed. Austin, who was leaning his elbows on his knees, looked to his left and said, "He knows you're here, Axe. You both have gotta face this someday… why not now?"

"Fuck, Aust," Axel rasped. Austin dropped his head in his hands, breathing hard.

Eventually, Austin looked up at Axel, his dark eyes filled with emotion and said, "I want the three of us to be brothers again. I want all this fucking hatred between y'all to stop…" Austin rolled his lips together, his nostrils flared and tears filled his eyes. On a ragged breath, he added, "It would tear Mamma apart if she could see her sons acting like this. All she ever wanted was for us to have each other… think of her proud face as she watched us all together, Axe, and tell me that ain't the truth."

I blinked rapidly so I wouldn't breakdown. I could only imagine how a statement like that would affect Axel. His mamma and Levi were the remaining two walls to fall from around his heavily guarded heart. Axel's arm around my shoulders pulled me in closer and as our gazes met, I could see the severity of his hurt staring back at me.

I knew he wanted my support, so I gave him a smile and nodded my head, "It's time, *querido.*"

"Okay," Axel said in a broken voice, as his attention went back to Levi who still hadn't moved from his position in the middle of the field.

Austin released a long relieved sigh. Together, we walked toward Levi.

As we approached, Levi's head snapped up and his gray eyes locked on Axel who was holding my hand. We stood behind Austin and Lexi.

"Good game, Levi," Lexi said trying to be upbeat. Levi ignored her, having eyes for one person only.

Axel's hand was tight in mine. As Levi continued to glare at Axel, his hand adopted a slight shake. I closed my eyes briefly anticipating how this was going to go down.

Levi rose to his feet, dropping his helmet on the field. His sandy colored hair was in disarray, his face still flushed from the exertion of his game. Towering to the same height as Axel and Austin, his torso slightly leaner, Levi looked every inch a Carillo.

"Lev," Austin said cautiously, "I knew Axe was coming, I helped plan it. He wanted to see you play. Nothing wrong with your brother wanting that, is there?"

Levi's face beamed bright red and his lips tightened. "Yeah, but it all depends which brother, don't it, Aust? You, or the fucking loser."

Axel flinched at the venom in Levi's tone. Austin shook his head in annoyance at his little brother. I almost said something myself as Axel kept his silence. But Axel suddenly released my hand and stepped forward.

338

Lexi threw me a panicked look and I quickly moved beside her. Austin stiffened as he watched Levi prep himself for a fight.

I had no idea what Axel would do if Levi lashed out.

Axel walked slowly to stand just a few feet from Levi. Levi fumed, legs unable to keep still.

"Back the fuck off, Axe," Levi snapped, but Axel didn't move.

"I ain't going nowhere, *fratellino*. You're my little brother and I wanted to see you play."

Levi scoffed and inched forward. "Yeah? You wanted to see me play? You wanted to see me play the same way you wanted to see me in your precious crew."

"They ain't my precious crew, Levi. I get that now."

Levi laughed in Axel's face. My blood ran cold at his condescending tone. "You get it now? Mr fucking Heighter of the century, gets that those fuckers he did anything for are poison? Tell me, Axe, why couldn't you fucking get that before you made me shoot someone!"

Axel paled, then went to say something. Levi cut him off. "No! You'll fucking listen to what I've gotta say!" he screamed, his voice echoing around the stadium. "You, my big brother, the brother I looked up to, the one who should've had my back, made me shoot someone! I was fourteen and you made me shoot him! Do you realize how

339

much sleep I've lost remembering that night? How many nightmares haunt me, torturing me as I wonder if I killed him?" Levi ran his hands down his face, tears streaming from his eyes. "Shit, Axe, you stood behind me pushing me do it! What the fuck kind of brother does that? I killed someone because you told me to. I worshipped you, *trusted* you and you made me kill someone! But now? Now I fucking HATE YOU!!!"

Axel dropped his head. I pictured the sculpture with the daggers; 'Exsanguination'. Every one of Levi's words were a dagger he couldn't remove, cracking him slowly. I could see the pain in Axel's face. Levi stepped closer still, and this time his fists clenched as his body pumped up... he was gonna fight Axel.

"Nothing to say, *fratello*?" Levi spat, the word *'fratello'* sounding like a gunshot on his lips. When Axel said nothing in response, Levi launched forward and pushed square on Axel's chest. "Speak, Goddamn you!" Levi shouted and pushed at Axel again. "FUCKING SPEAK!" Levi bellowed. Then I saw something snap inside Axel.

Whipping his head up, Axel grabbed the neck of Levi's football pads in his fists and shook him, then slammed him to his chest. Levi went ashen as Axel's face met his. "Don't fucking push me, Lev, don't fucking push me."

Then to my surprise, Levi smiled, but there was pure rage behind that fake smile. "Why, Axe? 'Cause you'll kill me too, ruin me too?" Levi leaned forward until their noses almost touched, then whispered coldly, "Well it's too fucking late. I fucking died when I was fourteen... when I lost everything because of you!"

Axel, reacting like he had just been burned, dropped his hands from Levi's pads and staggered back a few steps. Levi laughed at seeing Axel so defeated. He continued, "Aww, what's the matter, Axe? You feeling sorry for yourself now? Is the great 'Axel Carillo' pitying himself?"

Axel breathed in and out to control his breathing. He, then looked to Levi and rasped, "I'm sorry, Lev. I'm so fucking sorry for what I did to you... what I made you do. I'm so fucking sorry."

Lexi gasped beside me and reached out to hold my hand. Austin dropped his head, and I realized that was probably the first time Axel had ever apologized for his past choices.

Levi's teeth were gritted together with fury. Suddenly, he staggered back like he'd been shot. His gray eyes showed panic at Axel's confession. His gaze fell on the rest of us and he raked his hands through his hair.

"Don't," he warned Axel. "Don't you dare apologize!"

But Axel moved forward, his hands held out in surrender, and repeated, "*Fratellino,* I'm sorry. I'm so sorry for everything. I love you, Lev. I love you so fucking much."

Tears ran like rivers down Levi's cheeks. He choked back a sob, his fists clenching again. "No! Don't tell me that, Axe. Back off. Back the fuck off!"

But he didn't; Axel strode forward. "I love you, kid. I always did. I fucked-up, but I love you, I've always loved you, more than my own life…"

Levi raised his head to the darkening sky and screamed.

He stormed to Axel and pushed him back. "I said don't say that! You don't love me, you love no one but yourself! You never put us first! You fucking led us to hell!"

Axel stood his ground, his chest wide and repeated. "I know I did, but I do love you… so fucking much…"

Levi snapped, his body shaking. Tightening his fist, he drew back his hand and rammed it straight into Axel's jaw. Axel stumbled back, but he didn't retaliate.

Levi's eyes darkened. "Fight me! Fight me, you fucking pussy!" Levi boomed as he struck Axel again. Axel's head snapped back; then he took blow after blow. Levi's actions became frantic as Axel refused to fight, and he screamed, "I'm big enough now for you to face, so fucking fight me!"

Blood ran from Axel's lip, but he kept his hands by his side. He coughed out through his bruising mouth. "I love you, and I'm sorry, Levi."

Levi struck Axel again and I openly wept as more blood ran from Axel's lips and nose. Austin, at last, jumped forward, but Axel, on seeing his approach, held out his open hand to stop him. "No!" he shouted, as he bent over spitting out blood.

"Fuck!" Austin hissed and planted his feet on the ground in front of us… he was breaking apart watching his brothers fight.

Levi's cries were low and loud, and he paced in front of Axel like he couldn't stand all this emotion, like it was driving him insane. As Axel, bloodied and beaten, approached him again, Levi roared and took another swing, but Axel dodged it this time. Instead, Axel wrapped his arms around Levi's waist, refusing to let him go.

Levi thrashed around, trying to throw off his brother, but Axel was stronger and kept a tight hold, repeating, "I'm sorry, Lev, I love you," over and over. Each time Axel said those words, Levi's face contorted in pain more and more, his sobs becoming louder and louder.

"I love you kid, I fucking love you so much…" As Axel bellowed those words into Levi's ear, something suddenly changed in Levi. Losing all fight, Levi sagged against Axel who held up his baby brother in his arms.

Levi's eyes squeezed shut as his cries consumed him. After resisting for as long as he could, Levi suddenly wrapped his arms around Axel. The emotional impact caused Axel to fall to the ground with Levi still in his arms. Axel was crying his heart out too.

Unable to fight back a trapped sob in my throat, I put my hand over my mouth and cried with them. Austin and Lexi did the same.

"Axel," Levi cried and squeezed his arms tighter against Axel's neck, "You left me, you fucking left me," he said brokenly. "You left all of us… we needed you… and you left us... alone…"

"I'm sorry," Axel wept, "I'm so fucking sorry, kid…"

"And Mamma…" Levi said breaking as he said her name, "Mamma needed you there when she passed. She loved you. You were her eldest, her heart… and you left us all alone… you left *her* alone as she faded, as she laid there dying wondering where you were… you never got to say goodbye to her… you never got to kiss her goodbye… to pray with us… to kiss her cheek…" Levi wailed. Axel broke down further.

Axel sagged against Levi as he completely fell apart and Levi, feeling this, sat back and cradled Axel in his arms.

Their roles suddenly switched. Obviously unable to take it anymore, Austin ran to where his brothers sat on the ground and wrapped his big arms around them both. The three Carillo brothers were purging their pasts and healing through their shuddering tears.

"Oh God, Al…" Lexi whimpered beside me, burying her face in my side.

I looked up at the clear night sky. The stars shone brightly but I closed my eyes. I thanked God that tonight had actually happened. I looked down at the three Carillo boys, shrouded in pain, but finally... together.

Then I heard the sweetest sound of all…

"I… I love you, too, Axe… I forgive you," Levi said quietly as the brothers' sobs turned to soft cries, "I've missed you so damn much… nothing was ever right with you gone…"

Sniffing, Axel raised his head. Holding the back of Levi's head, he pressed a kiss on his younger brother's forehead, then Austin's. For the first time since I'd met Axel, he looked like he could breathe, as if his ton of burdens had been lifted from his soul.

Axel wrapped his arms around Levi, and Levi looked up with red-rimmed eyes. The adoration I saw in Levi's stare almost brought me to my knees.

"I killed that King, Lev," Axel admitted quietly. Levi's gray eyes widened in shock.

"Wh-What?" he stuttered in a hushed voice.

"Was no way that sin was gonna be on you, so I killed him first. You can sleep soundly, *fratellino*. Your conscience is clear."

My heart skipped a beat at the confession. It was always going to be the hardest thing for me to hear Axel say. I knew he'd killed, he'd told me so, but I had to confine it to the past, along with everything else.

"Axel…" Levi cried as he slumped forward. Austin wrapped his arm around Axel's shoulders. "Why didn't you tell me? It's haunted me for so long."

Pain flashed across Axel's face. "I… I didn't know you… didn't know you felt that way… I was… shit, Lev, I fucked up so bad… I'm sorry… shit…"

Axel squeezed Levi tighter, Levi looking up at Axel like he was a miracle, his savior.

"Lev?" Axel said. "We good now, kid?"

I could see the desperate hope in Axel's gaze. Sighing, Levi nodded his head. He rose to his knees and pulled Axel tightly to his chest.

Blowing quietly and steadily out of my mouth, I tried to relax. I squeezed Lexi's tiny hand. She looked up at me, wearing the biggest smile I'd ever seen on her face and whispered, "I don't care what anyone says about you two being together. You've saved Axel…" she pressed a kiss to the back of my hand and continued, "you've saved all three of them."

I fought to swallow down my emotion, but I couldn't. I was just so happy that Levi had come around, so happy for Axel that he'd got his baby brother back. Austin got to his feet, pulling Levi up too. Looking down, Levi held out his hand to Axel. With a big smile, Axel took it and stood up, ruffling Lev's hair.

Levi couldn't take his eyes off Axel. Looking at the three Carillo brothers in front of me, I pictured them as kids, Levi and Austin seeing Axel as their hero. Axel taking on the world to make sure they were safe.

Levi's face dropped, then he said, "Sorry for hitting you, Axe."

Axel, like he's just remembered his bust lip and bruising jaw, pressed his hand to his mouth, wiping away the blood. He huffed a laugh. "Don't sweat it, kid. I've had worse." His eyes met mine then. Only I knew what he'd suffered.

"So," Lexi said, stepping forward, "Shall we all go out for dinner?"

All three of the Carillo's, all tall and intimidating in size looked at my little friend. Austin's eyes showed all the love he had for his wife in his stare, and they all started to laugh.

"Yeah, Pix," Austin said, flicking his head to the side, urging her to go to him. Lexi laughed and ran into Austin's open arms, but not before she made time to pull Levi in for a tight hug... Nervously, she walked to Axel and, placing her hands on each of his cheeks, she pulled his head down to kiss him on the forehead.

Axel smiled in surprise. Lexi smiled back, so wide it was infectious.

Still looking shell shocked, Axel held out his hand, looked at me. I brushed past his hand to wrap my arms tightly around his waist. Axel sighed at my touch and kissed my hair.

Fifty minutes later, we were all sitting in a restaurant, the Carillo brothers breaking bread for the first time in years.

Everything seemed to be going right... at last.

Chapter Nineteen
Axel

As I sat at the dinner table with Levi, Lexi, Austin, and Ally by my side, I struggled to believe this was all true. I knew we had a ways to go, but we were all here, *trying*; trying to piece what was left of this family back together.

And I knew who to thank for it all… the fucking angel who had smashed into my life with the force of a T11 tornado. And somehow, against all the odds, she'd made it better.

My chest constricted as I watched her laughing at something Levi had said, her beautiful face glowing. I couldn't breathe as I watched her, she had become my everything… fuck, she *was* my *everything*.

Shifting on my seat, I tried to keep it together, but I caught Austin staring at me with a shit-eating grin.

Asshole…

As we left the restaurant later that night, we walked to Ally's car as Levi, Austin and Lexi went to theirs. As we said goodnight, Levi suddenly ran up behind me. Awkwardly, he pulled in me in for a hug.

Sighing in fucking happiness, I hugged him back. Pulling away, he dipped his head shyly, to quickly say, "Don't do anything that takes you away from us again, okay, Axe."

I firmly nodded my head. "*Lo giuro, fratellino,*" I said, meaning every damn word.

Levi smiled. "*Bene, molto bene. Buono notte, fratello.*"

Austin, Lexi and Levi waved goodbye just as Ally returned to my side. She pressed a kiss to my neck, using the distraction to snatch her keys out of my hand.

I raised an eyebrow in question. She dangled her car keys at me. "I wanna show you something," she said excitedly.

"Okay," I agreed, and the biggest teasing grin spread on her face.

Ally led me to the car and jumped in the driver's seat. Just as I went to slide in the passenger seat, I clocked a car parked in the distance. I frowned. I'd seen that black car round the city for the last couple of days.

"Axel?" Ally called from inside the car. I looked down at her frantically waving me in. Casting one more glance at the parked car, my chest lost tension when I saw it pulling out onto the road and away from the restaurant.

I sighed in relief and shook my head. I was being paranoid.

As I slipped in the car, Ally asked, "Everything okay?"

Taking her hand, I brought it to my lips, pressing a kiss on her smooth skin. "Fine."

A short drive later, we arrived at the gallery. My heart started slamming my chest as soon as we pulled up and Ally put the car in park.

The exhibition was in a couple of days' time and I knew she'd finished the design. I didn't know why, but I'd been too chicken to come here of late, seeing everything done, seeing the exhibition fully designed.

I guess it just made all this change in my life that bit more real. Like I was finally gonna be leaving my past behind. I was still afraid to believe this life I was now living was true; like it would all be pulled out from under me the minute I let myself just be content. I had my sculpting, I had Ally, and now, because of tonight, I had both of my brothers back in my life.

I couldn't bear to lose it all again.

"*Querido*, will you come with me?" Ally urged softly. Taking a deep breath, I got out of the car and walked behind her to the staff entrance.

As we entered, the guard that was usually on duty waved at Ally, and as always, ducked his head from me. Ally looked back and playfully rolled her eyes making my lip hook into a grin. I fucking adored this woman.

As we approached the black curtains, I started as I looked up at the huge title hanging above the entrance, *'Elpidio'*. My stomach flipped with an unknown feeling as I saw my artist name drawn in a simple black script. Then I realized that the unknown feeling was excitement. I was fucking *excited* about the show.

Smelling Ally's Jasmine scent, I glanced down to see her smiling up at me. But I could also see anxiety on her stunning face. She was nervous I wasn't gonna like what lay on the other side of the curtains. That was impossible. She knew me better than I even knew myself. It would, no doubt, be perfect.

"You ready?" she asked.

"Ready," I replied, and Ally drew the curtains apart to reveal the gallery, completely changed from the last time I'd seen it.

My feet began moving forward as my eyes drank in the space. It was... *incredible*... surreal... out and out fucking crazy that this was all for me.

My sculptures looked perfect at all the different heights. They were spread out so visitors would be able to see every part of them back and front.

"Well?" Ally asked anxiously.

Taking her hand in mine, I lifted it to my mouth and kissed along her warm skin. "Fuck, Ally," was all I could think to say. Her responding smile almost knocked me on my ass.

"Can I guide you round? Can I take you on the journey?"

I frowned not understanding what she meant by 'the journey'. Ally, clearly seeing it on my face, began to lead me forward.

"I set the flow of the gallery out in a certain way, in themes. As you told me what each sculpture meant, and what inspired it, I put them in a certain order. I started with this piece first because it felt like the beginning to me."

Ally brought us to the statue I made of us Carillo boys as kids. Austin and I were laid down, Austin pointing up at the sky, and in my arms, I held a baby—Levi. Beneath us was fire and faces screaming in pain… those faces belonged to my mamma, screaming from inside the trailer because of my papa as I tried to keep my brothers safe from his fists.

Ally pulled on my hand and next brought us to a marble stidda, a marble stidda the corners of which were choking a heart, it's sharp edges drawing blood. "Next is how

353

things began to go wrong, an innocent heart being punctured by this star."

I didn't say anything, *couldn't*, as we next moved to three brothers stood in a circle, heads down, the eldest brother gripping the necks of the younger two, dragging them alongside him.

"Then comes the demise of the boys from the beginning, the eldest leading them astray."

My heart pierced with shame as Ally said that, but she was only repeating my words back to me. Next we came to my newest sculpture, the boy crying bullets. Ally stood next to me and said, "We need a title for this one, Axel. Any thoughts?"

I nodded my head as I stared at the boy's face, too terrified to shoot. Levi's words from today circled my mind, about how he had nightmares believing he'd killed someone.

"Hamartia," I said gruffly. Ally looked up at me in confusion. "It means to sin, to do wrong, to miss the mark. It's an event that happens to main characters in a story which ruins their lives or sets them along a path that can only ever end badly."

"Axel…" Ally whispered sadly.

I looked to Ally and said, "You know the inspiration behind it. I don't need to explain it, right?"

Ally nodded at me in understanding. We walked round the rest of my sculptures, each one more gutting than the last.

"So we start with fear, then despair, then sin, guilt, and finally… this…" Ally trailed off. I didn't need to look up to know we were at the angel.

"Darlin'," Ally said soothingly, her hand on my back, "we need a title, we need something for the text boards. It's the last piece to talk about."

Feelings I was no longer able to hold back surged forward, suffocating me. I gasped, my eyes squeezing shut as I tried to get my breath.

"*Querido*," Ally whispered quietly and I pushed back my hair, opening my eyes.

"I can't, Ally, I can't talk about… *her*…" I said, my voice breaking on my last word.

Ally was suddenly before me, her hands gripping my wrist, forcing them from my face. "Baby," she said quietly, "It's time for you to face it. You need to talk about your mamma. It's eating you alive."

My heart swelled in my chest and I struggled to breathe, my lungs constricting. But I knew she was right. For five long years I'd blocked out my mamma from my head to keep my sanity. But it was killing me. I couldn't stand it anymore. It was hurting me, not being able to remember the good things: her face, her smile, how much she loved me, without feeling like I was being tortured slowly in the process.

Drawing in a strained breath, I forced myself to look up at that statue. A tidal wave of grief and guilt rushed through my body, physically bringing me to my knees.

Suddenly, Ally knelt down on the floor beside me, arms wrapped around my back. Tears started pouring from my eyes as I pictured the last time I'd seen my mamma. She was lying on her bed, her speech almost non-existent and her frail body weak and still. She stared at me leaving to go to the Crimson Tide's National Championship after party at Austin's school. I'd given her her meds, and picked up her clothes in her room. The entire time she'd just watched me with tears in her huge eyes from her broken position on her bed.

She worried for me. She was always worried for me. But that night, there was something different in her stare. It was as if she *knew* it was the last time we'd be there together… like she *knew* I was about to fuck up so badly that it was gonna change everything for us all…

*****

As I hung Mamma's clean nightgowns in her closet, I turned round to find her watching me, her face soaked with tears. My heart cracked at the sight of her so tiny and sad on that bed. She was always sad. Always lying down, unable to move, crying buckets of tears. As I stood there watching her breaking, I remembered what my mamma had looked like before. She'd been beautiful, so full of life, but the ALS robbed her of her every muscle and worst of all, her smile. All that remained unchanged were her huge brown eyes. The same brown eyes that could tell you all she was feeling with just one look. Those brown eyes that were gutting me as they stared at me right now.

I walked to where she lay, my heart racing in my chest, something inside of me making me sit on the edge of her bed and take her cold bony hand in mine.

As our gazes met, tears escaped the corner of my eyes just at the sight of hers. I couldn't fucking take her crying, it broke my heart. It broke my heart knowing that those tears were out of worry… out of disappointment in me.

I lifted Mamma's hand to my lips and pressed a kiss on her thinning skin. "Sorry, Mamma," I whispered as she stared up at me, her body unmoving, her tears coming thicker and thicker the more I spoke. "I know I'm not the son you wanted me to be. I'm sorry I'm such a huge fucking failure."

Mamma closed her eyes, blinking away the sadness filling her gaze as I told her those words. My head fell to her hand and I whispered, "I just wanted to help you, Mamma. Even as a kid, with Papa beating you, I always wanted to protect you, to keep you safe… to

357

save you from having such a shit life. But I know all I am to you now is a letdown. I ain't the sports star like Aust. I ain't like that young sweet kid in the next room that you just know is gonna be somebody someday..." I choked on a breath and met her eyes again, moving my finger to brush away the fresh warm tears from her cheek and the damp hair from her face. "But I love you all the same, Mamma. I love you so much that I don't know how to deal with all this shit you're going through, this fucking disease. I just can't stand what's happening to you. I can't stand not being able to do shit about it. I've always protected us all, but I can't protect you from this... and I can't fucking handle it." I squeezed my mamma's hand tighter and paused so I could breathe. "And I ain't sure what the hell I'll do when you leave me... when you leave us all..." A sob ripped from my chest as I thought of what it'd be like to live in a world where she didn't exist and it fucking broke me.

Mamma's breathing increased, and as I looked at her face, even though her muscles couldn't move, I saw the grief in her expression... I saw the gutting truth that she didn't want to leave us either... that it was eating her that she had no other choice but to slowly fade away.

"I ain't sure how to do this life without you, Mamma. I've fought for so long to keep us going, to keep you going, that I don't know what the hell I'll do when you go... how I'll cope..."

I cried an age on this bed with my mamma's hand so weakly in mine. I didn't think I could move from sitting here, just holding

Mamma's hand, but Gio pounded on our trailer door, telling me we had to leave.

Wiping at my cheeks, I stood and washed Mamma's face with the wet cloth I kept beside her bed. Leaning down, I kissed her on her forehead and whispered, "Ti voglio bene, mamma… sempre."

Just before I left, I moved to her old record player and switched it on. "Ave Maria" immediately began playing from the speaker.

Walking to the door, I left without ever looking back.

And I never saw her again…

*****

"Shh…" Ally whispered in my ear as she rocked me, crying into my hands.

Lifting my face, I met Ally's sympathetic gaze and said, "I never got to say goodbye, Ally… I never fucking got to say goodbye to Mamma…" Louder cries burst from my mouth and I fought just to breathe through the racking guilt.

"I was selfish… so fucking selfish, and I ran, I ran and left her all alone, left them all alone. She must have been so afraid for me, so worried about where I was as she laid there unable to get up and come find me. Because she always worried about me, Al. Even as she was dying, years of slowly wasting away, I didn't give her any peace. What

359

the fuck was I thinking? She died in that hospital room without me there to tell her I loved her, to tell her to finally leave this shitty life and be at peace… and that I'd miss her for the rest of my life… Christ, Ally, how the fuck do I get past that? There's no going back and I don't know how to go on."

Ally's tears splashed on my head and she said in a cracked voice, "She knew you loved her, baby… she knew that one day you'd be someone."

"But she didn't live to see any of it, did she? All she knew of me was disappointment. She died thinking that all she'd raised was a piece of shit coke dealing son. The guilt… the guilt of that just fucking rips me apart. She must have died thinking she'd failed as my mamma… but the truth was, I'd failed as a son…

"Axel…" Ally went to speak, but I looked up at her and said, "I don't even know what it was like when she passed. I've never been able to ask Austin about it. I don't know how she looked, what time she died, what was said. I can't ever forgive myself for it… for as long as I live, I'll never forgive myself."

All the color drained from Ally's face and her arms tightened around me. Then she opened her mouth and confessed quietly, "I was there, Axel…"

Still trying to stop my chest from suffocating me, I didn't understand what she meant. Ally's shaking hands pressed on my cheeks and she explained, "Baby, I was there when your mamma died… I saw her… I was in the room as she took her last breath."

Confusion made me freeze. Ally's face broke into soft cries. "I've wanted to tell you for so long that I was with Austin and Levi when your mamma passed. We were all at the hospital for Lexi when she relapsed and your mamma was brought in. Austin almost broke having his mamma dying and his soulmate fading away. He couldn't cope, so we all stayed to support him and Levi."

All I could do was stare at Ally as she spoke.

Fresh tears filled her eyes. "You could never talk about her and I was afraid if I mentioned it, it would chase you away. But I was there, *querido*. I was there when she passed."

Unsure how to react to what she was saying, I asked, "Was it peaceful? Was she in pain? I can't bear the thought of her fighting death, desperately trying to live."

Ally's lips pursed as she fought not to break down further. Then she added, "Your mamma was sleeping peacefully and then she just drifted away… it was painless, Axel. She looked like she was sleeping… she looked beautiful… like an angel…"

The image of my mamma's beautiful sleeping face filled my mind, and unable to hold it back, I collapsed into Ally's lap, shedding five years of pent up grief. I cried until my throat and chest were raw and aching. The whole time, Ally just held me in her arms, stroking back my hair and crying with me… still fucking treading water beside me.

"I wanted to tell her goodbye, and now she's gone it's impossible…" I croaked, purging my guilt.

Ally's cheek pressed on my head and she whispered, "Death isn't goodbye; it's simply goodbye for now."

My lungs paused in breathing and I raised my head to look right into her dark eyes. "Do you really believe that? That this isn't the end?"

Ally stroked back my hair. "With every part of my heart."

I don't know how long I stayed wrapped in her arms, but when I finally lifted my head, my chest felt lighter. And as I looked into Ally's loving eyes, my hands on her perfect face, I knew my mamma's prayer for me had come true…

Io prego perché tu possa trovare la tua luce, mio figlio smarrito… I pray you find your light, my lost son….

I had.

"*La Mia luce…*" I murmured through my scratched and raw throat. Ally's face softened in adoration. The next words I spoke came straight from my heart without any conscious thought. "*Ti amo, carina*… I love you so damn much that sometimes I can't fucking take it."

Ally dragged in a shocked breath, and as her bottom lip quivered, she leaned down to kiss my dry lips and murmured in reply, "I love you too, Axel. So so much. You're all of my heart."

Fuck. She loved me too…

Our kiss became deeper, until I pulled back. Feeling exhausted, I laid my head on Ally's lap, my eyes looking straight up at her face.

As I watched her happily stroke my face, I thought over mamma's prayer and I froze.

Ally, sensing something was wrong, asked, "What is it, baby?"

Shaking my head in disbelief, I said, "Just something that came to mind."

Ally's dark eyebrows pulled down. "Tell me," she urged.

I glanced over to the marble angel of my mamma and said, "Do you believe in fate?"

Still looking confused, she entertained me and shrugged. "I don't know, maybe. I think sometimes things happen that seem so planned out by an outside force that what happens can't be simply coincidence." Her head tilted to the side. "Why do you ask, baby?"

Clearing my throat, and feeling pretty damn stupid for saying it, I decided to tell her any way. "My mamma used to pray that one day I would find my light, the thing to change me, to *save* me. She would always call me her lost son, and her biggest wish was that I would find my way."

Ally smiled and reached out to take my hand, playing with my fingers. "But I didn't. In fact, things only got worse. She died and I went to prison."

"Axel..." Ally said in sympathy, but I stopped whatever she was going to say by holding up my hand.

"Ally, when I went to prison, it forced me from the Heighters, which led to me being shanked."

Ally blinked fast and I rushed to make her understand. "*Carina*, if I hadn't gone through all that... all that pain, that rage... I would never have talked to the nurse in the infirmary about my tattoo designs. I'd never have been forced into the art class to rein in my anger. I wouldn't have fallen in love with clay sculpting, that then led to my marble sculpting, into which I poured my pain. I would never have met Vin, who published pictures of my works, who then took my marble angel to an exhibition at the Met—"

"Where I saw it in a magazine and flew to New York to see it in reality. Where I then wrote articles and journals on your works and methods—"

"Where Vin read them, and when he went to put the show together, hired you to curate it… the woman that was friends with my brother… the woman who understood my soul before I even did…" I took a calming breath, "the woman who was in the room with my mamma as she passed when I couldn't be… that same woman who answered my mamma's prayer… she became my light, she saved Mamma's lost son."

"Axel… I… I don't know what to say…" Ally whispered, as more tears fell from her eyes. I pulled her to my chest and breathed in the lavender shampoo scent of her hair.

"I always wanted this," she said tightly, "I always wanted this kind of love, this intense love… I just never realized it could be so much more… *until you*."

I closed my eyes as she said those words and for the first time ever I felt… unburdened.

I fixed my attention on my mamma's marble statue and said quietly, "Ave Maria."

Ally tensed against my chest, and asked, "What?"

"The angel, its title should be "Ave Maria.""

"Axel," Ally sighed, "It's beautiful… it's perfect."

Ally pressed kisses all along my neck and I closed my eyes, relaxing at her touch. "The broken angel is my mamma in this life. Trapped in a body she couldn't escape from, praying for death rather than living in that hell. The ashes she's holding are symbolic for death."

Ally's lips had left my neck, her body so still. "And the other side?"

I smiled, almost feeling the warm sun on my mamma's face. "That's the next life, heaven, paradise, whatever you wanna call it. That's my mamma waking after death, fully healed, feeling the bright sun on her healthy body… free… it was always my dream from when she got sick. That she would once again be free."

A sense of peace filled me as I looked at the statue and I took a deep breath. All the titles and information were given. I'd gotten through it. The exhibition was finally complete.

"Axel?" Ally said.

"Mmm?" I murmured, my attention fixing on the bright stars of Orion's belt through the glass roof.

"It's time to tell your brothers about your sculptures."

I waited for the apprehension, the shame and the dread. For once, it didn't come. As I stared up at the stars, I realized I was ready to tell them about the real reason I was in Seattle, and what I'd really been doing with my life.

"Yeah," I said in response. "I'll tell them tomorrow."

I could feel Ally smile against my chest, and she whispered, "*Te amo, querido.*"

A rush, an almost crippling feeling of love ran through me, filling my every muscle and I whispered back, "*Ti amo, carina. Sempre.*"

Chapter Twenty

Axel

As I sanded the final curve of the hand, then washed the Carrara marble down with water, I stood back on the riverbank and exhaled.

This was my favorite piece yet.

I'd worked around the clock to get this done over the past week, the quickest I'd ever completed a sculpture, but I had no choice. I had to get the image from my head and into marble… I needed this piece to be seen forever. I needed it to complete my first show. It was the perfect end to the journey Ally had created.

As the afternoon wind whipped around me, I covered the sculpture with its tarp, padlocking it to the plinth and texted Vin that I'd finished. Only he knew I was adding it to the exhibition last minute. He had the text boards made up in private, the title board, colored backdrop and everything else I needed to make this perfect.

A beep came through my cell, telling me that he was on his way with his men. I told him where it was and that I'd be out. More than that, I trusted him to make the placement of it in the gallery.

Vin assured me everything would be fine and Ally would never know of it until opening night. It was my surprise for her.

My soul's gift to hers.

Moving into my studio, I smirked at the still messed up linen on bed. Every morning I'd usually wake up and make my bed before anything—years of being in prison giving me habits too hard to shake. But after last night, after making love to Ally last night, her telling me she loved me over and over in my ear as we came together... I couldn't bring myself to change a thing.

Seeing the Camino keys on the workstation, I walked over, picked them up, as well as my smokes and made my way out to my car. Nerves were shredding my stomach. The thought of telling Austin and Lev all about my sculptures; more than that, about my opening tomorrow night had me almost puking.

What the hell would they think? *Me.* A sculptor with his own show in a real fucking museum.

A new wave of something new hit me as I imagined their happy reaction… relief, excitement… *want*. Fuck, that was it; I *wanted* them to be proud of me. I wanted them to finally see me as more than just their older brother who'd only ever shown skill in pushing coke.

As I weaved through the streets of Seattle, I thought back to when Ally told me she'd be leaving to do her next commission after my show. The thought of not having her next to me every single day made every part of me fucking ache. I wanted her to stay. I wanted her to stay here in Seattle with me.

I had to figure out a way of making it happen. I couldn't let her leave. We'd come too fucking far.

As I drew closer to Austin's house, the nerves returned making my hands shake. I laughed that I was shaking. I was a damn pussy.

In minutes I'd parked up the Camino and walked through the front door… then immediately stopped dead at seeing Levi and Austin sat on the stairs, with my bag full of clothes sitting at their feet.

Both of my brothers had their heads down, but when they heard the door open, Austin looked up, a stony expression on his face.

"What's all this?" I asked, feeling the temperature in the room drop about fifty degrees.

Austin got to his feet and walked over to stand at the bottom of the stairs, arms crossed over his chest.

When his eyes met mine, I could see how much pain he was in. I almost moved forward to wrap my arm around his shoulders to ask him what was wrong, but the shitty way he was looking at me kept me rooted to the floor.

Austin lifted his foot, and rested it on top of my bag. "Went to the fish market this morning, Axe, the one you said you were working at."

The blood drained from my face.

"Yeah, Axe. The market where the managers had no fucking idea who I was talking about."

Austin looked down at Levi. Levi kept his head down, his hands gripping his hair.

I opened my mouth to explain, but—

"I couldn't believe it, Axe, so I went to every market I could find. None of them knew you. None of them. One of them remembered seeing someone of your description. He said he thought he'd seen you hanging around, but you sure as hell weren't working."

Austin clawed at his dark hair, his eyes shining. Meeting my eyes again, he said, "I thought there had to be some mistake. There *had* to be, because my brother had changed. He'd got out of prison five years early and was doing real good. He was a different guy than the one who used to be

371

Heighter tight." He pulled in a ragged breath and his face flushed red with his pain.

I stepped forward. "I—"

"*Then* I get home, fucking talking myself out of what I prayed wasn't true, and I go into your room, hoping you'd be there to explain all this shit. You weren't, as always. So I started going through your stuff, looking for some reason why you'd lied to me. Lied to all of us for fucking months!"

Austin reached into the back pocket of his jeans and pulled out the second bag of coke I'd bought after his game. I must have left it in my jeans.

My stomach fell, and I instantly knew what they were thinking.

"You're dealing again, Axe? After everything?" Austin's face contorted in a mix of both anger and pain. He threw the bag of coke at my feet.

I struggled to breathe as I stared at it. As I looked up, Austin was staring at me, all anger gone, just crushing disappointment on his face. But I couldn't speak. I couldn't get my head around how I'd come here today to tell them about my show. Instead my kid brothers were asking me to explain why I wasn't at the market, why I had this coke, and of course they immediately thought the worst.

Austin suddenly pushed my duffel bag to my feet. "I came to see you today to tell you that you're gonna be an uncle, a *Zio*, Axe. Lexi's pregnant. We've been trying for two years but because of the damage to her body through her anorexia, they weren't sure we'd be able to ever have kids. She woke me up this morning to tell me I was gonna be a papa. A fucking papa, Axe. Against the odds, we're having a baby. It's a fucking miracle… and the only two people I couldn't wait to tell were you and Lev."

My heart beat faster… Austin was gonna be a papa.

A fucking thrilled smile pulled on my lips, but Austin didn't see it, he was too busy glaring at the floor.

"I can't have you here no more, Axe. I got more important things than you to consider now." His dark eyes met mine. "I need you to leave. I can't have my baby, my *wife*, dragged into all the dealing and gang shit… my kid's gotta have a better life than we did… they've gotta be safe. We all need to be safe."

Levi lifted his head, his eyes bloodshot, his face pale and he rushed up the stairs.

"Lev… I can exp—"

Levi immediately stopped on the stairs, but never looked back. "You swore to me you wouldn't do anything to take you away from us again. I let you in, I opened my heart to you again, and you have to fuck it all up! I let you in,

373

Axe… and now I've lost you again…" he snapped and disappeared from sight. Austin turned his back on me and walked up after Levi.

Feeling real fear run through my veins, I stepped forward and called, "Aust…" but my foot landed on the bag of coke, busting the fucking thing open all over the floor.

Austin, hearing the bag split, sighed and, without looking back, said, "Just leave, Axe. Just fucking leave…"

My entire body filled with ice at how cold those words sounded coming from his mouth. I looked down at the mess of coke at my feet and felt nothing but shame… shame that I'd had a moment of weakness and bought this coke all those weeks ago.

But I was so fucking angry they hadn't heard me out.

They didn't even fucking let me speak.

Turning on my heel, I left my bag of clothes where it was and fucking raced outta the house, my head reeling.

What the fuck was I thinking in coming back here?

I was done. So fucking done with trying to make shit right.

I drove my Camino fast through the falling rain—a perfect fucking reflection of my mood—and headed for my studio. In my rush to tell Austin and Levi about my art, I'd brought nothing with me, not even my damn wallet or cell. I was getting them and then getting the fuck outta Seattle. And I wanted Ally to come with me. Just her, me, and the fucking road.

Letting the heavy metal music from my stereo fuel my rising anger, I didn't realize for a good few miles that the black car was tailing me. Frowning, my suspicion back, I turned down random streets just to see if it would follow—this time it did.

Feeling my pulse spike, I narrowed my eyes and picked up speed. The car followed, its bumper almost rear ending me.

"Fuck," I hissed under my breath. There was only one fucker I knew would be after me like this: Remo.

SHIT!

I pulled my car to a stop on a quiet road, a pit in my stomach as I realized this was it. He was here for my blood. The heavy rain bounced off my windshield like bullets and I cut the music, eyes glued on my hands.

I always thought I'd die at the hands of my crew. But what was tearing me apart right now was picturing Ally. I couldn't even call her to tell her goodbye. FUCK! I'd just gotten my shit together, finally making some fucking headway in my life… and now…

The sound of a car door opening made me sit up straighter, and for the first time ever, I felt fear. Real fear.

Today I had something to lose, the thought of leaving Ally behind, fucking terrified me.

Wrenching open my car door, I jumped outta the car just in time to see Remo Marino strutting my way. He looked older. Had gained weight, gained lines on his face, but he was still the intimidating fuck he'd always been. My stomach dropped… This fucker had been trailing me for days.

I stood my ground and watched as Remo's lips pulled into a smirk. "Fucking, *ragazzo!*" he said, faking a laugh and smile. "Almost didn't recognize you with the fucking hippy hair and beard covering your Heighter tattoos on your neck. It's taken me a few days to make sure the lead I was given wasn't bullshit." He waved his hand at me. "And your stidda, Axe? You lost that too?" he nodded in approval, "You done a real good job of hiding yourself from me. Almost had me thinking my intel was wrong. But when I saw Austin and Lev again, I knew for sure it was you."

Grinding my teeth at him mentioning my brothers, I spat, "What the fuck are you doing here, Rem?"

Remo dropped his shit eating grin. "I'm here to pay my family's debt, *ragazzo*. You know that… you must have been expecting it. You know the street code: blood for blood."

"You're on the run, Rem, fucking wanted for all kinds of charges, yet you come all the way here for me? The feds will have tracked you crossing state lines. You'll be going down for life."

Remo spread his hands wide. "Already on borrowed time, Axe. Gonna be going down for the rest of my life... what's one more felony when there's no chance of release anyway?"

Remo's eyes narrowed as he closed in on me. "But you, you got my cousin killed. Your fucking best friend! How could you, *ragazzo*? Gio fucking loved you."

"I was protecting my family," I said tightly. Remo even nodded his head like he understood.

"I get it. And now I'm avenging mine."

We stared at each other in the rain for what felt like hours, when, suddenly Remo rushed me, his fist connecting with my face, before he tackled me back against my car. Managing to push him away, I hit him back, Remo facing me with blood running down his face. He smiled and my blood ran cold. The bastard was insane.

Rushing forward, dragging us into the middle of the road, I went to strike the fucker's face again, when the sound of a gun going off broke through the night.

For a second I stood still, just staring at Remo stood before me... then as my eyes traveled down I saw a gun held out in his hand, his gun with its barrel pressed against my stomach. A sudden sharp pain sliced through my stomach stealing my breath, and blood was beginning to soak through my shirt. Remo stepped back, and lifting my hand to my stomach, I pulled it back and saw bright red blood coating my palm. My legs buckled beneath me and I smacked onto the asphalt.

The sound of sirens wailed distantly in the background as Remo stood above me and spat on my face. My lungs felt like they were in a vacuum as I tried to get up… but I couldn't move my legs.

"Blood for blood, Axe," Remo said again and disappeared from my sight.

Laying the back of my head flat to the pavement, I stared up at the gray skies, slews of rain drumming on my body. Pictures of Austin and Levi ran through my head and I felt my eyes prick with tears.

I'd never see them again… never got to tell them one last time how much I fucking loved them both…

Time seemed to slow and my thoughts drifted back to when we were kids. To a promise I'd made my mamma… I was reliving it like it was yesterday…

*****

"Dormi, Dormi, O Bel Bambin…"

Levi laid in my arms, wrapped in his faded blue blanket, his wide gray eyes staring up at me as I rocked back and forth on the bedroom floor. Quietly, I sang his favorite lullaby, a Christmas song, the one that always calmed him down, the one that helped him drift off and forget this horrible world for a while.

"Perche piangi, o mio tresor?
Dolce amor, dolce amor,
Fa la nanna, o caro figlio,
Tanto bel, tanto bel,
Fa la nanna, o caro figlio."

As I trailed off the last line, I heard soft breathing and I sighed. Leaning down, I pressed a kiss to my baby brother's soft forehead.
He was finally asleep.

Taking a huge inhale of breath, I leaned back against my bedroom wall and held Levi tightly in my arms. As I glanced down at his sleeping face, I closed my eyes and prayed to God that all this fear would end soon. That Papa would stop coming home drunk, that he'd stop hitting Mamma… and that he'd stop trying to 'shut up' Levi because he couldn't stand his crying.

Every night I would bring Levi into our cramped room. Every night I would bathe him, feed him, change him and rock him to sleep

379

by singing that lullaby… all so my mamma could stop papa from hurting him when he came slamming through the door, looking for a reason to fight.

I prayed to God every night that one day Papa would just stop coming home. That he'd leave us alone so we could all live in peace.

Just as I'd let myself relax some, the sounds of footsteps came running along the narrow hallway, and a second later, Austin ran through the door. His face was flushed red and his dark brown eyes were wide. Every part of me froze and I heard the front door slam closed.

"He's back," Austin said, fighting back his fear. He was only eight, I was eleven, and Levi, barely a few months old. "And he's real drunk tonight. I watched him swaying down the park road. He was screaming at everyone he saw."

My stomach fell and, looking at Levi again, I jumped when I heard my mamma scream from the other room.

Levi's eyes snapped open at the noise and his little face screwed up as he began crying in my arms.

My gaze met Austin who was frozen in the doorway. "Take our fratellino," I ordered. He ran forward and took Levi from my hands, then slumped down to our tiny shared bed.

A crash sounded in the TV room and Austin looked up at me, tears filling his eyes too. He looked so helpless that a lump clogged my throat. "He's gonna hurt her again, isn't he?" he said in a shaky voice, "then he's gonna hurt us."

Pulling in a deep breath, I said, "He won't. I swear it." I pointed at my two younger brothers sitting lost and scared on that bed and I said, "Look after Lev, yeah? Try and keep him quiet."

Austin nodded his head as I left the room, pulling the door to a close. My heart beat fast in my chest as the sound of my mamma's screams came drifting down the hallway.

I could hear my papa cussing and my mamma begging him to stop. As I reached the end of the hallway, I saw my papa pinning my mamma to the floor, her face bloody as her hands tried to push my papa away.

Her eyes were closed, but like she could feel me standing here watching, they opened. Her gaze met mine and she slowly shook her head. I knew she wanted me to go away, I knew she wanted me to run and hide. But I couldn't. He was hurting her, and I knew he'd come after my brothers next. I had to protect them. I had to make him want to hit just me.

Levi screamed from our bedroom just as Papa kicked Mamma in the stomach. Hearing the cries from the baby, my papa whipped round, his face fierce.

"That fucking kid!" he slurred, heading toward me.

He was going for my brothers… I couldn't let him get to my brothers.

Stepping forward, my papa saw me and he tried to push me out of the way. "Move!" he snarled. But I didn't. I looked to my mamma gasping for breath on the floor, her body curled in, I heard my baby brother crying in the bedroom, and heard Austin begging for him to stop.

Meeting my papa's dark eyes, trying not to shake, I stepped forward again and watched a slow grin spread on his face. Nothing was said. Nothing was said as he raised his fist and hit me across my face. Nothing was said as he lifted me off the floor and threw me against the wall, my back cracking the thin plaster.

I tried to block it all out. I focused on my mamma and brothers crying... I focused on my papa using me as a punch bag so he wouldn't go near them.

I didn't know how long it lasted, this beating, but it felt like forever. Eventually Papa's breathing slowed and his hits became weak and slow. He dropped me to the floor and I could taste blood running down my mouth.

I lay still praying this was the end of his anger, when the front door opened and slammed shut.

He'd gone… at least for now.

"Mio caro," my mamma croaked and I lifted my head enough to see her pulling herself to her feet. Using my hands, I made myself stand and moved across the small room to help her walk.

"Help me to my room, mio caro," she said on a whisper and, wrapping my arm around her waist, I helped her into her bedroom and into her bed.

I went into the bathroom and wet a cloth, bringing it back to wipe the blood off her face.

As I cleaned up her swollen lip, my mamma's shaking hand lifted to run down my face. I flinched as her fingertips touched a cut on my cheek and tears fell down her cheeks.

"I'm so sorry, mio caro," she said painfully but I shook my head.

"It's okay, Mamma, I'm not hurt."

A sad smile pulled on her lips and her fingers ran through my hair. "Such a brave boy. You are hurt, yet you show no fear or pain."

I pulled the cloth away from her lip so she wouldn't feel my hands shake. I didn't her want to know I was scared... that my face hurt. "I'm not hurt, mamma. I swear it."

Mamma silently watched me and, all the time she cried I tried to not to cry too. I knew if I did it would break her heart, and I didn't want to break her heart... she was already sad enough.

I only ever wanted to make her smile again.

I missed her smile.

"There, Mamma, you're all clean now," I said and Mamma lay back on her bed, holding her bruised stomach, but her sad eyes never left mine. I turned to go wash up in the bathroom when she reached out and grabbed my arm.

As I looked back, she said, "Axel, mio caro, you don't always have to be so tough, so strong."

Looking at my mamma broken on the bed, I said, "But I do. I have to protect you all from Papa no matter what."

Mamma quietly gasped. "That is not your job, mio caro."

I didn't say anything and the trailer went silent. But then I heard Austin quietly singing Mamma's favorite lullaby to Levi and I nodded my head. "Si, Mamma. This is my job. I need to look after you all, and I promise I always will… I'll never let anyone hurt you or my brothers ever again. I will always keep you safe…"

*****

Thick tears fell down my cheeks, mixing with the cold rain as that memory played in my mind.

I will always keep you safe…

As I pictured Axel and Levi, I suddenly felt at peace. With me gone, they'd be safe. There'd be no more ties to our past. With me gone Austin's new family would be safe and Levi wouldn't be in any more pain.

I will always keep you safe…

I smiled as the rain fell harder. I'd finally done it. They'd finally be safe.

Closing my eyes, numbness taking hold, I saw Ally with her chin on her fist, her hair pushed to one side as she smiled down at me on the bed. I fucking thanked God in that second that I'd had her… that I'd had her, even if it was only for a short while. At least I got to feel what that kind of love was like, even if it was just a brief moment of time.

I tried to hold on to the picture of Ally's face, until I couldn't hold on to Ally's picture no more... until everything faded to nothing.

Chapter Twenty-One

Ally

"You haven't seen him either, Vin?"

"Not since yesterday," he replied.

"Okay, thanks," I said and ended the call. As I stared at the floor, a peculiar feeling turned in my stomach.

I'd waited at Axel's studio for hours, but he didn't show. I'd tried his cell, but the battery must have died. Vin hadn't seen him, so I assumed he was at Austin's house.

A whisper of a smile spread on my lips as I thought of how nervous Axel was about telling his brothers about his show, his art… what he'd been doing for years. In my purse I had their invites for the opening tomorrow night, one for Austin, Levi and Lexi. They had to be there. I still wasn't sure if Axel would make an appearance. I'd guessed not, he was still against people knowing who he was, but his family should see his work… after all, they were the source of his inspiration.

In minutes I'd turned into Austin's driveway and parked up my car. I rapped on the door and after a short wait in the rain, Austin opened the door.

Ducking in from the downpour, I rushed into the hallway shaking off my trench coat. "It's damn soaking out there!" I yelled and finally looked to Austin.

His face was pale and he was staring at me with sad eyes. "You okay, Aust?" I said and glanced upstairs. Levi was walking down, his eyes rimmed with red.

My stomach fell.

"What?" I whispered. Lexi walked in from the kitchen. "What's wrong? Where's Axel?"

Shivers ran down my spine at the way they were all watching me, when Austin put his hand on my arm. "He ain't who you think he is, Al." His voice was hoarse from what sounded like hours of crying.

My gaze darted around the three of them and I asked, "What the hell are you talking about?"

"Axe," Austin said, "He's been pushing coke again."

Feeling like the floor had vanished from beneath me, I said, "What? What the hell are you talking about? He would never do that again."

Austin shook his head. "I'm sorry, Al, but it's true. I didn't wanna fucking believe it either, but I went down to that fish market he was working at as part of his parole and they hadn't even heard of him. He lied, Al. He's been lying all along."

"No!" I said shaking my head, trying to imagine what the hell must have happened here this afternoon. Austin held up his hand.

"I found a bag of coke in his room, Al. Cocaine! He's been dealing since he got here, and worse, he brought that shit into my house. I asked him to leave. I can't have that shit around us no more. I can't have my family involved in that kind of life no more."

A mixture of dread and sympathy flooded my chest and my hand flew over my mouth. "You... you asked him to leave?"

Austin nodded his head.

"Did you even let him speak to you? Did you give him a chance to explain the coke, the market?"

Austin's eyes dropped. When I looked to Levi he dropped his head too.

"You didn't, did you?" I asked. Tears began filling my eyes. My God, he came here today to tell them all about his art and they'd thrown him out and accused him of dealing because they'd found a bastard bag of coke... that damn coke he'd only ever bought because he was drowning in this new life… drowning in their rejection of him, of *my* rejection of him.

"God…" I cried and pressed my hand to my forehead.

Austin stepped forward but I stepped back. "Where is he now? I haven't been able to get in touch with him all day."

A flash of worry crossed Austin's face, but it quickly turned to stone when he said, "I told him to leave. He did. He didn't even take his things, he just cut and run." I choked on a breath. "Al, he'll be long gone. It's what he does when the shit hits the fan. He runs away."

Anger swirled within me, and I backed toward the door. "You have no idea," I said in devastation to them all. "You have no idea what he's done for y'all, no idea how much he's sacrificed and how much he's changed his life."

Austin's eyebrows pulled down at my words, but before he could speak, I reached into my purse and pulled out the invites. If Axel wasn't able to tell his brothers what he'd been doing, then I would.

Slapping the invitations on the side table, I looked each of them in the eye and said, "Invites for my gallery opening tomorrow night. You need to be there."

Austin shook his head and Lexi walked to join him at his side. "Al, I'm really happy and proud of you but, fuck, I just don't think the timing's right to—"

"You *need* to be there," I said interrupting him and Lexi frowned at me.

"Why Ally?" she asked and my anger dropped some. Shit, I could never be mad at Lexi. She hadn't done anything but accept Axel into her home, and out of everyone, she had cause to reject him.

"Just please, Lex. Please be there… there's something y'all need to see."

Reaching for my keys, I turned the doorknob, just as Austin said, "I know you liked him, Al, but Axel's always been this way. He's always been drawn to the darker side of life, the illegal shit. I'm just sorry you got hurt in all this."

Glancing back at Austin with incredulity, I replied, "I didn't just like him, Austin. I'm head over heels in love with him. He's changed my life *in every way* for the better, and I'm real sorry that you are so blinded by his past that you can't see him for the damn honorable guy he is today." Tapping my hand on the invites, I demanded, "Be there tomorrow night."

As I rushed out to my car, I pulled out my cell and dialed Axel's number again. It went straight to voicemail. I pressed END and stared out of the wet windshield.

Tears ran down my cheeks and my hands trembled with panic. Closing my eyes, I rested my head back against the headrest and whispered, "Axel… where the hell have you gone?"

*****

The following night I stood in the bathroom of the museum, staring at myself in the mirror. I looked tired and pale; the effects of feeling like my heart had been shattered.

Axel hadn't appeared. It was starting to become more than apparent that he'd gone. He'd actually left me. Part of me screamed that it wasn't possible, that he *couldn't* have left me, even though Austin and Levi were convinced it was his usual M.O. He loved me… he wouldn't leave me behind.

But then another part of me said it was entirely plausible. He'd been rejected by his brothers *again*. Of course he wouldn't want to stay. How much rejection could one person take? But I thought he would have at least called me. Told me he was leaving for a while, that he loved me and, at some point, he would come back to me.

On top of that, Vin had been in the Gallery all day, working on something in a cornered-off section at the back… on opening night! I was livid. I was exhausted, and I was racked with worry. I had no idea what he was up to,

391

but as a patron and the sole funder of this exhibition, I didn't really have a choice.

Hearing the hustle and bustle of museum and University stakeholders, fans and students alike, waiting for the show to begin, I forced myself to stand straight and shook my shoulders.

You can do this, you're a professional, I tried to convince myself.

Brushing back my long dark hair, styled straight and hanging down my back, I then ran my hands down my black knee length column dress. Finally, I checked my Louboutins were free of dust.

I was set.

Moving out of the bathroom, I walked to Bridgette, the museum director, and nodded to her that I was ready. I scanned the crowd for Vin, wondering where the hell he could be, but there was no sign. My hands were damp as I raced through an introduction in my head.

Bridgette introduced me as the curator, and I stepped up to the mic, a sea of eager eyes all looking my way.

"Good evening, everyone," I began. My name is Aliyana Lucia, and I am pleased to be here tonight to celebrate the inspiring and truly once-in-a-lifetime talent of Elpidio."

I paused when I saw Lexi, Levi and Austin enter the gallery, along with Molly, Rome, Cass and JD. My heart fell at how sad and forlorn the two Carillo brothers looked. I could see that the pain of their confrontation with Axel yesterday was weighing heavily on their hearts.

Focusing back on the crowd, I continued. "Elpidio began his journey with Carrara marble only a few years ago. In that time he has become a master in his field, capturing our hearts with his soul shattering depictions of despair, grief, guilt; indeed every facet of raw emotion and the human condition.

"Tonight you will see works that have yet to be published in magazines, and you will also see recent sculptures that will…" tears filled my eyes as I thought of the boy crying bullets, "that will challenge the emotions of even the most stoic among you."

Taking a deep breath, I added, "Tonight, you will also be able to read what inspired the creation of his flawless sculptures. Elpidio is notoriously reclusive, and as such, won't be making an appearance tonight," the crowd murmured in disappointment, "but he has shared with me his inspirations for the pieces which I'm sure will both astound and inspire you."

I nodded at Bridgette who was standing by the large red velvet curtains that would draw back to reveal the show. Turning back to the crowd, I said, "It is my pleasure to present to you, Elpidio!"

Bridgette drew the curtains, revealing the bright white of the show and I moved aside as the crowd eagerly filtered into the space.

Forcing myself to stay strong, I watched Austin, Levi, Lexi, Molly, Rome, Cass and JD approach me.

Molly walked over and wrapped me in her arms. I had to fight back the lump in my throat at the heartfelt comfort from my best friend. My heart was broken and it was taking everything in my power to not give in to deep sadness.

Axel should be here. He should be seeing how many people have turned up to view his show. He should be seeing his family's reaction.

"I'm so proud of you," Molly said and moved aside to let Rome hug me too. He hadn't said anything about Axel running off. I could see in his expression that he'd always expected him to fall back into his old ways.

All the gang congratulated me on the success of the show, but I only had eyes for Levi and Austin. Austin saw me watching them and asked, "Why did you want us to be here so bad, Al?" His voice was still raspy and he looked so tired. My heart clenched when I thought of how much kicking Axel out must have hurt him. Austin loved Axel, it was all a huge damn mess.

"It's about Axel, Aust," I said and walk forward put my hand on his and Levi's backs. Ushering them forward toward the gallery, both brothers were frowning at me in confusion.

Stopping at the entrance way, I turned to them, my other friends trailing at the back, and said, "You were right, Austin, Axel didn't come to Seattle to work at the fish market as part of his parole." Levi tensed, as did Austin, then I added, "But he also wasn't selling drugs either..." I dropped my head and huffed a humorless laugh. "You see, Axel is exceptional... he's so talented and amazing, yet never felt he could tell you. He felt he didn't deserve any praise or acclaim after what he'd put y'all through."

"Praise for what?" Austin pushed. Levi nodded in agreement,

"Praise for his work."

"What work? Al, what the fuck are you talking about?" Austin said curtly. Rather than tell him, I moved aside to face the gallery and gestured to the stunning show with my hand.

"This work, Austin... Axel... Axel is Elpidio..."

I scanned the shocked faces of my friends and watched as they took in the exquisiteness of the marble sculptures.

Lexi stepped forward, her hand over her mouth and said, "Axel... Axel created all these... Axel is... Elpidio...?"

Her green eyes brimmed with tears and she whipped her head to Austin. "My God, Austin… Axel did all this… and we all thought… oh God!" she cried.

"You didn't lie," Molly said. I met her knowing gaze.

"No, I fell in love with Elpidio… it just so happened that he was Axel Carillo too; both the hero and the villain."

Molly's expression filled with sympathy and Rome stood beside her gaping at the packed gallery.

"Come see," I said to my friends, holding back my tears. Walking forward, we came face to face with the marble boys pointing up at the stars. I heard Austin suck in a sharp breath.

"*Stelle*," I said, revealing the title.

Austin took a step forward, gazing down at the marble boys lying on their backs, smiles on their faces. "Fuck…" he said through a tight throat. "That's us," he looked to Levi who was pale and rooted to the floor. Levi was completely dumbfounded by it all. "Lev, that's you as a baby."

Lexi wrapped her arm around Austin like he needed the support and she asked, "You used to look at the stars with Axel, baby? Like you do with me?"

Austin nodded, unable to tear his gaze away from the sculpture. "Yeah… Axe used to take us to the top of the trailer when my papa would come home drunk and hit my mamma." Austin's face scrunched up like he couldn't bear to remember those times, but he added, "He would make me look up at the stars and tell him the constellations… he would distract me so I didn't hear my mamma's screams." Austin looked to Levi, and wrapping an arm around his shoulder, he pointed to the baby. "That's you, Lev. At night, Axel would take you from Mamma so when Papa came home piss drunk, he wouldn't hurt you. Axel would keep you in our room, feed you, change and bathe you… fuck, he'd hold you all night long in his arms just in case papa came in for us. When the fighting got real bad, he'd take us both on the roof and we'd look at the stars…"

Levi's gray eyes were huge as he leaned forward to inspect the baby in Axel's arms. "He… he looked after me? Protected me when I was a baby?" Levi asked innocently. I watched as tears began dropping down their faces.

"I… I don't know why I forgot all that?" Austin said numbly. He looked at Levi, then his wife, "He practically raised Levi until papa left… and me… he was always looking after me."

Clearing my throat, my heart breaking at the love shining in their faces, I led them to Axel's newest piece. As I walked in front of Levi, I heard a painful whimper escape his mouth.

I stood in front of the sculpture and looked to my friends. Rome was running his hand down his face. "Shit," I caught him whisper to Molly who was studiously reading the text board.

"Hamartia," I announced, pointing at the statue.

"That's me," Levi claimed. I could see the agony on his face as he relieved that moment. "Shit, Aust, that's me and Axe when I was younger."

Austin was drinking in the piece with disbelieving eyes. "What does Hamaria mean?" he asked gruffly.

"Sin," Molly said from behind us and everyone turned to face her. She blushed as she realized she'd said it out loud. "It's Aristotelian philosophy. It means taking someone to a dark place, missing the mark, to err, or doing wrong is how it's normally interpreted today."

"Sin…" Levi said.

I heard Cass whistle low in her throat. "That's some powerful shit right there," she said quietly. I wanted to look to her, but I couldn't take my eyes off Levi. Tears were streaming down his handsome face.

As though sensing my stare, Levi looked to me and asked, "How, Al? How did he go from the Heighters, to prison… to this? How is it possible?"

Glancing away from his penetrating gaze, I debated how much to tell them. But deciding that secrets and lies had been the source of so much misunderstanding, I came clean with it all.

"Axel… went through some things when he was in prison."

"What things?" Austin snapped, his body stiffening in apprehension.

"Beatings, being ostracized by his former crew members. The Heighters inside branded him a turncoat. They pinned him down and blotted out his Stidda with a needle and ink." Austin paled and he squeezed Lexi tighter.

"A guy called Alessio was sent down to the same prison as him," I explained. Levi gasped, his eyes shooting to Austin.

"Did you know that, Aust? Did you know Alessio was inside too?"

Austin shook his head. "Ally, when—"

"Two years into his sentence. It was the reason he started refusing your visits. He was worried Alessio would get to you when you came back to Bama, so he cut off all ties."

Austin looked like he was going to be sick, so I decided to tell him everything at once. "Long story short, Alessio attacked him over Gio's death and Axel got hurt… bad.

They stabbed him in his neck, held him down and shanked him."

Lexi turned her head and nuzzled into Austin's chest. She cried.

"It's the reason he has long hair," I informed. "It hid the scar so you wouldn't ask questions."

"Christ…" Austin rasped.

"He nearly died," I said sadly. "He was in the infirmary for a real long time. He was so angry, so bitter at the world… so angry at himself for everything he'd done… especially for missing your mamma's death. To try and help him cope with his anger, they sent him to an art class. He was a natural, and quickly gained the favor of the teacher, who sent pictures of his first piece to Vin Galanti, a marble sculptor. He took Axel under his wing and the rest is history." I looked into the eyes of every single one of my friends and said, "He came to Seattle for this show. He just never felt he deserved it enough to tell y'all. He's crippled by guilt and shame."

"Austin," Levi croaked, unable to hold back his cries, "We were wrong. We made him leave and he hadn't done anything wrong!"

Austin was lock still, until his eyes snapped to mine. "But the coke I found?"

Dipping my head, I worked on not letting my anger show, but I snapped, "He bought it after the Seahawks game… when everyone ignored him… including me. I hadn't known he was Axel Carillo until that day. I'd met and fallen for Elpidio, then when he was introduced to me as Axel, I freaked out. I hurt him so badly."

"I knew I saw something between you that day," Molly suddenly said. I offered her a weak smile. "They way you both couldn't keep your eyes off each other… I should have put two and two together, but I never ever dreamed Axel could do this." She gestured in awe to the gallery of his works. "The talent he possesses is astounding."

I nodded and my tears came thick and fast. "I hurt him, Levi hurt him… all of us did, and he stupidly bought the drugs from some street gang. He just wanted to escape the pain for a while… he was so lost and reverted to what he knew best."

"But he didn't take the coke, did he?" Austin asked, knowingly.

"No… he didn't."

"Shit!" Levi said, "How do we tell him we're sorry? How do we get him back?"

Everyone looked as helpless as I felt, when Austin suddenly asked, "Which piece was his first? The one that got him recognized? Which one is it?"

Taking calm breath, I led them toward the angel, which was the study of many admirers. But I heard the moment the Carillo's had seen it. Sobs and anguished cries ripped from their throats.

"It's Mamma…" Levi said, his voice breaking.

"It's called *Ave Maria*," I explained. "It's how he saw your mamma in this life…" I pointed to the other side of the sculpture, "and how he dreamed she would look meeting the next."

Reaching out, Austin crushed Levi to his chest as they both broke down at the feet of the marble depiction of their mother.

It was heartbreaking, gut wrenching and I couldn't take looking at it. Turning away, I tried to breathe despite my tightly coiled chest, when I noticed many of the guests looking my way and smiling as they exited a darkened, cornered-off display. A door separated it from the rest of the gallery. I suddenly remembered Vin putting something together here. Hell. I'd been so preoccupied with Axel's disappearance that I had forgotten all about it.

Walking toward the door, I heard Molly and Rome following behind me, but I didn't turn around, couldn't turn. Suddenly, I heard the melodic sound of my favorite piece of music drifting to me from behind the wall.

My heart hammered in my chest as I slowly opened the door, the sound of Yiruma's "Kiss the Rain" seeping into my every cell.

Flashbacks of me playing this, my favorite piece of music, for Axel in his studio raced through my mind. With every memory, I felt my heart break just that little bit more. A sizeable crowd had gathered around the sculpture, lavender lights creating a soft glow from above and the scent of Jasmine permeating the air.

As I moved closer through the crowd, many smiled at me as "Kiss the Rain" played on repeat. As if the visitors sensed I needed to be alone, they quietly dispersed. My feet abruptly ground to a halt…

Staring back at me was… *me*…

"Oh, Ally," I heard Molly sigh from behind me, but I couldn't look away. I was transfixed by the sculpture in front of my eyes.

A Carrara sculpture, of my smiling face, my chin balanced on my fist and my long hair flowing to one side was staring back at me.

Shivers ran down my spine and butterflies rattled around my stomach as I realized this must have been the piece he was working on this week, outside… this was what he so desperately wanted to carve… this beautifully crafted face… was how he viewed me….

403

"Hope," Molly's said, in awe. My glistening eyes followed the sound of her voice and she looked at me, her eyes watering beneath her glasses as she added, "This piece is called '*Hope*'."

Choking back a sob, I noticed that the room had cleared apart from my friends, a pained and sullen Austin, Levi and Lexi entering the room.

I watched as they saw the sculpture, and Austin had to turn away.

"What have I done?" I heard him whisper to his wife. "What the fuck have I done? Look at what he's created. Look at all this, what he's achieved and I made him leave because I jumped to the wrong fucking conclusions… I never gave him the chance to explain!"

Making my way over to the title, I ran my finger along the word 'hope', then noticed the text board…

"Hope is a fervent, silent wish that everything will turn out just as you dream…"

Unable to hold anything back, I cried as I read the words Axel had used to explain the inspiration for this piece.

Two strong arms wrapped around me, and I knew it was Rome. "Shit, Al, I… I don't know what to fucking say," he said apologetically and I cried harder into his chest. "I was fucking wrong. I was so wrong about him."

The room was silent apart from tears being shed for all the wrongs thrust upon the love of my life.

As I pushed away from Rome, I looked to Austin and Levi and said, "Axel, or Elpidio, is seen as one of the most talented and inspiring Contemporary Modern Artists in the world. But *Axel* doesn't see it. He doesn't see how anyone can think he's worth anything. Doesn't see that he deserves a second chance because he can't move past all the wrongs he's committed in his past."

Sniffing, I glanced back at my marble face and said, "It's time to put the past to bed. Stop judging him on yesterday, and accept the man he is today… the most amazing man I've ever known, ever *will* know."

Austin and Levi lowered their heads, seemingly in regret. Suddenly, Vin rushed through the door. Seeing me beside my sculpture, he rushed over to me, flustered and breathless. The look on his face...

"Vin? What's wrong?" I rushed out.

Vin's face was flushed and his hand lay on his chest. "I've… I've just received a call from the hospital. It's Elpi…"

My hands instantly started shaking. "What… What's happened?" I asked, breathlessly.

Vin stilled. "Elpi's been shot."

405

Staggering back at his words, I ran into Rome's chest. His strong arms stopped me from falling to the floor.

"What?" I whispered. Austin and Levi ran forward. Austin gripped Vin's arms and said, "Axe? Axe has been shot?"

Vin, clearly seeing the family resemblance, nodded his head. "Yesterday afternoon. He was shot in the stomach. He's in the hospital now. He had no ID on him at the scene. They took his fingerprints and because he was here in Seattle under my guidance, they called me. It took a while to track me down, I've been here all day getting this piece ready for the exhibition."

All I could visualize was blood and guns, when suddenly a name entered my head. "Remo..." I called out in panic, "Remo must have found him."

Austin and Levi's head's whipped to mine. "Remo? What do you mean *Remo*? What's Remo Marino got to do with anything?"

My lips and voice quivered, but I was able to say, "He told Axel he was going to kill him. He got word to Axel in prison that he would kill him in revenge for Gio's death."

"*SHIT!*" Austin bellowed, his deep voice breaking, echoing off the gallery's walls. "Why didn't he tell us? Why the fuck did he keep *this* from us?"

"He... he never wanted you to worry about him... he was trying to protect you... all he wanted to do was to keep you safe."

Snapping his head back to Vin, Austin demanded, "Which hospital?"

In a fluster, Vin told him. In seconds we were all running out of the door.

Chapter Twenty-Two

Ally

"Mr. Carillo took a gunshot straight to the stomach. He lost a lot of blood. When he was brought in we had to operate straight away. We managed to repair the wound and successfully remove the bullet. He's been transfused with blood and is now stable."

The doctor had yet to let us see Axel. My nerves were shot. I felt sick to my stomach as the doctor explained the extent of his injuries and how it could have killed him if the police hadn't found him when they did.

"Give us a few minutes to get him into his new room and he'll be ready to receive visitors, but only two at a time."

The doctor left the room. As I tried to breathe, a police officer walked in. "You're Axel Carillo's family?" he asked and looked at Austin.

"Yes, sir," Austin said and got to his feet. "You know what happened to him?"

The police officer closed his notebook and nodded his head. "You know a Mr. Remo Marino?"

I closed my eyes feeling my world was falling apart. I was numb, totally numb knowing that I could have lost the love of my life. The love of my life who deserved this *new* life he had—literally—carved out for himself.

Remo… Remo Marino. That bastard almost took my heart from me.

"Yeah, I know Remo," Austin said, the tone of his voice dropping to arctic temperatures.

The officer raised his eyebrow. "Old crew member?"

Austin stared at the officer, but didn't say anything. The officer swallowed and nodded his head. "Okay, I get it."

"What happened to Remo?" Levi asked, seeming to take himself by surprise.

The officer ran his hand down his face. "Mr. Marino was wanted on five counts of drug related felonies as well as two homicides. He's been on the run for years. He crossed state lines in a stolen vehicle and it was only a matter of time before we caught him… unfortunately he managed to attack Mr. Carillo before we discovered his whereabouts. Another car passing by saw the incident and called it in."

"And?" Rome asked. "Where's the prick now?"

"Mr. Marino open fired on the attending officers. He had no intention of going to prison. He was shot dead on the scene."

The silence that followed the officer's news hung heavily in the room. But I couldn't help but be thankful that Remo had died… that meant… that meant Axel was finally free.

He was finally free of his past.

The officer opened the door and said, "I'm sorry your brother was injured. It seems he's turned his life around. I hope he pulls through."

As the door shut, Austin slumped against the wall, sliding down to floor. He covered his face with his hands. "Christ…" he said in a gutting voice that made fresh tears spring from my eyes. "That fucking Heighter cunt. If he wasn't dead already, I'd kill him myself."

Austin raised his head to me. "Ally?"

I met his gaze.

"Alessio?" he questioned. I knew what he was asking. He wanted to know if he was a danger to his brothers.

"Serving life. Three counts of Homocide," I replied, and saw a ton of tension leave his muscles. "He's never ever getting out."

Just then, the doctor walked in the door. "Mr. Carillo can have visitors now."

I immediately jumped to my feet, as did Levi and Austin. The doctor looked at the three of us and his shoulders sagged. "No more than you three, okay?"

We followed him out of the door and with every step I took, my heart beat faster and faster. I wanted to see Axel so desperately that I almost broke into a sprint. Clearly feeling my anxiousness, Levi reached down and took my hand. Startled, I met his gray eyes and saw the fear and sadness in their depths. He was just as afraid of walking in that room as me.

The doctor led us to a room at the corner of the hallway. Chest tight and feeling numb, I followed him through a door, when I immediately froze in my tracks, as did we all, Levi's hand grasping mine like a vise.

Axel...

Like a dam breaking, water poured down my face as I looked to my broken love in a hospital bed. Wires were poking in and out of his skin, blood being transfused into his arms.

His beaten eyes were closed, his lips were swollen and bruised and his long hair was brushed back off his face.

Even like this he was beautiful... my dark and tortured anti-hero... the man I was always destined to adore.

As Austin's back bunched at seeing his older brother, I held his hand too. Austin's eyes closed briefly at my touch,

411

but they opened and kept focus on Axel. None of us could look away… we'd come too close to losing him.

"He's been waking up more and more, so you should be able to talk to him soon."

In some part of my brain, I registered the doctor leaving, leaving us alone, but my eyes were glued to the other half of my soul lying on that bed.

"How's he ever gonna forgive us, Aust?" Levi said through a tight throat. "We treated him like shit, never gave him a damn chance to explain anything… and look what he's been doing… look what he did for us both and we never knew. He nearly died in that prison trying to protect us, and he's done it again… he's protected us *again*…"

Levi's voice cracked. "He's always been protecting us, hasn't he, Aust? From when we were kids, he's always tried to keep us close… and we turned our backs on him when he needed us most…"

In the aftermath of Levi's confession, the drips from the IV sounded like clashes of thunder as they dropped down into the liquid gathering in the dispenser.

I opened my mouth to tell him it would all be okay, when we heard, "Ain't got… nothing… to be… sorry… for…"

Time seemed to stand still as the gruff timbre of Axel's hoarse voice cut through the sadness of the room. As one, we all leapt forward. Axel and Levi ran to one side of his bed, and I the other.

Stroking my hand across Axel's forehead, I watched him struggle to swallow and open his eyes. A tear from my eye splashed on his cheek, right on his crucifix tattoo. I used my thumb to brush it away.

As I ran the damp pad of my thumb along his jaw line, I felt that delicious sensation of a pair of Italian dark eyes watching me. Inhaling a fortifying breath, I blinked and glanced up to meet those beautiful eyes full on.

Top lip twitching into a hooked smirk, Axel opened his split lips and rasped, "*Carina…*" with a relieved sigh.

The endearment sounded like an answered prayer to my soul as it met my ears. Sniffing back my emotions, I gave him a watery smile, "Welcome back, *querido…*"

"What… What?" he tried to ask. I shushed him and shook my head.

"Everything's okay, *you're* okay." I looked up at Austin and Levi standing anxiously on the other side of the bed. And reassured, "We're all okay."

Axel slowly followed my gaze, bringing him to Austin and Levi. "*Fratelli…*" he said quietly, slowly lifting up his hand.

Austin was the first to reach for Axel's hand, his head lowering until his forehead touched their clasped fingers. "Axel... I'm so fucking sorry..."

"*Vai bene*," Axel replied. He next looked at Levi. "Lev..." he said with feeling. I could see Axel's eyes shining with unshed tears. He loved that kid to death.

Levi slumped to a chair like his legs could no longer take his weight, then his head hit the mattress, back shaking with the force of his tears. "I'm sorry, Axe... I'm so sorry..." he cried. Austin released Axel's hand. Axel laid it on Levi's head.

Levi looked up as he did so and wrapped it in both of his hands. "We should have trusted you."

Axel closed his eyes then opened them a second later. "Ain't ever... given... you much of a reason... to trust me in your lives... I... get it."

Austin shook his head. "You've only ever protected us, Axe... I get that now..." Austin wiped his eyes with the heels of his hands and asked, "those sculptures, Axe... why didn't you tell us...?"

"Shame..." he replied in embarrassment, "I didn't deserve it..." His head rolled on the pillow to me, his eyes wordlessly telling me how much he loved me, "none of this. I've been... unfairly blessed."

Feeling my heart swell, I leaned down and kissed his lips. "You're wrong."

"I'm a sinner," Axel said. I could hear how much he believed that statement. I could see it in his honest expression.

"No," I soothed, "A sinner is a man who doesn't recognize his wrongs. You have, *querido*, you've recognized them and done everything in your power to fix them… you're not a sinner. You're redeemed."

"She's right, Axe," Levi said and his breath caught, "*Mamma*… she would be so proud of *you*."

"Lev," Axel whispered. Austin sat beside Levi, adding his hand on top of theirs. "I'm so proud of you… I *have* pride that you're my blood."

Those words seemed to resonate with Axel, they meant something to the two of them and tears escaped Axel's eyes. The sight of the three Carillo's together was my undoing.

After minutes of the Carillo boys mending fences, Levi suddenly said, "Only good things for us from this point on, yeah?"

Axel exhaled and I could see the pride for Levi's show of strength glittering in his dark eyes.

Levi looked up and met the eyes of both Austin and Axel. "Swear it."

Austin wrapped an arm around Levi's shoulder, pressing a kiss to his head and said, "*Lo giuro.*"

They both then looked to Axel. Axel smiled through his swollen cut lips, a full genuine smile that I'd not seen him display before and he whispered. "*Lo giuro.*"

*****

Several hours passed as the three of us kept vigil by Axel's bedside. He was tired, slipping in and out of sleep, but we stayed. The three brothers talked about Axel's time in prison, Austin unable to believe that Axel hadn't told him how he'd suffered. But they managed to move past it. Levi spoke of his fears of losing them both, but admitted he had bottled up his feelings for far too long, wrongly blaming Axel for all his pain.

They laughed, they cried, and when the night wound down, a peace had been found.

When the doctor entered to tell us visiting hours were over, Austin and Levi reluctantly rose to their feet, but before I could join them, Axel gripped my hand. "Don't go," he asked sleepily, and my heart melted.

I looked to the doctor and threw him my sweetest smile. "Can I stay the night? He needs me."

The doctor sighed and I begged, "Please? I… I almost lost him…"

Seeing sympathy in his expression, he said, "Just you." Austin and Levi both kissed him on the forehead and promised to see him tomorrow.

As they reached the door, I asked, "Will you please tell Molly and Rome I'll see them tomorrow?"

Austin nodded and smiled at me. I staggered back at the power of that smile and, casting a last glance to his brother on his bed, he said only so I could hear, "Look after him, Al. Never thought I'd see the day, but that brother of mine fucking loves you to death. He may not show his feelings much, but he can't hide how much he adores you."

Reaching up to my tiptoes, I pressed a kiss on Austin's cheek and whispered, "*Siempre.*"

Austin laughed. I kissed Levi too before shutting the door. Everyone but the two of us had left the room.

As I moved to the bed, Axel was staring at my shoes and met my eyes with a smirk. "I love those fucking shoes," he said sleepily. I moved to the bed and, just as I was about to sit down on the nearby chair, Axel firmly shook his head and weakly patted the bed.

He began shuffling to the side to make room for me and I jumped forward at seeing the pain etched on his face. "Axel!" I hissed, as he winced in agony and held his stomach wound. Beads of sweat formed on his forehead as he relaxed back into the mattress… a space for me now at his left hand side.

"Lay down," he said through gritted teeth and I shook my head.

"No! Look at the pain you're in."

"Ally, I was shot and could've died. Please, just lay the fuck down… I need you."

I stood there debating what to do, but when I glimpsed vulnerability in his gaze, I gave in and carefully lay down beside him.

As I rested my head on his pillow, I reached down and threaded my hand through his. Axel squeezed my hand real tight, and when I looked up, I could see worry lines creasing his forehead.

"Hey," I asked. "What's wrong?"

Axel stayed quiet and I was sure I wasn't gonna get an answer from him. But on a ragged breath, he looked up and pulled my hand to lie under his cheek. "Last night, for the first time ever, I was fucking scared."

My heart sank as I saw how much that cost him to divulge. "Baby…" I whispered and, with my other hand, I stroked down his cheek. "It's understandable. You were shot."

Axel leaned into my touch and kissed my palm. "I wasn't scared of getting shot, Ally, I was fucking terrified I would never get to see you again."

My breath seized. I leaned in to kiss at his pale bruised lips. "Axel," I cried, "I was so scared too. Austin and Levi told me they had thrown you out and you'd ran away. I felt like my soul had been ripped out. I couldn't believe you would leave me like that… without even saying goodbye."

"I was gonna leave," he said sadly. His hand tightened around mine. "And I was gonna take you with me."

"Axel—"

"But then Remo followed me." Axel breathed through his nose as though he was reliving the entire thing in his head. "He'd been following me for days… I knew I wouldn't be walking away from him alive. He was there for revenge, and all I could think of was that Austin and Levi would never see me again after leaving on a misunderstanding… and that you… that I'd never see this fucking beautiful face ever again… that I would never get to live the life I couldn't believe I'd finally been gifted."

Tears ran down his stubbled cheek into his beard. "Shh…" I soothed, "You're alive. You survived and Remo's dead… all the threats to you and your brothers are gone... once and for all."

Axel inhaled deeply as though he couldn't comprehend that fact. Shuffling even closer to him on the bed, being careful of his injuries, I added, "And you have me... all of me... forever, if that's what you want."

Axel's eyes widened and releasing a long sigh, he nodded his head. "Fuck, Ally, that's all I want. You're everything to me. You're my *forever*."

"And you're my forever too," I replied. The image of my sculpture suddenly came to my mind, and I said, "Axel... your new sculpture..." I trailed off unable to find the words to express how I felt.

"Did you... like it?" he asked hesitantly, his rugged face for a moment racked with a nervous innocence.

"Did I like it?" I asked with a single laugh, "I can't... I can't believe that's how you see me... your *hope*... your wish come true..."

"You *are* my hope, Ally. You're every hope I've ever dared to have... *la mia luce*."

"Axel," I murmured. Carefully leaning down to his bruised mouth, I gently melded my lips to his. The kiss was everything I wanted to convey, but was unable to say with words.

As we broke away, I smiled. "Your show was a hit, baby. Vin's already had offers for it to go on tour. Just think, your exhibition in the biggest art museums in the world… the entire world will stand witness to your genius."

Axel glanced away, then looked back to me, a nervous expression on his face. "Axel? What is it?" I questioned, "Aren't you happy? This is life changing. It's a dream come true."

"I don't know," he replied and I frowned. "My happiness all depends…"

Rearing back, I asked, "On what?"

Rolling his lips, wincing at the painful cuts, he said, "On whether you're gonna be the official tour curator."

I blinked, then blinked again, before a wide elated smile pulled on my lips. "Axel, are you asking me to go around the world with you?"

Axel smirked at me in that devastating way that only he had mastered and said, "I ain't fucking going nowhere without you, *carina*. I know what I want… and it's you. You're the only one who's ever *got* me. Fuck, baby, you really have got me in every possible way."

Feeling like I could die from happiness, I tilted my head and said, "*Lo giuri?*"

He huffed a laugh back and nodded his head. "I fucking swear it on everything I am."

"And where would we live?" I asked, the surreal turn of this conversation was becoming difficult to track.

"Wherever you want, but—"

"But what?"

"But I'd kinda like to be near my brothers here in Seattle. Weirdly, I'm getting used to the gray clouds and rain."

I relaxed in relief. "Good, 'cause I wanna be here too. I wanna be here when Molls has my nephew or niece in a few months' time."

"Then you're gonna be living with me," Axel firmly instructed.

Warmth flooded my body and I nodded my head. "Of course. *Te amo*," I said in a state of perfect contentment, and curled into Axel's arms.

Hearing a peaceful sigh from Axel too, he whispered back, "*Ti amo, carina.* You've got all the love I have."

As I closed my eyes, safe with the man whose soul was forever fused to mine, I sent a silent prayer to Axel's Mamma…

I have him now, Chiara. Your lost son is found. You can finally rest in peace.

Epilogue
Axel

Seattle, Washington

Three years later…

"It's okay, *carina*, you can do it."

"I'm so tired," Ally whispered, her beautifully tanned face pale and her body exhausted.

I ran my hands down her cheek. "One more push, baby. One more push and she'll be here."

Love sparkled in Ally's Spanish eyes. She nodded her head. The doctor looked up at my wife. "This is it, Ally, one more push and you'll meet your daughter."

Clutching her hand in mine, Ally squeezed my fingers tight and pushed as hard as she could. My heart beat so fast I thought it would burst from my chest. Ally gasped

423

for breath, and the most amazing sound hit my ears—the sound of high-pitched crying.

My legs turned to jelly as I caught sight of the doctor holding a tiny baby. The nurses wiped her clean, just before they lifted her and placed her on Ally's bare chest.

Ally's face was streaming with tears as she looked down at our newborn daughter, a jet-black crop of hair already on her head. As I moved to the head of the bed, looking down at my two beautiful girls, I couldn't describe the overwhelming sense of home that hit me with the force of a Mack truck.

Ally's glowing face looked up at me and broke into a disbelieving smile. "Axel... we have a daughter," she said, her voice hoarse from all the hours of labor.

Unable to speak, I leaned down and pressed a kiss to her head, then, nervously leaned down and kissed my daughter on her cheek. As I pulled away, she squirmed in Ally's arms, and opened her eyes to stare straight up at me... her dark brown eyes meeting mine... and floored me where I stood.

Gasping, I stared down at her and a sudden fear rippled through me. Was I fucking worthy of being her papa? Did I deserve something this good to happen to me?

"She'll adore you, Axe," Ally assured me, catching my eye, immediately stopping the crippling thoughts slamming into my mind. "She'll adore you as much as I do."

Swallowing back the lump in my throat, I made myself relax and sat down on the bed. I wrapped my arms around my two reasons for living.

"*Ti amo, carina. Sempre*," I said brokenly and turned Ally's head for a kiss.

"I love you too, *querido*," she whispered back and ran her finger down our sleeping daughter's red face.

"She needs a name," Ally said softly, but I kept quiet. There was only one name I wanted to call her. A tribute, an honor I wanted my daughter to own.

We sat there for an hour before Ally squeezed my hand. "You'd better go and tell everyone the good news, my mama and daddy will be climbing the walls."

Smirking at the thought of Ally's Spanish mother wreaking havoc on the ward, demanding to be let in here ran through my mind.

"Okay, baby," I said, and kissing my wife and daughter one last time, I walked out of the room and into the wait area, where all our family was gathered.

As I opened the door, Ally's mama was on her feet in seconds and rushed my way. "Axel," she said in relief, her strong Spanish accent as thick as ever, "How are my girls?"

Her pretty face was just an older version of Ally's. I could see the worried apprehension in her brown eyes.

Unable to keep from smiling, I replied, "They're perfect... fucking perfect."

Mama Alita broke down into tears and she wrapped her arms around my neck. I closed my eyes and took a deep breath, laughing at her relieved response. Alita and Gabe had become my parents. They'd never judged me, just accepted me as the man Ally loved and welcomed me as their son. They were as perfect as in-laws as their daughter was the perfect wife... and they adored Austin and Levi too.

"She's waiting for you," I said. In a heartbeat, Alita was off down the hallway, practically running into the delivery room. I could hear her happy shriek all the way from in here.

Gabe, Ally's papa approached me and shook my hand. "Congratulations, son. Welcome to the daddy of a daughter club." He laughed like it was an inside joke. Pulling me to his chest, he patted me on the back and whispered, "Good luck."

As he left, two little people suddenly ran under my legs and I reached down to pick them both up. "*Zio* Axe!" Dante called, his chubby cheeks red and his green eyes huge.

426

"Hey buddy," I said and pressed a kiss to his cheek. He giggled, but just as he did, Taylor hit at my face wanting attention too. "Me too, Uncy Axe. Me want kiss too!"

Laughing, I pressed a kiss to her cheek and she pushed on Dante's arm making him scowl.

"Okay, okay, missy, enough," Molly said sternly and lifted her daughter from my arms, but not before pressing a kiss to my cheek. "Congrats, sweetie. I can't wait to meet her."

Lexi moved forward next and took her son from my arms who was still glaring at Taylor. Lexi shook her head at her son and beamed up a smile at me. Leaning down I kissed her on her cheek. "I'm so happy for you, Axe," she said.

Rome came over next and put out his hand, "Congrats, Axe," he said and squeezed my hand. "Make sure you look after them both, yeah?"

I nodded my head and he moved away. I would never be fully okay with that guy, and him me, but at least we'd moved past the wanting to kill each other stage and we could at least be in the same room... even get on, in some circumstances.

My eyes searched out Levi and Austin. As one, they barreled over and both wrapped their arms around my neck. Laughing, I held them tightly too.

"Auguri, fratello!" they each said and moved back with happy proud smiles. I saw Levi's girlfriend Elsie over his shoulder. She got up and wrapped her arms around my waist. "Happy for you, Axe," she said and I laughed at the blonde's cute face.

"Thanks, Elsie."

"So?" I asked, "Who wants to meet my daughter?"

All my friends and family headed for the delivery room, Dante and Taylor once again finding their way into my arms.

My beautiful daughter won them all over in seconds.

*****

As night hit, I stared at my sleeping wife on the hospital bed and moved to press a kiss onto her cheek. Ally stirred, her eyelids cracking open. I held my daughter in my arms, her brown eyes unable to stop watching me.

Ally lifted her hand and wrapped it in my long hair. "You okay, papa?"

I smiled and looked down at our daughter. "I'm perfect, *carina*. Fucking perfect," I whispered.

I glanced at the door, feeling the need for fresh air. Ally must have seen it in my face. "Go, baby, show her the night sky."

I tilted my head to the side, and said, "I love you, Aliyana Carillo."

Smiling sleepily, she murmured, "I love you too, Axel Carillo. You're all of my heart."

Pressing a final kiss on her head, I headed to the door. Just as I was about to leave, Ally whispered, "You need to pick a name, Papa. Your daughter can't be Baby Carillo forever… and I think I know what you want it to be. You just haven't worked up the nerve to ask them, have you?"

I briefly closed my eyes. As always, my wife knew me too well.

Looking at my daughter swaddled in a pink blanket, I took a deep breath and headed out of the door. The hallway was quiet and I headed for the OB unit's private garden. Walking to the nurse's station, the older nurse who'd been looking after my little family looked up and her face melted into a grin.

I held up the band around my arm that was electronically linked to the tag on my daughter's ankle. It told the nurses I was her father. "This ain't gonna go off if I go into that garden just there is it?" I nudged my chin to the garden entrance.

The nurse shook her head. "No, you can go out there. It's all fenced in and secure. So unless you can sprout wings and fly away, no alarms will go off."

429

"Nah, no wings," I said as I walked forward. Feeling all kinds of surreal as I held my child in my arms, Ally's child and mine, I kept looking down at my daughter to make sure I wasn't dreaming. Dreaming that all of this, my life, wasn't just one real fucking good dream that I didn't wanna wake from.

How the hell a sinner like me deserved all of this I had no damn idea.

As I opened the door to the roof garden, the summer night wrapped around me, the warm air seeping into my skin. The small private garden was deserted at this hour, so I moved to the patch of grass and sat down leaning against a wall, holding my daughter in my arms as I stared up at the clear night sky. All the stars were out tonight and a nostalgic smile pulled on my lips.

Looking back down, my daughter's nose scrunched up in her sleep. Running a finger down her cheek, I opened my mouth and sang, *"Dormi, Dormi, O Bel Bambin…"* I sang the Italian lullaby softly, rocking back and forth just as I'd done all those years ago with Levi. As I sang each word, I couldn't stop the tear that escaped the corner of my eye.

She was mine. This sleeping perfection was the best thing I'd ever done in my life.

Hearing the door to the garden open, I sat up straight, wiping my eyes, only to see Austin and Levi walking through, Dante sitting happily in Austin's arms.

"What the hell are you two still doing here?" I asked in a graveled voice. It must have been at least two in the morning. I flicked my chin to Dante. "And how the hell is he still awake?"

"He refused to leave, kicked up a storm when Lexi tried to take him away from us. I didn't mind, he never sleeps anyway. He's the damn energizer bunny," Austin joked, shaking his head, but holding his son tighter in his arms.

Dante slapped his hands on Austin's cheeks. "En-er bun... bun-*ee*," he tried to repeat, sounding too fucking cute.

Austin playfully nodded at his son. "Yeah, you are. The energizer bunny."

Dante squealed in laughter, throwing his head back, making us all laugh too.

Austin sat beside me on the dry grass, Dante perching on his knee, staring down at my daughter in fascination. Levi dropped to my other side and he wrapped his arm around my shoulder. "You didn't think we'd leave, did you?"

Feeling my chest tighten, I went to answer, when Austin said, "We're your brothers, we leave when you do. You know that, Axe."

Clearing the emotion from my throat, I glanced to my sleeping daughter, holding her in my arms and I asked, "How did you know I'd be out here?"

"You walked right past us, Axe. You were staring at your daughter so much that you didn't see us sitting right in front of you."

Dante leaned over to look at my daughter and he then looked up at me, his pink lips pursed. "What her name?" he asked in his cute ass baby talk. He was so fucking adorable.

"Yeah, Axe," Levi said, "What're you calling our niece?"

As I stared down at my daughter, I got lost in her pretty sleeping rosy face and said, "I wanna call her Chiara."

Silence met my words and I tensed. I wasn't sure if my brothers would be okay with my daughter being named after our mamma.

That's until I looked up and both of them were watching me with tears in their eyes. "Axe," Levi said, his voice breaking. "Mamma would be so damn proud that your daughter shared her name. I can just imagine how happy she'd be if she was here right now."

"Yeah," Austin said, equally as choked up. "Mamma's looking down at her now and she's fucking smiling, Axe. Smiling so big." Austin looked at my daughter. He leaned down and kissed her forehead. "Chiara," he said lovingly then Levi followed suit. "Little Chiara Carillo."

My heart was so full as the five of us sat here in silence. All three of us brothers unable to speak until Dante suddenly pointed up at the sky and said, "Papa... big star!"

Austin laughed at his son shattering our poignant moment and squeezed him to his chest, ruffling his dark hair. "Si, Dante. A big star. *Le stelle grande*," he said in Italian.

Dante watched Austin's lips and said, "*Lee stel ee gan de.*"

We all laughed as Dante tried to speak Italian. "*Bene!*" Austin told his son, and tickled Dante until he burst into fits of giggles. "*Molto bene!*"

Turning to Levi, I watched him squinting up at the stars and realized he never got to remember stargazing with Austin and me all those years ago, he was too young. But it should be something he got to share with us now.

Closing my eyes, I took a deep breath and leaning back against the wall with my daughter cradled in my arms, I said, "Austin, tell us what those stars are."

Austin looked over at me, and I could see his eyes gloss over at the request. We hadn't done this since we were little kids trying to escape our abusive papa.

Austin carefully placed Dante higher on his lap, Dante squealing with excitement. He stared up at the night sky.

I turned to Levi. "Look up, Lev."

Shaking his head and smiling at us, Levi leaned back and looked up.

Austin pointed at three stars in a row. "The three stars there are called Orion's Belt. You can tell it's Orion's Belt by the way they're all in a row. You see?"

I listened to Austin explain constellation after constellation, Dante and Chiara now part of our Carillo tradition. And as the minutes passed, a sense of peace and calmness washed over me.

We'd made it.

The three of us, lying here staring at the stars like we did so long ago, had made it. ,

We were the Carillo boys. Three brothers born into chaos and pain. Three brothers who'd endured tragedy and loss. Brothers until the end, bound by blood, our bonds unbreakable by unconditional love.

And I was sure that up in that sky, there was an angel looking down on her sons, a smile on her face and a prideful happiness in her heart.

The End

TILLIE COLE

Bonus Chapter
Axel

The Guggenheim Museum
New York City

Fifteen years later…

This shit never got any easier.

As I stood behind the scenes of my exhibition, hearing the hundreds of voices on the other side of the wall, my heart raced.

The Museum Director was out there now, giving the crowd his talk to introduce my show. Years of doing this hadn't taken away my opening-night nerves, my apprehension about how the show would be received. I closed my eyes and drew in a deep breath.

Just then, that familiar hand ran down my back, the scent of jasmine filling the space around me. My shoulders immediately lost their tension and I exhaled in relief.

"Ally," I breathed out on a sigh.

As I opened my eyes, I saw that my beautiful wife had moved to stand before me, dressed in her long fitted red dress, her long hair falling over her shoulder.

She placed her hands on my face. "Breathe, *querido*. The people love it. Most are too blinded by their tears to even speak."

Wrapping my arms around her waist, I pulled her to my chest and pressed my lips against hers. Ally melted into my arms and her fingers raked through my long hair.

Pulling back, her dark gaze met mine and tears filled her eyes. "I'm so proud of you," she whispered and gently pressed her forehead to mine. "A permanent exhibition at the Guggenheim. Axel. It's what every contemporary artist dreams of. There's no greater honor."

I nodded and blew out a long breath. "I know," I said and nudged my chin to the direction of the gallery. "Is it full? Did they get the turnout they wanted?"

"Packed," Ally replied, excitedly.

Just then, the door opened behind us. I turned to see my two beautiful daughters entering my hideout. Their faces lit up with ear splitting grins as they ran toward me, nearly tackling me to the ground.

Unable to hold back a laugh, I wrapped them in my arms. When I looked up, Ally was staring at us with a watery smile on her face. After all these years she was still my biggest cheerleader... and this, my own little family, surrounding me... they were my everything... my light, my world and my hope all brought to life.

With one final squeeze, Chiara, my fifteen-year-old daughter pulled back; Violeta, my youngest, followed suit. At age twelve she did everything her big sister did. It seemed to be a Carillo trait.

"Papa," Chiara said breathlessly with glossy dark eyes, "It's beautiful. The people are all going crazy for the sculptures..." her face became flushed as tears began to run down her cheeks, "*your* sculptures, Papa," she proudly announced.

Feeling my throat close at seeing her show of emotion, I lifted my hands and wiped her cheeks with the pads of my thumbs.

Hearing a sniff from my right, I glanced down to see Violeta staring up at her big sister, also shedding tears.

Leaning down, I asked, "Hey, not you too, *mia cara*. What's all this?" My voice cracked, my throat tight at seeing my daughters' reactions.

Violeta, who was every inch the image of her mother, looked at me and pursed her lips, deep dimples popping in her cheeks as she tried to catch her breath. "We're just *so* proud of you, Papa. All these people… they're here for *you*. Mama told us how special they think you are. And you're our *papa*… it… it makes me feel so proud," she managed to say and completely destroyed any hope I had of not breaking down.

Water blurred my eyes, and wrapping my hands around the back of my daughters' heads, I pulled them to me, tears now pouring down my face. "*Grazie*," I rasped, "I'm *so* proud to be your papa."

Immediately, I felt Ally ghost to my side.

Glancing up, I shook my head at my wife who was looking down at me and my girls, her expression full of love. "I can't see them cry, *carina*, it fucking breaks me."

Ally smiled as I pulled back to look at our daughters. Their huge eyes never left mine. "It's all for you, you do know that, don't you? All this, you're what inspires me. You two and your mama. Everything I do is for you."

Both my daughters nodded their heads at my words and wiped their cheeks. "*Ti voglio bene*," I said, and kissed each of them on their heads.

"*Ti voglio bene, Papa*," they replied in unison.

My heart melted just that little bit more.

440

Ally leaned over me and kissed Chiara then Violeta on their dark-haired heads. Wrapping her arms around their shoulders, her Spanish gaze met mine. "Have you heard enough? Are you ready to go?" she asked, knowing that my tradition was to listen to the reactions of the opening night crowd as I hid away behind the gallery. I couldn't stay at the galleries for more than about thirty minutes without nerves shredding me. And I still had no fucking desire for the art world to know who I was. I liked that I'd managed to keep my anonymity even after all these years.

Eager to get the hell out of the museum and away from all the craziness, I nodded my head. Catching Ally's gaze again, I asked, "Have our friends all left?"

"They left about ten minutes ago. I gave them a personal pre-show tour without the crowds," Ally informed.

Glancing at the floor, a tidal wave of nerves spread through my stomach and, looking back at Ally, I asked, "What did they think?"

Ally tilted her head to the side. Then that damn stunning look she always beamed at me when I needed her to calm me down drifted across her face. "They adored it, *querido*. Your brothers… they were blown away by your talent, as always." I closed my eyes as Ally added, "They are so proud of you."

Opening my eyes, I exhaled a relieved breath and held out my hand. Ally placed her hand in mine. Chiara went to Ally's side and Violeta came to my side, wrapping her arm around my waist.

I had to pause for second. I just had to take a moment to fucking breathe.

Listening to the impressed voices on the other side of that wall, fucking bowled over by my work, I stood here proudly, my wife and two beautiful girls by my side. I couldn't believe *this* was my life. I had a woman who loved me more than I deserved. For as long as I lived, it would never make sense to me. And I had two daughters who adored me... Two beautiful bright, happy daughters I adored right back.

A squeeze on my waist made me look down. Violeta's concerned tanned face was staring up at me. "Are you okay, Papa?"

Clearing my throat, I nodded my head. "Never better, *mia cara*. Never better."

*****

"You booked out the whole place?" I asked Ally as we walked into the empty New York restaurant.

Ally shrugged. "You don't like crowds, and everyone flew here for the exhibition. I wanted it to be special. So I booked the whole place."

Shaking my head at my wife, I took her outstretched hand. Chiara and Violeta walked into the restaurant first. Ally and me quickly followed behind.

Entering the rustic traditional Italian restaurant, our friends and family stopped their conversations and turned to face us. When Ally waved her arms, they got to their feet and started clapping.

Every single one of them...

I couldn't move.

Cassie, seeing I wasn't dealing so well with their congratulations, slid out of her chair and stood up. "Well if you ain't gonna move, I'll friggin' come to you!"

She barreled forward. Before I had a chance to do anything, she wrapped her hands around my neck. "You kicked ass, darlin'!" she yelled and pressed a kiss on my cheek.

JD wasn't too far behind her, along with their five kids... all boys, who lined up to congratulate me on my show. Molly and Rome Prince came next. Molly hugged me tightly, Rome holding his hand out for me to shake.

"Hell of a show you put together," he said and we shook hands. Before I knew it, Rome had pulled me to his chest and patted me twice on the back. "You did good, Axe, real damn good."

He immediately stepped back as their four kids came over and gave me hugs and kisses. I stood there fucking dumbstruck. Rome and me? Although we were okay, we'd never been close. I stared at him as he walked away... then he looked over his shoulder and gave me a proud nod.

I had no fucking clue what to do with that shit.

Feeling a hand on my arm, I looked to my side to see Levi with this wife, Elsie. They each held hands with one of their five year old twins; a boy, Jackson, and a girl, Penelope. Shaking his head, Levi held me tightly in his big arms. The Seahawk's number one ranked Wide Receiver squeezed me so hard I stopped breathing. Stepping back, I watched him swallow hard as he fought to speak through his tight throat.

Patting him on his cheek, I kissed his forehead. "*Grazie, fratellino*," I rasped, not needing any words to see how proud of me he was. As Levi stepped back, Elsie stepped forward and kissed me on the cheek, before wrapping her arm around Levi's waist.

Austin came next. Without a word he brought me to his chest. "Shit, Axe," he said through a clogged throat, "I got no fucking words. I'm just so fucking proud," he said and tears filled my eyes.

"*Grazie, fratello*," I struggled to say.

Austin pulled back, his dark eyes met mine. He shook his head. "I can't believe all this..."

"Same here, kid," I agreed.

"Can I get a kiss?" a voice asked from behind Austin. A second later, Lexi pushed through, making Austin laugh.

"Hey, Lex," I said on a laugh as she reached up to wrap me in her arms.

"It's beautiful, Axel, truly. There wasn't a dry eye in that gallery as all of us looked at those sculptures."

"Thanks, Lex," I said, just as Dante came to stand next to his papa. Dante was nearly eighteen and the double of Austin... shit, the double of me.

Slapping my hand, he pulled me closer and tapped my back. "*Zio*, it's incredible. Always knew it would be."

Throwing my arm around his shoulders, I clapped my hand on his chest. "It'll be you one day, kid."

"You think so?" he asked. Austin and Lexi nodded their heads in agreement and beamed with pride.

Ally leaned over me to kiss Dante's cheek. "Sure will." She adored our nephew. She adored that he wanted to be a sculptor like me. He was always at our place back in Seattle, watching me work.

"I know it. My nephew learning how to be a sculptor from me? Ain't no way you'll fail as my apprentice. You're a Carillo. We always pull through."

"I'm a Carillo too!" a little high-pitched voice shouted from behind Lexi. Daisy pushed Lexi out of the way to run to me. But as soon as she saw Ally, Daisy changed course and jumped into her arms. Ally lifted up our six-year-old niece. She immediately began playing with Ally's long hair.

Just then, Levi back came over with his twins, and asked, "We eating or what?"

*****

A couple of hours later, after food was eaten, the tapping on glass got everyone's attention. When I looked to my left, Molly Prince was standing. Rome stared up at her with a wry smile.

Looking at all of us around the table, Molly sucked in a deep breath. "Sorry for interrupting, guys." Ally reached down to take my hand, a happy smile on her lips, as she guessed what her best friend was about to say.

"Go on, Molls, you sexy beast!" Cassie shouted and took a swig of beer.

Molly shook her head, laughing, and took a long deep breath. "I'm not really one for public speaking, at least not

446

outside of the classroom. But I couldn't let this night pass without a toast or two being shared."

Molly fixed her eyes on me. "Firstly, I wanted to offer huge congratulations to Axel for what is one of the greatest achievements a sculptor could hope for... his very own permanent exhibition in The Guggenheim. I'm truly proud of you, sweetie. We all are." Molly raised her glass. Ally squeezed my hand as everyone raised their glasses and took a drink.

As Molly lowered her glass, she looked down to her husband and held out her hand. Rome took it immediately.

Turning back to us, Molly continued. "Just this week I was working in my office, trying to plan a release date for my next textbook. When I glanced at the calendar, I actually sat back in my chair in shock." A small smile pulled on her lips and she pushed her black glasses up her nose. "It's twenty-five years this very month since I flew to the USA... to the University of Alabama... to study for my Masters."

"God, Molls," Ally exclaimed. She shook her head in disbelief. "Twenty-five years?"

Molly nodded in disbelief and Lexi laughed. "I remember that day as though it was yesterday, Molls. You moved in with Cass and me. You were so nervous."

"Yeah, but we soon knocked that shit right outta you, didn't we, Molls? Soon made you one of *us*."

Molly laughed. "You sure did, Cass," she said happily, then glanced down at the tabletop. "I bring this up because... as I look around this table, at all of us... I can't believe how far we've all come. What we've all accomplished... and the obstacles we've all had to overcome."

Molly's face grew serious. "The reason I decided to go to Alabama was because I had no one in England, no family, no real friends... nothing."

Ally's hand squeezed mine as she looked at her best friend, sadness clear on her face.

"Baby..." Rome whispered, edging forward on his seat. Molly lifted her hand to cut him off.

"No, I'm not looking for sympathy, Rome. Quite the opposite." She faced the rest of us again. "My first day in Bama I met Lexi and Cass. And without judgment or expectation, the two of you took me on as your best friend and you changed my life." She then looked at Rome. "Then on my very first day of studies, I ran into you... *literally*... and that was it. I was yours and you were mine from that day onward."

This time, nothing was stopping Rome from leaning up and kissing his wife. Molly ran her hand down his face.

448

Then she turned to Ally. "Through Rome I met the most lovely girl in the world... his cousin, Ally. Ally, you fast became, and still are, family to me. You're the sister I never *had*, but always *wanted*."

"You too, Molls," Ally quickly agreed through a throat tight with emotion. Molly laughed as she wiped away a stray tear. Leaning in closer to my wife, I put my arm around Ally's shoulder and she immediately melted into my side.

"I remember the day I was asked to come to America by my professor. I remember thinking it through... wondering if it would be the right move for me to make. In the end I thought *'what the hell'* and jumped in with both feet. And because of that leap of faith, I'm now living a life I could barely have imagined. In truth, I honestly think we *all* are."

Molly pointed to Cassie and JD. "Cass and JD met the same night as Rome and I... and now you're the proud parents of five beautiful boys... and run one of the most successful ranches in Texas."

She next looked to Lexi. Tears fell down her cheeks. "Lex, you know what I think about you. Hands down, you're the bravest... the most courageous person I've ever met in my life. You overcame an illness that I can't even imagine coping with. Yet you do so with grace... and a fierce determination. You're my inspiration, my faith that a person can overcome anything."

"Molls," Lexi cried, unable to speak any further. Austin pulled his wife tightly into his arms and kissed her head. My chest tightened at the sight... my emotions fucking working overtime.

"It's true, Lex," Molly assured, "And on your journey you fell in love with Austin. Austin who, along with his two brothers, faced a kind of hell that no human being should ever have to endure." Molly fixed her eyes on me and Austin and Levi. "The three of you have overcome so much grief... so much heartache. But in the end, your love as brothers... your love for each other... pulled you through and made you the men you are today."

Molly then smiled at Ally, Elsie and Lexi. "Along with your wives, of course... three women whose tenacity and ability to love fiercely showed you that there was happiness and joy to be had in this life... and that life is far too short to stay stuck in the past.

"Levi plays in the NFL... Austin and Lexi run centers in Seattle to help troubled teens... and of course, Axel and Ally, who have taken the art world by storm." Molly turned to her husband. "And us, baby. You, the Tide coach. And me, a professor... and our four beautiful children who complete our lives."

Molly laughed to herself and shook her head, blushing. "I'm rambling. I know I am rambling. But sitting here in this restaurant tonight makes my heart fit to burst with happiness and pride." She went quiet and I watched a single tear run down her cheek and splash onto the tabletop.

Everything was silent as Molly kept her head low. But inhaling a breath, she continued. "Twenty-five years ago I had no family... I had little hope. And now? Today I am blessed with the best family and friends in the world... and a bucket load of hopes and dreams."

Lifting her head, a smile spread on her lips and she huffed a watery laugh. "In my head, I picture all of us growing old, our friendships never fading. I picture our children's weddings, Christmases and birthdays shared together... the years rolling by filled with love and happiness... and I picture all of us as grandparent's telling our grandchildren stories about how we all met, about all the journeys we took in our lives—both the good and the bad."

Ally was full on crying beside me. In fact, as I scanned round the table, everyone was fighting to keep their shit together. Even the kids were silently watching Molly talk, her daughter, Taylor, and three sons, Isaac, Archie and Elias, looking at her like she was their sun.

"What I'm trying to say is that the day I took a chance with the move to Alabama was the best thing I've ever done… because it brought me to you guys. I love you all so much that some days it's almost too much to contain." Raising a glass, Molly announced, "A toast… to taking a chance, because that chance taken may be the very path that leads you to your happily ever after."

All of us rose to our feet, toasting with a glass of champagne and all the girls ran over to Molly to hug her. As I watched Ally kissing and holding her best friends, I glanced to my right, only to see Austin and Levi moving to stand by my side. Silently, I put my arms around the shoulders of my brothers.

It was at that moment I knew I couldn't regret a thing. Not one thing that happened in my life, because this moment, *right now*, this *feeling*, was worth every bit of pain and heartache.

At that moment, Ally turned and caught my eye. Leaving her friends, she walked over to where I stood looking as damn breathtaking as the day I met her. Levi and Austin clapped me on the back and moved aside. As my brothers headed back to their wives, Ally wrapped her arms around my neck.

Holding her tightly in my arms, she moved back her beautiful face. Searching my eyes, she asked, "Are you happy, *querido?*"

Sighing, feeling the most content I had in my entire fucking life, I pressed my lips to hers, pulling back only to whisper, "*Sono felice insieme a te... Sempre.*"

Playlist

The playlist can be found under 'Sweet Hope' on:
http://tilliecole.com

Tainted Love — Marilyn Manson

Amor Prohibido — Selena

Live With Lonesome — Little Big Town

Kiss The Rain — Yiruma

Boot of Spanish Leather — Amos Lee

Roses — James Arthur (ft. Emeli Sande)

Mess Is Mine — Vance Joy

Bright — Echosmith

You Hurt The Ones You Love/I Don't Believe That — Maria Mena

Brother — NEEDTOBREATHE (ft. Gavin DeGraw)

Tutto L'Amore Che Ho — Jovanotti

The Prayer — RyanDan

Heartbeats — Jose Gonzales

Run — Leona Lewis

Lips Of An Angel — Hinder

Something Good This Way Comes — Jakob Dylan

Brother — Edward Sharpe & The Magnetic Zeroes

What I've Done — Linkin Park

Sweet Dreams — Beyonce

El Camino — Emos Lee

My Silver Lining — First Aid Kit

Sigh No More — Mumford & Sons

L.I.F.E.G.O.E.S.O.N. — Noah and The Whale

Say Anything — Tristan Prettyman

Shattered & Hollow — First Aid Kit

Acknowledgements

Sweet Hope was difficult to write knowing that it was the final book in the Sweet Home Series. This series launched my career as an author, and I will be forever grateful to the characters that lived in my head, urging me to put their stories to the page, and also, the magnitude of people that have helped me along the way…

Mam and Dad, we're now chugging full steam ahead! Thank you for setting me on course, and for riding shotgun beside me! Love you both!

To my husband. You encourage me, push me to always make every novel my best, and love me for the person I am, flaws and all. I love you to the moon and back. You're my Rome, Austin and Axel all rolled into one childhood sweetheart package… we just need to keep building up your tattoos!!! Full Carillo coverage is the goal! ;)

Sam, Marc, Taylor, Isaac, Archie and Elias. Love you all. And, Isaac, I'll keep working on the theme park at Universal Studios!

To my fabulous beta readers: Thessa, Kelly, Kia, Rachel and Lynn. Your comments and advice were invaluable. You always have my back and are not afraid to tell me straight. I love you guys for that. The best team a gal could ask for. *Onward!!!!*

Thessa, my sweet sweet friend. Thank you for manning my Facebook page and keeping me in check. Thank you for the endless meme's and promotional teasers/pimping you do. And a HUGE thank you for encouraging me to write this novel. Your love for Axel convinced me that I was on the right lines and that he desperately deserved this story. Love you, missus! Don't know what I'd do without you!

Kelly, and *Have Book Will Read Book Blog* for hosting my blog tour and just being a fabulous friend. I appreciate everything you do for me. And I love that you have my back, defending my honour and championing me all the way. The day I met you was a blessing. Cannot wait for more!

Cassie, my fantastic Bama editor. Thank you so much!

Lysa, my wonderful web designer. I love your Bostonian ass!

Liz, my fabulous agent. Wow. That's all I have to say. I can't wait to show my amazing readers all we have in store for 2015 and beyond… *World Domination!!!!* Thank you for taking the leap with me… it's gonna be a helluva ride!

Gitte and Jenny from *TotallyBooked Book Blog*. Where do I start? You know how I feel about you two, my fave Viking and Aussie duo! I say it in every book. AND I forever will, because you mean so much to me. You have become such fabulous friends over the past couple of years and I love you both to bloody bits!!!

Neda from Sub Club Books, my Carillo boys enthusiast. Love you girl! Hope you got your Carillo fill!

And a huge thank you to all the many, many more wonderful book blogs that support me and promote my books. I adore you all. Sincerely. You rock!

To all the fabulous authors I have befriended over the last year and the support you give. I love you guys! And thank you especially to the wonderful gals who sprinted alongside me so I could make this deadline. There was a copious amount Red Bull, Coffee, Chocolate and breakdowns along the way, but it was worth it. Not sure my digestive system agrees, but who cares about that! ;)

Tracey-Lee, Thessa and Kerri, a huge thank you for running my street teams, **Tillie's Hot Cole's** and **The**

Hangmen Harlots. Y'all kick ass! And to all of my street team members—LOVE YOU!!!

Jodi, Chelcie and Alycia, I adore you girls. You are not only supportive readers, but are now my sincere friends. Love you to bits!

My IG girls!!!! You give me nothing but support and smiles, and everyday have me racing to my app to see what you're all up to! You're my meme queens!!!!

And lastly, my wonderful readers. Your support, your enthusiasm and your love means the world to me. Thank you for all the messages of support you send me, the amazing reviews you leave for my novels, the beautiful meme's and teasers you make in honour of my work, and the tattoos you get of my words. You leave me utterly speechless. Gosh darn it! You're all so bloody brilliant that I could burst!

And even though The Sweet Home Series has come to an end *wipes tear*... I CAN'T WAIT to share with you what's coming up next!

Ti amo... sempre...

Tills xx

About the Author

Tillie Cole hails from a small town in the North-East of England. She grew up on a farm with her English mother, Scottish father and older sister and a multitude of rescue animals. As soon as she could, Tillie left her rural roots for the bright lights of the big city.

After graduating from Newcastle University, Tillie followed her Professional Rugby player husband around the world for a decade, becoming a teacher in between and thoroughly enjoyed teaching High School students Social Studies for seven years.

Tillie has now settled in Calgary, Canada, where she is finally able to sit down, write (without the threat of her husband being transferred), throwing herself into fantasy worlds and the fabulous minds of her characters.

Tillie writes Romantic comedy, Contemporary Romance, Dark Romance, Young Adult and New Adult novels and happily shares her love of alpha-male leading men (mostly with muscles and tattoos) and strong female characters with her readers.

When she is not writing, Tillie enjoys nothing more than strutting her sparkly stuff on a dance floor (preferably to Lady Gaga), watching films (preferably anything with Tom Hardy or Will Ferrell—for very different reasons!), listening to music or spending time with friends and family.

Follow Tillie at:

https://www.facebook.com/tilliecoleauthor

https://www.facebook.com/groups/tilliecolestreetteam

https://twitter.com/tillie_cole

Instragram: @authortilliecole

Or drop me an email at: authortilliecole@gmail.com

Or check out my website:
http://tilliecole.com

51564886R10279

Made in the USA
Middletown, DE
03 July 2019